CHECK, PLEASE!

Yvonne broke her M&M's cookie into four pieces, picked up one, and covered the other bits with her napkin. She finished the first piece and reached for the second. Though she'd said she needed to talk to me, she didn't seem eager to begin the conversation.

Which could only mean there was something she didn't want to tell me. I considered possibilities. Due to seasonal affective disorder, she never smiled when it was cloudy. Or, thanks to family issues, she'd need to bring—I scanned her face, trying to estimate her age—her daughter to work three times a week. Or, due to a bizarre medical problem, her doctor had said she shouldn't operate a computer keyboard. Or—

"I was in jail."

Or she'd been in jail. If I'd had a month, I might have come up with that possibility, but probably not.

"Actually, it was prison." She gave me a darting glance. "There's a difference."

Prison. Yvonne? She didn't look as if she would swat a mosquito that was poking its pointed nose into her skin. What could she possibly have done to end up in prison?

She pulled out the third piece of cookie. "I was convicted of murder."

Also by Laura Alden

Murder at the PTA

FOUL PLAY at the PTA

Laura Alden

AN OBSIDIAN BOOK

OBSIDIAN
Published by New American Library, a division of
Penguin Group (USA) Inc., 375 Hudson Street,
New York, New York 10014, USA
Penguin Group (Canada), 90 Eglinton Avenue East, Suite 700, Toronto,
Ontario M4P 2Y3, Canada (a division of Pearson Penguin Canada Inc.)
Penguin Books Ltd., 80 Strand, London WC2R 0RL, England
Penguin Ireland, 25 St. Stephen's Green, Dublin 2,
Ireland (a division of Penguin Books Ltd.)
Penguin Group (Australia), 250 Camberwell Road, Camberwell, Victoria 3124,
Australia (a division of Pearson Australia Group Pty. Ltd.)
Penguin Books India Pvt. Ltd., 11 Community Centre, Panchsheel Park,
New Delhi - 110 017, India
Penguin Group (NZ), 67 Apollo Drive, Rosedale, Auckland 0632,
New Zealand (a division of Pearson New Zealand Ltd.)
Penguin Books (South Africa) (Pty.) Ltd., 24 Sturdee Avenue,
Rosebank, Johannesburg 2196, South Africa

Penguin Books Ltd., Registered Offices:
80 Strand, London WC2R 0RL, England

First published by Obsidian, an imprint of New American Library,
a division of Penguin Group (USA) Inc.

First Printing, July 2011
10 9 8 7 6 5 4 3 2 1

Printed in the United States of America

PUBLISHER'S NOTE
This is a work of fiction. Names, characters, places, and incidents either are the product of the author's imagination or are used fictitiously, and any resemblance to actual persons, living or dead, business establishments, events, or locales is entirely coincidental.

The publisher does not have any control over and does not assume any responsibility for author or third-party Web sites or their content.

For Jon, forever and ever.

Acknowledgments

First off, I want to thank everyone who read my first book, *Murder at the PTA*. You took a chance on a debut author—always a risky business—and I deeply appreciate your plunge into the world of Rynwood, Wisconsin.

A bottom-of-the-heart thank-you goes to my parents-in-law, Bob and Lois Koch, who have done such a fantastic job of promoting my books that they should hang out a sign and go into the business.

Thanks to Julie Sitzema for buying more copies of *Murder at the PTA* than any rational human being should ever consider doing. And to Bob Fitzgerald, because he does, in fact, know about Girl Stuff.

To all my fellow CozyPromo members and Killer Character blog writers. You have taught me so much in the last year that my head is about to explode. Since there is no way whatsoever that I'll be able to teach any of you anything, I instead vow to pass my new knowledge on to other writers.

To Sofie Kelly (aka Darlene Ryan) and Susan Evans, who are always there to show me what really counts. To Avery Aames, Janet Bolin, Krista Davis, Kaye George,

Marilyn Levinson and Meg London (aka Peg Cochran). May we continue to hatch plots for years to come.

To the Sisters in Crime organization, and most especially to the Guppies chapter, who taught me the meaning of the word "perseverance." Lorna Barrett, Leslie Budewitz, Sandra Parshall, Elizabeth Zelvin, Hank Phillippi Ryan; the list of Guppy friends goes on and on. Gups rock!

To the Jessicas: my fabulous agent, Jessica Faust, and the best editor in the world, Jessica Wade. To all the librarians in the world, to all the teachers in the world, all the booksellers, and to PTAs and PTOs everywhere. Without you, the world would be a miserable place.

And, of course, the biggest thanks goes to my husband, Jon, for support above and beyond the call of marriage vows. Thanks, sweetie. I couldn't have done it without you, and I wouldn't want to.

Chapter 1

"You've got to get rid of her."

I ignored my best friend. Once again, she was trying to arrange my life for me, and I was much more interested in planning the Thanksgiving menu. Maybe I could swap the butter-laden, sugar-saturated squash for a simple broiled version. But the sugared version was the only kind of squash that Jenna, my eleven-year-old daughter, would eat.

"Beth, are you listening to me?" Marina scrubbed at her temples, frizzing her light red hair. "When was the last time Marcia was worth what you're paying her? It's time for her to go."

"Um." What I really wanted to put on the menu was a platter of cute little Cornish hens instead of a monstrous hormone-laden turkey, but that wouldn't fly with my family. "It won't fly," I murmured, and chuckled at my own stupid joke.

"This isn't funny." Marina waggled plump fingers at me. "Hey, pay attention. What are you doing over there, anyway? Tell me you're not making a list."

"Okay, I'm not making a list." What about the rutabaga casserole? It was an Emmerling family tradition to have rutabagas at Thanksgiving. Not that anyone ever ate them, but if I didn't have a panful, I'd be taken to task by my mother, my two sisters, brother, and assorted spouses. Maybe I could blame my lapse on being a Kennedy for the last twenty-one years. I squinted into the future and saw my sister Kathy cross her arms as she stared me down. "You've been divorced for two years," she'd say. "That's plenty of time for the Kennedy influence to wear off."

"You are too making a list." Marina looked over my shoulder. "Rutabagas? Who eats those?"

"No one," I said darkly.

She shot me a quick glance but didn't say a word. There are some places where even Marina dared not tread.

"Okeydokey." She pushed herself to her feet. "I'm going to get myself another cup of your tea. How'd you get me hooked on Earl Grey, anyway?"

The two of us were where we often were on Saturday mornings: in my kitchen, where Marina was collecting my children. This habit had developed in September when my problem employee, Marcia, began refusing to work on weekends. I'd worked out a schedule with the other employees of the Children's Bookshelf, only it somehow ended up that I worked two out of four Saturdays. It felt as if Marina, who was also my day-care provider, saw more of Jenna and Oliver than I did. What I was going to do in a few weeks when the Christmas rush started, I had no clue.

"You've got to get rid of her," Marina repeated. The teakettle shrilled its signal and she yanked it off the burner. "Want to know what I'm getting you for Christmas?"

"No."

"A new teakettle. Your Evan Garrett showed me this nifty one at the hardware and it's just the ticket. It has birds painted all over, and instead of a whistle that brings back nasty memories of high school gym class, it chirps like a little bird."

"I don't want a bird teakettle." I didn't have to ask to know that gym hadn't been Marina's favorite class. Her idea of exercise was using a manual can opener instead of an electric one.

"Don't you dare tell me you like this thing." She flicked her hot pink fingernail at the stainless steel kettle.

"Yes, I do."

She opened her mouth to argue me out of my opinion, so I jumped in ahead of her. "No bird teakettles," I said. "If you give me one I'll take it back."

"You are no fun."

"Because I don't want birds chirping in my kitchen?"

"No, because you won't try anything new."

Clearly, she was delusional. Maybe that fish oil supplement she'd started taking was giving her bizarre side effects. "What are you talking about?"

"You're stuck in the mud. Content with the status quo. A woman destined for ruts."

I shoved the menu into my voluminous purse. If it didn't take long to put the final touches on my upcoming PTA presentation, maybe I'd have time to work on the menu during lunch. "Need I remind you that in the last two years I've divorced a husband of two decades, brought my bookstore solidly into the land of profits, become secretary of the Tarver Elementary PTA, and helped put a killer behind bars?"

"All thanks to me." She nodded, congratulating herself so thoroughly that her hair scrunchie fell out. "Some people would be weeping with gratitude."

If I was going to be completely honest with myself—and I always tried to be, even if I hardly ever succeeded—there was a lot of truth in what she said.

It had been Marina's shove that pushed me to run for PTA secretary, and now I was glad to be making a difference in Tarver Elementary School. Providing bookstore customers with hot cider had been Marina's very successful brainstorm, and she had unquestionably been influential regarding my role of putting away the person who'd murdered Tarver's former principal.

"Some people might call you an interfering busybody." I opened the closet door and took out my coat. "Jenna? Oliver? I'm leaving!"

"But with a heart of gold." She cast her eyes heavenward and clasped her hands together. "And the best intentions in the world."

"You know what they say about intentions. The road to you-know-where and all that."

"Pish." Marina waved off the aphorism. "They also say that a wide brown stripe on woolly bear caterpillars means an easy winter." She frowned and put an index finger to her lips. "Or is it a narrow stripe?"

"You and the kids can make finding out today's mission." I buttoned my navy peacoat.

"Plans for the young brood are already afoot." She waggled a large and imaginary pipe.

"Do I want to know?" Much as I disliked leaving the kids on Saturdays, they were enjoying their outings with Marina and her youngest son. Jenna was eleven, Oliver eight, Zach was ten, and the trio were slowly forming a friendship that, with some nurturing and a lot of luck, would last a lifetime.

Marina put her nose in the air. "Tell you now and spoil the stories upon your return from the trenches? I think not."

"Bye, Mom!" Jenna yelled from the family room. Sadly, her freely given hugs were diminishing in quantity.

"Bye, Mrs. Kennedy!" Zach called.

"Yeah, bye, Mom!"

And Oliver was following suit.

I stifled a sigh. Why did growing up require growing away? I put the thought into a distant corner of my mind and picked up my purse. "There is one new thing I've done absolutely positively all by myself."

"Yeah? What's that?"

"I found Evan."

Marina laughed and flapped her hands at me. "Oh, get to work."

I left, and an Evan-induced smile stayed on my face all the way downtown.

Though Wisconsin is wonderful in many ways, the state isn't at its best in late fall. The bright leaves are gone, the days are dark and dreary, and windy nights hint broadly of the coming winter. Matter of fact, the only good thing about this time of year is Thanksgiving.

After all, what could be better than a day of cooking when it was growly and wet outside? What could be better than gathering your loved ones round and giving thanks for the year's blessings? What could be better than a holiday for which you didn't have to exchange presents, cards, or cookies, and at the end of which you waved good-bye to your family and bolted the door behind them?

My pencil gouged a hole in the menu. *Bad Beth!* I scolded myself. You don't really mean that.

Around me, the bookstore was quiet. It was almost closing time and I'd finally had time to think about the coming holiday. Last year Mom had announced that she'd cooked her last Thanksgiving dinner, and it was time for us kids to step up to the plate.

Through a process of elimination, my place had been chosen for the event. I lived in a pseudo-Victorian house in Rynwood, a small town just east of Madison. Kathy and her husband lived in a Tennessee condo. Darlene lived in Michigan, not too far from Mom, but she and her husband, Roger, had moved recently, and they were still unpacking. Their children were grown and scattered from California to Virginia. If any of them showed up to Aunt Beth's for dinner it would be a minor miracle.

Also in the Not-Enough-Room-to-Host-Thanksgiving category was my brother Tim. When they'd divorced a few years back, he and his ex-wife had renovated their house southwest of Chicago into a duplex. It made the custody arrangements with their teenage son a little odd, but it seemed to work for them.

Not that I'd know. Long ago my physicist brother had been nominated the World's Worst Correspondent. When he'd been married, his wife hadn't cared much about cultivating Emmerling family relationships other than sending the obligatory Christmas card, and since their divorce, we didn't even get those. I came across my nephew on Facebook every once in a while, but I suspected all those properly spelled posts were on the sanitized Max page he showed to his parents and not the real Max page he shared with his friends.

How old was Max these days? I tapped my teeth with the pencil. Thirteen? Fourteen? I tried doing the math in my head and came up with twenty-six, which had to be wrong. I scribbled dates next to "Green bean casserole," subtracted, and came up with fifteen. Good heavens, the kid was almost old enough to have a driver's license. How on earth had that happened? Wasn't it last year that—

"It's ten after."

Shrieking, I jumped straight up out of my chair, tossing the menu and pencil high. I tried to speak but my fluttering breaths wouldn't let me get out more than a word at a time. "I—didn't—hear—"

Evan retrieved the paper and writing implement and laid them on the counter in front of me. "Didn't hear the bells jingle as I came in? Didn't hear me call your name? Twice?" He smiled at me.

Smiled down at me, actually. If I stood on tiptoe I could look him directly in the chin. While I wasn't short, I wasn't tall, either, and learning how to kiss a man with such a height differential had given me a stiff neck more than once.

We were the same age—a smidge over forty—and had attended the same kindergarten class. I'd been the Goody Two-shoes and he'd been the kid to point out that the rules for adults should be the same as the rules for children. But that long-ago classroom had been in Indiana. Was it fate that had allowed us to meet up again when we were both single? It was a question I pondered when I should have been sleeping.

Now his smile, instead of slowing my rapid pulse, was making it pound faster. Though our first official date had been months ago, I still wasn't used to the physical closeness of a male. Especially one this good-looking. Last year I'd tried to quell my romantic feelings for Evan by remembering my oft-proven theory that Beautiful People were jerks. I leaned over the counter for a quick kiss and was glad that Evan had proven to be the exception to the rule.

"Sorry," I said. "Last time I looked at the clock it was a quarter to."

He'd returned the sheet of paper without reading it, and I wondered how many people could have done that. Not me. Certainly not Marina. Though maybe the action of nonlooking was a leftover from his former profession.

Not that I knew much about the habits of lawyers. To me, the law was a big scary thing, and I tried to stay as far away from it as possible. I pushed the menu back over to him. "Thanksgiving. I know you can't be there, but see what you're going to miss?"

"Hmm." He scanned the paper. What had once been a simple, straightforward listing of food items was now decorated with strikethroughs, circles, stars, and arrows. "Rutabagas?"

I'd crossed off the rutabagas at least twice and had, twice, returned them to the dinner plan. "It's a family thing."

"Ah." He gave me a glance, then went back to the list. "Oyster dressing? Same side of the family?"

I thought a moment. Family lore said Uncle Rolly, my mom's bachelor brother, had started bringing the rutabaga casserole. The oyster dressing had come from Grandma Chittenden, an East Coast transplant. "No. And unlike the rutabagas, most of us eat the oyster dressing."

He frowned. "If no one eats the rutabagas, why—"

We were saved by the ringing of the telephone. I picked up the receiver. "Good evening, the Children's Bookshelf. How may I help you?"

"Beth?"

"Hi, Marcia." I made a dead-bolt-turning motion to Evan and mouthed the word "Please."

"Oh, good, I caught you before you left." Her words ran together. This was unusual for Marcia, who normally wouldn't, couldn't be rushed.

"What can I do for you?" Maybe she'd forgotten to tell me something. This wasn't necessarily a phone call that meant trouble. Why did I assume the worst?

"It's about Wednesday night," she said.

Or maybe I assumed the worst because that was what so often happened. "What about it?" Wednesday night was the sole evening that all the downtown retailers were open, a tradition handed down in the mists of time. Marcia had worked Wednesday nights for years.

It worked out well because Wednesday was PTA night. I dedicated that evening to secretarial duties, even if we didn't hold a meeting. If there weren't minutes to work on, there were letters to write or fund-raisers to plan or parental e-mail to answer, and I was almost keeping up with it. This Wednesday there was a meeting, and since I'd asked to get something on the agenda, attendance was an absolute must.

"I can't work Wednesday night," Marcia said. "It's not going to be a problem, is it?" She didn't wait for an answer, but plunged on. "You'll figure out a new schedule. It shouldn't be too hard, one extra night. See, my grandson is starting swim lessons and I'd never forgive myself if I miss seeing him learn. You used to swim yourself, didn't you? I knew you'd understand."

"Are you talking about missing just this Wednesday?"

Marcia gave a peal of laughter. "It takes longer than one time to learn how to swim. No, these lessons run until March. Or is it April? Do you want me to check right now?"

No, I didn't. What I wanted was an employee who actually wanted to work. I said good-bye and hung up the phone. Marina was right: Something had to be done about Marcia. Too bad I hadn't a clue what it was.

"Problems?" Evan put his elbow on top of a nearby bookshelf. At the end of a long, busy day in retail he still managed to look unrumpled and drop-dead gorgeous. Curly blond hair going gray at the temples, long lean body, and a smile that quirked up on one side of his face, he was on track to become a Distinguished Older Man.

Some days—okay, most days, to be truthful—it was hard to believe he was interested in plain old me. What he saw in Beth Kennedy, age forty-one, divorced mother of two, and busy owner of a children's bookstore who'd been endowed with mousy brown limp hair and had accumulated an extra fifteen hip-area pounds, I had no idea.

Well, twenty pounds.

"What makes you think there are problems?" I asked.

"When you're worried you get little lines right here." He stretched out and tapped his index finger above the bridge of my nose.

His touch sent a cold wave down my back. Why did I keep feeling like a love-struck teenager around this man? I was Beth Kennedy, once voted Least Likely to Scream at a Rolling Stones Concert. "Lines?" I lurched backward, frantically scrubbing at my forehead. "I'm not old enough for lines. I'm not gray enough. I'm not *lined* enough."

Evan chuckled. "Then you'd better stop worrying. They might stick."

I stopped my fake rubbing. If I got wrinkles, would he still want to be seen with me in public? If I got any uglier, surely he'd stop—

The phone rang. Automatically, I reached to answer. "Hello, Children's Bookshelf."

"Beth."

Instantly, my senses went on red alert. "Kathy." My sister had never in my entire life called me at work. That she did so now could only mean . . . "It's Mom, isn't it?" She was sick. Why hadn't she told us earlier? Though Mom and I didn't have the ideal mother-daughter relationship, she was still my mom. If something had happened to her, I'd never forgive myself for not getting back to Michigan last summer. "How is she?"

"Mom?" Kathy's round voice sounded puzzled. "Fine. At least she was this morning when I talked to her."

"Oh. Good." My spine lost its stiffness. "So, um, how are you?"

She laughed. "Same old Beth. Small talk isn't one of your strengths, is it?"

Never had been, and thank you very much for reminding me, biggest of all sisters.

"It's about Thanksgiving," Kathy said.

"Oh, good. We should talk about the menu." I scrabbled around for the pencil. "Ron's allergic to green beans, right? And is it the red or the orange Jell-O you can't stand?"

"Sorry. No can do."

The pencil rolled out of reach. "What do you mean?"

"I mean we can't make it on Thanksgiving. Ron's company gave him an early Christmas bonus. Can you believe it?"

"Um . . ." Kathy's husband worked for a large financial services firm and made obscene amounts of money. I tried very hard not to be jealous and succeeded almost half the time.

"Anyway," Kathy said, "part of this year's bonus is a Thanksgiving cruise to the Caribbean. The U.S. Virgin Islands, St. Kitts, St. Lucia." She sighed dramatically. "It's going to be heaven."

I did not want to go on a cruise, I told myself. Especially not at Thanksgiving. Who would want to take a vacation on this most honest of all holidays? Thanksgiving was about gathering around a crowded table with as much family as you could shoehorn in, knee to knee and elbow to elbow, praying, laughing, and having the same arguments you had every year. Thanksgiving wasn't about shiny cruise ships and smiling waitstaff.

I'd almost convinced myself when Kathy said, "Ron's company is telling us the whole family is invited, so the kids are coming, too, plane tickets and all!"

Her voice was alive with excitement, and in spite of my jealousy—not that I was jealous, of course I wasn't—a smile spread across my face. "How long has it been since all the kids were in one place at the same time?" I asked.

"Three years and five months," Kathy said. "Ron thought you might be mad about us missing Thanksgiving, but I knew you'd be fine with it."

"Um . . ."

"Oop, there's the call waiting. Got to go. I'll send you a postcard from the ship!" She hung up, laughing.

"More problems?"

I debated how to answer Evan's question, and finally said, "Nope." The menu lurked on the counter. I pulled a pen out of a coffee mug decorated with cats and rewrote "Green bean casserole." Then I underlined it. Twice. "I just need to make a phone call."

My purse was in a drawer back in the glorified closet I called my office. I fetched it out front, extracting my cell phone on the way and finding the phone number for the PTA president. "Erica? Beth. It's about Wednesday night."

Chapter 2

I spent Wednesday night at the store. My manager, Lois, had bowling league that night, and my two part-time employees were both students at nearby University of Wisconsin. I didn't want Sara or Paoze to sacrifice study time for the sake of a job that didn't pay much more than minimum wage.

Lois said I was dreaming if I thought college kids did nothing but study on weeknights. "Most of them are out spending Daddy's money on video games and iTunes and beer. Not necessarily in that order."

"Do you really think so?" But I was happy in dreamland, so it was easy to picture blond, blue-eyed Sara chewing the ends of her hair while working on arcane organic chemistry equations. Even easier to see the brown-skinned, brown-eyed Paoze sitting in the library surrounded by the novels of dead white guys as he scribbled away on a paper for his latest English literature class. "Even Paoze?"

She relented. "Well, not him. If he was freezing to death he wouldn't have two quarters to make a spark." She grinned evilly; quite a look on her sixtyish face. "Say, do you think I could get him on that?"

Lois had developed a habit of playing on the gullibility of young Paoze. From snipe hunts to Paul Bunyan exploits, Lois worked hard at her tall tales. Even I got caught once in a while. She'd nailed Paoze multiple times—the fact that he'd fallen for the snipe hunt story still rankled with him—and for a week she'd had Sara believing in a left-handed wrench.

Despite the fact that Paoze was born in Laos and didn't move to the United States until he was a teenager, he probably knew better than most of us that flint is what sparks. "Remember last spring?" I asked. "He had that American Literature of the Early 1900s class and did a term paper on Jack London."

"That's right." Lois looked thoughtful. "'To Build a Fire' and all that. Hmm."

I made a mental note to warn Paoze about stories set in Alaska, and waved good-bye to her when she left at five.

The clock ticked time away slowly. A woman came in and asked if we had anything by Jackie Collins. "There's a bookstore in the mall," I offered, but she wasn't mollified and went away empty-handed and annoyed. The course of running a children's bookstore never did run smooth.

After she left, I did some alphabetizing, jotted down a few books to order, and was about to haul out the feather duster, when Marina breezed in.

"Hail, fellow! Well met!"

Along with my bigger-than-life best friend, the front door ushered in a blast of winter-cold air that made the back of my neck tense up. I cast a longing look toward the thermostat, which was resolutely set at sixty-eight degrees, and sighed. I loved Wisconsin, I told myself. There's nothing prettier than sun sparkling on snow and nothing better than skating and skiing and seeing white puffs of air coming out of your mouth six months of the year.

Marina shivered, sending waves of damp chill over

me. "Nasty out there," she said. "Remind me again why we live so far north?" She shook back her hair and droplets of water scattered in every direction.

"Because this is where my house is?"

She unbuttoned her bright pink coat. The color clashed horribly with her red hair, but a few years back Marina had decided that she liked pink, that she *loved* pink, and she wasn't going to let any out-of-touch fashion traditions dictate what she was going to wear.

Though I admired her attitude—I still found it hard to wear white shoes before Memorial Day—sometimes fashion rules were rules for a good reason. I trotted out that point of view when we were coat shopping, but she said I had no sense of adventure. In my experience, limited though it was, adventure meant uncertainty, discomfort, fear, and pain. None of those seemed like very sensible things to pursue on a regular basis.

"You, my dah-ling"—Marina was back in Greta Garbo mode—"could use a large dose of excitement."

"How can you tell?"

"You have a wistful cast to your dainty features. You have that air of faint discontent." She put her nose high and sniffed. "And, yes, the scent of ennui."

"It's the smell of burning leaves, and the last time you said I needed excitement in my life we ended up sitting in traffic for three hours and overheating your engine."

"Minor annoyances must be expected. Especially during Chicago's St. Patrick's Day parade. It was an excellent time and you're everlastingly grateful that I kidnapped you."

She was right. Watching the parade, seeing the cheerful crowds and the greened river, even sitting in a traffic jam had been the stuff of which fond memories are made. But saying so would just encourage her. "That was only eight months ago," I said. "Talk to me about excitement when the snow melts."

She brushed an infinitesimal piece of dust off the counter, and when I saw the way her pinkie was extended—high etiquette style—I knew the argument was far from over. She sighed. "It's so sad."

I looked at her warily. "What is?"

"Your precious children."

The kids were with their father, having a great time stuffing themselves with fat-laden pizza, drinking sugar-saturated soda, and playing video games guaranteed to rip half an hour off their attention span. "What about them?"

"Growing up without any adventure in their lives." Mournfully, she straightened a pile of bookmarks. "When they're old and gray, they're going to bow their heads and say, 'Remember when we were young? We never once did anything that wasn't sanitized, supervised, and structured. Why weren't we ever allowed to be kids? Why didn't we have any adventures?' "

I rubbed my forehead. "One minute you're saying I'm boring, the next you're wringing your hands over Jenna and Oliver's old age. If there's a connection, I'm missing it."

She slammed her open palm on the counter. "You! You're the connection, dear silly one."

"Um . . ."

"Don't you see?" She looked me solid in the eyes. "If you don't teach them that life is to be lived to the fullest, that it's worth wringing out every last drop of enjoyment, that there are no small parts, just small players, who will? Richard?" She snorted.

I leaned against the cash register. "So I should be something I'm not for the sake of my children?"

Marina crossed her arms. "Why did I know you wouldn't take me seriously?"

"Because I've known you more than ten years. And, thanks to those years of precedent, I know you have something up your sleeve."

"Me?" She tugged at the cuffs of her pink coat. "Nothing up there except air."

"You invoked the specter of future unhappiness for Jenna and Oliver. You never do that unless you're trying to convince me to do something I don't want to do."

"Poor Beth." Marina shook her head sadly. "Always believing the worst in people."

"Poor Marina," I said. "Having her past actions remembered so clearly."

She reached across the counter and, with her index fingers, pushed at the corners of my mouth until I wore a stretchy smile. "Much better."

"Quit that. Just tell me what you're after, okay? I know you enjoy the convincing game, but I have work to do."

She pounced. "Exactly! Too much of it."

"That's the fun of owning your own business. You get to pick which eighty hours a week you work."

"No, no, no." She swatted away my words. "I'm not talking about the oppressive hours you slave without just compensation; I'm talking about the work you're doing right now that should be done by someone else who shall remain nameless but her initials are Marcia Trommler."

I tried, and failed, to diagram Marina's last sentence in my head. "That again."

"Yes," she said, nodding so hard that her hair fell forward across her face. She hooked it back over her ears with impatient hands. "The problem isn't going away."

"I know that." My voice gained an unattractive edge. "But where am I going to find someone to replace her? It's not easy to find someone who'll work long hours for low wages, no benefits, and no bonuses."

"Long hours, you say?" Marina cupped a hand to her ear. "How many hours are on Marcia's time sheet? And now she's taking Wednesday nights off? Wednesday nights are PTA nights, remember?"

"It's her grandson," I said lamely. "How can I not let her have time off? She shouldn't have to miss watching him grow up."

Marina scoffed. "Then she should quit and spend all day with him instead of wreaking havoc with the store's work schedule."

I busied myself with straightening a stack of postcards. It could have been Lois standing there. Actually, she had been standing there, just a few hours earlier, and had said almost word for word what Marina was saying.

"She's been here a long time," I said. "No one knows the picture books as well as Marcia. And she has great rapport with the customers." At least the ones she knew. Strangers she didn't much care for. "And kids like her." Well, some did. The clean ones. Kids who came in with dirty hands were marched to the bathroom to wash.

Marina gave me a look. "You've never let anyone go, have you?"

"Um . . ."

"Hah!" She grinned triumphantly. "This isn't about Marcia's inability to fulfill her duties as an employee; this is about your fear of firing!"

"Is not." But my gaze slid away from hers.

She shook her index finger at me. "Prove it."

"It's not fear." So what if I hadn't ever fired anyone? So what if the thought of firing Marcia made my stomach hurt? So what if the idea of inciting confrontation went against everything my mother ever taught me? If I had to fire Marcia, I would.

"No?" Marina looked at me askance. "Then what is it?"

"Timing. It's too close to Christmas. And I'll thank you to remember that this is my store, not some playground for your management theories."

Marina shook her head, sighing. "Poor Beth, still afraid of life. You need to show your daughter and son how to overcome fear. Show them how to push through the anxiety and come through on the other side. Fear is nothing," she said solemnly. "If you're scared, it means whatever you're scared of isn't happening. If it was, you'd be too busy working your way out of trouble. . . ."

As she talked, I studied her, trying to figure out what was really going on in that busy brain. Clearly, she had an ulterior motive. And, just as clearly, she wasn't going to tell me what it was. Ah, well. Time would eventually tell. It always did. Marina couldn't keep a secret for beans.

The next night, Thursday, I sat at the front of a classroom in what I'd come to consider my spot. Thanks to some fast phone calls, a fair amount of pleading, and some outright begging, I'd convinced the PTA board to change the meeting night from Wednesday to Thursday.

To my right were my three fellow board members: Randy Jarvis, treasurer and owner of the downtown gas station; Erica Hale, president, attorney, and grandmother; and our new vice president, Claudia Wolff.

The four of us had our knees under a rectangular table at the front of the room. It was a fifth-grade classroom, so the furniture was close to adult-sized, but Randy's size was far from normal. Erica, Claudia, and I fit our bottom halves under the table without any trouble. Randy, on the other hand, kept whacking his knees on the bottom of the table. There was a reason I taped the meetings, and it wasn't because the board had voted to do so. Many a night I'd studied my handwritten notes, eyeing the jigs and jags due to Randy bumps, and turned on the tape recorder.

Erica put on her half-glasses and banged the gavel. "The Tarver Elementary School PTA meeting will come to order." Erica, silver-haired and slim, with just the faintest trace of a Southern accent, was one of the first grandparents to join Tarver's PTA. A dearth of volunteers had called for drastic measures, and allowing extended family to join had swelled the Tarver PTA's ranks nicely.

I took roll and tried not to wince when I called Claudia Wolff's name. Our former vice president, Julie Reed, a perky young mother, had come down with twins last year and, understandably, had to resign. In her stead was Claudia Wolff, the PTA's perennially underappreciated volunteer.

Well, underappreciated according to Claudia, and to be fair, she was probably right. She labored for hours on PTA projects, but spent just as much time asking people to feel sorry for her because she was working so hard on PTA projects.

I tried to like her, honestly I did. One night when the kids were in bed I even sat down and made a list of Claudia's good points. "Works hard," I said, writing the words on a yellow legal pad. She was a tireless worker. She'd come early for setup during bake sales, and she'd stay late to help put things away.

"Reliable." Never once had Claudia forgotten to bake cupcakes or call her branch of the phone tree or missed a PTA meeting.

"Sincere." Claudia wasn't the type to say things behind your back. No, she'd tell you to your face what she thought of your ideas, your choices in clothing, and your parenting methods. No one had to wonder what Claudia thought; it was out there front and center.

I'd never gotten any further with the list because Oliver had woken with an earache and I'd had my hands full the rest of the night. Now, as I finished taking roll, I tried to keep the three things I'd written down in the forefront of my mind. If I could continue to think well of Claudia, and if I could stay away from Randy's pant leg, the meeting would be a rousing success.

We pushed through the only old business item, the upcoming Father-Daughter Dance, and all through the dance committee's report my mouth grew drier and drier. If I tried to talk, would my voice work, or would it just squeak?

"Next up is new business," Erica finally said. "Item number one is a new spring project."

My hands were sweating. What if everyone thought my idea was dumb?

Erica looked at me over her glasses. "Beth, you have the floor."

"Thanks." I took a deep breath and looked out at the audience. Isabel Olson was in her son Neal's seat. Sam Helmstetter, dubbed the Nicest Guy on the Planet, his nice brown plaid scarf still around his neck, had his head tilted toward Tina Heller, who was giggling. Sam's expression was one of patient fortitude. He was used to Tina. The Hellers and the Helmstetters, in addition to their close proximity in the alphabet, lived backyard to backyard.

Also out there was a mother newly arrived in town, though I couldn't remember her name. Plus there was Debra O'Conner, formerly known as the Rynwood Woman Who Most Intimidates Me; Heather Kingsley; and CeeCee and Dan Daniels. Marina was home, watching over my children.

I knew almost all of these people. Most of them I knew very well. I sold them books and stickers and stuffed animals, for heaven's sake, so why was I suddenly so nervous?

"First off," I said, "please accept my apologies for changing the meeting date at such short notice. What I'm proposing"—my throat froze shut for an eternal moment—"is a story session between the children of Tarver and the senior citizens of Rynwood."

"At Sunny Rest Assisted Living," Erica added.

"That's right." My face lost its heat and my potential embarrassment suddenly seemed like a silly thing to worry about. "I think we'd all like more interaction between generations. My idea is to match Tarver students with Sunny Rest residents. The students will write stories about their residents, and the end product will be a book that both Sunny Rest and the PTA can sell as a fundraiser."

"Lovely idea," Erica said.

I breathed a little easier. There'd be at least one vote for my motion. Well, two, including mine. When I'd first come aboard as secretary, I'd asked who made a tie-breaking vote. Erica looked thoughtful, Julie started paging through the bylaws, and Randy said he couldn't think about things like that on an empty stomach. The question hadn't been answered, and I'd forgotten all about it. Until now.

Debra O'Conner raised her hand.

"Yes, Debra?" Erica asked.

"You said stories. What kind of stories?"

I leaned forward, eager to explain. "The kids decide. But they'll have a list of questions that need to be answered. Where the resident was born, what they liked to do as children, what music they listened to—oh, all sorts of things. We'll decide on a minimum and maximum length, and the PTA will edit them." I'd do the editing, probably, but the project was my idea, so it was only fair.

"So more like an interview than a story," Claudia said.

Why did a comment that was factually accurate come across as derisive? I tried to separate tone from content and focused on the meaning. "Exactly. The kids will learn about lives very different from their own, and the residents will get their stories in print."

The room went quiet. I picked at my cuticles. Should I make the motion? Wait for someone else to make the motion? If no one else did, I'd have to, but that would look like failure from the get-go.

Randy stirred, but said nothing.

I pulled off a too-big piece of cuticle and watched red ooze to the surface.

"Okay," Claudia said. "I guess I'll make a motion that the Tarver Elementary PTA coordinate with the school and Sunny Rest for a story session between the kids and the residents, details to be determined at a later date."

"Second," Randy said.

"All in favor?" Erica asked.

There was a chorus of ayes.

"The motion has passed." Erica adjusted her glasses. "Next on the agenda is a gluten-free bake sale."

I tried to look interested, but on the inside I was doing cartwheels and pumping my fist into the air as if I'd won the Stanley Cup. They'd listened to me and paid attention to me and by golly they'd voted for the idea I'd proposed all by my lonesome. I couldn't wait to tell Marina.

The rest of the meeting passed by in a rosy haze. Finally, Erica said, "Meeting adjourned," and banged the gavel.

A general leave taking commenced. People stood, pulled on their coats, and went out into the cold, dark evening. I gathered up my legal pad and tape recorder and pushed them into the worn bag that had, once upon a time, carried diapers.

"Beth, do you have a minute?" Erica asked.

Except for Harry, we were the last people left in the building. Harry, the janitor who doubled as security guard, always checked that the doors were locked. I'd caught sight of him on the way into the meeting, walking like a shadow through the halls in black pants, black long-sleeved shirt, and black sneakers so old they were back in fashion again. Ever since Harry and I discovered a mutual passion for hockey, we'd never run out of things to talk about. He cheered for the wrong team, but I was working on that.

"Um . . ." I glanced at the wall clock above the whiteboard. There was a push to purchase interactive whiteboards, but the school's budget barely allowed replacement of worn-out regular whiteboards, let alone anything technologically cool. The Tarver Foundation, funded by the estate of the late Agnes Mephisto, had been approached by the interactive advocates, but as yet there was no answer. "Marina's watching the kids, but I have a few minutes."

"Excellent." Erica, slim, elegant, and gray-haired, was the woman my mother had wanted me to be. Assertive without being aggressive, kind yet not a pushover, with the courage to stand up for what she thought was right.

She'd been widowed as a young mother and parked her three children with her parents while she attended law school. She graduated with high honors, one of two women in the class. Erica found a job at a midsized firm in Madison and moved herself and her children north. Ten years later she was a partner. Five years after that she'd become senior partner and led the firm to be the largest in the region.

Only now, in her retirement, did she have time for joining the library board and the garden club, and heading up the PTA. It was a good thing she was retired; otherwise, I would have had to reevaluate my vow to keep all lawyers at a quarter-mile distance.

"This project of yours," Erica said. "How deeply are you committed?"

Deep? I blinked. What would be a good answer—five feet committed, but not six? "Um, deep enough to see the project through."

Erica chuckled. She did this regularly, but I was always surprised to hear such rich, easy laughter come out of the patrician framework. Bad Beth, for clinging to limiting stereotypes.

"You've been spending too much time with lawyers," she said. "Even recovering ones maintain a particular mind-set."

"Um . . ."

"Back to your project. You came up with the idea yourself, correct?"

"Yes, but I doubt it's original."

"Hmm." She drummed her fingers on her leather briefcase. "We can put our own spin on this."

I got the stomach dropping feeling that "we" meant me. "What do you mean?"

Erica buttoned her black coat. How she managed to have a dog and three cats and own a coat free of pet hair, I had no idea. Between the black from our cat George and brown from Spot the dog, pet hair was a permanent part of my wardrobe. "How big do you think?" she asked.

Yet another open-ended query. Maybe I'd missed the e-mail that today was Hard Question Day. "Bigger than a breadbox, smaller than the solar system."

She laughed. "Do you think in terms of the entire state?" She lifted her leather case off the table, I picked up my ratty diaper bag, and we headed for the main entrance. "I think it has the potential to get big," she said. "Fantasize with me for a minute."

My fantasies usually had more to do with grandchildren or a certain tall, blue-eyed man, not the PTA, but I could play along.

"The Tarver PTA completes its first senior story session in June. We send out press releases across the state. We get newspaper, television, and blog coverage. We are suddenly the PTA to watch."

The two of us pushed through the metal double doors

and the outside air slammed hard against our bodies. Erica kept talking, as if she hadn't felt a thing.

"Think of it, Beth. We could start a program that sweeps statewide. If we organize this well, it could go nationwide."

We walked across the lonely parking lot. Erica's high-heeled boots made clicking noises on the asphalt. My clunky trail boots made a quiet *thud-thud* as I hurried to keep up. Another mystery of life—how did any woman walk in high heels, let alone walk as fast as Erica did? I'd have to ask my physicist brother about it someday. Or not. If I asked, he'd tell me, and I'd be required to feign interest throughout the explanation.

"Your story sessions," Erica was saying, "could open a national conversation on ways to improve relationships between generations. And it all starts here." She stopped at her car, a silver sedan from some foreign country. "It starts with you, Beth. How big do you think?"

Why did my friends keep trying to talk me into doing things? More specifically, why did they try to talk me into doing things I didn't want to do?

A gust of wind blew down from the north, slithered around my neck, and snuck between my layers of clothing to hit skin. I shivered and the small of my back tightened with cold.

"We have time to consider the ramifications," Erica said. "But we should agree on how far we want to take this by the January meeting."

I'd turned to put my back to the wind, and doing so gave me a view of the far corner of the parking lot. An SUV sat all alone, surrounded by nothing but empty parking spaces and dormant grass.

"This has the potential to be a life-changing project, Beth. Think of the people who could be touched by these stories."

Whose SUV was that? I squinted at it, trying to see in

the gusting wind. What I noticed most about cars was size. After that, color. After that . . . well, there wasn't anything after that. I frowned. It was hard to make out true color underneath the orangey hue cast by the parking lot lighting.

"The possibilities are tremendous," Erica said. "I have a few ideas for—"

"Sam," I said.

"Helmstetter?" She flipped up the collar of her coat. "I hadn't considered him, but you're right. No reason not to tap into the business community."

I shook my head. "No, over there. That SUV is Sam's." He often took the parking spot the farthest away. The walk did him good, he always said. Plus, he'd add, why not leave the closer parking spots for someone who didn't have two good legs.

Erica turned. "Sam left long before we did."

The wind was rising, roaring with the threat of winter. A small sliver of a moon appeared briefly through the scudding clouds, then disappeared as if it had never been. There was no good reason for Sam's SUV to be sitting there. If he'd been having car trouble, the hood would have been up and he'd have been waiting for a tow truck inside, where it wasn't thirty-five degrees with a wind chill that cut to the bone. If he was having an illicit assignation, he wouldn't have left his vehicle out for everyone to see.

Not that Sam would be having an affair. He and his wife still held hands in public and sat shoulder to shoulder whenever seating arrangements allowed.

"I suppose . . ." Erica sounded uncharacteristically indecisive. I glanced over and, even in the poor light, saw anxiety and concern on her face.

"I'll go check," I offered. "Probably he had car trouble and someone gave him a ride home."

"Yes." Her relief was obvious even in the one syllable.

"How clever of you to come up with a likely explanation." I started walking, and after a half-step hesitation, she came along. "My mama always said I made things more complicated than they needed to be. She said I was born to be a lawyer."

My mother had told me I was born to make her hair go gray, but I didn't pass that comment on to Erica. I'd never understood Mom's exasperation until I had children of my own. Oliver probably hadn't understood my reaction when he shoved his multitudes of stuffed animals in the washing machine and added a bottle of detergent. And Jenna probably hadn't understood how I could be angry when she'd taken the scissors to her bangs. "It's my hair," she'd said, weeping. I'd wept, too, over the quarter-inch-long tufts sticking straight up out of her head.

Erica and I approached Sam's SUV, her boots clicking, mine thudding. "Do you have any plans for your garden next year?" she asked. Erica was a master gardener and her garden was so spectacular that the Madison newspaper had done a Sunday feature on it.

"Oliver wants to plant cucumbers." The SUV's windows were tinted slightly; I couldn't see through them at all.

"He's eight? An excellent age to have his own gardening space. Old enough to have full responsibility and old enough to understand the direct relationship between hard work and the payoff hard work can bring about."

Why was Erica talking about gardening? She almost sounded nervous. "Old enough to pull weeds?" I couldn't quite see into the driver's seat. To gain some elevation, I walked on the balls of my feet for a few steps, but it didn't help.

"Old enough by far to detect the difference between a weed and a desirable plant. I had my children taking care of their first tomatoes by the time . . . ah, it appears that he just fell asleep."

"He's been putting in long hours, trying to get his business off the ground."

"Well, he can't sleep here all night. His wife will worry, and besides, he'll freeze to death." She rapped on the window. "Sam, wake up." Her knuckles made a dull sound against the glass. "Sam?"

I edged closer. Inside, a shadowy form sat in the front seat, slumping forward against the shoulder strap. If he slept like that much longer, he'd get a horrible stiff neck. As a business owner myself, I understood all about long weeks and fatigue and wearing myself thin, but I'd never fallen asleep in my car. At my desk, yes. On the couch trying to make sense of invoices, yes.

"Sam!" Erica pounded on the window with her fist.

Unease prickled at the back of my neck. I'd had this feeling before, and it hadn't turned out well. "Um, Erica?" I dropped the diaper bag, pulled off my mittens, and reached into my purse for my cell phone. I flipped it open, trying to ignore the tightness in my chest. "Erica, something's wrong. There's no way Sam is asleep." Not even Jenna, my out-like-a-light daughter, could possibly sleep through all that window whacking. I punched the first number. *Nine.*

"Sam?" Erica called. "Are you all right? Sam!" She grabbed the door handle and lifted it.

I stabbed at the second number. *One.*

Erica yanked the door open. "Sam? Are you—" Her question ended in a gasping shriek. Sam fell toward her, his scarf too tight around his neck. There was no life in his slumped body and his open eyes were seeing nothing but death. "Sam!" Erica screamed. She jerked off her gloves and felt for a pulse, then dragged Sam's body out of the SUV and onto the cold ground. As she started the pointless job of CPR, I pushed the last button. *One.*

There was a single ring. Then: "Dane County dispatch. What is your emergency?"

Chapter 3

Gus Eiseley, Rynwood's chief of police, looked at me. "I hear you have the perfect alibi."

"It's all my fault." I clutched a cup of coffee as if it might be the rock that would sustain me. It wasn't, of course. It was a blistering hot liquid that, thanks to its caffeine, would keep me awake most of the night, but after seeing poor Sam like that, it wasn't likely that I'd be able to sleep anyway. I blew at the coffee, making small ripples.

"Your fault." Gus turned a chair around and sat, putting his arms on the back and looking as comfortable as he looked in his living room. "Are you ready to make a confession?"

I shook my head and almost slopped coffee over the side of the foam cup. "It's my fault that Sam's dead."

Gus propped his chin on his hands. "This, I can't wait to hear."

The coffee's temperature had dropped to merely scalding. I took one sip, then another, as I tried to think out a way to say what I had to say without sounding like a complete idiot. No matter what, Gus would be kind and understanding because that's the way he was, but he would also poke me in the back at the next church choir rehearsal and make fun of me.

I took another sip of coffee. "It's my fault because if it hadn't been for me, he would have been home tonight."

"And you think that would have made a difference?"

"Well, yes." I took another swallow. My drink of choice was tea, but Gus didn't believe in anything brewed from leaves. "If he'd been home maybe his wife would have seen the signs and called 911 before he died." Even though we were inside the school, I could see the revolving lights of the ambulance that arrived much too late to save Sam's life. Around and around they went.

"Signs?" Gus asked.

I gestured with my cup. "Of a heart attack, or whatever it was. PTA meetings are always on Wednesdays. It was because of me that we met tonight." Me and my dumb story session idea. I'd wanted the project approved, I'd wanted to get going on plans, I'd wanted to—

"He didn't die from a heart attack," Gus said.

"Oh." I stole a look at my watch. Barely an hour had passed since I'd called 911. How Gus could know cause of death already, I wasn't sure, but maybe forensic conclusions really did happen as fast as they did on television. "Um, stroke?"

Gus spoke softly. "Sam was murdered, Beth."

I heard the words, but they didn't make sense. "No, he wasn't. He must have had one of those silent diseases they talk about. Scary, to think every one of us could be walking around with a little alarm clock inside, and one day the alarm will go off but we won't hear it. All we'll do is not wake up the next morning." I was babbling. This is what I did when nervous, scared, or uncomfortable. When I was all three, like now, the effect expanded geometrically. "Back in college there was this professor who died of an aneurysm. Here one day, gone the next. You just never know, do you? And I once knew a—"

"Beth." Gus interrupted my steady flow of words. "Sam was murdered. There's no question about it."

"How can you be so sure?" Everyone made mistakes. I made them every day. I even did dumb things in my dreams. "Shouldn't a coroner or a medical examiner or a doctor or somebody be the one to say?" Not another murder, I pleaded silently; my children had only recently recovered from the last murder in town. Oliver was sleeping with only one stuffed animal instead of a bedful, and Jenna hadn't woken in the middle of the night, shrieking, in weeks. "Are you certain? I mean . . ."

"Am I qualified to say how anyone died?" A smile came and went on his weather-worn face. "Normally I wouldn't. But in this particular case the signs are clear."

I shut my eyes. Sam's wife would be devastated. And the poor children. To lose your father to disease was bad enough, but to have him taken away from you by another human being? I looked at Gus. "You're absolutely sure?"

"Classic signs of strangulation. They were so obvious even I could figure it out. The scarf around his neck helped."

Shame filled me. "Gus, I didn't mean—"

He patted my arm. "You're not questioning my skills; you just don't want there to be another murder in Rynwood."

I nodded thankfully.

"You're not alone in wanting Sam's death to be from natural causes, believe you me. But facts are facts." His demeanor shifted from normal, friendly Gus to that of a law enforcement officer at the scene of a crime. "Now. I'll need to ask you a few questions."

I opened my mouth, but he was ahead of me.

"Just like last time," he said, "the Dane County Sheriff's Department will be taking over the case. But that hasn't happened yet, and until it does I'm in charge of the investigation."

I wondered when the sheriff's department would show up. Tonight? Tomorrow? And would Deputy Sharon Wheeler be in charge of the investigation? She'd headed things up when Agnes died, and, while she and I hadn't been outright enemies, we weren't kindred spirits, either. But Dane County was big, and so was the sheriff's department. The chances of Deputy Wheeler being assigned to this particular matter were—

"Good evening, Chief Eiseley."

—were apparently quite good. Deputy Wheeler strode into the room, trim and fit in her brown and tan uniform. Even the bulky brown coat flattered her figure. The deputy shook hands with Gus, who'd stood to greet her, and looked at me. "Mrs. . . . Kennedy." She dragged my name out of a year-old memory, something that would have taken me fifteen minutes of hemming and hawing. "How are you?"

Tired, sad, scared, and filled with a need to hug my children. "Fine, thanks. Yourself?"

She gave a short nod, then turned to Gus. They started talking about crime-scene contamination and estimated time of death.

I sat in my chair, trying not to hear what they said, trying to make myself small. If I were really small, they would forget I was there. They'd leave the vacant office Gus had commandeered and I'd be able to pick up the kids and go home. I probably shouldn't have been listening to their conversation, anyway, as it might have been privileged police information. The thought must have occurred to Gus and Deputy Wheeler at the same moment, because they both swung around to look at me. Under their steady gazes I felt like a butterfly stuck onto an insect collection.

"What time did you and Erica leave the building?" Gus asked.

"After seven. The meeting started at six and lasted until . . ." Suddenly I remembered my secretarial role. "Hang on." I sorted through the contents of the diaper bag, pulled out my yellow legal pad, and scanned my notes. "Here it is. Meeting adjourned at six forty-seven p.m."

"Six forty-seven exactly?" Deputy Wheeler sounded amused.

"According to my watch, yes." Even at the time I'd thought writing down the exact minute was silly, but it had been 6:47, and rounding either up or down didn't seem right. The time was the time and, thanks to my stickler-for-accuracy son, our household set clocks and watches a minimum of once a week.

"And Mr. Helmstetter stayed the length of the meeting?"

"Yes. No, hang on." I thought back. "He left at one point, then came back."

"Cell phone call?" Gus asked.

I frowned, trying to remember. "I don't recall hearing a phone ring." At the beginning of every meeting Erica asked everyone to turn phones off or to vibrate. Most of the time it worked, but every so often we'd get someone with a new phone and the meeting would be interrupted by the digital notes of Beethoven's Fifth, or the University of Wisconsin fight song, or (my personal favorite of the year) "Mary Had a Little Lamb."

"But he might have had his phone set to vibrate," I said. "Tina Heller was sitting next to him. Maybe she'd know."

Deputy Wheeler scratched some notes on a pad. "Thank you, Mrs. Kennedy. A couple of more questions and we'll let you go for the night. Did you see anyone in the parking lot when you and Mrs. Hale walked out? A person, a car, anything?"

"We were the last ones to leave the building. Well, except for—" I came to a screeching halt.

"Except for Harry?" Gus asked.

I blew out a small sigh of relief. He already knew about Harry. I didn't have to worry about being a tattletale on the only other person I knew who understood the importance of the Selke Trophy.

"Harry clocked out at six thirty," Gus said, "and was standing in line at Sabatini's, waiting for his pizza, at six forty-five. He met up with a friend who came in at six fifty, and they sat down in the restaurant to eat."

"Good," I said, but I was wondering who Harry's friend was. Last I knew, the only real friend he had was the late Agnes Mephisto. "Fast work." I looked from city police officer to sheriff's deputy, not sure where to aim the compliment.

Gus shrugged. "Not really. Harry came back a few minutes ago to check the doors and to make sure a classroom floor was drying okay. Some kid's lunch hadn't sat right and it went all across the floor." He made a sweeping motion with his arm. Deputy Wheeler and I winced simultaneously.

"One more question, Mrs. Kennedy," the deputy said. "Can you think of anyone who might have wanted to kill Sam Helmstetter?"

Any lightheartedness that had slid back into me disappeared. "No. I can't."

"No one?"

I shook my head, and the weight felt too heavy. My neck wasn't big enough to support the leaden thoughts inside. Poor Sam. His poor family. All their lives they'd have this sadness hanging over them. "No one." I looked up at her. "We call him the Nicest Guy on the Planet. Everybody likes Sam. No one could possibly want to kill him."

Deputy Wheeler slid her notebook into the pocket of her coat and didn't say a word. She didn't have to. "Same phone number as before, Mrs. Kennedy?" I nodded, and she headed over to the next office to talk to Erica.

It had been Erica's suggestion that the two of us split up. "It'll make things easier for all of us," she'd said. All of us, except for me. I hadn't liked sitting alone in the empty office of the former school psychologist. As I looked at walls once covered with photos of wildflowers and baby birds and lambs and chicks, I wondered who we'd get next. Good school psychologists were worth their weight in five-year-old cheddar; the search had been going on since June.

And now we had another murder in our midst and no one to help the kids deal with it.

"Tired?"

Somehow I'd forgotten Gus was in the room. "Why do you ask? Do I look tired?" I pushed my eyelids apart. "Wide open, see?"

"Keep doing that and your eyeballs will dry up and fall right out of your head."

I smiled, but didn't laugh. Couldn't, really. I released my eyelids and blinked away the sandpapery dryness. "Gus, why would anyone kill Sam?" I desperately wanted an answer to my plaintive question. Please give me a reason. Please put some order back into this tragic night. Please give me a world that makes sense.

But I should have known better. Gus and I had known each other a long time, and never once in all those years had he dusted sugar coating onto any truth.

"I don't know, Beth. Tonight there are a lot more questions than we have answers. But what I do know is that he didn't deserve to die." Gus's lips were set in a straight, firm line. "Not so young, and not that way."

I shied away from the reality of murder. "They'll find out who killed him, won't they?"

"It's not my case." He put up a hand to stop my protest. "It's not my case," he repeated. "But Sam was one of Rynwood's own. None of us will rest until his killer is put where he belongs."

"Promise?" I held up my right hand in the Girl Scout salute, palm out, thumb holding down my little finger, three middle fingers standing straight. Scouting was another thing Gus and I shared.

Gus returned the salute. "I promise."

And, oddly enough, I felt better.

The night Sam was killed, I lay staring at the bedroom ceiling far more than I slept. Every time I started to drift away, I'd jerk awake with unwelcome images. Sam's scarf. The SUV, forever lonely. A wife, bereft of her lifelong helpmeet. Crying children.

When the alarm clock beeped, fatigue hung on me like a heavy overcoat. Then I made the mistake of working out how much sleep I'd had. "Four hours," I said out loud, thumping downstairs in the only clean clothes I could find: a pair of khaki pants coated with black cat and brown dog hair, and a bright green sweater given to me by my mother.

Until now I'd worn it only when St. Patrick's Day fell on a day I didn't have to leave the house. My mother's choice of clothing gifts always made me look sallow and slightly jaundiced. My personal rule for unsuitable clothing gifts was to wear the article a minimum of six times before giving it away, but Mom's gifts were an exception. Three times, tops.

"Passing on the right!"

Jenna clattered down the stairs ahead of me, her long hair bouncing against her back. The sight normally would have made me smile, but today . . .

"Jenna! Did you comb your hair?"

My daughter stopped at the bottom of the stairs, one hand on the newel post. Without looking back, she said, "Sure. What's for breakfast?"

"Did you comb out your hair this morning?"

"You mean like *comb* comb?"

"What other kind is there? Back upstairs, young lady, and bring that comb to the kitchen. I want to see it slide through your hair from roots to ends without stopping."

I didn't want to scold her. I wanted to be compassionate and thoughtful; I wanted to be the mother we all dreamed of having. But my dreams last night had been bad and today's mothering was headed the same way.

Jenna's bright face soured. She stomped back up the stairs, each footfall making the house shudder.

I wanted to call her back, to say I didn't mean to be this way, that I hadn't slept well, that I was sad about Sam, that I was confused and scared and needed a hug to make my scary thoughts go away.

Instead, I went into the kitchen and hauled out bowls and boxes of cereal.

Oliver skipped into the room and slid into his chair. "What's Jenna so mad about?"

Her pathetic excuse for a mother. "That's Jenna's business," I said, "not yours."

His eyes went wide and, for the second time in five minutes, I wanted to take back what I'd said. This was not shaping up to be a good day. Don't make that a self-fulfilling prophecy, I told myself. Dream your day and live into it.

As long as the dreams weren't like last night's.

"Jenna," I told Oliver, "is angry with me."

"For how long?"

I put bowl and spoon in front of him. "Not very, I hope."

"Like only until after breakfast?" His face was a mixture of curiosity, hope, anticipation, and wariness.

Jenna clumped into the room, brandishing a comb. "Is this good enough?" She inserted the comb into her hair, then dragged it all the way through with a flourish that would have done Liberace proud.

Oliver gave me a look. This one was much easier to interpret. It said, "You've made Jenna mad so I'm going to be mad at you, too." The entire situation was all my fault, which made three of us who were angry at me.

But I was the grown-up in the room, so I had to make at least a pretense of knowing what I was doing. I didn't, of course—never had and probably never would—but it wouldn't do to let my children know that. Not now, anyway. Maybe when they were older. Like when they turned thirty.

"Jenna," I said, "I'm sorry for snapping at you about your hair."

She halted, comb halfway through her second demonstration, and looked at me sideways.

Another breath. "I didn't sleep well last night and I'm still very tired. Sometimes when you're tired it's easy to get mad and scold lovely daughters when they don't deserve it."

Jenna dropped into her chair and crossed her arms, tapping the comb against her upper arm. "Well . . . okay." She flashed me a bright smile.

"You should have a glass of warm milk tonight," Oliver said seriously. "That's supposed to help people sleep."

The thought of drinking warm milk was about as appealing as the thought of eating pea soup. Ick. I smiled at my son. "What a nice idea. Thank you."

Jenna poured a stream of cornflakes into her bowl. "Why couldn't you sleep?"

I pushed the pitcher of milk her way. Jenna asking about my personal welfare? This was a first. She was a kind and sunny child, but she'd never been inclined to put herself into someone else's shoes. Could part of her growing up and growing away include a growing empathy with others?

"Thank you for asking, sweetie. That's very thoughtful."

She shrugged and poured about half a gallon of milk on her cereal.

Last night they'd both been on the verge of sleep when I'd picked them up from Marina's, and I hadn't said anything about Sam's death. I'd told two people: Marina, via shocked whispers in the kitchen; and Evan, via a phone call after the kids were in bed.

I considered what to tell them, couldn't think of anything very good, then just started talking. If I kept at it long enough, maybe I'd eventually figure out the right thing to say. Last year at the breakfast table I'd told them about the murder of their principal. A year and change later, here I was doing it again. This was turning into a macabre tradition and it needed to stop immediately. "Do either of you know Blake or Mia Helmstetter?"

"The Blake who plays the piano?" Jenna asked. Once upon a time she'd taken piano lessons, but soccer and now hockey had left no time for lessons, let alone practice.

"The Mia with the yellow hair?" Oliver asked. His sister and I both stared at him. Never once had Oliver commented on a girl's appearance.

Jenna opened her mouth, but I cut her off. "Yes, that Mia and that Blake. They probably won't be in school today."

"Are they sick?" Jenna asked.

Sick at heart, I wanted to say. "No, their father died last night."

My two children looked at each other, communicating a silent message that I couldn't intercept. Jenna plunged her spoon into the cereal. "Mr. Helmstetter's dead?" She shoved the flakes into her mouth, and, chewing, asked the question I'd been dreading. "Dead like Mr. Stoltz, or dead like Mrs. Mephisto?"

Though the murder of Agnes Mephisto had made an impact in their short lives, so had the death of Norman Stoltz, an elderly neighbor who'd had a killing heart attack. I took one of her hands and one of Oliver's in my own, stroking their knuckles gently with my thumbs, trying to rub my love into them. "Like Mrs. Mephisto."

"Killed dead?" Oliver's eyelids opened wide enough to show white all around his blue irises.

I let go of his hand and reached out to put my arm around his bony shoulders. "Chief Eiseley told me himself. The police will find out who killed Mr. Helmstetter. There's nothing to worry about."

"So there's a new bad guy." Jenna pulled her hand out from under mine and went back to eating breakfast.

"I'm afraid so."

Oliver looked up at me, his long eyelashes curling in perfect arcs. "How many bad guys are there?"

How was I supposed to answer that? Option one: Tell him evil lurked everywhere and it would be best to lock the doors and never venture outside. Option two: Tell him that there were only a couple of bad guys out there, that one was already in jail, that the other one would be soon, and that after that he wouldn't have to worry about bad guys ever again.

I rubbed Oliver's back and waited for an option three to come along.

"Are there lots of them?" His voice quavered and he edged up onto my lap. Eight years old was still young enough to want to be on Mommy's lap when monsters threatened.

Option three, where are you?

"No, there aren't," I said firmly. "Most people are very nice. It's kind of like"—Bingo!—"like dogs. There are big dogs and little dogs. Yellow and brown and white and short-haired and long-haired dogs."

He nodded into my armpit.

"A few of those dogs," I went on, "are mean ones. Can you think of any?"

"There's a big dog by the school soccer fields," Jenna offered. "He growls at us through the fence."

Wonderful. I made a mental note to talk to Gary Kemmerer, Tarver's principal. "But other than a few nasty ones, most of them are good dogs, right?"

"Like Spot!" Oliver bounced up and down on my lap. I winced as his weight pounded my thighs. If the kid kept growing at his current rate, my lap was going to be too small by Christmas.

"That's right," I said. "Like Spot."

The three of us looked around for our dog. Spaniel-sized, and as mellow as a dog could come, the solid brown Spot had already been named when we picked him up at the animal shelter a year ago. His name had either been a joke or he'd been named after the puddles he used to leave on the floor.

Spot was in his bed by the garage door. He looked up at the sound of his name, thumped his shaggy tail, and grinned doggily.

"He's a good dog," Oliver said. "Like most dogs. Only a couple are bad."

"Just like people," I said.

"Like people," he repeated and slid to the floor. In seconds he was slurping cereal just quietly enough to keep me from scolding.

"Should I be extra nice to Blake?" Jenna asked.

This, apparently, was the day for hard questions. I'd been handed two of them already and it wasn't even eight o'clock. "How well do you know him?"

"For a fourth-grader, he's good at kickball."

"How do you think you'd want to be treated if you were him?"

Jenna looked thoughtful. "Like normal. I wouldn't want them to treat me any different."

My daughter, my child, my heart. She really was growing up. "Then maybe that's how you should treat Blake."

Oliver laid down his spoon. "But I want to be extra nice to Mia. Is that okay?"

"Being nice is always good," I said. "Just don't . . ." My advice hit a dead end.

"Don't be a weenie about it." Jenna reached for the cereal box. "She'll never like you if you're a weenie."

"Who said I wanted her to like me?" Oliver's cheeks flushed pink.

"Look! He's blushing!" Jenna giggled. "Oliver and Mia sitting in a tree—"

"Time to scoot." I got up from the table. "Jenna, it's your turn to take Spot out. Hurry; we need to leave in ten minutes."

"But I don't have time. I need to call Alexis about our social studies project." Jenna plopped her bowl and spoon next to the kitchen sink.

"You could have done that last night. Spot is your responsibility," I said. "Yours and Oliver's, and it's your turn."

She grabbed her coat and Spot's leash from the hooks by the back door. "If I had a cell phone I could take out Spot *and* call Alexis. It makes *sense* for me to have a cell phone. So, can I?"

This was not a hard question. I smiled at her. "Nope."

Chapter 4

After I dropped the kids off at school, I debated about heading home for a nap. The store didn't open until ten, so there was an hour and a half before I needed to put on my happy bookstore owner face. I sat at the school's curb in the idling car, undecided, until the parent behind me tapped her horn. "Sorry." I waved an apology and turned right out of the school, headed downtown.

Usually the drive through Rynwood made me smile. My adopted hometown was the kind of place that, when you heard the beep of a car horn, you looked around to see who was waving at you. Today, though, downtown, with its warmly red brick buildings, colorful awnings, Victorian streetlights, and quirky window displays, passed by as a faded background.

Poor Sam. And poor Rachel. How was she going to go on without her beloved husband at her side? How many nights would Blake and Mia cry themselves to sleep? I rubbed at my eyes, thinking about the permanent empty ache Sam's family was going to have to make room for.

I parked in the alley and came in the back door, turning on only the minimum of lights, and headed to the tiny kitchenette. It held a small microwave, the hot plate for the teakettle, a cube refrigerator, sink, hooks for our coats, and a door into my office.

I took my brewed and milked (two percent) tea to my desk. There were a couple of ways to combat fatigue. One was to get some sleep, but since I'd taken that option off the table, I was left with option two. Get busy. I toasted the towering pile of paperwork with my tea mug, put my head down, and got to work.

When the phone rang, I was engrossed in accounts payable. "Good morning, Children's Bookshelf. This is—"

"Beth," said a sobbing woman. "Is it true? About Sam?"

I laid down the invoice from Ingram. The voice was too high-pitched for Marina, and besides, I'd told her about Sam last night. Debra O'Conner, in spite of her recent transformation from perfectly smooth to slightly rumpled, would never call without identifying herself. Claudia wouldn't be asking questions, she'd be demanding answers. "It was on the news this morning," the woman wailed. "I just can't believe it. Who would kill Sam? It doesn't make any sense."

"No, it doesn't—"

"Who would be so horrible? I thought we were safe here in Rynwood. I thought this was a nice place to live."

"Well, I—"

"After Agnes was killed I wanted to move away, but Dan said don't be silly."

Got it. "CeeCee, the police will—"

CeeCee Daniels gave a high-pitched laugh. "The police? The police didn't figure it out last time. You did. You and Marina."

We should have left well enough alone, and I said as much.

"But nobody liked Agnes," CeeCee said. "Everybody

likes Sam. He's so *nice.* No one would kill him except some nutcase. So there's a nutcase who's wandering around free. They say it's easier the second time."

I liked CeeCee, I really did. But when she got worked up, she came across like a bad combination of too many soap operas and too many cop shows.

"The police will figure it out," I said. "Marina and I were only a step or two ahead of them last time, and that was mostly luck." Bad luck, if you asked me, but no one did.

"Do you realize I was one of the last people to see Sam alive?" CeeCee's voice shook slightly. "Did you see who left last?"

So CeeCee had no idea that Erica and I had found Sam. A tension I hadn't known I'd been holding released in my chest. She didn't know and I wasn't about to tell her, as I had zero desire to relive the event.

I glanced at my watch. Five to ten. "CeeCee, I have to go. I'll talk to you later, okay?" I put the phone down on her squawking noises and went to open the store.

At eleven, when the slow trickle of Friday morning customers became a steady stream, I picked my head up and looked around. I was still the sole staff member in the store. Lois wasn't scheduled until twelve, but where was Marcia? She should have been here long ago. I leapt to the worst conclusions. Stroke or car accident. Accidental fall of grandchild, sudden illness of grandchild, disease symptoms in grandchild so outlandish that an emergency trip to Mayo Clinic was required, fast driving on a dark highway with a sobbing child, or worse, a quiet one. Driving through the night to—

"Good morning!" Marcia breezed past me, smiling and waving to the customers.

The cowardly part of my personality wanted to let this go, to forget Marcia's increasingly tarnished work attendance record, to forget how little I cared for her attitude toward out-of-town customers, to forget the whispering conversations of which the only word I could hear was an indignant "Beth."

Most of me wanted to forget all that, but there was a rising tide of ire that was sweeping Spineless Beth off to the side. In her place—at least for now—was Forthright Beth.

I gave the store a practiced look. Everyone was browsing contentedly. I put my shoulders back and sallied forth to the back of the store. It wouldn't be completely private, but if we kept our voices down, no one would know my problem employee was getting a dressing-down.

Marcia was hanging up her coat with one hand and handing me photographs with the other. "Look, isn't he the cutest thing?"

I took the pictures and felt my forthrightness slipping away.

"Just printed these this morning." She smoothed her overly blond hair. "Mrs. Tolliver is going to stop by today, and last time she was in we were talking about my grandbaby. I took these last night. Isn't he the most adorable child ever?"

Marcia's daughter and her family had moved back to Rynwood last summer, and Marcia had gone from a life of bookstore clerking and bridge club and dinner at the country club to clerking and grandson adoration, with a concentration on the adoration.

I looked at the photos. The boy was almost three, with blond hair, chubby cheeks, and a big smile. "He's a good-looking kid." Just as he had been in the previous thousand photos she'd shown me.

She snatched the pictures away. "Good-looking doesn't do him justice. Oh, you're just poking a little fun. Always the jokester, aren't you?" She giggled.

"Marcia, weren't you supposed to be here at ten?"

"Oh, that." She made a *tsk*ing noise. "The printer was giving me trouble. It took me forever to print those. Sometimes I wonder if these digital cameras are all they're cracked up to be. Computers are such a pain in the you-know-what."

I tried not to look at my watch. "You were scheduled to be here at ten." But why shouldn't I look at my watch? I did so, ostentatiously. "It's after eleven."

"Family is more important than work," she said, smiling. "You're a mother, so I know you understand. Did I tell you what he said last week? It was the cutest thing, he—"

The irritation I'd woken up with came back full force. I tried to tamp it down, but the anger had been building for months and had only needed a night of poor sleep to set it free.

"Ten o'clock means ten o'clock." I tapped my watch. "It doesn't mean whenever you see fit to come in—it means ten o'clock."

"Well, I know that." Marcia had a puzzled look in her eyes. "And I'm always on time, except for once in a while."

I held up my hands and started ticking off fingers. "Monday he had a haircut you couldn't miss. The week before you had to leave early to shop for a new bib. Before that you had to help interview a new babysitter. And the day we had a rainbow you rushed out of here with hardly a word."

"He couldn't miss seeing the rainbow," she said indignantly. "What kind of grandmother would I be if I let him miss his first rainbow?"

One who has a job? "Emergencies are understandable and perfectly acceptable reasons for coming in late and leaving early. But the definition of the emergency is 'urgent necessity,' and I don't see that clipping your grandson's fingernails is a necessity."

She picked a stray hair off her sweater. "Oh, look. It's one of his! See the curl?"

"Marcia, I need dependable staff. A store can't function without reliable employees, and reliable doesn't mean rushing off for things that aren't important."

"Not important!"

Finally, I had her full attention.

"How can you say that picking out his first tricycle isn't important?"

"It's no emergency," I said.

"Well, when you're a grandmother, maybe you'll understand that the definition of emergency changes when there are grandchildren involved." She smiled tolerantly.

"I hope I never consider anyone's bowel movement anything I need to leave work for."

Marcia's eyes thinned to slits.

Oh. My. I'd said that out loud, hadn't I? Time to move this conversation elsewhere. "Let's go into my office." I took a step to my right, leading the way. "We'll talk this over and—"

Marcia stayed rooted in place. "Some things are more important than work," she said distinctly. "I always thought of you as a sympathetic employer. With children of your own, I thought you would understand."

"I do." I tried to diffuse the ratcheting tempers by trying to relax, trying to smile. "But if you commit to working, you have to put your job at a higher priority than most other things in your life."

She gaped at me. "I can't believe you said that! What kind of mother would put a mere job ahead of her own flesh and blood?"

A mother with a mortgage, two college educations that needed funding, and a child support check that, though it had once seemed generous, now didn't seem to cover the needs of two rapidly growing children. "There's a balance," I said as evenly as I could.

"That's what I'm talking about. And now is as good a time as any."

"For what?"

"I need the week of Thanksgiving off. Plus, I won't be able to work the week after Christmas, and not the week before. There's just too much to do!" Marcia wafted off into descriptions of turkeys drawn in the shape of hands and Christmas cookie baking and present wrapping and stocking hanging.

When she got to marshmallow making (*making?*) I made a rolling motion with my index fingers. "Wait a minute. Did I hear right?"

"I don't know." Marcia smiled, dimples showing in both cheeks. "Did you hear that I need the week of Thanksgiving off? And the weeks before and after Christmas?"

My ears felt as if they were on fire. "I can't possibly give you that much time off."

"Why not? Lois can work a few extra hours. Sara and Paoze will be off school. And look at this place." She waved a languid hand at the bookshelves. "It's not like people are packed in here Walmart tight."

I chose my next words carefully. "Christmas is our busiest time of the year. Our annual profit depends on doing well in December."

"Your annual profit, not mine. All I get is a paycheck." She shrugged. "A small one, at that. My husband keeps saying I should ask for a raise. I've been here longest, other than Lois. So I'll ask now. Can I have a raise?"

In the same conversation she was asking for three weeks off smack in the middle of the busiest time of year, she was also asking for a raise. I had a pet theory that, if spontaneous combustion truly existed, it was caused by having too many contradictory points of view in one body. I slid back a few inches, but Marcia didn't burst into flames.

"And come to think of it"—she leaned her head to one side—"why don't I take the first part of January off, too. All we do that week is inventory, and you don't need me for that."

"If you care about this job so little," I said quietly, "why do you work here at all?"

"Because I love books." She gave me an indignant look.

"I need you to commit to working at least twenty hours a week. Twenty-five between Thanksgiving and Christmas."

"Twenty-five hours?" She compressed her lips, making small vertical lines appear all around her mouth. "During the holidays?" she asked. "Weren't you listening? I need that time off."

"And I need you to work twenty-five hours a week."

Her mouth moved, but nothing came out for a while. "But I can't work that much!"

"Then maybe you should quit."

There. I'd said it. Out loud, calmly, coolly, and without too much squeak in my voice.

Marcia frowned. "Maybe I . . . ?" The sentence trailed off into the place where sentences go to die when the speaker (at last) clues in to the fact that she hasn't had any idea what was really going on. "Quit?" she asked. "You want me to quit?"

Yes, please. But I couldn't say that out loud. Or . . . could I? "Yes, I do."

Her face went still. "After all these years? All the days and nights and weekends I've worked for you, and just like that you want me gone?"

Not nearly as many nights and weekends as she'd been scheduled to work, but whatever.

"All the things I've done for this store, and when I ask for a little time off, it's time to get rid of me?"

There wasn't any point in answering. She'd decided to cast herself as victim, and I was the villain. It was a new role for me, outside of the times I was dubbed the Meanest Mom in the Whole Wide World, and I already knew I didn't like it. At all.

"You're firing me, aren't you?"

Her voice was loud now, and I tried not to think about how many customers were listening in. A smart bookstore owner would have had this conversation in her office behind a closed door.

"Aren't you?" Marcia's white face had gone a blotchy red.

"Yes," I said. "I'm firing you. I'll pay you through the rest of the week and—"

"You can't fire me." She snatched her coat off the hook and forced her arms through the sleeves "I quit!"

She stomped through the store, head high, the edges of her long woolen coat swinging open, catching at the occasional low-shelved book and pulling it to the ground. At the front door she turned and made determined eye contact. "I hope you have a good lawyer!"

And she was gone, leaving behind a trail of animosity, pain, and a few picture books. The picture books I could put away, the others . . . I sighed.

A female face peeked up over the top of the Middle Grades books. "Is she gone?" she asked in a stage whisper.

"Afraid so." My smile was weak. "I'm sorry you had to listen to that."

"Good heavens." The customer straightened and walked around the end of the shelving, and I ran through names until I found a set that fit. Barb. Barb with a W. Two syllables. Walker. Wilhelm. Wylie . . . Got it.

"Mrs. Watson," I said, "that conversation should have

been private and I apologize. It couldn't have been very pleasant."

"Hah!" Mrs. Barb Watson came close and thumped me on the shoulder. As she was six inches taller than I was and sturdy as an overengineered bridge, I rocked back on my heels and tried not to wave my arms about.

"Best eavesdropping I've had in years," she said. She thumped me on the shoulder again. This time I was prepared for it and leaned into the blow. "Top-notch moment in the history of this store, if you ask me." She guffawed. "You hit a high note at the bowel movement. Good girl!"

"I liked the 'Why do you work here at all' part." A short, stoop-shouldered woman edged closer. Her white hair curled up and around the wildly colored knit hat she wore. "That was my favorite."

"No, the best part was 'And I'm always on time, except for once in a while.' Please." A middle-aged man in a suit and tie leaned against an endcap of stuffed animals. "I would have fired her then and there. Your restraint is admirable."

I looked from customer to customer to customer. "You think so? I mean, I've never fired anyone before. It's not . . . not a very nice thing to have to do."

"Course not," Barb said.

The man shook his head. "It never is. That's why it's so important to hire the right people in the first place."

"Wait a few days," advised the elderly woman. "Things will settle down and you'll find the store operates fine without a clerk like that."

"You think so?" Management consultants lurked everywhere; you just had to open your eyes.

Barb chuckled, a rich, throaty noise that rose up out of her body like a warm fountain. "Know so."

The stoop-shouldered woman edged closer. She looked left and right and we all drew close. "I probably shouldn't say this, but . . ." She looked at the floor and we leaned farther in. "But Marcia once told me that *Anne of Green Gables* took place on an island." She paused dramatically. "*Long* Island."

My male consultant looked puzzled. I was appalled. Barb threw back her head and laughed. And, since her laughter was too big to stay inside one person, it spread first to the elderly woman, then to the man in the suit, and finally to me.

We held on to bookshelves to keep from falling to the floor, and laughed and laughed and laughed.

A mere four hours later, I was sitting in a freshly empty Tarver classroom. Erica placed her half-glasses on her nose. "This special meeting of the Tarver Elementary PTA will come to order," she said, managing to convey disapproval without so much as a sniff.

I looked out across the minimalist audience, which consisted of three of the four dance committee members and no one else. Marina, the fourth member, was in the gym, babysitting the kids.

Erica forged ahead. "Our vice president, Claudia Wolff, called this meeting. Claudia, you have the floor."

"Thank you, Erica," Claudia said gravely.

I glanced down at the agenda: "Thanksgiving Father-Daughter Dance." The PTA had sponsored this dance every year for eons. Always held the second Saturday in November, it was consistently the PTA's most successful fund-raiser.

What on earth could be so important that Claudia needed to call a meeting? The dance committee had met a few days ago; all the dancing ducks were in a row. There was the small matter of who was going to play deejay, but I was almost sure the issue would be settled without bloodshed. CeeCee Daniels was committee chair, and though she didn't always present herself as someone who could sort a sock drawer, she was, in fact, a very competent organizer.

"Having this meeting was a difficult decision for me," Claudia said. "I've had hardly any sleep as I've struggled with what's the right thing to do." She bit her lower lip. "I'm not sure I've ever had such a hard thing to decide."

Erica started tapping her index finger on the tabletop, a sign to "get to the point or I'll make your point for you."

"Some things are easy to decide," Claudia said, "but the tough decisions are hard."

Maybe it was the deejay. Or maybe . . .

Erica couldn't stand it any longer. "Please. We all have other places we'd rather be."

A sudden flash of Claudia insight filled my brain. "Oh, no," I whispered, too softly for anyone to hear. "Please, no." But the universe is a cold, hard place and my plea went unanswered.

Claudia focused her big wet eyes on our PTA president. "What are we going to do about the murder of Sam Helmstetter?" She swung around to look at me.

I wanted to put my head in my hands. Almost by accident, I'd once helped put a killer in jail. The odds of doing it again were about as good as the chances of me losing ten pounds over the holidays. The odds of me *wanting* to do it again were roughly the same. I wanted the murderer brought to justice, of course I did, but I wasn't going to risk life and limb to do so, not with two children depending on me.

Firm thoughts. Excellent. Keep it up, Beth. Don't let your mind wander off into investigations you aren't going to pursue. Stop wondering about who knew of the change in the meeting date. Stop wondering about that white van you saw on the way home that night, parked where you'd never seen any vehicle parked before. Stop wondering about any of it.

"We are all troubled about Sam's death." Erica, as always, was ready with the right thing to say. Maybe in a million years or so some of her ability would rub off on me. "But this agenda"—she held up the sheet of paper—"is related to PTA business."

"I know." Claudia dabbed at her eyes. "That's why this is so hard. The dance is important, but not as important as Sam."

Erica folded her hands and spoke in a patient voice. "Claudia. What are you proposing?"

"I think . . ." Her mascara was almost, not quite but almost, smearing. "I think we should cancel the dance. In honor of Sam. It wouldn't be right for us to dance the night away with poor Sam dead."

Since the event closed down at nine o'clock, it was hard to square reality with her statement, but I suppose I knew what she meant.

"Especially when you think about where he was killed." She drew in a raggedy breath. "In this very parking lot. Think about it. Poor Sam was killed right there!"

I'd been trying very hard *not* to think about it. Thanks to Claudia, however, my internal gaze went out the door, down the hall, out the front door, and to the dark far corner of the parking lot, where Erica and I had . . .

"We're all having a hard time with Sam's death," Erica said. "But let's stay on topic, shall we?" There was velvet steel in her voice, and I got a glimpse of what she'd been like in the courtroom. "Now. You are proposing a cancellation of the twenty-third annual Tarver Elementary PTA Father-Daughter Dance, correct?"

Claudia rubbed her cheek. "That's right. It's the least we can do for poor Sam and—"

"Does the dance committee have a recommendation?" Erica asked. "We've advertised the dance. It's scheduled for Saturday, eight days from today. If we're going to cancel, we need to do it now."

CeeCee had that deer-in-the-headlights look. The other committee members were two mothers I didn't know very well. All I knew about Ursula was that she'd had triplets. I couldn't even remember the name of the other woman. Something to do with the weather. Stormy? Autumn?

"Ladies?" Erica asked.

I considered going to fetch Marina, but Marina's response would be: "Cancel the dance? Is Claudia insane?" She'd cross her eyes, say, "That's the stupidest idea I've heard since they decided to revamp the lunch menu and get rid of Tater Tots," and the meeting would go downhill from there. Much better to sit quiet and let events roll out without the benefit of Marina's opinions. She'd be annoyed at my high-handedness, but she'd been annoyed before.

The mother whose name I didn't know slid to the front edge of her seat. "I . . . I think having the dance would be okay. It's a tradition. The girls and dads look forward to it. And it's a very profitable fund-raiser."

I looked at her curiously. She was probably ten years younger than my forty-one, and had straight brown hair like mine. If I cut off my feet to lower my height a few inches and lost twenty pounds, we could look like sisters. Not that I needed another sister.

Claudia straightened. "Why do we let money rule our decisions?" Her voice grew strident. "Is holding a good fund-raiser more important than Sam's memory? Is that what you're saying?"

The unnamed mother slid back. "No. I didn't mean . . . I mean . . ." She shrank into herself and nearly disappeared.

"Ursula?" Erica asked, taking no prisoners. "What do you think?"

"Well . . ." Ursula's gaze darted from Claudia to CeeCee to Erica and back around again. "Maybe we could hold off until December? Or January? After the holidays, anyway. Would that be a problem?"

Of course it would, I thought.

"Yes, it would." Erica was writing, but I couldn't see if she was writing notes or doodling. Sketches of flowers would be my guess. "Rescheduling a large fund-raising event is impossible. We have a Valentine's mother-son dance the first week of February, and holding two dances within a three-week span isn't the best use of anyone's time. Canceling the dance or holding it are the only two realistic options."

As surreptitiously as I could, I craned my neck around the front of Claudia to look at Erica's notepad. Daffodils and tulips.

"Anyone else?" Erica asked. "CeeCee? You're the committee chair. Surely you have an opinion. Currently we have one opinion for holding the dance and one for postponing it. Where do you fall?"

CeeCee pushed her hair back behind her ears. This could be interesting. CeeCee and Claudia had been friends since they ran around in their backyards in diapers and nothing else. I'd heard (from Marina) that their husbands didn't get along, so their friendship was limited, but CeeCee often bowed to Claudia's will.

The last time I'd seen it in action was when they were shopping in the bookstore and Claudia had scoffed at the graphic novel CeeCee was reading. "That stuff's awful. Your kids read too much of that and their brains will rot." And though CeeCee had put the novel back in the rack, she'd come back a week later—alone—and bought it for her son. "It's all he likes to read," she explained. "It's better for him to read this than nothing at all, isn't it?"

"Absolutely," I'd said, and wrapped the novel in special glitter paper, no extra charge.

Now, she opened and closed her mouth repeatedly

without saying a word, and looked as miserable as a cat in a rainstorm.

"CeeCee?" Erica put on a patient smile. "Do you have anything to say?"

"I . . ." Her eyes darted left, right. And down to her lap. "No," she said softly. "Nothing."

Erica's eyebrows rose into high peaks. "No opinion? You've been active on the dance committee for years, headed it the last two, spent hour after hour on the preparations, and you aren't speaking in support?"

CeeCee kept her attention on her lap and shook her head.

"Well." Erica sat back. "Do we have a motion?"

"Yes," Claudia said. "I move that, due to the death of Sam Helmstetter, we cancel the Tarver PTA Father-Daughter Thanksgiving Dance."

"Is there a second?" Erica asked.

My learned response was to wait for Randy, who could always be relied on to second anything. But Randy wasn't here; during the winter he didn't have anyone to cover him at his gas station.

"Do I hear a second?"

I shuffled my feet. Licked my lips. "I second the motion."

Erica stared at me. I could feel the intensity of her unspoken question: *What are you doing?*

Between us, Claudia was smiling as if she'd gotten top score in a spelling bee.

"The motion is seconded. Is there any further discussion? No?" Erica kept her gaze riveted on me. "Roll call vote, please. Those in favor signify by saying aye. Those against, signify by saying nay. Will the secretary call the roll?"

My throat suddenly felt clogged. I coughed once, then again. "Wolff?"

"I hope," Claudia said, "that the rest of the board understands the rightness of canceling this dance. I vote aye," she said, smiling at me.

"Hale?"

I expected Erica to launch into a concise yet detailed summary of the reasons for her vote, but all she said was a short nay.

"Kennedy." I scribbled my vote and looked up. Erica, Claudia, and our small audience were all waiting expectantly. Erica, with her eyebrows still lifted; Claudia, smiling with happy confidence.

But it was a confidence born from a lack of knowledge regarding parliamentary procedure. Seconding a motion does not mean support of a motion. It merely means you agree that the topic of the motion should be discussed. Not many people understood the intent of a second, but thanks to an online course I'd recently taken, *Robert's Rules* and I were as one. "Sam loved to dance with his daughter," I said. "My vote is nay."

Erica's brilliant smile was completely eclipsed by the storm cloud on Claudia's face.

"You can't do that!" she shouted. "You seconded! That means support. You have to vote in favor. Point of order!"

"The meeting is still in order." Erica put on her lawyer face. "A second to a motion merely allows discussion about the motion to take place. *Robert's Rules of Order* is very clear about this, and our bylaws state that we operate under those rules. I have the tenth edition, if you'd like to borrow it."

"She supported," Claudia said. "She has to vote in favor."

"No, she seconded." Erica clicked her pen. "Your objections will be part of the minutes. Beth, are there any communications? No? Then this meeting is adjourned. Thank you for coming."

I hurriedly made a note of the time and started stuffing papers into the diaper bag.

"How could you do that to me?" Claudia asked. She'd stood and was looking down at me with red anger flaring in her eyes.

Confronting hostility was so low on my priority list it might as well not have been written down. "I'm sorry we disagree, but—"

"Sorry? If you were that sorry you'd have voted the right way. But no, you vote with Erica. President's pet, that's what you're turning into. You don't have a mind of your own."

Even I could be pushed only so far. I put the tape recorder into the bag, then stood, surprisingly calm. For years I'd held insults and slurs tight in my stomach, letting them color my days and nights with a dull gray. Tonight her words didn't touch me. Was it possible I was finally growing up?

I looked Claudia full in her flushed face and my mouth went dry. Possible, but not probable. I smiled and shrugged. "Looks like we'll just have to agree to disagree."

"No way am I agreeing with you on anything." Claudia's hands had turned into fists. "You can bet your last dollar that I'll never vote for anything you want. Ever!" She tossed her nose in the air and stomped out of the room.

My hands trembled slightly as I watched her go. From now on Claudia would do her best to make PTA meetings miserable for me. I hated being miserable.

Erica buttoned her coat, chuckling. "President's pet? Nice alliteration. Shall I have a name tag made up?"

I summoned a smile. "Choosing the color would be too hard. I need to be color-coordinated at all times."

"Black on white," Erica said. "Goes with everything."

"Please. Those colors would look atrocious against my sleeveless silver lamé gown." I shuddered.

Erica laughed. "Wear it to the dance." She lifted one eyebrow. "Wonder what Claudia is going to wear." She laughed again, hefted her briefcase, and walked out.

Which left two people in the room—me and the woman whose name I couldn't remember. Awkward situation number two, coming right up.

She carried a light blue ski jacket that, though it carried the logo of an expensive manufacturer, looked as if it had seen a lot of winters. Her jeans were scuffed at the bottom hems, but that didn't mean anything. I'd recently discovered that the worn look was considered cool, even for adults. So either she was trendy or she didn't have a lot of money to spend on clothes. Or maybe she was like me and cared about clothes as much as she cared about the current price for a share of Berkshire Hathaway stock.

"Hi, Beth," she said. "I don't know if you remember me. Summer Lang?" She lifted the ends of her sentences, making everything she said sound like a question.

"Hello, Summer." I slid a glance at my watch. "What can I do for you?" If I knew my best friend, right now Marina would be shooting baskets with the kids. She was the worst basketball player ever, but that didn't stop her from having a good time. I could just hear her: "She shoots! She misses for the three hundred and thirty-seventh time!"

Since I was the second worst basketball player in the world, and since I didn't find nearly as much fun as Marina did in playing horribly, it didn't tweak my mom guilt too much to let them play on without me.

Summer dropped a glove, picked it up, then dropped it again. "I just wanted to say how much I admire you for standing up to Claudia like that. That took real courage."

I blinked. "Courage?" Laughter burbled up inside me, but the earnest look on her face made me lock it inside.

"You wouldn't say that if you knew how much I wanted to let Claudia have the vote."

Summer dropped another glove. "If you wanted to back down but didn't, that makes you even braver."

I didn't agree, but she was entitled to her opinion. "Well, thanks."

We stood there in silence, and I came to the sudden realization that we were both feeling the same thing. Awkward.

"So," I said, "it seems as if we're having a dance. Do you have much left to do?"

"Oh, gosh, yes. I'm in charge of food. Lots of food to buy and bake. Which reminds me . . ." She plopped her purse on the table and pulled out a multifolded piece of paper and a pen. "Muffin papers," she said, writing. "Can't forget. Sorry, but I have to make a list if there are four things we need at the grocery store."

"It's three for me." I laughed. "Do you title your lists?"

In answer, she handed me her sheet of paper. At the top in block letters she'd written "PTA Dance Grocery List."

I dug into the diaper bag and showed her a sheet of yellow paper I'd torn off the legal pad at work. Its title: "Tentative Thanksgiving Menu."

"Nice title," Summer said. "Wonder what else we have in common?"

I felt the stirrings of friendship. "How do you feel about politics?"

She shrugged. "Ignore them as much as I can. Coffee or tea?"

"Tea, except for an occasional cup of decaf with dessert."

She nodded. "I love movies with intermissions."

"Books with illustrations."

"Swing dancing."

I held out my hand and she shook it firmly. "Speaking of dancing," I said, "does the committee need any help?"

She fished into her purse for another piece of paper. "Let me look at the master list." She scanned the page. "As long as everyone does what they've promised to do, we're all set." The paper went back into her purse. "Is this dance really the best moneymaker the PTA has?"

"Yup. Something about dancing with their little girls gets the dads to fork over wads of cash." I smiled. "If the moms were around to keep the wallets in the pockets, we'd make a lot less money, but it usually turns into a contest."

Her eyebrows drew close together. "What do you mean?"

"They wind up seeing who can hand over the biggest cash donation."

"Huh. Must be a guy thing. What's the next best fund-raiser?"

"Let me think. We try to hold an event every month of the school year." I ticked off the months on my fingers. "September is the Relay for Tarver. October is the Spook House. November is this dance. February is the mother son dance. March is the carnival. April is the Spring Fling and May is the Fun Run.

"Plus," I went on, "we're going to work on the senior story project this spring and present it in June." At least that was my general plan. One of these days I had to get going on a real schedule. Names. Dates. All that. But there'd be plenty of time after Christmas. Lots of time.

"How about January?" Summer asked.

"Um . . ." Did we have a January event? For me that month was a blur of postholiday recovery and store inventory. "I don't think there is anything."

"Do we want to do anything?"

I looked at her. The question was astute. Summer might be young, but she knew her way around a PTA.

"We always want to do more projects," I said, "and projects cost money. Do you have something in mind?"

She reached into her bag and pulled out another piece of paper. "Since you mentioned it, yes."

Where the other papers had been white, this one was pink. I wondered if she had a color-coded system for her lists, but decided not to ask. Envy wasn't an attractive trait, and list envy was even worse. I plucked the paper from her hand and read the loopy handwriting.

"Summer," I said, "this will have to be run by the board, but I think you have a winner."

Marina and the kids and I walked the three blocks to her house. The kids, as usual, were running half a block ahead. A couple of weeks ago, during the dedication of the new Agnes Mephisto Memorial Ice Arena, we'd enjoyed unseasonable warmth. Blue skies, calm winds, light jackets and no gloves. Those days were long gone. Now the wind whistled through the naked trees, rattling the branches against each other in a rhythm that sounded almost like speech.

I wondered what trees would say to each other. Did they discuss us humans? Did they wish they had our freedom of movement, or did they pity us? "Poor humans," said the trees. "They have such a narrow range of comfort."

"What's so funny?" Marina asked. Even in the sporadic light cast by streetlights and porch lights, she'd seen my smile.

"Oh, nothing." Best friend she might be, but she'd hoot at my whimsical thoughts. She opened her mouth, undoubtedly to say that no woman could truly be thinking of nothing, so I jumped ahead of her. "I fired Marcia."

"You . . . what?" She stuck her mittened index finger into her ear and twisted it around. "Did I hear you correctly? Tell me true, dear heart."

Marina had been on a Shakespeare kick lately. The Southern belle of last year was sooo twelve months ago. I'd spent half a morning dreaming up what she might do next and had come up with possibilities too horrible to consider. Fractured and inaccurate Shakespeare was preferable by far to affecting fake street slang. Or speaking in tongues.

"You heard me the first time," I said. There were reasons I hadn't told Marina yet, and most of them had to do with the very real possibility of hearing "I told you so."

"Forsooth, verily."

"That's redundant."

"If you hadn't given me such good news, I'd call you a nitpicker, but today I won't." She took a couple of quick steps to get ahead, then turned around to face me. Walking backward, she said, "Did you really get rid of that leech on the store's profits? That personality-challenged clerk who couldn't sell a Harry Potter book to a kid with a lightning bolt tattooed on his forehead? That incompetent present wrapper? That"—she groped for a suitable epithet—"that *giggler*?"

"She didn't want to work the week of Thanksgiving."

"Tsk, tsk, tsk." Marina's smile was wide.

"Or the week of Christmas. Or the week after."

"Away, you moldy rogue, away!" Marina made sweeping motions with her hands.

"Since I'm a mother, she thought I'd understand that she wants to spend a lot of time with her grandson."

"Pish!"

"That's not Shakespeare." I stopped walking. "And quit going backward or you're going to trip and land on your keister."

She patted the body part in question with both hands, but slowed to a halt. "Lots of cushion. And I never said 'pish' was Shakespeare."

"Then you need to wave a flag when you're out of the William S. zone."

"Where are you going to find another clerk?"

"Aye, there's the rub."

Marina clapped her mittens together. "Beth's playing? Hooray!"

I winced. "It was an accident."

"You are no fun. But I bet that has much to do with the unlamented but certainly painful departure of your former employee. Tell me when I'm wrong." She threaded her arm through mine and we started walking again. Ahead, the kids had jumped into the gutter and were scuffing through the last leaves of the season. "Your hands were shaking. You had to take deep breaths. Your mouth was dry." She patted my arm. "Do I have the symptoms right so far?"

"Three for three. Am I going to live, Doctor?"

"Only if you promise not to torture yourself for firing her. This was a long time coming, and the only thing you should regret is not doing it sooner."

"But—"

"Promise."

"Yes, Doctor."

"Good." She did the arm pat thing again. "Luckily, I have a surefire guaranteed cure."

"I don't have time for a pedicure."

"Now, now. Let the doctor finish."

I looked at her. For years Marina's guaranteed solution to anything had been a pedicure. "Yes, ma'am."

"That's a good patient. Dr. Marina knows best."

"What about the time she prescribed dinner at that run-down restaurant because it would be good for me to see the seamy side of life, and I got food poisoning?"

"You ended up losing a few pounds, as I recall. Would you like to thank me now or later?"

"I still can't eat hamburgers." The very thought made my stomach heave.

"Thanking me later will be fine." She hopped a step to make our footsteps match. "The current situation requires a serious level of doctoring. Please pay attention."

This game had gone far enough. Withdrawing my arm from hers, I stopped dead in the middle of the sidewalk.

"Uh-oh," Marina said. "I went a little too far, didn't I?"

"About twenty feet ago."

"Oh, dear." Her face drooped into lines of sorrow. "It's the bane of my existence. The Devoted Husband says that's why the older offspring never visit. That they're afraid of their mother's games."

"The kids never visit because one of them goes to college in Boston, one is stationed in Germany, and the other is in Africa with the Peace Corps."

"Why, that's right, isn't it? I should have known the DH was teasing."

"You do, however, tend to get carried away. It's irritating that I always have to be the responsible one."

"I know." She hung her head. "I promise never to do it again."

While on the surface it sounded like a great idea, on the whole the idea was a chilling one. No spur-of-the-moment Marina excursions? No more coin-flip trips? Some of my favorite adventures had played out from the flip of a coin. We'd pack the kids into the car and, whenever we came to an intersection where we were required to stop, someone would flip a coin. Tails, we'd go left, heads, we'd go right. If the coin was lost on the floor or in the upholstery, we'd go straight. Jenna still talked about the "best root beer float ever" we found on a coin-flip trip. A year later we tried to find it again, but couldn't. Marina's theory was that things appeared magically for a coin-flip trip and faded away like Brigadoon when we left the premises, and I almost believed her.

"If you keep a promise like that," I said, "you'll wither away to mere normalcy, and no one wants that."

"Not even Zach?" She indicated her youngest son, who was showing inclinations that he might be taking after his father, a civil engineer. I was reminded of the old joke: At a party, how do you tell the difference between the introverted engineer and the extroverted engineer? The extroverted one stares at your shoes instead of his own.

"Zach loves cooking night," I pointed out.

Marina brightened. "He does, doesn't he?" She'd begun cooking nights last winter. We gathered together leftover ingredients from both of our refrigerators and, with the kids' help, brewed up a meal. Some dinners were hits, and once we'd had to order out pizza when not even iron-stomach Jenna could eat the unappetizing mix of corned beef, eggs, hot dogs, and chicken noodle soup, but overall, cooking night was a great success.

"Yes, he does," I said. "And once you tell me what you have planned for me, I'll try and be more spontaneous myself."

"Promise?"

I tried not to think about what I might be getting myself into. Though as I almost always went along with Marina's ideas after short bouts of dragging my heels, I didn't see that I was taking much of a risk. "Promise."

"Hot diggity!" Marina jumped into a little dance, humming what might have been an Irish sea chantey. "Then I will relent and taunt you no longer. You will be glad to know that I have solved all of your problems."

"It's about time someone perfected cold fusion."

"That's next week. This week I found you . . ." She

spun around. Then, with a stomp of a foot, arms outstretched, she presented her announcement. "Ta-dahh! I found you the perfect bookstore clerk."

"You did . . . what?"

"You heard me. She's my new neighbor and she'll be perfect for the job." Marina smiled widely, sure that her offering was the best present I'd ever received.

"I'll find my own employees, thank you."

"Now, don't go all annoyed at me," Marina said. "What's this?" She stretched her arms high and stood on her tiptoes.

"If you're trying to call a cab, we're only half a block from your house."

"No, silly. It's me, being high-handed. Get it? High-handed? Come on, laugh. You know you want to."

I let my laughter rise up and out and into the night air. Marina knew nothing about clerking and, in spite of the fact that she'd raised three and a half children, knew very little about children's books. She had a tendency to think her friends were smart, capable, and good-looking, and she had the best intentions in the world. Who could ask for a better friend?

Chapter 5

The following Wednesday was the opening of firearm deer season in Wisconsin. It was also the day the Children's Bookshelf put out Christmas books. The previous owner had started the custom and I, after a private war with myself over stocking Christmas items before Thanksgiving, had continued the tradition. Thousands of men drove north to hunt, and thousands of "hunters' widows" stayed behind to get started on their Christmas shopping. Who was I to deprive these poor women of the chance to cross a few items off their lengthy lists?

In the past, Marcia had helped customers while Lois and I rearranged the store. Today it was just Lois and me. Sara was coming at noon, but that was hours from now.

"How in the heck are we going to get this all done?" Lois, dressed in her Deer Day costume of Day-Glo orange turtleneck, neon green pants, and pink hair band, stood in the doorway to the back storeroom. She pursed her lips as she surveyed the towering stacks. The boxes had been opened and inventoried as they arrived at the store, but we hadn't had time to sort them into categories. "And I can't believe you ordered this many books.

Last year we were selling holiday books at half price the week before Christmas just to get rid of them." She slid me a glance. "Or . . . *did* you order these?"

I sighed. "No. I let Marcia. She asked and asked. I thought maybe . . ."

Lois gave an eloquent sniff.

"We'll do it in bits and pieces," I said. "If we don't get it all done today, the world's not going to end."

Lois shook her head, clearly not convinced. "We always have these books out by two o'clock."

We looked at each other. I'm sure the anxiety I saw in her face was mirrored in my own. If we didn't have the books out by two, we'd be facing the combined wrath of Mrs. Tolliver and Auntie May.

Mrs. Tolliver was the blue-haired matriarch of one of the founding families of Rynwood. As far as she was concerned, her wishes were law, and one of her wishes was to buy a Christmas book for each of her grandchildren for a Thanksgiving present. "The gift of a book about Christmas," she'd said more than once, "is pointless after the holiday has arrived."

Auntie May was May Werner. The entire town of Rynwood called her "Aunt," and the entire town was afraid of the tiny ninety-one-year-old woman. While her memory of what happened last week might be fuzzy, she could recall every embarrassing incident in every person's life, even if she hadn't been present at the time. She had an uncanny memory for scandal and cackled with delight when someone was caught in a lie.

She was a resident of Sunny Rest Assisted Living, two blocks away, and when the mood struck, neither snow nor rain nor heat of summer would keep Auntie May from getting some unlucky nurse's aide to push her bright purple wheelchair downtown.

Auntie May liked to see the Christmas books in the store before anyone else bought a single one. Two years ago, I'd made the mistake of letting Mrs. Tolliver choose a book before Auntie May had had her fill of gazing at the display. The mental wounds I'd received from the resulting scolding had healed, but I wasn't sure of the thickness of the scar tissue.

I looked at the pile of books, at Lois, back at the pile of books. There was no possible way we were going to get it all done by two o'clock. I closed my eyes and briefly considered fleeing the country. No, that wouldn't work; I didn't have passports for the kids. "All we can do is try our best," I said. "No one can expect more."

Lois make a rude noise. "Want to bet?"

"No."

By one forty-five, the three of us were exhausted from moving around so many books, cranky from trying to be nice to customers who said they'd be buying the book online but it was nice to see it in person first, and nail-biting anxious about the impending deadline.

At one fifty, I decided we were overreacting. Mrs. Tolliver and Auntie May would understand why the books weren't out. They were both reasonable human beings who knew that circumstances occasionally blew out of control. It was silly for us to be scared, just plain silly.

I said as much to Lois and Sara, and Lois nodded emphatically. "You're right. It's ridiculous to work ourselves to a frazzle over this."

Sara looked up from a box of board books. "They're just two people. And Auntie May hardly ever buys anything, anyway."

"Exactly."

We nodded, a trio of wise women agreeing on the state of the universe.

At one fifty-nine we were rushing around like crazed cats. To the back of the store for armfuls of books; to the front of the store to shelve them; to the back for more books; back and forth, back and forth, our breaths growing short, our arms growing tired.

When the bells overhanging the front door pealed out their merry jingle at two o'clock sharp, we exchanged despairing glances. We'd cleared out the shelving in front, and we'd set out the middle-grade and young adult Christmas books, but there were still huge stacks in the storeroom. There were the Christmas picture books, the illustrated books, and the boxed-set books. There were stencil books, coloring books, and cookbooks. Then there were the Christmas-themed stuffed animals, the cellophane bags, the stickers, and the bookmarks.

Why had the previous store owner ever thought that getting all this done in one day was a good idea? Why had I continued the tradition? Why did I continue to do things that made life hard for me?

But maybe it was someone else walking in the door. Rynwood had a population of five thousand. Dane County had upward of half a million people. Surely someone other than Mrs. Tolliver or Auntie May was standing at the front of the store right now. Maybe it was a first-time mother, newly moved to town, who needed to stock up on Sandra Boynton books. Or maybe—

"Well!" said an imperious voice.

Or maybe it was Mrs. Tolliver, winding up for a slap shot down the middle.

"It *is* two o'clock, isn't it?" She pulled off her black leather glove and cast a dramatic glance at her thin wristwatch.

I tried out my apologetic smile. "Yes, it's two. I'm so sorry we don't have all the books out, but we're running shorthanded today. We're doing our best to—"

"I'd say your best isn't good enough," she said in clipped tones. "My father always said a store that doesn't live up to its promises isn't a store worth patronizing."

Frantically I tried to think of when I'd ever promised

anyone that the Christmas books would be out on Deer Day. "I'm sorry you feel that way, Mrs. Tolliver. Is there—" The stack of books in my arms suddenly shifted. I took a dancing step to my left, trying to keep them from tumbling to the ground in an untidy heap.

One step . . . almost there . . . another step . . . and that's when I ran into Mrs. Tolliver. The books cascaded onto her, onto me, and onto the floor. After them fluttered a packing slip.

The quiet that followed was a very loud one. I couldn't tear my gaze away from Mrs. Tolliver's shiny black boots, their toes covered with a thin layer of books. I closed my eyes and waited for the storm to break.

"Hah!" Auntie May rolled herself forward. "Where's a video camera when you need one? Funniest thing I've seen in weeks. Young Beth there looked like a vaudeville routine, and Adelaide, your eyes were big as the night your daddy caught you on the front porch swing with Johnny Schwartz."

Adelaide? I'd never even known she had a first name.

"I'll thank you to never mention that again, May." Mrs. Tolliver smiled thinly. "There is no reason to dredge up old tales."

"Hoo, hoo, look who's talking." Auntie May peered up at her with sharp eyes that had seen everything from iceboxes to iPhones. Her skin had the transparent sheen of age, but it was surprisingly unlined. She'd been raised in a place and time where ladies wore hats and gloves, keeping their faces and hands white, and it showed.

Auntie May must have rolled in the door when the books were dropping to the ground, and here she was distracting Mrs. Tolliver from crushing me with caustic comments. For the first time ever I was grateful that Sunny Rest Assisted Living was within wheelchair-pushing distance.

"Aren't you the one," Auntie May went on in her thin

but strong voice, "who didn't let go of that story about Marlene Upshaw?"

Mrs. Tolliver's chin went up. "That was decades ago, and it was a different situation altogether."

I looked at Lois. "Marlene Upshaw?" I mouthed. I'd never heard of her.

"Before my time," Lois whispered.

"Hah!" Auntie May thumped her fist on the arm of her wheelchair. "Like heck it's different. Marlene's life was ruined because you wouldn't stop telling everyone in town that she was no better than she should be. No wonder she couldn't get married." *Thump*. "No wonder she couldn't get a job." *Thump*. "No wonder she had to leave town."

Mrs. Tolliver smoothed her gloves. "If I recall correctly, and I'm sure I do, she married quite well. I shed no tears for her."

Lois and Sara and I flipped our attention back to Auntie May, attendees at a riveting game of gossip.

"He was fat, bald, and thirty years older than she was." She pointed a knobby-knuckled finger at Mrs. Tolliver. "Are you still fool enough to think all his money could make her happy? What she wanted was to marry Dale Crowley, but you put a stop to that, didn't you? And then when Eddie Tolliver decides you might be good enough for him, you toss poor Dale away like a dirty handkerchief. What good came of all that gossip?" She leaned forward and fixed her victim with a hawklike stare. "What good?"

Mrs. Tolliver gave a genteel sigh. "And what good comes of dredging up the events of decades past?"

"Good?" Auntie May cackled. "None. I just like seeing you squirm."

Underneath the expertly applied Tolliver makeup, red spotted her cheeks. Her chest rose and fell and I got the inevitable feeling you get when watching a bad comedy—the feeling that this was going to turn ugly in a hurry.

Mrs. Tolliver drew herself tall and opened her mouth. I winced. Lois winced. Sara closed her eyes. Auntie May smiled. But before she could utter a word, a smooth voice interrupted the incipient storm.

"Oh, dear." A slim dark-haired woman darted between Auntie May and Mrs. Tolliver. "You've dropped some books. Let me help." She stooped and gathered a few into her hands. "Is this yours?" She stood and handed Mrs. Tolliver *The Gift of the Magi*. "And this looks like it could be yours." She slid a copy of *A Child's Christmas in Wales* onto Auntie May's lap.

"Don't you just love Christmas?" she asked, smiling out of skin almost too white to be real. "And the books this time of year are so beautiful. Now, *The Polar Express* is nice, but it doesn't hold a candle to the classics. Do you know *The Pint of Judgment*?" She looked at the two combatants expectantly. "My mother read it to me every year. It's one of my earliest memories. What was yours?" And then they were sharing stories of childhood Christmases.

We watched, mouths agape. No one had ever successfully ended an Auntie May vs. Mrs. Tolliver battle. To the best of my knowledge, no one had even tried since 1987.

"Who is she?" I whispered. But Lois shook her head.

We marveled as she had the two women interacting without verbal jabs, then chatting together, and then—wonder of wonders—laughing. I wasn't sure I'd ever heard Mrs. Tolliver laugh. It had a rusty sound, but was pleasant enough.

"It sounds as if you two ladies had wonderful childhoods," said our knight-ess in shining armor. "Thank you for sharing your stories. And speaking of stories and books, it seems as if today is a big day in this store." Her brown eyes smiled into mine.

I swallowed. Maybe she could wade into deep waters without a qualm, but I wasn't that brave. "We usually have all the Christmas books out by midafternoon, but we're, um, a little shorthanded these days."

"Is Marcia taking time off again?" Mrs. Tolliver asked.

"No," I said. "Well, yes. Kind of. She quit. Kind of."

"Fired her, is what I hear."

Auntie May chuckled. Or a noise that I assumed was a chuckle. If it wasn't a chuckle, she was probably choking to death, and it had been a long time since I'd had any first aid training. "Marcia Trommler," Auntie May said. "That girl is a piece of work."

"Goodness knows why you kept her on this long," Mrs. Tolliver said. "If I owned this store, she would have been let go ages back."

"Really? I thought . . ." In truth, I'd thought Marcia had been such a fixture in Rynwood that firing her would cause irreparable damage to the store's profit margin. It sounded stupid, even in my head. Saying it out loud in front of the town's two rival matriarchs would be equivalent to a social death sentence.

Auntie May cackled. "Bethie, honey, if you don't like someone, you have to figure you're not the only one."

"Words of wisdom," Mrs. Tolliver said.

I cast a cautious glance heavenward. If there was ever cause for the world to end, it was Mrs. Tolliver paying her sworn enemy a compliment.

"Ah, shucks." Auntie May grinned, revealing dentureless gums. "That Marcia was a giggler from the time she was two. Can't abide giggling in girls, let alone grown women. Makes our whole breed look silly."

"Marcia babysat my children once," Mrs. Tolliver mused. "But just once. Bernice Klein recommended her."

Auntie May shook her head. "Bernice was a dab hand in the garden, but she was never going to win the Mother of the Year award."

"I was much younger then." Mrs. Tolliver slipped her gloves into her coat pocket. "I'd been taught to respect my elders, and Bernice was a decade older than myself." She looked at the frail woman in the wheelchair. "Shall we look at what Christmas books the girls have put out? I'm sure they'll finish in due time."

"Long as I get a copy of *How the Grinch Stole Christmas* before leaving," Auntie May said. Mrs. Tolliver took firm hold of the wheelchair handles and the two moved off, chatting as if they'd been friends for years.

Our angel of mercy looked at the stack of books she was holding. "These are from the floor. Where do they go?"

"Oh, you don't need to . . ." I glanced at the beckoning empty shelves. "I mean, here, I'll . . ." Flustered was my new middle name.

"Here?" She set them on the shelf, fanned them out expertly, and started alphabetizing. "I love the Tomie dePaola books, don't you? Such wonderful illustrations. Here, let me take those." She reached for the stack Lois held. "All picture books, right? On these displays?"

I watched, mesmerized, as she unerringly put Patricia Polacco before Elise Primavera and M. Christina Butler after Jennifer Liu Bryan, chattering away about the merits of each book and the life of each author. When she alphabetized Fran Manushkin ahead of Angela McAllister, I found my voice.

"Do you want a job?"

Her eyes widened, showing white all around the brown irises. Small veins of red marred the pale color in a way that seemed wrong. A woman this capable of taming brutal adversaries should have perfectly white whites.

"Well . . . I . . . well . . . that is . . ." The power that had granted her the perfect thing to say seemed to have deserted her.

"I'm Beth Kennedy, the store owner." I smiled, feeling a trifle relieved that she could, in fact, be caught off guard. Oh, the ugliness of humanity.

"Yvonne Ganassi."

"Nice to meet you, Yvonne." I held out my hand. "If you give me a minute I'll print out a certificate for you."

"A . . . what?"

"A proclamation of courage for preventing open warfare." I looked over my shoulder at the two women, who were happily debating the merits of illustrators Brian Selznick and Barbara Lehman. "I've never seen anything like it."

"Oh." She let out a long, shaky breath. "It just seemed like the thing to do." She glanced at the happy pair. "It won't last, though," she said in a low voice.

"Cease-fires never do. But we can enjoy the peace while it lasts, right?" I grinned, and, though it took some time, a smile spread across her features, changing her face from wan, pinched, and pale to pretty and pale.

"So how about it?" I asked. "Are you looking for a job? Low pay, long hours, and you get to work with the finest citizens of Rynwood." I tipped my head toward Auntie May and her new sidekick. "No benefits, naturally, and the only perk is you get to read any book in the store."

The phone rang. I looked around. Lois wasn't in sight and Sara was headed this way, weighed down with more books than she should be carrying. "Excuse me." One of these days I'd have to get the book cart's broken caster fixed. Right after I got the car's oil changed. Which would come right after I mended Jenna's hockey sweater. But, really, did a hockey jersey need to be mended? I mulled over the allure of a tattered sports uniform as I hurried to the phone.

"Good afternoon, Children's Bookshelf."

"Yo, Beth."

I held the phone a few inches from my head. After I'd pushed the volume button half a dozen times, I put it back against my ear. "Hey, Marina."

"Hey, yourself. Is she there?"

"My store is packed with people, O Red-haired Ray of Sunshine. Please be more specific."

"Perky today, aren't we? Did we have lunch with the handsome Mr. Garrett?"

"No, we did not. Today is Christmas book day."

"I forgot all about that."

I lowered my voice. "It was ugly for a while, but a small miracle happened and all is well."

"Miracle? Tell me all."

"Later. I'm trying to interview someone, and I really want to hire—"

"But you can't!" Marina wailed. "I told you. I know the perfect person for your store."

"And I have the perfect person standing fifteen feet away from me. Yours will have to find another job."

"No, listen to me. She'll be great, I know she will. She's smart and personable and knows a lot about books and—"

"And she's too late. I've made up my mind, Marina," I said firmly.

"But you can't do that!"

I pinched the bridge of my nose. The morning headache I'd staved off with ibuprofen was coming back. "Marina, this is my store. Last I checked, I get to make the decisions."

"Well, sure, unless they're stupid ones, and I'm telling you—"

"Marina, I've decided."

"Won't you even talk to her?"

"Not if Yvonne takes the job."

"Fine," she snapped. "Then you might lose the chance of getting your best employee ever. Yvonne would be . . ." She finally listened to what her ears were hearing. "Did you say you want to hire a woman named Yvonne? Is she really pale and about five feet tall?"

All was becoming clear. "Dark-haired and soft-spoken."

Marina's sigh blew loud in my ear. "I don't know whether to kiss you or cut you off from my brownies."

"Oliver says kisses are yucky."

"Then a kiss it is." She smooched a long wet one into the phone. "Got to go, kiddo. Love ya!"

I replaced the receiver. Yvonne was on her knees, helping to shelve fluffy polar bears. Though I'd decided to hire her the minute she'd picked the copy of *Carl's Christmas* off Mrs. Tolliver's feet, there was something a little off about her.

Her difference wasn't in the way she dressed: Her jeans were standard denim, her shoes were dark brown trail boots of the type ninety-nine out of ninety-nine adults wore through Wisconsin winters, and her coat was the standard Lands' End navy blue.

I watched her chat with Sara. What was different was the nearly infinitesimal pause that came before she said anything. The swift mental calculation that could only come from a history of saying the wrong thing.

There was something else about Yvonne, too, and it tugged at my mothering instincts. She had that bruised look, the look kids get when they've had too much to bear. It was in the set of her shoulders, in the way she held her hands close to her body, in the wariness of her gaze. A thousand things could have caused this, but all I wanted to do was help make it go away.

The bells had jingled while I was on the phone with Marina. By the time I tracked down a special order and finished helping a substitute teacher find the perfect book to calm unruly children, Sara and Lois and Yvonne had finished displaying all of the Christmas gewgaws and most of the picture books. After I'd answered the phone another half dozen times, rung up a few sales, and wrapped two books in Christmas wrapping paper, it was four o'clock and the Christmas display was complete.

"Well, looky there." Lois flung her arms wide. "It's done. Two hours late, but no one died, and the Ladies Who Tongue-Lash went away happy."

"It looks marvelous," I said, and it did. We didn't have room to display all the books face out, but they'd picked and chosen the most attractive covers to display prominently. Dancing snowflakes hobnobbed with a jolly Santa who looked benevolently upon a baby Jesus who was making a Christmas tree chuckle with delight. "If this doesn't help people feel Christmasy," I said, "nothing will. You've done an outstanding job."

"It was all her." Lois jerked her head at Yvonne. "I don't have an artistic bone out of my two hundred and six. Are you going to hire her, or what?"

"I've already asked, Ms. Manager."

"And she said what?" Lois demanded.

In fact, she hadn't said anything; the phone call from Marina had interrupted the offer I'd been underselling.

Yvonne was toying with the collar of her crewneck sweater. "You want the job," Lois barked. "What could be better than working for minimum wage evenings and weekends? And holidays. Low man on the totem pole gets holidays, you know."

I caught Lois's eye and frowned, shaking my head. She was acting as if Yvonne was already a long-term employee, and I didn't even have a W-4 for her. As that thought came and went, another took its place." "You are an American citizen, aren't you?"

Yvonne started. "I what? Oh . . . yes." Her smile was small and brief. "Born and raised."

"Not around here," Lois said. "You don't have an accent accent, but the way you talk isn't quite right."

"Lois," I said.

"What?"

Honestly, sometimes she was as bad as Marina. "Yvonne hasn't said if she wants the job."

Lois gazed at the tin ceiling. "Of course she does." She shifted her gaze and skewered Yvonne with a laserlike glare. "Don't you?"

Yvonne's shoulders lifted and fell. "I . . . I just . . ."

"Take it," Lois commanded. "You'll regret it every time you open your paycheck, but"—her voice softened—"you'll love every minute you're in this store. It's a magical place."

"I . . ." Yvonne clasped her hands, then unclasped them, then clasped them again, wringing her hands in classic nineteenth-century gothic style. She looked up at me. "Can I talk to you?"

"Um, sure. I know just the place." I glanced around at the empty store. "Can I bring back a cookie for anyone? Chocolate chip?"

Sara grinned. "Yes, please."

Lois heaved a martyred sigh. "Oatmeal raisin. Two of them."

Five minutes later, Yvonne and I were seated at a small round table, our shoulder blades resting uncomfortably against heart-shaped wire chair backs. We were surrounded by antiques of all shapes, sizes, and prices. The Rynwood Antique Mall was run by my friends Alice and Alan, and half the population came here on a daily basis to eat Alice's glorious cookies. "I cook 'em like I like 'em," she always said, and the couple was making more money from cookies than from selling antiques.

I'd told Alice I was gaining more weight from her cookies than from all the other food groups combined. What was she going to do about that? She'd laughed and said, "Have another cookie. The coconut chocolate chip turned out really good today."

Yvonne broke her M&M's cookie into four pieces, picked up one, and covered the other bits with her napkin. She finished the first piece and reached for the second. Though she'd said she needed to talk to me, she didn't seem eager to begin the conversation.

Which could only mean there was something she didn't want to tell me. I considered possibilities. Due to seasonal affective disorder, she never smiled when it was cloudy. Or, thanks to family issues, she'd need to bring—I scanned her face, trying to estimate her age—her daughter to work three times a week. Or, due to a bizarre medical problem, her doctor had said she shouldn't operate a computer keyboard. Or—

"I was in jail."

Or she'd been in jail. If I'd had a month, I might have come up with that possibility, but probably not.

"Actually, it was prison." She gave me a darting glance. "There's a difference."

Prison. Yvonne? She didn't look as if she would swat a mosquito that was poking its pointed nose into her skin. What could she possibly have done to end up in prison?

She pulled out the third piece of cookie. "I was convicted of murder."

The air in my lungs suddenly felt stale and empty. Murder? The cookie I was holding crumbled to bits. Murder? She couldn't have murdered anyone, she just couldn't have. Anyone who loved books as much as Yvonne clearly did couldn't possibly murder anyone. Which made no sense whatsoever, but how can you help what pops into your head?

"Fifteen years ago I was sentenced to life in prison for murder." Her tone was flat. Lifeless. "My husband and I and a woman named Sadie Florentino all worked at a big accounting firm in California." She named the company, but it meant nothing to me. Regional Beth, that was me. Marina still made fun of me for asking who Bergdorf Goodman was, but why should I care about a store hundreds of miles away?

"The prosecutor said I killed her because she and my husband were having an affair," Yvonne said dully. "It didn't take much to convince the jury."

"What happened?" I asked softly.

"Turns out there was a police officer who believed me all along when I said I didn't do it. He believed that I didn't know Sadie and my husband were having an affair. He believed me when I said if I had known I would've strangled my husband instead of Sadie." A half smile came and went. "He never gave up, which was more than I can say for my husband—I mean ex-husband—and my family and almost all of my friends."

Bitterness tinged her voice. "My mother died thinking I was a killer. Mom said she loved me no matter what, but that I wouldn't be in prison if I wasn't guilty." She nibbled at a bit of cookie. "I told her over and over I was innocent, but she just gave me that look."

I knew it well. The look came to women the instant they became caretakers of small, wriggling children. The "you know you've done wrong" look, which segued immediately into "I raised you better than this; I'm so disappointed in you," and ended with "Admit what you've done and things will go easier when your father gets home."

Yvonne went on. "Jake kept looking for evidence that would prove I hadn't killed Sadie. I never even knew he was doing it, until one day he showed up at visitation. He started laughing and pounding the table. 'I got it,' he said. 'I got proof.' " The memory shone on her face.

Curiosity battled with the recognition of her right to privacy, but since curiosity is one of the five major food groups, I asked, "What was the proof?"

"They'd never processed the car for DNA evidence."

Car? My skin tingled. And not in a good way.

"No one ever called for it," Yvonne said. "I couldn't afford an expensive defense attorney. All I had was an overworked public defender on my side. The prosecutor convicted me with motive and opportunity. Plus . . . well . . . back then I never saw any reason to hold my temper back." She looked at her hands, then at me. "It's different now."

I nodded, believing her.

"Anyway, when Jake heard the car was still parked back in the far corner of a police parking lot, he called in some favors and got a forensics team to go over it."

"What did they find?"

"Hair with follicles attached." She lifted a stray brown strand from her sweater and stared at it. "That's the good kind, they said. The DNA matched up with a guy who'd been convicted of a carjacking a couple of years before Sadie's murder. And in the backseat they found some skin cells that matched up."

"I can't believe they didn't run any of those tests for your trial." Indignation vibrated in my voice. "How can someone be convicted of murder without DNA evidence?"

"This was fifteen years ago." She shrugged. "And like Jake said, real life ain't *CSI*. DNA testing is expensive, and if the prosecutor thinks she can get a conviction without bothering, why spend the money?"

Her voice was calm and reasonable. Unreasonably, the aura of peace that seemed to surround her irked me. "How can you be so calm?" I asked. "You spent a huge percentage of your life in prison for a crime you didn't commit. Why aren't you angry? Why aren't you demanding . . . demanding . . ." But exactly what, I couldn't say.

"You see, don't you?" She nodded. "I could be angry at the prosecutor. I could be mad at my ex-husband for having the affair. I could be mad at the way our justice system works. But what good would any of that do? It wouldn't give me back those years, and I don't want to let anger take hold of my life." Her words were soft and imbued with a sense of tranquillity. "I want to leave it behind. All of it."

That made sense, and I said so.

"Thank you," Yvonne said. "Marina says you're the best listener ever."

"Marina tends to exaggerate."

"Maybe." She smiled at me. "But I doubt it."

The compliment made me twitchy, so I shoved half a cookie into my mouth, making myself even more uncomfortable. After I managed to swallow most of it without needing the Heimlich maneuver, I asked Yvonne if she knew anyone in Wisconsin.

"Not really. Just Marina," she said. "And now you."

"No family?"

"Native Californians don't leave the state if they can help it." She fiddled with her napkin. "Now that you know about . . . about me, do you still want to offer me a job? It might not look good to hire someone . . . like me."

Unease curled around the back of my neck and tried to whisper itself into my thoughts. I loosened my ponytail to cover my ears. No whispers allowed. "I'd love to have you."

"If you're sure?"

"Yup." I nodded. "Low pay, horrible hours, and all."

We shook on the deal and walked back to the store in amicable companionship. But while I was telling her about store hours and standard operating procedures, a little thought was growing large. The deaths of Sadie Florentino and Sam Helmstetter had an awful lot in common.

At half past midnight, I sat bolt upright in bed, panting with fear and covered in sweat. I yanked the sheet away from my neck—not a noose, just a sheet—and hoped I wasn't having a heart attack.

I sucked air in through my nose, and blew it out through pursed lips. In. Out. In. Out. In. Out.

A few hundred repetitions later, normalcy crept back. I wasn't being strangled to death, I wasn't going to die from sheer fright, and even without a paper bag, I wasn't going to hyperventilate. I blew out one last big breath and propped my elbows on my thighs, letting my head hang down.

In my dream, a wool scarf had wrapped itself around my neck, all cozy and warm, but then it turned into a rope and kept getting tighter and tighter and tighter. I put a hand up and was almost surprised that my neck wasn't tender to the touch. It didn't take much to figure out where that nightmare came from.

"Way too real." I said the words out loud, and was reassured that my voice sounded the same as it always did. Never had a little too high and a little too nasal sounded so good.

I slid back down between the sheets, disturbing George just enough to get him to start purring, and tried to find some sleep. But just as I started the long, slow fall into slumber, my eyes snapped open.

Sam. Did he normally wear scarves in winter? Some people did, but many people—especially men—didn't even own one. Did Sam? I couldn't remember. If he didn't normally wear one, how did the killer know a weapon would be so handy?

Ideas tumbled around in my head, and it was a long, long time before I found any sleep.

Chapter 6

Thanks to an unusual fall class schedule, Paoze often worked on Thursdays, so the next morning I gathered Lois and Paoze in my office and told them as little as possible about my new hire. Yvonne herself was at the computerized cash register, studying the software manual.

At the end of my narrative, Lois slurped at her tea. "Why did she move here? To Wisconsin."

"Why not?" I turned up my palms. "This is a beautiful state. We have scenic beauty galore, the excitement of four seasons—"

"Four seasons. Right." Lois counted on her fingers. "Fall, winter, spring, and construction season. Or"—she held up her other set of fingers—"winter and three months of poor sledding."

I ignored her. "We have opportunities in every market sector and we have a great educational system."

Lois scrunched her face. "Great? Have they taught our youth anything about sled dogs?" She swung around and faced Paoze. "Well, have they?"

Oh, dear.

"Sled dogs?" he asked.

Lois smiled and I could almost hear her thinking, *Gotcha!*

"Sled dogs are what settled the West," she said.

He looked at her. "It was the covered wagon and the plow and the oxen. I do not believe in sledding dogs."

"What?" She opened her eyes wide. "Here I am trying to teach you the stuff they don't write in history books and you're saying I'm making it all up?"

Paoze shot me a glance, but I held up my hands and backed away. I'd long since declared myself a noncombatant after a game had started.

"What is the history?" His mouth was firm, set in the "you can't fool me" stance that Lois took as a direct challenge. "I know of no sled dogs in Kansas. Sled dogs are in Alaska."

Lois nodded sagely, making her dangling earrings rattle. Today's ensemble, in contrast to the hunter's orange of yesterday, was a long brown skirt over brown boots and a tawny-colored sweater. She'd tied her hair back with a white silk scarf and added earrings made of tiny little cowbells.

The clothes I understood—she was showing her solidarity with the deer currently under siege by thousands of hunters—but I didn't understand the cowbell earrings. She'd told me they represented the deer's hope for survival. I'd said I wasn't sure deer had that complex a psychology, and she'd given me the old milk for my tea.

"Yes, indeedy," she said. "Sled dogs are in Alaska. But they're also raised throughout the upper Midwest. Not down here, we're too far south, but up there." She waved a hand northish. "And back in the day, there were sled dogs everywhere."

"How then and not today?" Paoze asked suspiciously.

Lois rolled her eyes, all attitude and melodrama. "Haven't you heard of global warming? There *used* to be enough snow around here to run sled dogs. We *used* to have long enough winters to ship supplies from Boston to Denver via sled dog. Kind of like the Pony Express, only different, see?"

Paoze was starting to nod. "Would not horses and big sleds have been a good choice?"

Scenting victory, Lois shook her head vigorously. "Horse hooves get too packed with snow on the long trips. Dog feet were better."

I was half convinced myself.

"The biggest problem," she went on, "was the food. When they're working, dogs eat a lot, and to feed the animals the drivers had to hunt. It took them too far out of their way and they lost so much time that the drivers' association decided to make a new breed of dogs. It started with breeding a sled dog with a wolf, but then some scientist got the brilliant idea to cross a sled dog with a camel. What a great idea!" Her eyes sparkled. "A camel crossed with a husky. They called it a huskel, and that, my friend, is how the West was settled."

"Huskel." Paoze crossed his arms. "I do not believe you."

"Well, it was only a little camel, and . . ." But Paoze was walking away. "Bugger," she said. "I had him, did you see it? Why didn't I stop?"

"No telling stories to Yvonne. At least not until spring."

Lois sighed. "I suppose we do want her to stay. Anyway, how did she end up here? Wait. She's had a yearning for fresh cheese curds and this is her chance to make the dream come true."

I loved cheese curds, those small bits of cheese that, when fresh, squeaked against your teeth. Without too much effort I could eat half a pound at a sitting. Unfortunately I would gain two pounds, which seemed to defy a basic law of thermodynamics—matter cannot be created nor destroyed—but I didn't feel up to the explanation my brother would give if I asked. "I doubt anyone would move for cheese curds."

"Kringles?"

Another Wisconsin treat. Kringles looked like a plate-sized race track made of pastry. They were topped with thin icing and came in a variety of fillings: cherry, pecan, cream cheese. All were the stuff of dreams and laden with fat. I stayed away from them at all costs. Except for special occasions.

"You can have Kringles shipped," I said.

Lois frowned. "Does she have family here? Maybe she has a thing for Frank Lloyd Wright architecture. The stuff is everywhere, you know."

"I didn't pry into her reasons." I gave Lois a stern look. "And don't you start, either. If she wants to tell us, she will."

We left my office and were starting our morning chores when the front bells jingled and Mrs. Tolliver marched in. "I hear you've hired a felon," she announced.

I gasped. How had the news spread so fast? But even as I had the thought, I figured out the answer. Texting. Facebook. Twitter. These days it only took an instant for bad news to travel around the globe. One post on someone's wall and your reputation was in tatters.

But who had let out the news? And why?

Lois was staring at me, round-eyed. Paoze had gone blank-faced. Yvonne had instantly become a statue, freezing solid in the act of turning a page. The few customers in the store were poking their heads above the shelves, eyes and ears alert.

Mrs. Tolliver nodded at me. "I thought it only fair to tell you in person that I will not patronize your store any longer. And I must say I question your decision. Hiring a convicted killer when there's a murderer roaming free?" She shook her head briskly.

I faced Mrs. Tolliver. Deep breaths, I told myself. You can do this. Be brave. Or at least pretend that you are. I smiled. "Yvonne is going to be nothing but an asset to this store. But you already know that, don't you?"

Her chin went up. "I beg your pardon. How could I possibly know such a thing?"

"You met her yesterday." I nodded at Yvonne. "Mrs. Tolliver, please meet Yvonne Ganassi. Yvonne, this is Mrs. Tolliver, one of our store's best customers."

The older woman's rounded jawline fell slack. "*You're* the murderer?"

Yvonne's shoulders slumped, her pale face a shade whiter. "I didn't kill anyone," she whispered. "Ever. I mean . . . I couldn't."

Mrs. Tolliver made a *tsk*ing noise. "I beg to differ. Anyone can kill, given the right set of circumstances. Even myself, but I would only kill to save one of my loved ones from death." She pierced Yvonne with a laser glare. "Were you or were you not convicted of the murder of your husband's mistress?"

Yvonne's fingers trembled. She slid the book she held onto a shelf. Into, I noted, the correct place. "Yes, but—"

"Then no more need be said." Mrs. Tolliver swept out of the store.

Of the three remaining customers, one scuttled out, her gaze skittering over and through Yvonne. Another edged to the back of the store. The third, a regular customer from Madison whose name I could never remember, looked at Yvonne, then looked at me. She shrugged and went back to perusing the early chapter books.

"I'm so sorry," Yvonne whispered. "I'll leave now. Maybe you can catch up with Mrs. Tolliver and—"

"Don't be ridiculous," I said, loud enough for everyone in the store to hear, including an openmouthed Lois and a very still Paoze. "You're not quitting. You didn't kill anyone. You're completely innocent. You received a complete acquittal."

She'd also, I'd found out during our walk back from eating cookies, been awarded a hefty compensation check and didn't need to depend on a paycheck from the Children's Bookshelf to make the mortgage payments. This was an excellent financial situation for a bookstore clerk.

Yvonne kept her head down. "It doesn't matter if I'm innocent or not. People will know I was in jail. I don't want to hurt your business, Beth, so I'll just—"

"Don't you dare walk out on me."

"I . . . what?" Her head popped up.

"You saw what happened yesterday. Lois and I can't do all the work that needs doing. We need a third full-time person and you're the person we need."

"There must be someone else."

"Everyone with the qualifications wants benefits, and the only benefit I can provide is the smell of new books."

She was starting to edge away and I didn't know what to do. If I'd been Erica, I could have pummeled her with sound logic and have her begging to sign a contract for indentured servitude. If I'd been Marina, I'd have thrown my arms around her and wept until she agreed to stay. But I was only Beth, and my powers of persuasion were limited.

"Please stay," I said softly. "We need you."

Five simple words, each one a single syllable. No way was that going to be argument enough. I heaved a heavy internal sigh. Yvonne would leave and never come back. The newspaper ad for a new employee would go answered. Lois and I would run ourselves ragged trying to operate the store ourselves. Lois would get sick from stress and have to be hospitalized. I'd rush from store to hospital to PTA meetings to home and would inevitably forget one of Jenna's hockey games. She'd never forgive me, and as we descended into her teenage years, our relationship would deteriorate to silence. All for the want of a bookstore clerk. I looked at Yvonne and couldn't think of anything else to say.

"You really want me to work here?" she asked.

My heart started beating again.

"Yes!" Lois shouted. Her head was peeking up over the row of middle-grade bookshelves. "Absolutely yes."

"Are you sure?" Yvonne asked. "What if Mrs. Tolliver tells three people not to come here again, and those three people tell three other people, and—"

"Don't be such a worrywart," Lois said, coming around the endcap. "It'll be fine. The three of us will make a great team." She draped her long arms over our shoulders. "Paoze, get over here. Add in Sara, and Beth will be franchising the place before you know it." She beamed.

Like I wanted the headache of franchising. Ick.

"Well, if you're sure . . ."

"Very," I said firmly.

"Hooray!" Lois cried, and slapped us both on the back.

We stood there, a perfect photo opportunity for anyone who wanted to take a picture of a young man and three women of varying ages. One tall and familiar man did walk in the door, but he didn't have a camera in hand. What he had was a concerned expression on his face.

"Beth, can I talk to you?"

I shut the door, wondering what was so important that Evan would leave his store in the middle of the afternoon. He'd spent the first year of his ownership of the hardware rearranging displays and adding items that would attract customers other than laconic contractors, and was starting to reap the rewards of his savvy instincts and immensely long hours.

I hoped there wasn't a problem with one of his girls.

Evan was divorced and had two children, but his daughters were grown. One was in the army, and the other was a sophomore at the University of Wisconsin.

But the look on his face wasn't that kind of look. I looked up into his blue eyes. Blue as the eyes of the Siamese cat I'd had as a child. Blue as a winter's dawn.

"Beth, are you listening to me?"

"Um, sorry. I was just . . . thinking." Daydreaming, whatever. For some reason, Evan's presence had that effect on me. One look into those light blue eyes and the real world fell away. In my imagination we were often on a desert island, or in Europe, or in the English book town of Hay-on-Wye with Evan cheerfully carrying all my purchases.

"Thinking is a good thing." He pulled out my desk chair and kissed me as I sat down. The spare chair was covered with catalogs and books and magazines, but Evan knew the drill. He picked up the pile, dropped it onto the floor, and sat.

"So I hear you've hired a convicted murderer." He draped one ankle over the opposite knee.

I'd been in the act of leaning back comfortably, but at his words I sat bolt upright. "Where did you hear that?"

He waved his hands. "You know this town."

This town, that town, every town, probably, when it came to news like this. "It's not true." Well, technically it was. I sighed and gave him the thirty-second summary.

"Interesting situation." He put his hands around his knee. "How do you feel about some unsolicited advice from a current business owner and former attorney?"

I put my hands over my abdomen. "My stomach hurts already."

"Your stomach hurts all the time."

"Only when I worry."

"You worry all the time." He gave me that lopsided grin.

I smiled back. "Not *all* the time."

We sat there making goopy-eyes at each other until my face got tired. "Okay, I'm ready for the advice. Hit me."

He dropped his foot to the floor and looked at me straight on and serious. "Hiring Yvonne is a mistake."

I felt as if he had hit me. "No," I said. "You're wrong." I started listing all the reasons Yvonne was perfect for the job, perfect for the store, and perfect for Rynwood, but Evan rode over my tally.

"Hear me out, okay?" He sat forward, elbows on thighs, letting his hands dangle together. "None of that matters. The only thing that counts in a business is that it makes money. Every decision has to have that as its focus."

I stiffened. He was using the patient voice. I hated that. "Are you saying I don't know how to run my own business?" Stupid Beth, floundering in her own ignorance. It was amazing the store had carried on this long.

Evan stood and walked over to my chair. He took my hands, pulled me to my feet, and enfolded me in his arms. "You're doing a wonderful job," he said into my hair. "You've created an almost magical atmosphere here. You think it's the books, but the crucial ingredient is completely different."

I pulled back and looked up at him, frowning. "What do you mean?" He wasn't making sense. Of course it was the books. Poor man; he'd been spending too much time with plumbing fixtures.

He kissed the tip of my nose. "It's you. Your quirky sense of humor and your sense of fun, but most of all your warm heart." His lips touched mine softly. I would have put my arms around him and leaned into the kiss, but I didn't want to get a stiff neck. Our height differential necessitated a couch for even mildly amorous activities. Either that or a step.

"You," he whispered, and kissed my forehead. "You make this store a haven."

He was wrong, but it was a nice thing to say.

"That's why I want to warn you about this decision." He kissed me again then released me. "Your sense of fairness is exceptional, and I'm afraid it could land you in trouble."

Back to Yvonne. Rats. I thought the topic had been successfully buried. "She didn't kill anyone."

"A lot of people think she did."

"They're wrong." I folded my arms.

"Your customers' perceptions count more than any fact," he said. "If we didn't have an unsolved murder in town, this issue wouldn't be so crucial, but the facts are undeniable. Yvonne was sentenced to life in prison for murder by way of strangulation. Sam Helmstetter was killed the same way." Evan took one of my hands between his two large ones, hiding it completely. "Let's think about this differently. If a pediatrician came to town and you heard that he'd been accused of malpractice, would you consider taking Jenna and Oliver to him?"

"Of course not," I said indignantly. And as I said the words, I realized what I'd said. "Um, not until I'd done some investigating . . ." My voice trailed off to silence.

"Point taken?" Evan asked. His tone was gentle.

I nodded, unhappy with myself for leaping right into the trap. "Some days reality stinks."

He laughed. "Ah, it's not so bad. We're alive, breathing, and in good health. What else could you want?"

My answer was automatic. "Full-ride college scholarships. Two of them, please."

"I'll see what I can do." He opened his palms and kissed the back of my hand. "Thanks for listening."

"You're welcome." I looked at my hand. The only other person who'd ever kissed my hand had been Uncle

Rolly on my thirteenth birthday. "Thanks for caring enough to voice your concerns."

"I care about you."

"And I care about you." This was as close as we'd come to saying the scary "I love you" thing. Stronger than "I like you," but much safer than the *L* word. "So I hope your feelings aren't hurt," I said, "when I ignore your well-meant advice entirely."

"You mean—"

"I'm not going to ask Yvonne to leave."

He sighed. "I had that feeling."

"If this town turns against the store, we'll survive. Over half of our customers are from Madison." Which I only knew because we'd started to ask for zip codes. Though I disliked asking, the information was helping us decide which advertising was worthwhile. My advertising budget was about the size of a twelve-year-old's allowance, which made wasting even a single dollar painful.

Evan looked unconvinced. "If you lose—let's just hypothesize here—twenty percent of your Rynwood customers, how would your monthly revenues match your budget forecast?"

I did the math in my head. Then, since I didn't like the way it turned out, I did it again. "Math isn't my strong suit." But even I could recognize impending doom when the edge of the cliff was rushing near. For once, however, I wasn't going to worry about it. "And it doesn't matter. Yvonne is staying."

"It sounds as if you're making this a statement of principle."

I hadn't thought about it in those terms. Principles weren't something I thought about on a daily basis. "I suppose I am."

He frowned. "Principles can be expensive. I hope the cost isn't too high."

"You and me both," I said, hoping to make him smile. "Stop worrying, or your face is going to freeze like that."

He didn't laugh, but he did smile a little. "Are we still on for Saturday night? I have—"

The phone rang. Then again. "Sorry," I murmured. "Children's Bookshelf, how may I help you?"

"Beth," said Richard, my ex-husband. "It's Richard."

"Hello, Richard."

As soon as the name came out of my mouth, Evan stood and headed for the door. "Wait," I said.

"What?" asked Richard.

"What?" asked Evan.

"Not you," I said into the phone. "You," I said to Evan. "Saturday is still good. Five o'clock?"

"How about four?" He smiled as he shut the door behind him.

"Okay, I'm back," I told Richard. As always after seeing Evan, I felt as if I could solve the world's problems and be home in time to cook dinner. "What's up?"

He said three short words and my life changed. There were other sets of three words that changed lives: "I love you," "It's a girl," or the pronouncement of "husband and wife." Those were all good changes, at least most of the time. No, Richard's three words were the bad kind, the kind you hoped you'd never hear. But maybe I'd heard wrong. I didn't always listen to Richard as closely as I might. Maybe he'd said something else. "I'm sorry, Richard. What did you say?"

"I've been fired."

Chapter 7

Marina's kitchen was bright and cheerful, a welcome change from the blustery Friday evening weather that had pushed me inside the door. I was flying solo tonight. Evan kept the hardware open on Friday nights, and the kids were with their newly unemployed father, doing the trick-or-treat thing. I'd taken them out last year, so this year was Richard's turn.

Poor Richard. I hoped they'd be able to distract him from his worries. He'd worked for the insurance company for over twenty years, been CFO for almost ten. A few months ago a merger had swallowed them whole, but he hadn't been worried. "I have too much corporate memory," he'd said, tapping the side of his head. Either the new guys didn't care about his memory or he'd been sucked dry.

Marina turned over a slab of pork and it sizzled in the cast-iron frying pan. "What did he say after that?"

My stiff-upper-lip ex-husband had broken down in tears, but I wasn't going to tell Marina. Two years of divorce didn't entirely stamp out the loyalty built in a marriage. "Oh," I said, "you know men."

"The gender is a blight on the planet." Marina

grabbed a potholder. She yanked open the oven door and pulled out a cookie sheet covered with potato slices. "What do we need them for, anyway?" The potatoes looked seasoned enough to me, but Marina grabbed her shaker of special spices and shook it furiously.

"Aside from the need to propagate the species?"

She tossed away the notion with a shower of the spices. "We'll figure out another way to reproduce. Name another reason."

The oven door slammed shut and I wondered what Marina's Devoted Husband had done to deserve such ire. "Opening jars that won't open."

"*Bzz.* When women run the world we'll adjust the machines so they don't get so tight in the first place. Next?"

"Taking the car to the mechanic. No matter what, I always feel like an idiot."

"When all the mechanics are women, that won't matter, now will it? You get one last chance for the continuation of male humans. Why, pray tell, should we keep them around?"

"To get rid of dead things."

Marina's mouth opened, then closed. A slow grin cleansed her stormy face. "Reason enough, mine friend. Since you've answered my question of the day, shall I answer yours?"

"Well, I am wondering how Mrs. Tolliver, and therefore the whole of Rynwood, found out so quickly that Yvonne was in prison for murder. I'd hoped it would take a few months to get around, but no, it wasn't even twenty-four hours. How on earth . . . um, are you okay?"

Marina was leaning against the kitchen counter, her face in her hands. "Oh, no. Oh no oh no oh no."

I was getting a bad feeling about this. "What did you do?"

She mumbled some words into her hands and I

reached over to pull her arms down. "Again. This time in English."

Her eyes darted left and right and up and down and everywhere but at me. "I had to tell CeeCee Daniels."

I stepped away so I couldn't give in to my urge to shake her silly. "Had to?" My voice echoed around the kitchen. I shut my eyes for a second, then started again, cool, calm, and somewhat collected. "Could you have picked a more inappropriate person to tell?"

"Cindy Irving," she said instantly.

My irritation zipped up, then came back down again. "Okay, Cindy would have been worse." Cindy did landscaping and janitorial work for city hall and a number of downtown area businesses. She probably talked to more people in a day than walked into the bookstore in a week. "But why did you tell anyone?"

"I didn't want to," she wailed. "CeeCee was here one day and Yvonne stopped in and they hit it off, and the next day CeeCee calls asking if I thought Yvonne would be okay babysitting her kids. I said sure she would, she's great with rug rats. Half an hour later CeeCee's in here about ready to roast my gizzard. She'd looked Yvonne up on Google and there it was, all bright and shiny. Convicted of murder. CeeCee didn't read anything after that. I tried to explain, but I don't think she heard a word I said."

It all made a Marina-based sort of sense.

"CeeCee must have told Claudia, and who knows who she told? I'll call Yvonne tonight and apologize," Marina said. "I should have known what would happen, it was stupid, and I am really, really, really sorry."

She certainly looked apologetic. The word "contrite" didn't begin to cover the drooping eyes, the slumped shoulders, and the overall attitude of dejection. It was so unlike her that I couldn't stand it. I poked her shoulder with my index finger. "Well, everyone's entitled to one mistake a decade. Too bad you used up yours so early."

Her smile came a moment after mine. "Yeah," she said. "Too bad. I'd better be on my best behavior the next few years. Think I can do it?"

"Not a chance."

Five minutes later we were seated at her kitchen table, our bright red plates laden with meat, potatoes, and a small heap of beans. It was just the two of us since Marina's young son, Zach, was staying overnight at a friend's. After her earlier behavior, I wasn't about to ask what her DH might be doing. We'd slid into the habit of Friday night dinner and a movie soon after Richard and I separated. The evenings had been a lifeline in those first lonely months, and it would take a thousand years to repay what she'd done for me.

"So with Richard joining the ranks of the unemployed, what does that do to you?" Marina stuck a fork into a piece of pork that had the faintest of pinkish hues in the center. "Did he get a bag of gold or a boot out the door?"

"His severance package is generous." I tried to sound unconcerned. "We'll be fine for a long time."

My attempt at nonchalance didn't fool Marina a bit. "Long being what?" she asked. "Weeks? Months? Years?" As in, you have a mortgage payment affordable only via child support payments, so how long are the severance bucks going to last, because foreclosure is an ugly thing?

I didn't want to think about this. I wanted us to laugh ourselves silly over nothing and then pop a huge bowl of popcorn and chomp our way through *The Sting*. "Six months," I said.

"Well," Marina said slowly, "that's kind of a long time."

"Absolutely."

"And he has all sorts of skills. Like . . ." She pursed her

lips and stared at the ceiling. "Well, he can do lots of things, I'm sure. There are probably companies calling him about a job already."

"You could be right."

"You bet I am." She banged the butt of her knife on the table. "This will turn out just fine. Heck, Richard will probably find a better job with more money and massive benefits."

"Um . . ."

She ran over my hesitation. "And you said just the other day that business at the store was picking up. You're going to be rolling in—" She stopped and peered at the expression I thought I'd kept off my face. "What?"

"Nothing."

"Don't give me that." She pointed her fork at me. Unfortunately, it was laden with green beans, which fell to the table with a small plop. That didn't faze Marina. She speared each bean one by one and popped them into her mouth. "What's up?"

Maybe I could be vague. "Sales at the store have been falling off a little."

"At this time of year?"

Rats. Marina hid her capabilities beneath a swirl of personality and fractured quotations, but I knew better. Rather, most days I knew better.

Now I had to decide what to say. The truth would not only make her feel guilty, it would also spur her clever mind to the creation of great business-building feats, and I was quite sure I lacked the energy for any scheme she might dream up.

"Tell me, or I'll be forced to take drastic measures." Marina held her spoon in catapult mode, the spoon's bowl filled with potato.

Though I had no memory of finishing my meal, there was only a small scrap of potato peel for ammunition, not nearly enough to defend myself. Besides, I'd never actually participated in a food fight. I was probably a very poor shot. "Mrs. Tolliver says she won't come into any store that hires convicted killers," I said, "especially when there's a killer on the loose."

Marina's spoon clattered to the table. "But Yvonne's innocent! How can she say such a thing?"

"I didn't get a chance to explain. Mrs. Tolliver came in, made her pronouncement, and walked out."

"That's not fair!" Marina's hair was flying away from her head in a thousand different directions; she looked like a red-haired Albert Einstein.

"There's not much I can do about it."

"There is one thing," Marina said.

I shook my head. "I'm not going to let Yvonne go."

"Don't be silly. Your innate—and borderline obsessive, I might add—sense of justice eliminates that option. No, the thing to do is clear."

"It is?"

"And this time we have experience!"

She didn't mean . . . she couldn't mean . . . "No," I said. "You can't mean *that*."

"Yup. We need to find Sam's killer." She nodded sharply.

"Not a chance."

Marina's cheeks were flushed with . . . well, I didn't want to know what. I didn't want to think it was excitement that was getting her riled up. I'd had enough of that last year when we were trying to figure out who killed Agnes Mephisto. I'd come to care deeply about bringing the killer to justice, but the fun and games had ended abruptly when my children had been threatened.

"We did it before, we can do it again," Marina was saying. "Thanks to us a killer is behind bars."

"The police would have figured it out," I said. "They have procedures to follow, so it takes them a little longer, that's all."

"Procedures, my aunt Fanny." Marina *tsk*ed away hundreds of years of case law.

"Yes, procedures. You know, the laws of the land? Local, state, and federal? We have them for a reason."

But as private citizens, Marina and I weren't hampered by the myriad rules and regulations. We would be free to follow hunches. We could poke into people's coat closets and medicine cabinets, no warrant required.

"We don't need to prove anything beyond a shadow of a doubt," Marina said. "All we have to do is figure out who did it and let nature take its course."

"My nature is quite content to leave this to the police." Mostly.

"And how long will that take?"

As her right eyebrow went up, I thought about what she'd said. How long *would* it take for the police to find Sam's killer? Mrs. Tolliver's attitude could be contagious. The longer the murderer walked about free, the longer the Mrs. Tollivers of the world would consider my newest employee a menace to society. And the longer Yvonne was considered a threat, the longer my store's sales would suffer.

"Aha!" Marina pounced. "You're thinking about it, aren't you?"

"Am not."

"Are too. That little line between your eyebrows is a dead giveaway. It's only there when you're thinking that I'm right and you're wrong."

"No, I think my head is about to explode because of the completely opposing viewpoints in my head."

"Completely?"

"This side of my brain"—I tapped my left temple—"is committed to safety, security, and obeying authority. The other side"—I flicked my index finger at the right side—"has an affinity for anarchy. Is it any wonder I get a line in the middle?"

"There's only one solution." Marina reached for my plate and stacked it on top of hers.

"What's that?"

"Loose the blood-dimmed tide!"

I stared at her. "You just quoted Yeats." Sort of.

"That who it was? It's the only thing I remember from freshman English. That's where I met the DH, you know. That widening gyre poem was his favorite."

I didn't know which was more disconcerting, Marina quoting Yeats, or the idea of her DH even having a favorite poem.

"You're off work tomorrow, aren't you?" she asked. "Good. Be ready at ten."

"For?"

"Anything!" she said gaily, then sobered. "But you'd better wear black. Oh, quit looking like that. You thought there might not be a funeral?"

"It's been over a week. I thought maybe Rachel decided to have a memorial service later on." April would be good. The week I was out of town for spring break would be excellent.

"Somebody said they're short-staffed at the medical examiner's. Ew, you know?" She made a face. "And no trying to weasel your way out of this. You know we have to go."

I sighed. "Why is doing the right thing so darn uncomfortable?"

"Because if it were easy it'd be fun, and fun is never the right thing to have."

"Never?" What a depressing thought.

"Well, hardly ever." She took the plates to the kitchen, whistling the Gilbert and Sullivan tune from *H.M.S. Pinafore*. I followed after her, once again surprised at the things that bounced out of her mouth.

* * *

I'd hated every funeral I'd ever attended. Too much baggage, too much emotion, too much everything. Marina said it was my own fear of death, and she was probably right, but that didn't make it any easier to sit through a service.

Marina elbowed me. "Quit squirming," she whispered.

The organ was playing a quiet meditation as people filed in. We'd arrived early, but Marina had asked the usher for a seat in the back. I'd spent the next few minutes reading the service's bulletin, then a couple of minutes paging through the hymnal. Then I sat with my eyes closed, thinking about Sam. Which led me to think about Sam's wife, which sent me to thinking about the children. Which would have made me cry, so in the name of distraction I started inventing itches at the back of my knees.

"Stop that," Marina said quietly. "Don't think I don't know what you're up to."

"You don't?"

"Stop that."

"Stop what?"

She ignored my whisper, which showed how smart she was. I hadn't been looking at her; I'd been studying the church's stained glass windows, but now I heard an odd scratching noise that didn't at all belong in a church, let alone a funeral service. Frowning, I looked around to see what was making the noise.

It was Marina, cradling a small memo pad in her left hand. As an usher went past on his ushering duties, she wrote on her pad.

I bumped her with my elbow. "What are you doing?" I whispered.

"Writing down names." Her voice, though as quiet as it could get, held the "duh" tone.

"What on earth for?"

Our school superintendent and his wife, Mack and Joanna Vogel, went past, and Marina bent her head to scribble. "There's a good chance Sam's killer will show up, and I'm bound to forget someone if I don't write down the names."

I was appalled. "You're taking notes?"

"Shh!" Marina shot quick glances all around. "Do you want the whole town to know what we're doing?"

My best friend was an idiot. "The only time killers make an appearance at the funeral is in movies."

She watched Randy Jarvis, our PTA treasurer, lumber up the aisle. Writing, she said, "Movies are rooted in reality. The germ came from somewhere, yes?"

"So the movie plot where a suburban husband single-handedly fights off a small army of terrorists, rescues his wife, and disarms the ticking time bomb before his children are blown to bits is based in fact?"

"You're just being difficult," she said. Claudia Wolff and her husband went down on the list, followed by Tina and Tony Heller. "And we have to start somewhere."

It was a reasonable statement; we did need a place to begin. So why did I feel so depressed? "Oh," I said.

"What's the matter?" Marina looked at me, then saw where I was looking. "Who's that?"

"Pete Peterson. Remember?" I'd run into Pete last year after Agnes had been killed. It was Pete who'd been instrumental in putting the last piece of our investigative puzzle together. Sort of.

"Ah, yes," Marina said. "Shortish? Balding? All-around good guy who always makes you feel like smiling?"

"That's him."

Pete was alone, and the somber face he wore looked wholly unnatural.

Marina studied the back of his head. "You got to watch out for those nice ones. Do you think—"

"No," I said shortly. "Don't be ridiculous."

She clucked at me. "Just because you laugh at his jokes doesn't mean he's not a killer."

Her logic, though littered with negatives, was irrefutable. "Doesn't mean he is, either." But Pete's name went on the list in spite of my protests.

"Oh, my goodness." Marina perked up. "Look at that."

An usher was leading two couples toward the front of the sanctuary. One set I recognized as Bruce Yahrmatter and his wife, the other was—"Is that Dave Patterson?"

Just before I'd met Evan, Marina had tried to set me up with Dave. He was a nice enough guy, but whenever you talked to him he had this awful habit of saying your name over and over. "Hi, Beth. How are you today?" "How's business, Beth?" "How's that dog of yours, Beth?" It wasn't personal; he did it to everyone, but it set my teeth on edge.

"Who's with him?" I asked.

"Would you believe Viv Reilly?"

"No!"

Marina nodded, and when Dave stepped back to let his companion enter the pew ahead of him, I saw that she was right. "How long has her divorce been final?" I asked.

"A week."

Viv and her husband had married and started a family while still very young. Two and a half decades and three beautiful adult daughters later, Viv was one of those women who delighted in strangers assuming she was a fourth sister.

Her husband had found this amusing for a few years, but when she'd wanted him to pretend that he was her father, he'd declined to participate. From that simple beginning, exceedingly ugly divorce proceedings had commenced. Coward that I was, I'd avoided Viv for months so I didn't have to hear about it.

"I don't care how good she looks," Marina said, "she's got to be ten years older than he is."

The look she slid me was so open and innocent it could only mean one thing: She was trying to start an argument. Whether she wanted to fight about Viv's age or was trying to get me going on the double standards so common in female-male relationships, I didn't know. More likely she was trying to distract me from her note taking. No matter what her intent was, I wasn't going to be drawn into a verbal battle at a funeral service. I started to say so when the black-robed minister stood and put his hands on the pulpit.

I jabbed Marina in the ribs and pointed at the memo pad. She heaved a very small sigh and tucked it into her purse.

"We are here," the minister said, "not to mourn the death of Sam Helmstetter, but to celebrate his life."

I dug into my own purse and found the one thing I always brought to funerals.

A handkerchief.

On the way home, Marina handed me her memo pad. "Read, O comrade, and see if anyone twangs your instincts."

"But I was right there," I said. "I saw everyone you saw, and I didn't see anyone." Which didn't make any sense whatsoever, but since the sentence was inspired by Marina, she understood.

I was still a little startled by my post-funeral behavior. I'd stopped to talk to Sam's widow, Rachel, and had nearly cried at the emptiness in her face. On impulse I'd asked if she wanted me to stop by the next day. Rachel had nodded slowly and said that would be nice. Good move, Beth, making a condolence call the day after Sam's funeral. What were you thinking?

"Sometimes it takes more than one look," Marina

said, as if she had decades of experience in homicide detection instead of what she did have under her belt, which was years of movie watching. "Sometimes something just clicks and—"

My phone beeped.

"That's got to be the most boring ring tone in the history of cell phones," Marina said.

This was an old discussion and always ended with me telling her that if she wanted me to have a more interesting ring tone, she was welcome to read the instruction manual and reprogram the phone to her heart's content.

I dug into my purse for the phone. "Hello?" To my left, I could feel Marina rolling her eyes. "Hello?" I said again. "This is Beth."

"There's a problem with Thanksgiving," said a male voice.

"Hey, Tim," I said to my brother. "How are you?"

"How am I?" The puzzlement in his voice was thick. "Reasonably well. Why do you ask?"

Tim's social skills hadn't improved since he was fifteen. When asked by a girl to a Sadie Hawkins dance, he'd replied, "Why would I want to do that?" How he'd managed to date a woman long enough to get married—and stay married long enough to beget offspring—was one of life's great mysteries. Their son, Max, was, to the disappointment of his multidegreed parents, a completely average teenager. I loved him dearly. Not that I didn't love my brother; blood is thicker than water, or so they say. But with my lifetime knowledge of sibling behavior, Tim's question was a good one: Why had I bothered asking him how he was? "What's the problem with Thanksgiving?"

"My project team," he said, "had a procedure scheduled on Gammasphere for January. There was a cancellation and I can get in on Thanksgiving."

I waited. But that, apparently, was all he intended to say. No apologies, no remorse, no nothing beyond the bare-bones explanation. Typical Tim. "What about Max?"

"Max?" He sounded surprised that the name would come up. "What about him?"

I wanted to reach through the phone and twist my brother's nose. "What's he going to do for Thanksgiving?" As in, while you're closeted away with like-minded physicists, what is your sole offspring going to do with himself?

"That," Tim said, "is a reasonable question." There was a rustling sound as he covered the phone with his hand. "Max!" he called. "I'm going to be working on Thanksgiving. What do you want to do?"

I closed my eyes and prayed for strength.

There was muffled conversation, but I couldn't make it out. Eventually Tim uncovered the receiver. "Max will be fine," he said.

"Let me talk to him."

"Beth—"

I firmed up my voice. Too bad I couldn't do that to my hips as easily. "Put him on the phone."

Tim sighed and called for his son.

"Hi, Aunt Beth."

"Where's your father?" I asked. No way could we have this conversation with Tim in the same room.

"Um . . . he just made the signal. He's going over to Mom's."

The signal was a complicated series of taps on the joint wall between the two sets of living quarters. Morse code, I assumed, but had never asked. Even mild technical questions asked of Tim tended to be answered in fifty-minute lectures. He'd served as a teaching assistant while in graduate school and had never recovered.

"Let me know when he's gone."

There was a pause punctuated by the shutting of a door. "Okay, we can talk now. What's up?"

"Still working on that B average?" I asked.

"Every day."

"That's my boy."

"There's just one thing." Even though he was alone, his voice went quiet. "I really like my English lit class."

I pumped my fist in the air. "Yeah?"

"Yeah. There's this long poem about a monster. This guy decides he's going to kill it. He does, but the monster had a mother who's even meaner. The guy kills the mother, too, and he ends up being the king. When he's really old, a dragon wakes up. The guy kills the dragon, but he ends up getting killed, too. His people give him a huge funeral, though."

"How nice for him." *Beowulf* had never been distilled so completely. CliffsNotes had nothing on my nephew.

"Do you know it?" Max asked. "Dad didn't, but I think it's kind of famous."

"It sounds familiar. Listen, Max. About Thanksgiving."

"Oh. Yeah." His voice, which had been full of inflection and life when telling me about Grendel, went flat and lifeless. "He's going to be working, so I guess we're not coming up."

"What do you feel about coming up by yourself?" A good sister would have talked to her brother about the possibility before discussing it with the fifteen-year-old, but today I was being a better aunt than sibling.

"By . . . myself?"

"We'd have to clear it with your parents, but there is such a thing as Greyhound."

"Greyhound?"

"The bus. I'm sure you've heard of it. Service nationwide with reclining seats, tinted windows, and an onboard restroom." Not that I'd use one, but it was different for boys.

"Bus?"

"Max, stop being a parrot. I still want you to come for Thanksgiving, and there is a way to get you here."

"Mom's driving to Grandma's, you know, over in Iowa? I could probably go with her."

"Talk it over with your parents," I said. "We'd love to have you."

"Really?"

His teenage angst was palpable and I ached to pull him close in a great big hug. "Really." We said good-bye and I slid the phone back into my purse. In all likelihood Max would end up going with his mother. Maybe the kids and I would take a trip to Illinois during Christmas vacation. It'd be nice to—

"That's two down," Marina said.

"Huh?"

"Once so eloquent," Marina said, addressing an invisible crowd, "she now resorts to the monosyllables of youth. What lies in store for our fair maiden? Her future, I fear, is bleak."

I could fake Shakespeare as well as anyone. I cast caution to the winds. "What, pray tell, is the topic of yon conversement?"

"Hooray!" She clapped her hands. "Beth's in the game!"

"One sentence doth not a play make."

"Ooo, good one. What I meant was two down, two to go, with your family for Thanksgiving. At least you don't have to buy as much food."

"I suppose."

She slid me a glance. "Methinks I detect a smidgen of downcast spirits."

I was pretty sure "smidgen" wasn't a word in the vicinity of 1600, but I didn't feel like calling her on it. "Maybe a smidge."

"You're taking this personally, aren't you?"

"No." But I was. How could I not? "Kathy and Tim have good reasons for canceling. If I were either of them I'd do the same thing."

"Oh, you would not." Marina signaled and pulled into my driveway. "You'd move heaven and earth to keep a commitment. Especially a Thanksgiving commitment, even with that dysfunctional unit you call your family." She jammed the gearshift to Park. "You have a thing about Thanksgiving, don't you? Why?"

"Not sure."

"Bet you a hundred bucks you just don't want to tell me."

I casually reached for my earlobes, trying to feel if they were hot. Ever since I could remember, my ears turned red when I lied.

Marina was looking at me expectantly, doing the one-eyebrow thing.

"Everyone has a favorite holiday," I said.

"Sure. Mine's Flag Day."

"It is?"

"Yup. All you have to do is put out the American flag. No presents, no cards, no family get-togethers. Put out the flag at dawn, take it in at sunset, and recite the Pledge of Allegiance in there somewhere. Can't get much simpler than that."

Was she making that up, or telling the truth? With Marina it was hard to know.

"So what's your deal with Thanksgiving?" she asked. "Cook a bunch of food, invite a bunch of people. Who cares if they're blood relations?"

Straightening the strap of my purse suddenly became a huge priority. I fiddled with the leather. "It's because of Norman Rockwell."

"That guy who painted all those magazine covers?"

"*Saturday Evening Post*. Remember the painting of the mom putting the big turkey down on the table? She's wearing a white apron over her dress and Dad is in a dark suit and tie. He's standing at the head of the table and the rest of the family is leaning forward, all smiles and anticipation and happiness."

"Sure, I remember." Marina looked thoughtful. "It's one of those pictures that make you wistful for the perfect family Thanksgiving."

Exactly.

"It's impossible, of course." She squinted at me. "You know that, right?"

"That magazine cover was printed in March. The painting isn't really about Thanksgiving."

"Which makes it about every family Sunday dinner. Even worse."

"How's that?"

She made a face. "Please. Talk about setting yourself up for failure. Cooking a meal the volume of a Thanksgiving dinner every Sunday is the definition of insanity. Can you imagine eating with my in-laws once a week?" Her face scrunched so hard it looked inside out.

"That's not what I meant."

"I know." She patted my arm. "It's the hope that gets you," she said. "The hope that one day things will be better, that we'll grow out of our anger and drop all the baggage and just *be.*"

For all her poking and prodding, I knew she understood. "First time I saw that Norman Rockwell picture," I said, "was right after my Grandma Chittenden died. Once she was gone the family fell apart. Without her, there wasn't any pull to get together. Everyone went their separate ways and it hasn't been the same since. That picture reminds me of the way things once were."

Silence ticked away between us.

"Well, maybe someday things will be that way again." Marina grinned. "Say, how do you feel about a white apron for Christmas?"

I was laughing as I got out of her car, but by the time I got to the house my laughter was gone. Tomorrow's appointment with Rachel was already starting to sit in my stomach like an undigested ball of dough, and I had a feeling that the closer tomorrow came, the larger the ball was going to grow.

If tomorrow didn't come soon I might need surgery.

Evan and I sat on the couch in front of my fireplace, flames flickering, coals glowing. The radio was playing quiet classical music, and Evan's arms were around me. He was talking about the Thanksgiving plans he'd been making with his daughters, and, as I listened, I was enjoying how my house looked in the dancing firelight.

Here in the dark I couldn't see the dirty windows, or the dusty surfaces, or the baseboards that hadn't been cleaned since . . . well, I didn't want to think that the last time I could remember cleaning them was soon after Oliver was born, so I went back to paying full attention to Evan.

". . . but they're both concerned about another murder in Rynwood," he said. "How are Jenna and Oliver taking it?"

I'd almost become used to Evan's questions about my children. He'd been carefully casual the first few times he'd spent time with the three of us, never holding my hand, never telling them what to do, never once acting as if he had any right to be part of our group. Ever so slowly, he'd spent more and more time with us, and now his presence most weekends and occasional weeknights was a given.

The whole situation still felt strange, though, and I still wasn't sure if I was doing the right thing in seeing him. The kids were polite and seemed to enjoy his company, but every time I pressed either one about how they really felt, all I got was "I dunno" or "Okay, I guess."

"How are they taking Sam's death?" I asked. "As you might expect. Jenna won't talk about it and Oliver won't stop talking about it." Gender reversal had nothing on my children.

Evan brushed his hand against my cheek. "And how are you taking it?"

"Me?" This was something I hadn't considered. "Um, okay, I guess."

"Like mother, like daughter," he murmured. "Any ideas about who killed Sam?"

I hesitated. Was this a trick question? Last year our relationship almost ended before it began, thanks to my amateur investigations and Evan's inclination to dispense unwanted advice.

But even if he was trying to ferret out my intentions, the question was simple enough to answer. "No ideas," I said sadly, watching the fading fire. "No ideas at all."

Yet.

Chapter 8

I knocked on the Helmstetters' front door. Rynwood on a Sunday afternoon in November was never an active time, but this portion of this particular neighborhood was quieter than any neighborhood should be. There were no cars driving down the street and not a single kid was riding her bike in the semiwarm sunshine. Not a single home owner was out raking leaves.

Eerie.

I turned away from the sight. It was creeping me out. I knocked again and harbored a shameful hope that Rachel had forgotten I was coming over.

Just then the dead bolt slid back, the knob turned, and the door creaked open.

A young girl stared up at me, thick blond hair frizzed in all directions. "Hi," she said. "Are you Mrs. Kennedy?"

"Yes, I am. Are you Mia?"

She nodded solemnly. "My brother Blake is in his room and won't come out, so Mommy said I should answer the door."

The urge to flee grew strong enough to overpower social obligations. "I'll come back later." Or not. Not would be excellent. "Can you tell your mom—"

"Mommy said to sit in the living room." Mia abandoned the doorway and I was left with the choices of trailing in her wake, stay standing at the front door, or turning tail and rushing home to the comforts of hot chocolate and a good book. I sighed and went after Mia.

The house was a simple two-story: living room, kitchen, and family room on the main level, bedrooms upstairs. It had probably started as a plain builder box ("All neutral colors, folks!"), but the Helmstetters had created a cozy atmosphere with a judicious use of color, textures, patterns, and accessories. An antique quilt hung on a large expanse of wall, and a lamp was decorated with seashells. In the far corner, an upright piano had a bright red ceramic cat perched on top and Scott Joplin's "Maple Leaf Rag" on its music rack.

When I turned to face Mia, I spied a set of bifold doors next to the entrance, doors that could only be a closet. In there would be the answers to my questions about Sam's scarf-wearing habits. If I peeked in there, I'd know at a glance if Sam always wore scarves. If I opened those closet doors I'd see the coats of this girl's father . . . and so would she.

I looked down at Mia and my investigative urge vanished. There was no way I'd push more hurt on this child. Her vacant face was telling me too much about her pain, about her bewilderment, and about the problems she'd be facing for much too long.

"You can sit down here, I guess." Mia stood in front of a tweedy brown sofa, the best possible color for hiding kid dirt.

"Thank you." I smoothed the back of my skirt and sat down. "Would you like to sit with me?"

"Um . . ." Mia reached up for a tendril of hair. "Mommy said I should make sure you're comfortable." The word was a hard one for her and it stretched out into more syllables than it normally had.

"I'd be better if I had some company." I patted the seat beside me.

Mia continued to pull and twist her hair, and I continued to sit. After a long silence I asked, "Do you play the piano?"

"Sometimes Blake does. Mommy tries, but she gets mad and hits the keys." Mia released her hair and held her hands out, making crashing motions. "The piano makes a big noise and sometimes"—she lowered her voice—"sometimes she says a bad word. Once it was a *very* bad word."

"She probably felt sorry afterward," I said.

"Maybe." Mia looked doubtful. "Daddy came in and asked what key that was in and she started laughing. Then he sat down and they both started playing some song about a colored boat."

"Submarine."

I looked up. Rachel was standing at the bottom of the stairway, wearing a sad, sad smile. "Yellow?" I asked.

"The very one." She came down the last two stairs, her left hand white-knuckled on the railing. "Mia, honey, your brother is on my bed watching a movie. Do you want to watch it with him?"

Mia, still fiddling with her hair, walked to the stairway. Her mother dropped a kiss on top of her head. "I'll bring up some snacks in a little bit."

"Okay." Up the stairs the girl went, one slow tread at a time.

Rachel sighed. "At least she's talking. She didn't say a word for two days afterward."

"How's Blake?"

She shook her head and came into the living room. Two large armchairs flanked the sofa, and she sat in the closer one, kicking off her shoes and tucking her feet underneath her. "I have an appointment with the new school psychologist tomorrow. Have you met her?"

"I didn't know they'd made a final selection." Clearly, the PTA was the last to know.

"Last week," she said. "Or was it the week before?" She rubbed her forehead. "It's been hard to keep track."

Rachel was a few years younger than my forty-one, but today she looked a decade older. Grief tugged at the lines of her face and she'd moved with the stiffness of old age. Our circles of friends didn't overlap much; we knew each other only through PTA. I'd often wanted to ask her to lunch, but the busy-busy of my days kept me from reaching out. What was it someone had once said, that what we most often regretted wasn't the things we did do, but the things we didn't.

Smart lady, whoever came up with that one.

"It's hard enough," I said, "to keep track of days normally, let alone after what you've gone through. I am so sorry, Rachel."

Her gaze drifted to the piano. "My minister says someday it'll get easier, and I'm sure he's right, but I almost don't want it to, because that'll mean I'm forgetting Sam."

"Not forgetting," I said gently. "You'll never do that."

"How do you know? Your husband wasn't murdered." Her words were harsh, and as soon as she'd said them she looked stricken. "I'm sorry. I didn't mean—"

"Don't apologize. Please."

She put her knuckles to her mouth. "It's so hard. Every day, it's so hard. To have Sam dead is bad enough, but murdered? Mia is scared the bad guy is coming after her next." Her attempt at a laugh turned into a weak sob. "I keep telling the kids they're fine, they're safe, but how do I know?"

Her eyes beseeched me for help, and I had no idea what to do.

Tears trickled down onto Rachel's fist. I got up, sat on the arm of Rachel's chair, and took her free hand between mine. Her bones felt so brittle beneath the skin that I didn't dare squeeze, so I simply sat and stroked the back of her hand as she wept for her dead husband.

The sobs that wracked her body traveled down her arm and into me. I imagined her sorrow as a gray river, and, as I caressed her hand, I prayed that the grief-swollen water would lose its power and ease to a thread of a creek, then dry up from drought. I stroked, praying for her, wishing there was something else I could do, and knowing there wasn't.

Finally, she squeezed my hand. "Thanks, Beth," she said in a voice colored raw and red.

"You're welcome." I hesitated, then gave her shoulders a quick hug.

"I needed to cry." Still hanging on to me, she rubbed at her face with her tear-soaked hand. "I hadn't yet, can you believe it? Mom stayed until this morning, and every time I started crying she'd give me the stiff-upper-lip talk. You know, be strong for the kids, they can't see you crying, they need to know you're strong."

It seemed to me they also needed to see their mom grieving for their father. "Anytime you want to cry, just let me know."

She half smiled, and I gave her another hug. "Studies have shown," I said, "that crying releases all sorts of endorphins and toxins and antioxidants and who knows what else, so right now there's only one thing to do."

"What's that?" she asked.

"Eat."

Fifteen minutes later we were sitting at the round table in their kitchen. Rachel had taken a tray of snacks up to the kids—carrots, crackers, and grapes—while I'd examined the offerings in the garage's chest freezer. Church ladies had dropped off so much food that Rachel wouldn't need to cook for weeks.

I selected a medium-sized container of chicken soup and a loaf of homemade bread and carried them inside.

By the time Rachel came downstairs, the microwave had dinged and I was almost done with the creation of two salads.

"Oh, goodness, Beth, you didn't need to do all that."

"I know. And I'm going to be bossy for a while. Sit. No, no protests. Sit."

We sat, sipping soup, crunching on toast, and adding too many croutons to our salads.

"This single-mom thing," she said, drenching her salad with French dressing. "How do you do it?"

Easy answer. "Not very well."

"Oh, come on. Your kids are great, you run that wonderful bookstore, you have a beautiful house; you even have time to be secretary of the PTA. And you make it look so easy."

My spoon halted halfway to my mouth. "I do?"

"Well, sure."

The notion was so ludicrous that I couldn't think of an appropriate reaction. Rachel went on, concentrating on grinding pepper onto her salad. "You have this air of competency. You always seem to know what to say and do. If you want to know the truth, I've always been a little jealous of you."

A snort snuck out of my throat. Rachel looked up in surprise. "No, I mean it. I wish I was more like you. You're smart and funny and brave and—"

It was the brave comment that did it. I dropped the spoon back into the bowl, threw my head back, and howled with laughter.

Rachel started giggling; then, as I kept going, her giggle turned into an outright laugh.

"I'm the least brave person in the world," I said, wiping my eyes with a napkin. "At least I hope so."

Rachel popped a crouton into her mouth. "Last year you saved your kids from Agnes Mephisto's killer. You're very courageous."

She was making me sound like a Boy Scout. "It wasn't like that. Honest. My children were being threatened. I just reacted. I didn't have time to stop and think about the danger." If I had, things might have turned out very differently, and I didn't want to think about that, so I didn't. "Any mother would have done the same."

"Maybe." She didn't look convinced.

It suddenly seemed very important to make her understand. "Rachel, on the inside I'm a mess. Almost every minute of the day I'm sure I'm doing the wrong thing."

"You are?"

"Even today, I wasn't sure I was doing the right thing by coming over here. I couldn't decide if I was coming over too soon after the funeral, or if I was coming over too late after . . . well, after. Either way, I was bound to be wrong."

"You really thought that?"

"The only thing I know for certain is that I love my children." My voice was low and husky. "I would do anything, *anything*, to keep them safe and sound and whole and happy."

Rachel's gaze met mine. The look that passed between us was one of complete understanding and, in that moment, our relationship moved from acquaintanceship to solid friendship.

"Amen," she said softly.

I wanted to reach across the table and grip her hand, but I wasn't sure I could pull it off at all naturally. Then her fingers twitched in my direction. Hand outstretched, I leaned toward her, glad beyond belief that I hadn't poked around in the front closet. She met me halfway and our shared grip promised support and understanding and love.

We released at the same time and went back to slurping soup. One can maintain strong emotion for only so long.

"The problem," Rachel said between sips, "is how to do that. How do I keep them whole and happy? Love that phrase, by the way."

"Thanks." It had popped into my head out of the blue, but I was sure the thought wasn't original. A poem? A minister's sermon? "I don't know how to do it, either. I've made a lot of mistakes, but thanks to a lot of luck and the grace of God, they seem to be okay." The upcoming teen years, however, were lurking around a dark corner with sharp pointed teeth. I sighed.

"Your kids are fine," Rachel said. "Jenna is bright and pretty, and not only is Oliver the cutest little bug on the planet, but he's very intuitive."

I stopped with a forkful of salad halfway to my mouth. "You think so?"

"Didn't Oliver tell you about the time he helped Mia get the pinecones out of her hair? Robert Laird and his bully friends snuck up on her at recess one day last year."

No, Oliver hadn't told me. Intuitive he might be, but communicative? Not so much. I sent up an extra-special thank-you that Robert, once one of Oliver's special friends, had moved away. Hopefully far, far away.

I didn't want to say that I couldn't begin to guess at the virtues of her children, so I cheated. "I think Jenna has a crush on Blake."

She smiled. "He says girls are gross, but I overheard him talking with his dad and—" She stopped, tucked her lips between her teeth, and concentrated on stirring her soup.

I let the wave of grief break over her and pass through. Then I said, "Isn't it funny how we have them paired off already?"

She swallowed and nodded. "And how we picked careers for them when they were still in diapers. Sam . . ." Her voice caught and she started again. "One of Sam's hopes when he started his company was to pass it on to one of the kids. I kept telling him that they might want nothing to do with a mobile shredding business, but he'd laugh and say it didn't matter, that the only thing that mattered was teaching them how to juggle."

"How to . . . ?"

"Juggle." She smiled again. "It was how we met. Long story." Her smile faded. "Now here I am with his children and not the foggiest idea what to do. What do you think?"

"Um . . ." If she was asking my advice, clearly I hadn't impressed upon her the depths of my incompetence. I should have told her about the steak knife incident. Or better yet, the story of Beth and the Blender. If neither of those convinced her, surely the state of my closet floor would do the job. No one with so many unmatched shoes could possibly be considered a rational human being. Why I had a dozen solo shoes was one question; another was why I didn't get rid of them.

She put her elbows on the table and laid her arms flat. It was the first time she'd looked truly engaged in our conversation, and my mouth got a little dry around the edges in anticipation of what was coming next. On the way over I hadn't prepared for anything more than comforting the bereaved. I hoped she hadn't been serious about wanting my opinion on the path her life should take. My own path was more a series of deer trails wandering through the woods, circling back on themselves every so often, coming to dead ends even more often, and never going anywhere.

"For the last few months," she said, "ever since their secretary went part-time, I've been doing the bookkeeping for Sam and his partner."

I hadn't known Sam had a partner. I wondered who it was, but Rachel was still talking and I didn't want to interrupt.

"At first I wasn't sure I could do the work, but the guys were really patient with me, and it wasn't as hard as

I thought." She studied her left hand, wiggling her fourth finger, watching the sparkle of the diamond in her engagement ring. When she spoke again, her voice was quiet. "Do you think I can do it?"

Do what? I wanted to ask.

"Last night I hardly slept at all," she said. "I went from being sure I could do it to being sure I'd have to sell the house and we'd have to move in with my parents and the children would turn against me and hate me forever."

That was a sleep pattern I knew intimately. It wasn't the kids who tired me out so much as the worry that constantly plagued me. My ex-husband had never understood, but every mother to whom I'd confessed did.

She looked up. "Silly, isn't it? You've probably never had a night like that. I know you said you're not brave, but you're so nice I bet you said that just to make me feel better."

As if. I smiled and started to deny everything, but Rachel kept going.

"This morning I decided that even if Sam was gone, our marriage vows aren't. I owe it to us, to our family, to try."

Her words were full of bravado, but the expression on her face spoke of fear and a shaky stomach.

I only wished I knew what she was talking about. There was, however, only one proper course of action. Mom action. "You can do anything," I said. "You're young and strong and smart and fearless in your determination to do what's best for your children. There's no wall tall enough to keep you from achieving your goals." Whatever they might be.

Rachel puffed out her cheeks and blew a sigh of relief so big it fluffed her bangs back off her face. "You think so?" The soft question made her sound only slightly older than her daughter.

"Look at all you've done so far." I waved my arms,

indicating the homey kitchen, the living room, and the pile of financial printouts littering the small desk in the corner. "You've created a beautiful home, taught yourself a new career, and in your spare time raised two well-behaved children who, I've been told, can walk and talk and chew gum at the same time. If that doesn't qualify you for king of the world, I don't know what does."

She didn't laugh, but she did smile. "Thanks, Beth. You've been a big help. I couldn't have made this decision without you."

I hated it when people said things like that. It made me feel that I should do all I could to make the decision the right one. Which ended up with me making offers that ranged from babysitting infant triplets to helping a friend move in a January blizzard.

"Let me know," I said, "if I can do anything to help."

The referee dropped the puck and two hockey sticks darted out. "Go, Raiders!" I yelled, clapping my mittened hands together. Jenna's hockey team was on home ice here in the Agnes Mephisto Memorial Ice Arena, and they had a good chance to win this afternoon's game.

I sat down next to Marina. "Did you know Sam had a business partner?" I asked.

Marina huddled inside her capacious wool coat. "'Neither a borrower nor a lender be; / For loan oft loses both itself and friend, / And borrowing dulls the edge of husbandry.'"

Well, well, well. "That's a direct quote."

Marina tossed up her chin. "Thou dost soundest surprised. Methinks you underestimate this . . . this sprite."

Sprite? Marina was many things, but elflike was not one of them. Not unless elves came in tallish, widish, red-haired versions whose use of an indoor voice was limited to whispers about feminine hygiene products.

"Just going with precedent," I said. "Never once have

I heard you quote Shakespeare correctly." Not that I was the best judge—English lit had been a long time ago—but even I could tell when iambic pentameter was being beaten with a stick.

Her chin dropped. "Not even once?"

"Well, you get the 'To be or not to be' part right, but after that . . ." I shrugged.

She looked at me with narrowed eyes. "You're not going to bring up the York thing again, are you?"

Only Marina could turn "Alas, poor Yorick" into "Alan's poor York." "Would I do a thing like that?"

"In a New Yorick minute," she said.

"Pretty funny, aren't you?"

"Why, yes, I am." Her proud look made me laugh. "The DH and I are paying huge smacking sums for the second youngest child to learn five-hundred-year-old plays at the collegiate level, so I figured I might as well learn, too. Double instruction for the dollar." She grinned. "I'm driving the kid nuts."

"Good for you. So I take it you knew Sam had a partner?"

"Sam's partner is—oh, dear, I thought this was a no-hitting league—Brian Keller."

"No checking," I corrected. "Hitting is always illegal. Checking is different." Much different, but no matter how many times I explained the rules of hockey to Marina, they never seemed to sink into the long-term-memory part of her brain. Lately, however, I had suspicions that she understood much more about hockey than she was letting on. One of these days I'd catch her, and it'd be all over.

"So you say. You also say they wear sweaters, and if those are sweaters"—she pointed at the ice—"I'm a raven-haired string bean."

We could have entered into a debate regarding the merits of using outdated terms of reference—if she was going to make fun of the term "sweaters," I would ask her about the last time she physically dialed a telephone number—but there were more important topics on the agenda. "Who's Brian Keller?" I asked, then stood up and whistled loud enough to send an echo around the cavernous building. "Nice save, Jenna!"

"It was?" Marina's forehead was creased with puzzlement. "But she fell down."

My daughter had, in fact, thrown herself onto the ice, arms outstretched, in a last-ditch effort to keep the puck from sliding into the outside corner. "Quit that," I said. "Who's Brian Keller?"

"He was a friend of Sam's in college," Marina said. "Grew up in suburban Milwaukee, played baseball from infancy through high school, went to the University of Wisconsin to major in art history of all things."

My spine stiffened in preparation for the defense of all liberal arts degrees. "There's nothing wrong with majoring in art history."

"There's nothing wrong with declaring your major to be communications, but is it really going to help you get a job? I think not. Sam and Brian connected during a Western civ class—required, in case you wanted to know—and stayed in contact over the years. When they became disenchanted with their wage-slave jobs, they put their heads together and came up with the brilliant idea of selling cheese to the Chinese.

"Selling—"

Marina kept going. "Luckily for their net worth, their wives put the kibosh on that idea. Behind every successful man there is a woman who could say, 'I told you so.' Though if I remember correctly"—she tapped her cheek with an index finger covered in purple mitten—"Brian and his wife are divorcing. No children."

I looked at her in admiration. "How do you know all that?"

She picked a piece of invisible lint off her sleeve and dropped it onto the cold cement floor. "Some call it gossip, I call it information gathering."

"What else do you know?"

Her breezy manner fell away and her mouth twisted as she watched the players skate from left to right and back again. "That Sam was the nicest guy ever. That no one can dream up a real reason why he was killed. That without Sam, Rachel and the kids are going to have a tough time."

All true and very sad, but none of it was useful for finding a killer, saving my bookstore, or restoring order to the city of Rynwood.

"Anything else?"

"Why, yes, indeed, my sweetie."

"Don't tell me you've figured out how to end static cling."

She shook her head. "I've decided to let the next generation tackle that. It'll be good for them."

"Well, what is it?"

"I know who killed Sam."

Even though I was used to Marina's dubiously authoritative pronouncements, this one startled me. "Forty-five seconds ago you had no clue to the killer's identity. Now you know?"

"You didn't see the announcement flashing in big red lights on the scoreboard?"

It was my own fault; I knew better, but I glanced over at the scoreboard and saw only the score. Home 2, Visitors 1.

Marina cackled. "Caught you!"

I closed my eyes. Why did I do things like that?

"But in answer to your question, my razor-sharp intelligence homed in on the murderer's identity just as your dainty daughter whacked the puck clear to the other end of the ice. Brian Keller is the killer."

Sure he was. "And what's the rationale for this theory, other than the fact that it's fun to say."

She was repeating the phrase in a singsong fashion, tipping her head from side to side with the beat. "Keller is the killer, Keller is the killer. Rationale? I need no rationale. My instincts are keen and sure."

"Then how do you explain your former instincts about Dave Patterson being in love with me?"

She waved away the comment.

I grinned. Marina had a talent for ignoring what she didn't want to see. It was one of the many things about her that I loved. In contrast, the combination of nature and nurture that had created my personality forced me to look for the worst-case scenario in every situation. From late-running school buses on field trips to a child's wail after a loud thumping noise, my thoughts jumped straight to ambulances and emergency rooms and the fastest way to notify Richard.

"Dave Patterson was in deep like with you," Marina said, "but since you spurned his advances, he had to settle for second best."

I started objecting to the "spurned" comment, but a forward on the visiting team broke away from the defenseman and scooted up the ice toward Jenna. I jumped to my feet, shouting, my voice mingling with other parental calls. "Go, Jenna! Stop it! Stop it!"

The skater wound up and whacked the puck straight toward the goal. It skittered and danced on its way to my daughter. My breath caught, for a bouncing puck is one of the hardest to block. Jenna lunged, right leg extended, wide goalie stick on the ice, doing her bighearted best to keep the puck out of the goal.

Marina was screaming in my ear. "Block that punt! Block that punt!"

All looked good for the home team until the other player's shot took a bounce and headed for a spot Jenna couldn't possibly reach, high and far to her right. There was no way for her to correct, no time for her to move, no chance for—

Tink!

They didn't call the posts a goalie's best friend for nothing. With sighs of relief or disappointment, depending on which team you supported, the crowd sat back down in a semi-coordinated way.

"Brian Keller has a motive," Marina said.

"He does?"

"Partners always have motives." She made it a statement of fact, and, after thinking about it, I realized she was probably right. Marriage partners have motives, such as love, jealousy, and money. Were business partners—except for the love part—any different?

"So now what?" I asked. "And before you ask, I am not—repeat, not—calling the sheriff's department and telling Deputy Wheeler your theory."

"Not to worry, dearest of all friends. I am sure our fine law enforcement officials and I are as one on this issue." She held up her mittened hand, and I assumed she was holding her index finger and middle finger together as a single unit. "There is only one thing they need."

Ah. I knew there was a catch. "What's that?"

"Proof! Proof that will stand up in a court of law." She leaned close. "And I know just how to get it."

"You do?"

"Ah do, dah-ling," she said, sliding into Southern belle mode. "Y'all just leave it to me and mah blog."

"You mean—"

"Why, yes, ah do." She batted her eyelashes. "WisconSINs will rise again."

It sounded like a bad prophecy, and I was getting ready to say so, when the end-of-game buzzer went off. Making fun of Marina could wait; taking photos of Jenna and her team couldn't. Mom priorities won, every time.

* * *

That night, I gathered up the kids and met Evan at Sabatini's Pizza. Though I hadn't felt overly hungry, the pungent mixture of garlic, oregano, and basil made me forget the popcorn I'd eaten at the hockey game. And the nachos. And the hot dog.

As Evan let me slide into our side of the booth first, the kids had a swift scuffle over who got the spot next to the window. From that alone I got the feeling the evening was headed straight downhill. Moms can tell this kind of thing. Don't ask us how we know, we just do. One hundred percent accuracy, money-back guarantee.

A perky teenaged waitress delivered menus and red plastic glasses of ice water. "Here you go. I'll be right back for your order."

I saw Jenna playing with her straw. "Jenna," I said quietly. She looked at me, all innocence, and we had a short but silent meeting of the minds over whether she should blow her straw paper at her brother. Luckily, she saw the wisdom of tidying the paper up into a tiny ball.

Taking her cue, Oliver did the same, and I whisked the papers away to the adult side of the table before any escalation could begin.

My offspring started to read their menus, and I tried to read their faces. Okay, maybe I was wrong about the evening heading south. Maybe that one hundred percent accuracy was only ninety-nine—

Oliver peeked over the top of his menu, his gaze locked on Evan. "Are you going to marry our mom?"

I gave a small squeak.

Evan, bless him, did not glance my way. Instead he sat quiet and looked Oliver straight on. "I don't know."

Jenna leaned forward, leading with her chin. "Do you *want* to marry her?"

My face instantly turned a hundred shades of cringing crimson. "Jenna! You can't—"

"It's all right." Evan still wasn't looking at me. "Your mother and I are very good friends, and friendship is what a good marriage is based on. But marriage is a very serious commitment and it can take a lot of time to know if it's the right thing to do."

"Are you going to be our dad?" Oliver's chin trembled.

I longed to pull him into my arms and hold him tight, but he wouldn't want me to do that in public. Besides, the booth seating made logistics difficult.

"You only have one dad," Evan said. "I will never try to replace him."

Now it was Evan who I wanted in my arms.

"If you're not going to be our dad, then what are you?" Oliver asked.

There was a beat of silence.

Two beats.

Was it possible? It seemed that Evan didn't know what to say. I never thought I'd witness such an event. Only why did it have to happen at the expense of my son? I opened my mouth to say something—anything—but Evan beat me to it.

"I'm your friend, Oliver."

"Oh." Oliver's face was serious. "I guess that's okay."

Evan nodded. "Jenna, I'll be your friend, too. If that's all right."

She fussed with her wristwatch. "I suppose."

Evan glanced at me. I smiled and took his hand. Rome wasn't built in a day, and neither was the love of an eleven-year-old. "Let's order, shall we?"

That night, after I'd put the kids to bed and started a load of laundry, I fired up the computer. I launched my browser and navigated to WisconSINs, Marina's on-again, off-again blog. "Well, would you look at that?" I said to George. Though the black cat didn't move from his nest on the bookshelf, I was sure he was interested.

Sometime in the last few months—months in which I'd never once looked at the blog—Marina had revamped the look of the site. A new right sidebar had pictures of Rynwood and links to old posts. The left sidebar had links to local events and businesses, and there was the Children's Bookshelf, right at the top.

Classic Marina. Just when you were ready to yell at her for having less sense than a teenager on her first road trip, she did something wonderful. All the irritation that had been rising in me since she'd whipped out her notepad at Sam's funeral died as if it had never been.

Smiling, I shook my head and began reading her latest post. Title: "I'm Baaaack!"

"Greetings, Rynwood-ites! My long sabbatical is over and it's time for us to get to work. The task at hand is a sad one, yet necessary for the sake of peace, quiet, and tranquillity in our fair city. How much do you love Rynwood? We could count the ways, but today our time will be better spent in helping the police track down the person who stole away Sam Helmstetter's life."

This time she'd done it right. Last year the blog had pointed fingers at various people until one of them had retaliated. Not the smartest way to catch a killer. I was relieved to see her take a reasonable approach. She ended the post with a plea for anyone who might have any inkling about anyone who wished Sam harm to contact the police.

All well and good, but it was a passive game, posting and waiting, posting and waiting. Meanwhile, sales at the store were dropping, Yvonne was feeling wretched, and Richard's severance package wasn't going to last forever.

Maybe Marina's efforts would yield results, and maybe they wouldn't. Time alone would tell.

I turned off the computer and sat, staring at the dark screen. Time would tell a lot of things. It would take time to find out if I'd done a good job as a mother. It would take time to figure out if Evan and I had a future together. Given time, Richard would find a job. In time, we'd know who killed Sam.

All that waiting. I made a face and saw the resulting unattractiveness in the reflection of the screen.

"Only one way to fix that," I told myself.

Then I headed up to bed. The cure would start tomorrow.

Chapter 9

"Déjà vu all over again." Gus looked at me across the top of his battered desk. The piles of papers were, I was pretty sure, different than the piles I'd seen last year, but one stack of manila folders looks much like any other. Gus had never been good at cleaning out his church choir folder, so why would he be any better at cleaning his desk?

"So I suppose Marina has you poking around into Sam's death?"

I jerked my head up so fast I was bound to have a stiff neck the next day. "What makes you say that?"

Gus laughed. "I've known you for almost twenty years, I've known Marina for nearly thirty, and I remember what happened last fall. I'm no genius, but even a small-town cop can figure out a three-syllable word like 'precedent.' "

"Um . . ."

"Don't worry." His shoes went up on the edge of the desk and he put his hands behind his head. It was all designed to put the person in this seat at ease, but I'd learned a little bit about precedent, too. This was the position Gus took when he wanted to be friendly, disarming, and so confide-able that you'd willingly confess all your sins, including the one time you took a Popsicle from your grandmother's freezer without asking.

"I'm not going to scold you," Gus said. "Homicides are investigated by the county detectives. Deputy Wheeler is in charge."

It was just like the last time we'd had a murder in Rynwood. Local law enforcement was out of the investigative picture, and also like last time, I didn't have the least desire to talk to Deputy Wheeler directly. The woman reduced me to speechlessness, and if I could pass on any substantial information to my friend Gus instead, well, what was wrong with that?

"If I find out anything," I said, "it's okay to tell you, right?"

He moved his size twelves to the right—the better to see me with—and half smiled. "What's the matter, you too scared to talk to the big-city cop?"

"Yes."

He laughed. "You're not the only one. She scares the bejesus out of me, too."

As if. I smiled and decided to play along with the fiction that Gus could be scared of anyone. "It's that look she has," I said. "Like she knows I've done something wrong and it's only a matter of time before she figures out what it is."

Gus nodded. "We were talking about how criminals start small, and I almost told her about the time I stole my brother's favorite comic book."

I laughed, but Gus didn't laugh back. Maybe he *was* a little scared of Deputy Wheeler. I looked at him with knowledge gathered from thousands of mutually attended choir rehearsals, hundreds of Sunday services, dozens of funerals, and nearly twenty Christmas Eve services. When you sit in front of someone for that many hours, you can learn a lot. I knew Gus gnashed his teeth at the oh-so-common mispronunciation of "February," that he liked Billie Holiday, and loved the music of John Rutter. I'd also heard him weep during Maundy Thursday services and laugh with joy on Easter mornings. No, Gus wasn't scared of Deputy Wheeler. He just didn't like her.

"So what theory is Marina working on now?" Gus asked. "Let me guess. Organized crime is moving into the document-shredding business and Sam wouldn't pay the protection fee. No, wait. Aliens are trying to take over Earth, and they've decided the best way is to eliminate the nicest people first."

I sighed. "That's the problem, isn't it? Sam was too nice to have any enemies."

"He had one."

"Marina thinks Brian Keller did it," I said.

Gus laughed so hard his feet slid off the desk. "Leave it to Marina," he said through spasms that looked painful. "The one guy in the world with a perfect alibi and she targets him as the killer."

I could make fun of Marina's theories, but Gus didn't have the same rights I did. "What perfect alibi?"

"Keller was on television the night of Sam's murder." He wiped tears out of the corners of his eyes. "National television."

"You mean live?"

"He was at the hockey game that night. Minnesota Wild played the Red Wings. He had great seats right at center ice, just above the glass, and got caught upside the head with a puck." Gus slapped his temple with the heel of his hand. "He says he turned to look at a hot blonde and whammo! He was out cold for a couple minutes. It was all over the TV. The EMTs rolled him out to an ambulance and he ended up staying at the hospital overnight. Got twenty stitches to boot." Gus fingered stitches he didn't have. "Two days later he got served with divorce papers. His imminent ex says she was filing anyway, but the timing makes you wonder, doesn't it?" He chuckled. "I can't believe Marina hadn't heard about this."

I couldn't either, and my fingers itched to pull out my cell phone. "She's been . . . busy."

"Losing her touch, more like. Say, is she still doing that blog?" He sounded amused, which irritated me no end.

"Yes, she's still doing the blog." I rose. "See you on Sunday."

Though it left something to be desired as an exit line, at least I'd said something. But when I reached the door, Gus called me back. "Hey, Beth?"

I turned, one hand on the knob.

"If I tell you to leave this well enough alone, will you listen?"

A number of thoughts rambled around in my head. That he was probably right and I shouldn't interfere in what was essentially police business. That if Marina and I had left well enough alone last year, a murderer might still be on the loose. That if Sam's murder wasn't solved, Yvonne would become a pariah. But my primary thought was that I didn't like being told what to do.

"Will I listen?" I smiled. "What do you think?" And I left before he could get in another word.

"He *what*?"

Marina's voice screeched into my ear canal, making the hammer pound, the anvil bang, and the stirrup swing. Wincing, I pulled my cell phone off the side of my head, but it was too little too late; my ear was ringing with the echo of her disbelief. "Brian Keller can't possibly have killed Sam," I said. "He was on TV." I explained the incident, but Marina, who usually saw the funny side of everything, even when there wasn't a funny side, didn't laugh.

"There has to be a way," she muttered.

"Not unless you believe in time travel." Which I knew full well she thought was impossible. "If humans could travel in time," she said on a monthly basis, "someone would have gone back by now and made sure Philo Farnsworth stayed on the farm instead of inventing that idiot box we call a television."

Now she said, "Maybe Brian has a twin."

"And maybe you need to get a new theory." I told her I'd bring pizza to her house after work. We'd pack goody bags for Saturday's dance and be done with the job in no time.

I slid the phone back into my purse as I walked into the bookstore. Lois was sitting on the counter, leaning back on her hands, kicking the heels of her Earth shoes against the wood paneling. The first time she'd worn the shoes, I'd asked what else she had in the box labeled "1970." She'd huffed and said these were brand-new, thank you very much, and clearly I didn't know a thing about fashion trends.

True. But I did know ugly when I saw it. Luckily, the thought stayed in my head.

Lois started whistling. I cocked my head, listening. "'I've Been Working on the Railroad,'" I said.

"Bingo!" Lois slid off the counter and landed on the floor with a light thump. Sixty one years old and she was as limber as a teenager. It was the yoga, she said. Last year for Christmas she'd given me a yoga DVD. Sadly, the plastic wrapper was still wrapped tight around it.

"But I was whistling sarcastically," she said. "I haven't been working at all."

I glanced around the store. Not a single customer. My stomach lining rolled over and put another knot in itself. "Where's Yvonne?"

"In the back unpacking a box of special orders."

"Have we—" My cell phone rang and I fished it out. "Hello?"

"I know who killed Sam," Marina said.

"Excellent. Now hang up and call Deputy Wheeler. Would you like her number?"

"Don't you want to hear my theory first?"

"No. I want the killer in jail fast and—" I stopped. It wouldn't do to worry Marina about the customer-less state of the store. She'd feel guilty about Yvonne and double her investigative efforts.

"And what?"

"And I want life to get back to normal." Her nose was probably twitching like mad; Marina could scent a lie faster than a first-time mother picked up a dropped pacifier. But it wasn't a lie, not exactly. "I have to go, okay? There's a bunch of people coming in." I clicked off the phone.

Lois went to the door, opened it, and poked her head out. "Hellooo?"

"What are you doing?" I asked.

"Looking for that bunch of people."

On a normal day this would have made me laugh. Today I couldn't even summon a smile. "I have some errands to run. Call me if you need me."

"Aye, aye, Captain." She snapped to attention and saluted smartly as I went by.

The salute, silly though it was, made me pick up my chin. Today, if I couldn't smile, I could do my best to save my store. All I had to do was find Sam's killer. And to do that all I had to do was find a reason for Sam to be murdered.

Piece of cake.

Flossie Untermayer frowned at me. "Sam Helmstetter didn't have an enemy in the world."

"That's what everybody says," I said.

Flossie, who was seventy-six and proud of it, frowned at her clipboard and made a note with a pencil tied on with a shoelace. She was the only adult I knew who still used No. 2 pencils. She also knew everyone in town. She was one of my top ten favorite people.

"Quite a contradiction, isn't it?" She pursed her lips and looked at the ceiling of her downtown grocery store. "The only man in town without an enemy, and he's the man who is murdered. You and Marina are teaming up again, I imagine."

I sighed. "How can a reputation be made on one incident?"

Flossie laughed, a silvery run of light. She'd once danced ballet professionally in Chicago. When she'd aged out of that career, she'd turned to stage acting and singing, and when those roles dried up she came home to Rynwood to take over her family's grocery store.

"A reputation can be made even when the incident never really occurred." She crouched down, the better to view the bottom shelf of cereal boxes. "You should know that."

I did, but that didn't mean I had to like it. "So you can't think of anyone who'd kill Sam?"

She looked up at me from her crouch. If I stayed in that position for more than five seconds my thighs would be screaming, but Flossie looked as if she could stay down there, comfortably, for the rest of the day. "The rule is to look at the spouse first and business partners second," she said.

"That's what they say." The proverbial "they" also claimed that Nero fiddled while Rome burned. Ruthless and depraved Nero might have been, but the violin wasn't invented for another fifteen hundred years.

"Yes." Flossie adjusted her crouch to sink lower. "But even if Rachel wanted to kill Sam, I don't see how a woman her size would have the strength to strangle a man of Sam's size. Simple physiology is against it."

That's what Gus had said, back on the night of the murder.

"And we all know where Brian Keller was that evening." She chuckled. "Talk about building a reputation on one incident."

Everyone in town knew about Brian Keller. Why was I the last to know? Maybe Marina was losing her touch.

I watched Flossie write a few notes on her clipboard, then asked, "Who do you think killed Sam?" Behind my simple question was a plaintive plea for answers. Please tell me I've never met the murderer. Please tell me I don't go to church with him, walk the same streets, or have him walk into my store, and please, please, keep him away from my children.

Flossie stood, moving to an upright position without visible effort. "Are you all right?" She put the back of her hand to my forehead. "You're shivering."

I put on a smile. "Just a chill."

"Mmm." She gave me an intense look, but stepped back. "Who do I think killed Sam?" Her tone, usually full of rich inflection, was devoid of life. "I have no idea. He shouldn't be dead."

And on that, as on many other topics, Flossie and I agreed completely.

I left the grocery store and pulled back the sleeve of my coat to look at my watch. Just past eleven. Perfect. I walked across the brick street, checked my watch against the Victorian clock the chamber of commerce put up a few years ago, and opened the door of the Green Tractor.

The diner smelled of fried food and grilling beef. I stood by the cash register, eyes closed, breathing in the luscious scents, trying to convince myself that smelling it was just as good as eating it.

"Are you okay?"

I opened my eyes. Ruthie, the diner's owner, was looking at me in the same way Flossie had. "Why do people keep asking me that?" I asked.

"Maybe because you look like you're about to keel over." Ruthie handed me a mug and a plate filled with a cinnamon roll. "Sit down and eat."

Since I was constitutionally incapable of passing up one of Ruthie's rolls, and as my life seemed to be full of women telling me what to do, I sat on the closest stool.

The Green Tractor was a leftover from what had once been a dime-store luncheon counter. When the dime store had abandoned Rynwood for good, Ruthie and her husband had bought the building and divided it into two businesses. The other side evolved from a butcher shop to a men's clothing store to a furniture store and settled on being an eclectic gift shop. The Green Tractor side, after the initial renovation, hadn't changed a bit.

Ruthie's husband died a few years ago, clutching his chest with one hand and his trusty pancake flipper with the other, and Ruthie had marched on alone. The only difference was that instead of telling her husband what to do, she told her customers what to do.

I swiped off a fingerful of the roll's cream cheese filling and licked it down before Ruthie came back with a knife, fork, napkin, and etiquette lessons.

"Here you go." She set the implements of destruction in front of me and, after a glance across the mostly empty restaurant, sat next to me. "So what's up? Have you decided to toss in the bookstore towel and come be a waitress for me?"

My fork froze halfway to my mouth, a piece of cinnamon roll perched precariously.

Ruthie let out a burst of laughter. "You should see your face, missy. Have you ever done the waitress bit?"

"One summer I worked at a fast-food restaurant. It was the longest five years of my life."

Ruthie laughed again. "I don't see you as the waitress type. Now, don't take offense. Being a good waitress takes a special kind of person. You have to be willing to show people who you really are, and you're not like that. You keep yourself to yourself. Nothing wrong with that. It's just not going to get you good tips."

I'd never thought about it that way, and she was right. I'd never been comfortable engaging complete strangers in conversations that revealed too much. Marina said I was too uptight, that my upbringing was going to kill every chance of fun I was ever offered, but I liked Ruthie's interpretation better.

"So what's up?" Ruthie asked.

Frosting crumbled off the roll as I cut it into bits. "It's about Sam Helmstetter."

"Oh, you're playing the who-killed-Sam game, too?" She smiled, making the wrinkles at the corners of her eyes deepen. "You and Marina? Hey, after last year you two have experience in this kind of thing. Have the police asked for your advice?"

I peered at her over the rim of my tea mug, but she didn't seem to be laughing at me. "No," I said. "But Gus did say he'd pass anything along to the sheriff's department." I lifted up the end of my sentence so it sounded like a question. Meaning: Do you suspect anyone of anything? And if so, please tell me.

"Haven't heard diddley that makes any sense." Her face sagged. "People are saying, 'It's a darn shame about Sam,' and 'The police should be doing something.' Typical talk." She shrugged, but sadness showed in the set of her chin. "He never hurt a soul in his life. He was an Eagle Scout, did you know? And he went on so many mission trips to Central America that he ended up minoring in Spanish." Bewilderment colored her voice. "Why would anyone want to kill a man like that?"

Ruthie had known Sam his entire life. Had watched him grow from infant to toddler to young man to husband to father. "He shouldn't be dead." I put down my fork and put my arms around her. "He really shouldn't."

"I wish I did know who killed him," she said roughly. "I'd—"

"Shhhh," I whispered. *"Shhhh."*

We clung together, held close by mutual grief for Sam: husband; a father of two; not a person to light the world on fire, but after the age of thirty-five, it would be a rare individual who had the spare energy to light more than his own little corner. No, Sam hadn't been one of those dynamic, perk-up-the-room kind of guys, but he'd been someone you could count on, and really, what mattered more?

"Sam's killer won't be free much longer," Ruthie said. The quake in her voice belied the confident words. "The police are going to find out who did it."

I hugged her tight. "They sure are."

And if they didn't, I would.

I left the Green Tractor later than anticipated, my departure delayed by Ruthie's refusal to accept payment for the food. The only reason she took any money whatsoever was because she accepted my suggestion to set up a coffee can collection for a scholarship.

"I'll decorate it with the Rynwood High School colors," she said, brightening up a little. "Wouldn't it be great if Blake ends up wearing blue and gold, too?"

Traffic on the street was picking up now that lunchtime approached. I stopped just short of the hardware and stood on my tiptoes so I could see over the colorful display of bathroom sinks.

"You could just walk in."

I jumped, then spun around and looked up—way up—at Evan. "What are you doing out here? Don't you have a store to run?"

He smiled down at me and I went all mushy. A year

after we'd remet, it still happened every time the man smiled. Well, almost every time. I didn't mush out when he laughed at my attempts to repair drywall.

"My excuse is a visit to Debra O'Conner," he said. "What's yours?"

Debra was the bank's vice president in charge of business loans, and Evan, who'd retired at age forty from a very lucrative career as a corporate attorney, had more money than anyone I'd ever known. Which wasn't saying a lot, because I'd spent my adult life in Rynwood and didn't get out much. Still, I couldn't imagine that Evan needed a loan for anything.

Part of me wanted to ask why he needed to talk to Debra; another, larger part of me didn't want to know. My own financial problems were keeping me from getting a decent night's sleep. If Evan had troubles, I'd never get any rest at all.

I smiled brightly. "Errands."

"Hmm." He studied me. "If I were still a practicing attorney, I'd say you look guilty."

"It's the light." I glanced up at the clear November sky. "This time of year it always makes me look as if I'm up to something. Getting close to Christmas and all that, so don't ask too many questions."

"Hmm," he said again. "I'll let you go, then."

"Okay." I backed away. "See you later, okay? I mean, I'll see you. Um, later."

I made my escape.

Down the street and over one block, my favorite hairstylist snicked her scissors shut and dropped them into a jar of green liquid. "There you go, Mrs. Beuhrle," Denise said. "Better than new."

Mrs. Beuhrle, who, no matter what she wore, reminded me of my great-aunt Edith's sofa, patted her hair and smiled into the mirror. "You do *such* a nice job. I don't know what I'd do without you. Promise me you'll never retire." She handed over a check, heaved herself out of the chair, and made her way out the door.

Denise looked at the check left behind and made a sour face. "I'm not retiring any day soon on the tips that woman leaves behind."

I laughed. "All part of her plan."

"Huh." Denise dropped the check into the cash register. "She's just cheap. Do you know the difference between Mrs. Beuhrle and a canoe?"

"No, I don't." I knew the difference between a Dutchman and a canoe, but maybe this was another joke.

"A canoe can tip." Denise slammed the cash drawer shut.

Nope. Same joke.

"Did you want to make an appointment?" Denise flipped through her book. "I don't have any early slots until next week, but there's an opening Saturday afternoon. Want an updo for the dance? Bring Jenna in and I'll give her a French twist with ringlets. She'll look like a princess."

I tried to imagine my tomboy sitting in a hair salon chair for an hour straight. Couldn't manage it and tried again, this time with feeling. Still couldn't.

"Not this time," I said. "Put me down for the Tuesday after Thanksgiving."

"Pencil or ink?"

Oh, the commitment. "Ink."

"Okeydokey." She turned the pages. "Did you hear the hot money is on the Stulls for the next divorce in town? Five bucks will get you into the pool. You get a one-week window."

"Um, no, thanks."

"Suit yourself." She scribbled my name and looked up. "Say, are you and Marina poking around again?"

Flossie was right—one incident could indeed make a reputation. "What makes you say that?"

"Nothing. I just wondered if you were." She busied herself with straightening a stack of business cards that had never been straightened in their lives.

The hair at the back of my neck stood on end. Either Denise had something to tell me or I should have worn a heavier coat. "A little bit," I said. "Gus said he'll pass any information on to the sheriff's department."

"He will?" Her face cleared. "So I can tell you and he'll tell them? Sweet." She beckoned me close.

I leaned over the counter, close enough to smell the hair spray on Denise's stiffened bangs.

She slewed her eyes left and right, but no one in the salon was paying any attention to us. In the back, a fifty-ish woman was sitting under a beehive hairdryer and reading *True Confessions*. The two stylists who worked for Denise were both busy with clients. One was highlighting a teenager's hair and talking about the latest Lady Gaga news, while the other was concentrating on the curly, full-bodied style her straight-haired client had cut out of a magazine.

Denise spoke into my ear. "You know how everybody says Sam is such a nice guy? I'm not so sure."

My stare contained total and complete incomprehension. "What do you mean?"

She put her mouth an inch away from my ear. "I think he smoked grass. You know, marijuana?"

"What?" Other words bubbled up in my throat—no, don't be silly, how ridiculous, how can you say such a thing—but only the one came out. "What?"

"Shhh." Denise made quieting motions with flattened hands. "Don't let anyone hear."

I nodded; the town might not rise up and lynch her for slandering Sam, but she'd have a hard time getting anyone to believe her.

"You don't believe me, do you?"

No, I didn't. I started to frame a reply of sorts, but she went on without me.

"No one will," she said. "And if one more person says how nice a guy Sam was, I'm going to scream. No one is *that* nice. It just can't happen."

"But until a little bit ago," she said, pulling back a few inches from intimate revelations to whispered confidence, "I thought the same thing. That he's just so nice. Isn't it funny how your idea about someone can change with one sentence?"

Back to the topic of the easily made—or lost—reputation. I wanted to ask what sentence it was, and by whom it was uttered, but I knew better than to interrupt Denise when she was in full spate. If I diverted the flow, it might never get back to its original path.

"It's funny," I said agreeably.

"Yeah." Denise sighed. "And that's why I don't want to spread this around. Maybe I'm wrong about Sam. For the sake of the kids, I hope I am." She shook her head. "If he was only using, that would have been bad enough. But what I heard makes me think he might have been selling, too."

"What?"

"*Shhh.*" Denise made frantic shushing noises. "See why I want it hush-hush? If the rumor gets around, the guy could be scared off, and they'll never solve the murder, see?"

I wasn't sure I followed, but Denise's line of thinking was more along the line of Marina logic. Both had a habit of not letting facts interfere with their conclusions.

"So you'll tell Gus?" Denise asked.

I got an image of the meeting. I'd walk into his office and tell him I'd heard that someone suspected Sam of selling and using drugs. He'd politely take notes and then, as soon as I'd left, laugh uncontrollably and toss the notes into the trash.

"He'll want evidence," I said.

"Evidence?" Her face flashed with indignation. "I have the best evidence of all. Sam's very own—"

A woman's shriek rent the air. "Deniiiiise!" The front door banged shut. "You have to help me," she wailed. "I can't be seen in public like this, I just can't!" Though the temperature was up into the midforties, the thirtyish woman wore a knit hat that covered her entire head. Its cheerful strings tied under her chin were a stark contrast to the anguish on the woman's face.

"What's the matter, honey?" Denise hurried to her side. "Let me see, okay?" She sounded like an emergency room pediatrician. "Take that off and we'll take a look."

Sobbing, the woman untied the strings and, with all of us watching, slowly pulled off the hat.

A collective intake of breath drew all the oxygen out of the room, and I was sure we were all thinking the same thing: That poor woman. I'm so glad it isn't me.

Her hair was green. Not the bright green you got from the temporary color kids used to paint their hair school colors, and not the green that blondes get from spending too much time in the swimming pool, but a miserable mottled pea soup kind of green that was as unattractive as mold on the last piece of pumpkin pie.

"Oh, honey." Denise put her arm around the woman's shoulders and steered her toward the back of the salon. "It's bad, but I seen worse. We'll make it better, don't you worry." She called back over her shoulder. "Jenn? Call my clients and let them know I have a hair emergency."

"Sure thing," Jenn said. "Um, for how long? Mid-afternoon?"

With a grim visage, Denise studied the green tresses.

"Better make it the whole day." To the woman she said, "C'mon, honey. Let me get you in a chair."

The salon was filled with head shakes and whispers. There was no way I'd be able to talk to Denise now. Whatever she had to tell me would have to wait. But I was just as glad. I did not want to hear anything bad about Sam. Not an ideal attitude for someone trying to find a killer, but then I never claimed to know what I was doing.

When I returned to the store, a surprising sight greeted me: There were actual live customers browsing among the shelves. Not one, not two, but *three* people were picking up books and reading their contents. I counted them a second time and still came up with three, and all appeared to be shopping separately.

One, two, three. I smiled contentedly. This would all work out. Some people in Rynwood might stay away from the store because they thought Yvonne was a threat to motherhood and apple pie, but most would be reasonable. And a large share of my customers came from environs beyond Rynwood. How many people in Madison would know—or care—who was on staff?

With a heart much lighter than it had been two minutes earlier, I shed my coat and purse and waded into the fray. Lois had many superpowers, but even she could only be in one place at a time. Offhandedly, I made my way across the store, straightening books and realphabetizing as I went.

I approached Customer Number One, a sixtyish woman who'd laden herself with picture books, graphic novels, and two puppets. A grandmother, I guessed, but after the time I'd asked a gray-haired customer how old her grandchildren were, and she'd snapped that her *children* were five and seven and that if I had the sense of a toad I'd be able to tell she wasn't a day over forty-five, I'd taken to asking different questions.

"Hi," I said. "Could I take those up to the counter for you?"

She gave me a grateful smile. "That would be wonderful. I'm not sure I want them all, though."

"That's fine," I assured her. "We'll sort it out at the register."

Arms full, I headed to the counter. The phone rang, and one puppet tumbled to the floor as I tried to bring the goodies in for a landing and answer the phone at the same time.

"Good morning, Children's Bookshelf. How may I help you?"

"Morning?" Marina asked. "What time zone are you in?"

I glanced at the wall clock. "Pacific. I hear it's nice in San Diego this time of year."

"The only time it isn't nice in San Diego is during forest fire season."

I picked the fox puppet off the floor and slid it over my hand and made it bark silently. "When was the last time you were in San Diego?" *Bark, bark, bark.*

"Thou must not underestimate mine travels," she said airily.

"The only place outside of the Midwest you've gone in the last three years is Boston, and that was to take your youngster to college."

"Mayhap," she said. "However, travel is not only of the body, but also of the mind. Why let mere flesh keep you rooted in a single place?"

I tried to think of a reply, but soon gave up. Some days I just couldn't keep up with her. "Did you have something to tell me, or are you just going to be irritating?"

Marina chuckled. "Gotcha. Are you keeping score this month, or am I?"

If we actually kept score, the tally would be a six-figure number on her side and a big round zero on mine. "Numbers are merely symbolic approximations of reality. I care not for them."

"Nice." Faint applause noises came through the phone. "What I called to say is this." She paused dramatically. "Are you ready? Brian Keller didn't kill Sam."

As revelations go, this one wasn't stunning. Roughly one hundred percent of the interested population had reached the same conclusion days ago. "Glad to hear it."

"I knew you would be," she said. "Could I have a drumroll, please?"

"No."

"Now, Beth," she said patiently. "All good theories must be released with proper fanfare."

"Why?"

"Because I said so. Drumroll, please."

Sighing, I pulled the fox off my hand and tapped the phone's receiver with my fingers, simulating a drumroll with as little effort and embarrassment as possible.

"Is that the best you can do?" Marina demanded.

I kept tapping.

"Okay, okay. This time I really do know who killed Sam."

While Marina wasn't likely to posit that an alien from another galaxy had sucked the life force out of Sam, she could have come up with something almost as unlikely. "Great. Shall I notify the media?"

"Sam was killed by . . ."

She left the sentence unfinished, so I finished it for her. "The butler in the library with a candlestick."

"Do you want to hear this or not?"

Only if the killer was a complete stranger. If he was someone I knew, well, no, I didn't want to hear.

"Okay, then," she said into my silence. "Sam was killed by a jealous husband."

The idea was so unlikely that it was ridiculous. I

started laughing. "Come on, Marina, you don't really believe that Sam was . . . you know."

"Of course not," she said indignantly. "The man didn't have an adulterous bone in his body. But what if some poor misguided soul *thought* Sam was having an affair with his wife? What if Sam, nice guy that he was, stopped to help a woman change her car tire. What if she was so grateful that she sent him a card? What if her husband saw it, and he's the wacked-out type who can't stand if his wife so much as breathes in another man's direction? Ergo, he killed Sam."

As ludicrous as her theory was, there was a warped logic to it. And if morning talk shows were any reflection of reality—which they weren't—then she actually had a valid point. There was only one problem.

"Who's the jealous husband?" I asked.

"Who? You ask who?" She sounded like an owl. "How would I know? That's for the police to figure out."

I was getting a headache. "Marina, you can't honestly expect me to go to the police with—"

"Oopy," she said. "Hear those children screeching? Got to go play referee. See ya!"

In a very adult manner I stuck my tongue out at the phone. I'd see Marina soon enough, and in very certain terms I'd tell her there was no way on God's green earth that I'd take her harebrained theory to the police. I could just *see* the pitying look on Gus's face. "Did Marina put you up to this?" he'd ask.

No. I would not do it.

"You'll do it." Marina pushed a stack of cellophane bags across her kitchen table. "This is what investigating is all about. Pushing at things that don't want to be pushed, pulling at things that won't be pulled."

"Why am I always the one who's getting pulled and pushed?" From the piles in front of me, I chose six

Tootsie Rolls, two sets of stickers, a small sack of candy corn, and a miniature plastic turkey wrapped in clear plastic, then, frowning, put it all into one of the bags. The whole concept of goody bags irritated me. "Tell me again why we're giving candy and cheap gifts to kids who already eat too much sugar and have too many toys?"

"Ours not to reason why, my dear," Marina said sadly. "It is the will of the PTA's dance committee. We are mere minions to do their bidding."

"How can you be a minion if you're part of the committee?"

"Alas, I am only one vote."

True enough, but how had the whole goody bag thing gotten started? I hadn't received them when I was a kid, so when—

"You're thinking again." Marina tossed a Tootsie Roll at me. "Keep it up and those frown lines will become permanent fixtures. Then where will you be?"

"Same place I am now, only with frown lines on my face."

"And Evan won't be too pleased about that, now will he?"

She sounded a little snippy, which was completely un-Marina-like. I looked at her.

"What?"

Still snippy. "Are you feeling okay?" She did look a little flushed. Maybe she was coming down with something.

"I feel fine," she said. "What, can't I make a joke about Evan without you getting all defensive?"

She swallowed and I saw her throat bobble a little. Scratchy throat, for sure. Now came the tricky part: how to take care of Marina without her knowing I was taking care of her.

I stood up. "Do you still have that box of chamomile tea? A mug sounds good right now. And I was thinking, your theory about Sam being killed by a nutso jealous husband is a good one. Let's make a list." Not that I'd take it anywhere near the police station, but I'd find a way around that.

While I bustled about, doing tea-type things, Marina started naming the men who might be considered candidates. This included the husbands of every woman who had a child at Tarver, the husband of every woman who attended the Helmstetters' church, the husband of every woman who shopped downtown, because Sam's business was on the last block to the west, and the husband of every woman who shopped at the mall, because Sam often took the kids to the mall on rainy Saturday afternoons.

If Marina had run through the names alphabetically, she could have used the Rynwood phone book.

I placed two steaming mugs on the table and we both wrapped our hands around them, letting the warmth seep into our bones.

"Do you really think one of those men killed Sam?" I asked.

Marina put her face to the tea and breathed deep and long. "No. But we have to start somewhere."

And, of course, she was right.

Chapter 10

The day of the Father-Daughter Dance dawned like a lot of days in November, overcast with a spatter of rain. This time every year I was reminded of the vacation conclusion I'd come to years ago: November was the month I'd love to travel.

"It's raining," Jenna said morosely. She was kneeling on the family room couch, her arms hanging long over the back, chin propped up by the tweedy brown upholstery. Raindrops trailed down and wind gusts buffeted the glass.

She heaved a huge sigh. Either she was spending too much time with Marina or she was about to enter the eye-rolling stage. Since I couldn't do anything about either possibility, I opted for the next best thing. Distraction. "I saw a woman with green hair the other day."

No response. She didn't even turn around. I wasn't sure she'd even heard me, because the next thing she said was as thorough a non sequitur as I'd ever heard.

"Do I have to go to the dance?"

I blinked. A week ago she'd wanted me to teach her how to waltz. Two days ago I'd come into my room and found her holding up one of my dresses, swishing the black chiffon around her legs and humming. She hadn't noticed my approach, and I'd backed away with a smile of bittersweet happiness on my face.

Now I frowned at the back of her head. What didn't I know about? Trouble at school? Had something happened between her and her father?

Thousands upon thousands of my synapses were firing simultaneously, but even so, it was going to take some time to come to a conclusion. Luckily, Oliver was up in his bedroom reading *The Velveteen Rabbit* to Spot, and after that he was scheduled for a sleepover with a friend, so there was mother-daughter time aplenty.

"Mom?" Jenna turned halfway around, and I saw her profile against the gray morning light. For an instant, I saw the woman she would become. Her little girl nose lengthened, her cheekbones grew gracefully, and her chin—repositioned through the clever use of orthodontic appliances—accented her full lips. The sight took my breath away, and for a moment I couldn't speak.

"Mom?"

I shook myself out of the future. Which was too bad, because the future had been wonderful, and the here and now was a little troublesome. I still wasn't sure why Jenna didn't want to go to the dance, and guessing was always bad. Calm and cool, as if I didn't care about her answer, I asked, "Why don't you want to go?"

She sighed again, tipped her head back and forth, then flopped around and sat on the couch like a human being. "I don't know."

Which wasn't the answer I'd hoped for, though it was the answer I expected. Now I needed to probe mildly enough to make her want to talk, but hard enough to get an honest answer. Every mother is a master negotiator. "Did you want to try on the dress one more time?"

Last week we'd trekked to the mall and bought a dress for the occasion. Jenna had, at first, resisted the idea with all her stubborn might, but she looked interested when the salesclerk brought out a simple royal blue dress, no lace, no bows, no Peter Pan collar. She tried it on, and once she'd seen herself in the mirror, twirling around in a circle, the full skirt billowing out about her, just like in the movies, she'd caved instantly.

"You look very pretty in that dress," I said. "Your father will hardly recognize you."

My tomboy smiled a little. "I like it. A lot."

Cross dress off the list. Next item, please.

"Do you want to practice dancing? We could try that swing step again." Once I'd convinced Jenna that dancing improved agility and coordination, she was easily persuaded to learn a few basic steps. She'd learned fast and I'd had to borrow a dance DVD from the library to keep up.

"Noo." She slid a little lower. "I'm good."

"Have you talked to your friends? Alexis and Bailey are both going tonight, aren't they?"

"Yeah. They are."

Hmm. Jenna's concern couldn't be . . . couldn't possibly be . . . a *boy*, could it? She was barely eleven years old, for heaven's sake! She'd talked about Blake Helmstetter, but not as if she *like* liked him, not my little Jenna, not my little girl who—

"I think maybe I'm getting sick."

Of all the possibilities, that was one I hadn't considered. Bad mother. Jenna rarely got sick, but since Marina was coming down with a cold, the idea should have crossed my mind at least once.

I hurried to the couch and felt Jenna's forehead. Normal. "Does your throat hurt?"

"No . . . it's my stomach."

She held her hand to her lower abdomen, and I had the sudden and horrifying thought that she might be entering the first phases of Becoming a Woman. In spite of the admonishments of Marina, my mother, my sisters, and every other female who'd raised girls, Jenna and I hadn't yet had The Talk. Not completely, anyway. I'd told her that her body was going to change as she got older, that a baby was created when a man and a woman loved each other very much, and that a woman's body was designed for carrying children.

That's where the conversation either went vague or very technical. The morning after I told Jenna about how eggs travel down the fallopian tubes, her eyes went wide at the sight of two of them staring her in the face, sunny-side up. That had been a few months ago, and I wasn't sure she'd recovered.

I sat down on the couch and pulled her close. She was much too big to fit into my lap, but we made it work. What did I care if her elbow jabbed into my solar plexus? I could breathe. Mostly.

"Shall I get the pink stuff?" I stroked her hair.

"It's not that kind of stomachache."

I kissed her cheek. "What kind of stomachache do you think it is?"

"Um . . ." She snuggled in closer. "The kind I sometimes get before a big game."

Ah. The lightbulb went on. My Jenna was nervous, and it wasn't about a hockey game. Wonders, indeed, never ceased. "But your game this afternoon isn't a big one." I knew full well that it wasn't; I was using a common mom ploy. Pretend ignorance, and the kid will be compelled to enlighten you.

"Not real big," Jenna said. "I mean you never know what's going to happen, but this other team's only won once this whole year."

"Then why the funny tummy? You're all caught up with your homework, right?"

"Almost." She squirmed, and I smiled. Jenna was the worst liar on the planet, except for her mother. But while my ears turned red when fibbing, her skin went itchy all over. The bigger the lie, the itchier her skin.

"Don't you have some math homework?"

"A little, but it's easy."

For her, it probably was. "How's that social studies report going?" When I'd checked it on the computer last night it looked as if she was at the midpoint.

"Half done," she said. "I'll finish tomorrow."

So why, then, the stomachache?

"Mom?"

"What, honey?"

Could she be worried about Evan? Though the pizza parlor incident had troubled me, Evan had laughed it off, saying she just needed time. I'd figured he was right, but maybe I was wrong. Maybe I—

"Mom, are you and Mrs. Neff going to figure out who killed Mr. Helmstetter?"

Once upon a time I'd known with a ninety-five percent accuracy rate what was going on in my children's heads, but the older they got, the more difficult it was becoming. With Oliver it was still above seventy percent, but Jenna? Fifty, if I was lucky.

I kissed her hairline. "What makes you ask?"

"Well, last year you figured out who killed Mrs. Mephisto, so I was just wondering, you know, if you were going to do it again." Her question carried the casual tone of someone who was extremely interested in the answer.

I debated her question, trying to decide which path to take. The most attractive choice was the one of distraction. It wasn't the best path, but that hadn't ever stopped me before. For if I didn't use distraction, what was left was the truth, and it wasn't pretty.

Last year a killer had threatened my children. The only thing that had saved us was my unthinking animal instincts to get my children out of danger. How I'd managed that I still didn't know, and I didn't care to think about it too much. It had been my fault they'd come into danger in the first place, and my mother rarely let me forget the fact.

"It won't happen like that again," I promised Jenna.

"You mean you and Mrs. Neff aren't finding the killer?"

She didn't sound relieved; she sounded disappointed. I bobbled her ponytail around. "It sounds as if you want us to."

"Well, yeah," she said. As in, "Duh, Mom."

"Shouldn't we let the police do their job?" I asked.

"You'll be faster," she said seriously. "Real life isn't like a TV show, where they solve everything in half an hour."

I smothered a laugh in her hair. The wisdom of an eleven-year-old. "You're right, sweetie. Life isn't like television."

"Police need the help of everyday citizens," she said. "Chief Eiseley told us that when school started. He said we need to keep our eyes and ears open and to let a law enforcement officer know if you see something bad happen."

Bless Gus. Could a town have a better police chief?

"So Oliver wanted to know," Jenna went on, "if the bad guy was still around, and I told him you and Mrs. Neff were taking care of it. And you are, right?" She leaned back to look into my face. Her own was filled with hope and expectation and confidence.

There was no choice here, none at all.

"You bet your britches," I said, and hugged her hard. "Mrs. Neff and I will take care of everything."

"Cool!" She slid off my lap. "Can I try on the dress again? I want to show Oliver."

Obviously, I'd worked a miracle cure on her stomach-ache. She ran upstairs, her feet barely touching the treads, flying up as if she weighed nothing at all.

With love in my heart and anxiety everywhere else, I watched her go. Marina and I would take care of everything, I'd told her. Don't worry about a thing, I'd said.

I blew out a sigh and got to my feet. If I was going to be mom, PTA secretary, bookstore owner, *and* caped crusader, I'd better get busy.

Jenna and I stood side by side in the entrance to Tarver's gym, both of us wide-eyed with astonishment. What had been an everyday, ordinary, run-of-the-mill elementary school gymnasium had been transformed overnight to a barn stuffed full of a summer's harvest.

The metal joists overhead were wrapped with Styrofoam timbers. Brown canvas hung from fake timber to fake timber, mimicking a barn roof. On the stage, straw bales were stacked high to hide the slightly tattered curtain. Pumpkins, squash, and little teepees of corn were distributed all about, and tables made of barn wood held the punch bowl and cookies. It was a far cry from the brown and orange crepe and construction paper I'd been expecting.

"This is amazing." I wondered if the money for the decorations had fallen from the sky, or if someone had won the lottery.

"It's cool!" Jenna twirled, sending her dress out in a small circle. "I can't wait until Dad sees."

Since I was a volunteer minion for the dance committee, last week I'd told Richard I would bring Jenna to the school. "Not the most appropriate way for a man to pick up his date," he'd said, and I was glad this man was the father of my children. The next thing he'd said reminded me of why we'd divorced. "But efficient. You're learning, aren't you?"

"There she is." Jenna was waving at a girl in a pink dress that would have fit in nicely at a cocktail party. She was accompanied by a man who wore a pair of dress slacks, a dress shirt, and a hideously patterned tie. "That's Bailey and her dad," Jenna said. And she was off.

A year ago I'd almost worried myself to ulcers over Jenna and Bailey's exclusionary friendship. I'd gently encouraged Jenna away from being best friends with Bailey, and had been relieved when she started calling Alexis again.

"What do you think?" Marina dug her elbow into my ribs. "Not bad for a bunch of amateurs, eh?"

"It's gorgeous, but—" I stopped, not wanting to cast a stone into the still pond.

Marina winked. "But how—and more to the point *why*—are we spending money to decorate a gym for an elementary school dance?"

"Exactly."

She raised her right hand. "The committee members know nothing, I swear it. We got an unsigned letter in the mail with a list of conditions, if you can believe it. Change the name of the dance, put in all these decorations, spike the punch—you know."

I stared at her in amazement.

"We didn't really spike the punch," she whispered. "That was a joke."

"You kept a secret from me," I said. "You never keep secrets from me. You told me when Oliver lied for Jenna about who broke the lamp. You tell me what Claudia Wolff says about me. You tell me what you're getting me for my birthday two months ahead of time."

She gave me a pitying look. "There's a first time for everything, mah dear. Surely, y'all know that."

A return to the Southern belle, one of her favorites. I couldn't speak with a good Southern drawl if my life depended on it. The only accent I could manage was a bad Canadian one, eh?

"So what do you think of the sign?" Marina waved her arms, conductor style.

I turned. "Oh . . ."

"Yeah." Marina made a fist and thumped her chest. "Gets you right here, doesn't it?"

It certainly did. Hanging high over the stage was a wide banner. Painted on the beige canvas were red and orange and yellow leaves with a scattering of brown leaves and acorns. The words, bold black and two feet tall, proclaimed this dance to be "The First Annual Sam Helmstetter Scholarship Fund Dance."

"Beats our little Father-Daughter Dance sign all hollow, doesn't it?" Marina nodded at a stenciled poster board.

"But . . . who?" I gestured at the sign, at the ceiling, at the whole kit and kaboodle. "This must have cost hundreds. Thousands."

Marina shrugged. "Dunno. The letter was anonymous and the money came straight from the bank."

"Anonymous? Do you think—"

"Nope. The Tarver Foundation didn't have thing one to do with it. You should have heard that snotty-nosed lawyer when I called and asked. 'The Ezekiel G. Tarver Foundation funds important, truly educational projects. A dance does not come close to the scope of the foundation's mission statement.' You'd have thought I was asking if they'd contributed money for a field trip to an AC/DC concert."

That sounded like the foundation, all right. But if not them, then who? "Why would someone donate all that money?" I mused. "Why would . . ." My question trailed off.

"What's the matter?" Marina asked. "You look like your last friend just died, and since I'm standing right here I know that's not true."

"What if it was Sam's killer who sent the money?"

Marina put her hands on her padded hips. "Once upon a time I thought you were a smart cookie, but now

I realize it's all an illusion. Why, pray tell, would a murderer want to name a dance after his victim? Why do all this?" She flittered her fingers. "Why start a scholarship fund for the kids?"

"Guilty conscience."

Marina looked at me fondly. "You're projecting again."

"I'm what?"

"Like anthropomorphism. I know you think that Spot of yours is sad about being left alone all day. This is the same thing."

"Spot is a killer?"

Marina made a rude noise in the back of her throat. "That dog wouldn't know what to do with a squirrel even if he could catch it. No, silly one, I'm saying you're projecting your emotions onto the killer. If you killed someone accidentally, you'd feel guilty enough to sign over the store and its contents to the surviving family members and work for free the rest of your life."

"I'm not the only person with an overdeveloped sense of guilt."

"Name ten."

"One, my Grandma Chittenden. Two, Gus Eiseley. Three, Oliver. Four—"

But Marina had already moved on to another topic. "Say, did you hear about Brian Keller?"

"Um, he decided to leave his share of Rynwood Shredding to Rachel and is going to raise alpacas instead?"

She made a buzzing sound. "Wrong again. Someone posted on WisconSINs that Brian was in a car accident. Broken arm, which is nasty, but it could have been worse, so don't get your tender heart all worked up."

"What happened?"

"Who knows? It was dark, it was raining, some yahoo in a van ran a stop sign, and whammo!" She slapped her palms together with a meaty sound.

I winced.

"Worst part is the guy who hit him didn't stop," Marina said.

"Why do people do things like that?"

Marina shrugged. "Scared, probably."

My cell phone rang. After fumbling through a collection of toys, small packaged snacks, loose change, and a paperback, I pulled the phone out of my purse and looked at the number. Richard.

"Beth, is Jenna there?"

"Somewhere. Where are you? You're late."

"I'm in Atlanta."

That didn't make any sense whatsoever. Though maybe there was an Atlanta, Wisconsin. I knew there was an Atlanta in Michigan; maybe there were Atlantas scattered across the country. "Georgia?" I asked.

"Of course Georgia. What other Atlanta is there? I got a call on Thursday to come down for an interview on Monday, but when they found out that I golf, I was invited to their company tournament. That was today," he said pointlessly. "The banquet starts in ten minutes."

"A job interview? That's . . . great." The implications were too much to process, so I stuck firmly to the one thing I could grasp.

"It came up quickly. Tell Jenna I'm sorry and—"

I closed my eyes and thought calming thoughts. "You need to tell her yourself."

"Beth, I'm late for—"

"You could have called Thursday," I said, trying to keep the anger out of my voice. "You could have called Friday, or even today up until an hour ago. But you forgot, and your daughter is wearing a dress—a *dress*—bought especially for tonight. You're her date, Richard, and you're standing her up."

"It's only a grade school dance."

"This is the first dance she's ever attended."

He paused, then repeated, "It's only a grade school dance." This time, however, his voice was weak. He'd done his daughter wrong, and he knew it.

Marina had detected the impending doom and fetched Jenna. "Is that Dad?" She looked around as if he'd materialize any second. "Where is he?"

In the doghouse, I wanted to say. "Here's Jenna," I said into the phone, then handed it over. "It's your father." In those three words I wanted to communicate love, understanding, and empathy. But I'm pretty sure the only thing she heard was "It's your father."

She took the phone eagerly. "Dad? How far are you? You won't believe what they did to the gym. There's a—" With a suddenness that was heartbreaking, her animation disappeared. "Where's Atlanta?" Her face was still as a stone. "You mean you're not going to be here at all?"

I wanted to turn away from her pain, but I wouldn't, couldn't, leave her alone.

"No!" she shouted into the phone. "I don't want to see you on Wednesday. Or next weekend. Or ever. I hate you!" She hurled the phone onto a bale of straw and ran from the room.

I started after her, but Marina held me back. "Let her cry a minute," she said.

"But—"

She shook her head. "It's a hard thing, but let her cry. She won't always have Mom around to dry her tears."

I wanted to disagree with her—of course I'd always be there to comfort Jenna, I'd always have a handkerchief and a magical kiss, I'd always have a way to fix whatever was wrong—but part of me knew Marina was right. Somewhere along the line, children have to learn that pain happens and that there's not always anything we can do about it.

Well, except for the option of revenge, but that wasn't

behavior I wanted my children to emulate. There was, however, one thing I could do.

I retrieved the phone, blew off the straw dust, and dialed.

Half an hour later I'd explained the ugly facts of job hunting to Jenna ("It's not as if your dad *wanted* to go to Atlanta, honey"), washed off her tears, and led her out of the restroom to which she'd fled. We'd arrived early to help schlep the goody bags, and, as we approached the gym, we saw a long line of men and girls snaking out into the hallway. The girls were hopping from one foot to another in their dance dresses; the men, dressed in everything from jeans and T-shirts to suits and ties, were talking and joking with each other while they looked in their wallets.

"They all have their dads with them," Jenna muttered.

Normally I tried to squash her sarcastic comments, but I let this one go. She had a right to be angry.

Summer materialized at my side. "Hi, Beth."

"Looks like a great turnout," I said. "We should make a lot of money for Sam's fund."

A light hand touched my elbow. "Beth?"

I looked around. And up. "Evan, you look great!"

The kind, thoughtful man had interpreted my panicky phone call as the emergency it was. Not only had he turned off the college football game he'd been watching, but he'd tossed aside the bowl of popcorn he'd just popped, and changed out of the sweatpants and sweatshirt he'd been wearing.

"Wow." Summer looked at him from the perfectly formed knot in his bow tie to the pleats in his tuxedo shirt to the sharp creases in his black trousers to his shiny shoes. "I mean, *wow*!" She gave me a wide grin and slipped away.

My dejected daughter had wandered, slump-shouldered, up the line to talk to a friend. I called her back. "Jenna, I have a surprise for you."

She turned, and her eyes went wide. "Mr. Garrett? Are you going to a wedding?"

He moved swiftly to her side. "I heard of your distress and have come to offer my aid." He went down on one knee and took both of her hands in his. "Jenna, will you be my date for the dance tonight?"

My daughter—my athlete, my tomboy, my nothing-bothers-me kid—actually giggled. "You're silly."

He held one of her hands to his chest. "Please, mademoiselle, say yes."

Red-faced, shy, and stammering, she said the only thing possible. "Y-yes."

"With that one word you have made my evening an unforgettable one." Evan kissed the back of her hand, and, in one smoothly elegant motion, rose to his feet and twirled her in a circle. "Come, let us dance the night away!"

The line parted to make way for Evan and Jenna, dancing together as if they'd been practicing for weeks. Just before they spun out of the doorway and into the gym, Evan looked back at me, smiled, and winked.

It was a magical moment, a scene I knew I'd play over and over again in my memory. I wanted to laugh with joy and to cry with happiness. My mouth hurt from smiling so wide, and the warmth in my heart felt as if it would last forever.

Another light hand touched my elbow. "Beth?"

"Pete! What are you doing here? I didn't know you had a—" My next word should have been "daughter," but the letters forming on my lips were about to sound more like "wife."

Pete Peterson, stocky and balding, nice guy extraordinaire, was the owner of Cleaner-Than-Pete's, a cleaning service out of Madison that took care of everything from vandalism to murder scenes.

"Beth, I'd like you to meet my niece, Alison." Pete put his arm around the girl's shoulders. "She and her mother just moved to Rynwood. Alison, this is Mrs. Kennedy."

Niece. No wonder he'd never mentioned a daughter. I smiled and held out my hand. "Hello. It's nice to meet you."

Alison, who was already showing her uncle's trend to stockiness, also had his merry eyes. Her curly locks might have come from that side of the family, too, but it was hard to tell from what little remained of Pete's hair. She shook my hand. "Are you Jenna's mom? She's nice. She's not in my grade, but she helped me pick up the books I dropped once."

Pride in my daughter swelled my smile a little wider. After we exchanged a few more pleasantries, she saw a friend and, after asking Uncle Pete's permission, ran after her.

"Nice girl," I said.

"My sister's kid." He shoved his hands in the pockets of his wrinkled khaki pants.

I wanted to ask about her father—and if Pete had been a woman, I would have—but I kept my questions to myself. Cross-gender friendships have more rules than the official 112-page NFL rule book.

"That your boyfriend?" he asked, looking in the direction Evan and Jenna had taken.

In the line ahead of us, men were laughing and tossing bills onto the table where Summer was taking money. Tickets were five dollars, but additional donations were accepted with thankful smiles.

"Top that, Eric!" a man said.

"I'll see your hundred and raise you fifty." A bill slapped down. "What do you say, Dan?" the tallish man asked. "Put your money where your mouth is, pal."

Testosterone flourished in the most unusual places. Sometimes I truly felt sorry for men. At least women were only ruled by their hormones one week out of the month. "Boyfriend? Um . . . I suppose he is," I said. "Evan Garrett. He owns the hardware."

"Seems like a nice guy."

Pete sounded a little funny, and I felt compelled to explain. "My ex-husband was supposed to be here tonight, but he was called out of town. Evan stepped in at the last minute." I shifted from one foot to the other. Evan was my boyfriend, for lack of a better word. Why the delay in calling him that? And here was a better question: Why was I feeling so awkward about discussing him with Pete?

If I'd been a better person, I would have spent some time sorting out my feelings. Instead, I decided to enjoy the dance and shoved it all to the back of my head.

We stood there, inching forward in line, listening to the men ahead of us laugh at something Eric had said. Whoever Eric was. Through the bookstore and the PTA I knew most of the Tarver mothers, but I knew only a few of the fathers.

Summer reappeared. "Erica's here. Is this a good time to talk about, you know, my idea?" Since the last PTA meeting, the two of us had had numerous phone conversations about her brainstorm for a January fundraiser. I'd told Erica that Summer had a new moneymaking idea, and Erica said we'd talk about it at the dance.

I glanced at my watch. Somehow it was already seven o'clock. In front of us, the line dematerialized with that suddenness that sometimes happens in crowds. I laid down the admission fee—and a little extra—then headed into the gym. "See you later, Pete," I tossed over my shoulder.

He waved back amiably, and I decided not to worry

about him. Whatever I thought I'd heard in his voice must have been a trick of the acoustics, was all.

Moving away from the dancing and speakers turned a notch too loud, Summer and I and Erica found a small oasis of near quiet between a bale of straw and a screen made of barn wood.

"So I hear you two have another fund-raising idea." Though Erica was smiling and was dressed semi-casually in dress pants, low heels, and a silk shirt, both Summer and I straightened as if we'd been called up in front of a judge. Erica swung her steady gaze to me. "Beth. How are the preparations for your story session progressing?"

"Um, things are coming along." Slowly. So slowly, in fact, that you could say I'd done nothing at all. "I'm finalizing the . . . the outline."

Erica lifted her chin a fraction of an inch. She didn't believe me. "You'll bring a solid plan to the December PTA meeting?"

I nodded. "You bet." Who needed sleep, anyway?

The sharp eyes shifted to Summer. "I hear you're ready to head up a new project."

"Yup!" Summer chirped, sounding as if she'd never been nervous in her life. "Beth and I were doing some brainstorming about what we could do when it's cold and snowy and windy."

"Anything in January would be good," Erica said, nodding. "It's a slow time for Tarver PTA activities."

"How about if"—Summer pointed at the far corner of the room—"there was a windmill over there?" Nodding toward the stage, she said, "How about a little hill right here? And a standing bear over there?"

Summer laughed at the blank expression on Erica's face. "Miniature golf! What do you think of a mini-golf course?"

A loud squeal erupted behind us. A girl in pale purple

was jumping up and down, tugging on her father's hands. "Ooo, I *love* mini-golf! Daddy, can we come?"

Erica's face took on a pensive cast. "Hmm." She looked at the girl, who was now telegraphing the news to all her friends. She looked at the gym. Finally, she looked back at us. "Get it down on paper and bring it to the next meeting. If you want to do this in January, be ready for a lot of work." It sounded like a warning, but if so, it was delivered with a smile.

A PTA mother hovered. "Erica, do you have a minute?" The two headed off, and Summer and I grinned at each other. If Erica was behind the project, odds were good that it would happen.

"What do you think you're doing?"

I jerked around. Claudia Wolff was standing behind us, hands on hips, face redder than was healthy.

Summer turned a whiter shade of pale and moved slightly behind me. In front of me men and girls had stopped dancing. "It's too hard to talk over the music," I said pleasantly, and headed for the nearest doorway.

Claudia didn't budge. "You can talk to me right here and right now."

"That's fine." I kept a smile on my face. "What can I do for you?"

"You can quit taking over the PTA, that's what you can do."

"Excuse me?"

"Don't go all polite. I know what you're up to, don't think I don't!"

At least one of us knew. Unfortunately, it wasn't me.

She scrutinized me with slitted eyes. "It's written all over that pretty face. You want to be the next PTA president, don't you?"

I couldn't think of anything I wanted less, other than being elected president of the United States. Now *that* would be a wretched job. Except for the *Air Force One* thing. That part would be okay.

"See, you're not even denying it." She nodded, having found what she was looking for somewhere between my forehead and my chin. "You want to run the PTA. Going to Erica with this mini-golf thing without taking it to the board is just the first step, isn't it?"

There was no good answer to that question. My knee-jerk inclination was to laugh out loud, but it was unlikely Claudia would meet that reaction with an answering laugh. "Um . . ."

"See, you don't even know what to say, do you?" she said triumphantly. "I can always tell when I get things right when people don't know what to say."

Or else they went silent because otherwise they were afraid they'd bop her in the nose for being such an idiot.

"At the next meeting," Claudia went on, "I was going to talk about *my* idea for a January fund-raiser. *I* was going through the proper channels. *I* was going to follow our bylaws. *I* was going to do what was right, not what was politically expedient."

What politics had to do with the Tarver PTA, I wasn't sure, but Claudia seemed sure of the connection

"Mini-golf." She made a *tsk*ing noise. "What a dumb idea. As if you and your little friend there will get anyone to play golf in January. Puh-lease!" She rolled her eyes. "If you make ten bucks after expenses I'll be surprised. My idea was a winner, and now you've ruined it for everyone. Think of all the money the PTA could have made with . . ." She paused dramatically. "A casino night."

My mouth dropped open.

Claudia half smiled. "See, you're already jealous you didn't think of it first. Everybody loves Texas Hold 'em.

Everybody loves slot machines and roulette and the chance to win big." She shook a pair of imaginary dice and threw them across a phantom craps table. "What could be better than a casino night? It's a perfect idea!"

It was an absolutely awful idea. A PTA-sponsored casino? Not in this town. Erica would have a tizzy, Agnes Mephisto would spin in her grave, Mack Vogel, the superintendent of the Rynwood schools, would have a conniption fit, and the parental fallout would be horrendous.

"Just because you're buddy-buddy with Erica," Claudia said, "you think you'll be a shoo-in when her term's over. Don't you believe it. Between trying to take things over and hiring that murderer for your store, you've made lots of enemies in the PTA. You'll never be president. Never. You'll be sorry for this, mark my words!" She shook her fist at me and marched off, her feet stomping in time to the music. "Turkey in the Straw."

I stared at her receding back. Half of me wanted to rush up to her and explain my actions in great detail; the other half wanted to sit in the corner and cry. By age forty-one you'd think I'd be able to tolerate a high level of verbal abuse, but it knocked me down, every time.

Marina appeared. "That woman is a menace. If we held a vote for someone in town to be murdered, she would win, hands down."

Shades of Shirley Jackson's "The Lottery." I shuddered. "You don't really mean that."

"Want to bet? Anyway, don't let her bother you. She's all bluster and smoke with no flame."

"She shook her fist at me."

Marina moved in and looked at me closely. "Get that hollow tone out of your voice. Claudia Wolff isn't worth a finger snap of worry."

I tried to snap my fingers, but the noise was barely audible.

Summer had edged forward. "Let me try?" She snapped her fingers. Nothing.

"Oh, for crying out loud. You two are pathetic." Marina held out her hand and made the snapping motion. The result was a tiny thudding noise. "Well, shoot," she said. "Let me try my left hand. Maybe I'm becoming ambidextrous in my middleish middle age." But when she tried, the result was, if anything, even less impressive.

I stared at her hands, at mine, at Summer's. This was not an omen. The fact that all three of us suddenly couldn't perform the simple act of snapping our fingers didn't mean that Claudia's threat would turn into a hex that would end the PTA as we knew it, which would in turn create a gradual slowing of sales at the store because no mother would shop at a store owned by an ostracized PTA ex-secretary, which would in turn force me to sell the house, and, with Richard unemployed, the kids and I would move to a studio apartment above a video arcade, where Jenna and Oliver would spend too many hours learning how to shoot things, and by the time they reached high school their biggest concerns would be making high score in Halo 13 and what color of leather belt to wear around their necks. All for want of a finger snap.

"Ladies." Evan stepped into our small circle. "If I may?" He raised his hand, put thumb and middle finger together, and snapped. The noise was loud enough to make children stop whining.

"Hey." Marina gave an approving nod. "That's a good trick. Got any more?"

"All in good time." He bowed to her, to Summer, then to me. "Milady? Can I have this dance?" He held out his hand, palm up, and smiled into my eyes.

"Kind sir." I dropped a small curtsy and took his hand. We spun off into a waltz and all thoughts of Claudia, hexes, and tumbling bad luck fell away as we danced and danced and danced.

Chapter 11

"A waltz, huh?" Lois looked at me over the top of her steaming tea mug. "Are you sure?"

"No. What difference does it make if it was a waltz or a polka?"

"It's like flowers," she said.

After years of working with Lois on an almost daily basis, you'd have thought I'd be used to her non sequiturs. "Flowers?"

"Sure." She sipped the lemon-flavored brew. "You know how flowers have meanings? Roses are love, daisies are innocence, freesia is trust."

"Why is freesia trust?" I wasn't sure what freesia looked like, exactly, but how could any particular kind of flower mean trust? For that matter, how could a daisy mean innocence? I could see how roses meant love—as in I'd love to be able to grow roses free of mold or spots or bugs—but who dreamt up all the other things? "Are there flowers that mean death and destruction?"

"Just like flowers," Lois went on, "dances have emotions associated with them. A fox-trot indicates a platonic relationship. A tango is passionate love. A polka shows that your partner has a sense of fun."

"You're making that up," I said.

Lois drew herself up tall. Which today was very tall, considering that she was wearing four-inch-high platform shoes. On a purely period basis they went well with her bell-bottom pants, wide leather belt, and gauzy white shirt complete with square neckline.

"Questioning my veracity on a Monday morning? How can you do this to me, your loyal employee, your compatriot in arms, your friend and coworker of many years, your—"

"You're overdoing it," I said.

Her spine unstiffened and she sank down three inches. "It was the compatriot part, wasn't it?" she asked sadly.

"Over the top."

Lois sighed and took a sip of tea. "So what happened after that?"

"Claudia left in a huff." She'd tried to slam the self-closing door, which hadn't gone well. "After that, everything went fine." The air had seemed to clear, the atmosphere had felt brighter, and the music had sounded more playful. Jenna had taken her partner back, and Marina and I doled out goody bags and ladled punch the rest of the night.

"That Claudia Wolff is nothing but a bully," Lois said. "Has been ever since she was a toddler. Some tigers never change their stripes."

I looked at her. "Which tigers do?"

"Oh, you know." She waved her mug at me. "The ones who can. There's this breed in a remote province of India that has been known to have their stripes change to white if they've had a close call with death."

I was about to call her bluff when the bells on the front door jingled. "I'll get it," I said, and headed out front, a pleasant owner-of-the-store smile on my face. "Good morning, let me know if—" When I saw who'd come in the door, my words dried up and my feet stopped moving. The nightmares I'd suffered the last two nights weren't nightmares any longer; they were reality.

"My, aren't we nice when it's in our own best interest?" Claudia asked. "Be polite and get people to buy things so we can make a buck, right?"

Behind her ranged a group of women, all of whom I knew. Tina Heller, Claudia's best friend. Heather Kingsley, Isabel Olson, and Carol Casassa. At the back of the pack was Cindy Irving. She was well known for being Johnny-on-the-spot for whatever was happening in town, so I wasn't sure if she was here in support of Claudia or if she was here in hopes of catching some fireworks.

"What can I do for you ladies?" Smile, smile, smile. Defuse the anger, be their friend, show them there is nothing to fear but fear itself. Or something like that.

"You know perfectly well what you can do," Claudia snapped.

There were a number of things on my list today: finish the already late December newsletter, take the pile of flattened boxes out for recycling, inventory the picture books, call the gift wrap supplier and ask why we were delivered Valentine's Day paper instead of Christmas paper, and see if I had money to pay a few bills. However, I had a feeling none of those was what Claudia was talking about. In all likelihood, she wanted one of two things: me to resign from the PTA or—

"It's that Yvonne Ganassi," Claudia said. "I can't think what you were thinking when you hired her."

I'd been thinking she was my hero. "Yvonne is—"

"A convicted murderer." Tina Heller stood shoulder to shoulder with Claudia. The two of them created a solid, nylon-parka-covered wall. "A murderer in a children's bookstore is about the dumbest hire anyone could make."

My chin went up. "Yvonne didn't kill anyone. She was exonerated."

"Then why was she sent to prison?" Claudia demanded. "They don't send innocent people to prison." Her cohorts nodded; human bobble-heads, all in a row. "Innocent until proven guilty, and the guilty go away for life. Or they should." She glared at me.

I could see that any argument I made would be laughed at, ignored, derided, or all three. These women had made up their minds and nothing I said would convince a single brain cell to lean another way. Still, I had to try.

"Would you like to see a copy of her acquittal?" I asked. "The governor of California handed it to her personally."

In the back, Cindy's face lit up, but the rest of the group didn't look impressed. "Who cares what some politician did?" Claudia's scorn was so deep that she splattered a little spit on the *p* of "politician." "Everyone knows they issue those things at the drop of a hat for whoever contributes most to their campaigns. Pardons are a get-out-of-jail-free card; they don't mean you weren't guilty in the first place."

Any minute now she'd implode from having too many conflicting opinions. I just hoped it wouldn't be in my store. "But—" I stopped. If she didn't understand that an acquittal and a pardon were two different things, then it wasn't likely this would turn into a teachable moment.

"She was convicted of murder." Claudia's strident tones rang through the store. "There's been a murder in Rynwood. I have no idea why the police haven't arrested her, but I'm sure it's just a matter of time."

My head started to ache. "Yvonne didn't kill anyone," I said. "Ever. You're making a big mistake."

Claudia's eyebrows shot up. "You're the one making mistakes. First, thinking you can run the PTA. Second, hiring a killer. The streets of our town won't be safe—our children won't be safe—until that woman is behind bars." Claudia raised her mittened hand and, from what I could make out from the movements inside the wool, pointed her index finger at me. "And you can bet I'll do all I can to get her there. Ladies?"

She turned and the group filed out. As the last one left, a gust of wind grabbed hold of the door and flung it wide open. I hurried to grab the handle and tried to pull it closed, tugging hard against the wind.

The group was huddled together outside the store, and my movements caught Claudia's attention. Her gaze locked on mine and she pointed at me again. She mouthed some words, but since I was horrible at lip reading, I had no idea what she said. It could have been, "Have a nice day," but it probably wasn't.

I smiled at her pleasantly and shut the door.

"Hokey Pete," Lois said. "Looks like Claudia has taken a turn for the worse. Say, maybe she killed Sam. Wouldn't be the first time the real killer has tried to insert herself into an investigation."

I wanted to ask on which episode of *CSI* that had happened, but I stopped myself in time. "Gus said all the people at the PTA meeting that night were cleared."

"Well, shoot." Lois slouched and crossed her arms. "Just when you think you have things all figured out, the facts have to rush in and confuse things."

I knew exactly what she meant.

"Wonder what Claudia was talking about?" Lois mused. "How is she going to get Yvonne into prison?"

"She's not. She's just—" My mother's admonition against gossip bounded into my brain. Thanks so very much, Mom. I sighed and restarted the sentence. "She's just worried about her children."

Lois snorted. "All I saw was Claudia being seriously mad at you."

Which is what worried me. Claudia had been born and raised in Rynwood. If she started marshaling her troops against the store, we could be in real trouble. "Lois," I asked slowly, "who do you think killed Sam?"

She sighed. "Oh, honey. I wish I knew. He was just so darn *nice*."

"Didn't he ever get into a fight, even as a kid?"

"Not so far as I remember. Though there was one thing . . ." She pinched her nose, then shook her head. "Nope. Can't remember. Had to do with sports, though. So, high school?"

Or junior high, or elementary school. Or college, since he'd played baseball at Wisconsin. All it would take to figure it out was some time. Good thing there was a new day every morning. Twenty-four fresh hours to fill with kids, work, housework, starting up the PTA senior story session, and hey, let's solve a murder, too.

Beth Kennedy, Renaissance woman. Either that, or Beth Kennedy, overcommitted woman destined for a breakdown.

One of those.

I pulled out a notepad. With Lois's help and a phone call to Flossie, I'd soon have a new list, this one titled "Sam's Former Teammates." If I talked to enough of them, maybe, just maybe, I'd find a Clue.

All I could see of Todd Wietzel was his bottom half. His top half was so far inside a car's engine compartment that it was invisible. Todd's wife (Mindy, mother of ten-year-old Caitlin and five-year-old Trevor) had told me I'd find him in the garage. "I think it's the water pump," she said, "but he's sure it's electrical."

It could have been a flat tire, for all I knew about cars. All that mattered to me about any internal combustion engine was that it worked when I turned it on. But, as I traipsed down the few steps from kitchen to garage floor, even I could see that the car Todd was working on was something special.

It was what they called a muscle car—a nickname that had never made any sense to me—and probably looked better than it had when it was new. Dark red paint gleamed under the garage's fluorescent lights, and inside the red, small bright flecks caught the light and sparkled golden. The chrome rims shone, the tires were so black they seemed to swallow light, and the window glass was cleaner than any glass in a garage had a right to be.

"Hey, honey, could you hand me the timing light?"

I glanced at the array of tools spread across a nearby workbench. Looked at the stacks and stacks of red metal drawer sets that held a multitude of mysterious tools. Cast my eye at the floor, where a number of unidentified objects lay scattered about. "Um, what does it look like?"

Todd's head popped up. "Hey, Beth. I thought you were Mindy. What are you doing here?"

I knew Mindy from PTA, and I knew Todd because Caitlin and Jenna played on the same girls' hockey team. Caitlin played defense and was working hard on developing a wicked slap shot. Of all Sam's former teammates to talk to, Todd was the easy first choice.

"Aren't most show cars put away by now?" I asked, using the only thing I knew about the subject.

"Yah." Todd levered himself up and out, then leaned backward in a long stretch. "Out of the blue this guy calls about buying this girl and the electricals aren't right."

"But . . ." I looked from the vehicle to him and back again, remembering all the stories I'd heard. "Didn't you spend three years restoring this car? Didn't you enter it into the Rynwood Car Show and win first place?"

"Yup." He smiled at it fondly. "Judges said I could win car shows in this class all over the state."

"And you're going to sell it?"

"It's the restoring that's fun," he said. "Going to shows is fine for some people, but I'd rather be in the garage tinkering."

It made sense, in a warped and twisted sort of way. Kind of like raising children. You get them to where they might be rational human beings, and zoom! Off they go, to college or the military or the work world or into marriage or—

"So what can I do for you?" Todd wiped his hands on a rag.

Right. I wasn't here to look at cars, I was here to ferret out clues that could lead me to a killer, clear Yvonne's name, and keep me and my children out of that second-floor apartment.

"You know I'm secretary of the Tarver PTA? Well, we're starting a scholarship fund. Mia and Blake are the first two recipients, but if the fund gets big enough, it'll be endowed, and we can continue to give out scholarships forever." Unless every dollar contributed was matched by a thousand from the Ezekiel G. Fund, it was unlikely that it would ever grow large enough to be self-perpetuating, but Todd didn't have to know the whole story.

"I heard about that," Todd said. "Caitlin got a sore throat Saturday afternoon, so we didn't go to the dance." He fumbled in his back pocket. "Here. Let me see what I can do. Sam's kids . . . man, that whole thing is rough."

He handed over a fifty-dollar bill. After the dance, I'd marveled at the stacks of fifties and hundreds in the cash box. I'd had no idea that men carried that much cash in their wallets. And I still had no idea *why* they did.

"I wish they'd find the killer," I said. "That would help a little."

"They'd better catch him soon." His face was set in hard lines. "Sam and I went way back."

"You played baseball together, right?"

"Since we were this high." Todd held out his hand at belt level. "T-ball, Little League, heck, everything on up through high school. I started working for my dad the Monday after graduation, so no college ball for me."

"Was Sam nice even as a kid?" I asked.

"He should have been one of those kids that kids love

to hate, but everyone liked him. How could you not like a guy who'd take the blame for any trouble we cooked up?" He smiled. "Sam would tell the coach to let the second- and third-stringers play. That it wasn't fair they had to sit on the bench all the time. And his sister, Megan? She came to practices and he always walked home with her, every time."

"No one called him a sissy?"

"No sissy can knock a fastball into next week." He got a distant look on his face and I knew he wasn't seeing me any longer. "Or throw a rope from third to first."

Rope? What did a rope have to do with baseball? I made a mental note to Google it later. "What about on the other teams? Sam was such a good baseball player, weren't some of the other kids jealous?"

"Oh, sure, but . . ." He stopped and looked at me. "You're trying to figure out who killed him, aren't you?"

It suddenly occurred to me that my feet needed a close inspection, so I bent my head and studied them with great intensity. He was angry. How could he not be, considering I was rooting around in his past, trying to shake out a reason for murder that might have originated decades ago, which didn't make a lot of sense, really, but I had to try. "Well . . ."

"You think somebody from baseball hated him enough to kill him?" Incredulity sent his voice high.

I sighed. "Not really. I mean, how could sports be reason enough for murder?"

A flicker of something crossed his face. "People can get pretty uptight. Remember what happened at that second hockey game?"

I winced away from the memory of women whacking each other with their purses. "Your daughter hit my baby girl!"

"Your baby girl is twenty pounds heavier than my daughter!" Whack. Whack.

"Sam hasn't played ball in years," I said. "Lots of people carry grudges, but this seems a little extreme."

"Hmm." Todd rubbed his chin, leaving behind a small streak of black grease. "There was this one time. The pitcher beaned one of our guys and our guy charged the mound. Everybody was yelling, and before you knew it, the benches were empty and it was a real slugfest. I'm sure Sam got in a few good ones, he had a long reach."

"When was this?" My ears perked up.

He grinned. "I think we were maybe eight."

The small spurt of adrenaline faded away. If a bunch of eight-year-olds going at it hammer and tongs was what Lois hadn't quite remembered, this particular path of investigation was coming to a quick end. "No other fights?" I heard my own hopefulness and backtracked. "Not that I want there to be, but you never know what someone will get angry about."

"Ain't that the truth," Todd said, gesturing at the car with a jerk of his thumb. "Who would have thought my wife would get so mad about me spending five thousand dollars on a paint job?"

If there was ever a question that didn't need answering, that was it.

"Other fights, though." He shook his head. "I can't remember one."

"No grudges?"

"How could anyone have had a grudge against Sam? It'd be like hating Santa Claus."

There was a tiny rip in my heart. Todd had pegged it: In another thirty years, Sam would have made the perfect Santa. By then he'd have had a nice belly, his hair would have turned white, he could have grown a lovely beard, and his laugh . . . oh, his laugh.

Todd cocked his head. "You can hear it, can't you? He had that 'ho, ho, ho' thing down."

"He sure did."

We stood there, hearing the last echoes of Sam's laughter ripple through us, then fade away.

"If you find out who killed him," Todd said hoarsely, "you let me know first. Got that? Tell me first."

Not in a million years. But I nodded, then said goodbye. At the top of the stairs I glanced back. He was still standing in the middle of the garage, one hand gripping the dirty rag, the other hand holding tight to absolutely nothing.

The evening had turned from dusk to full dark while I was talking to Todd. Streetlights had popped on everywhere, and I was going to be late picking Jenna and Oliver up from Marina's. I glanced at my watch. If I hurried I'd be only a little late.

Mothering instincts satisfied—or at least muffled to a distant throbbing noise that resembled the unceasing noise of the ocean—I walked briskly down the sidewalk and headed to the next name on the list.

Gerrit Kole leaned back in his high-backed leather chair and shook his head. Gerrit was an attorney and single and ambitious; the only reason he wouldn't have been at the office at a quarter to six in the evening was because he'd gone to pick up a take-out dinner.

"There's no reason," he said, blowing out a sigh. "No reason at all for anyone to have killed Sam."

I sat perched on the edge of a companion chair and tried to keep from sliding off the front. "You've thought about this, haven't you?" I asked. Gerrit's troubled look was miles away from his typical expression that life was good, and if we all worked as hard as he did, that we, too, could own a BMW convertible for summer, a Cadillac SUV for winter, and a Harley-Davidson just for fun.

"Sam and I grew up together," he said, as if that explained it all, and I supposed it did. People didn't use that phrase lightly—at least people in Wisconsin didn't—and it often translated as "we were closer than most brothers."

"No ideas?" I asked.

He tapped a pen against his leather blotter. "I've spent hours I can't afford working on this. After I couldn't think of a provable reason, I looked for something that couldn't be proved. Nothing." He stopped midtap. "You talked to Todd Wietzel?"

"No ideas there, either."

Gerrit grunted and went back to tapping. "For a few days, I wanted to think Larry Carter had done it. Larry never got any decent playing time, thanks to Sam. He's a guy who can hold a grudge, Larry."

My ears twitched. Was this, could this possibly be, a Clue?

"But then I went to talk to him," Gerrit said. "Turns out Larry saw the news about Sam's murder on a hospital TV. He'd broken his ankle playing hockey the night before. Got three expensive screws in his ankle."

I made a mental note to talk Jenna out of playing hockey ever again. "Well, I'm sure the police will find the killer," I said.

Gerrit made a noncommittal noise, and I noticed that his hands were clenched into fists so tight that the tendons drew pale across his knuckles. "Not too soon, I hope," he said quietly. "There's a debt to be paid."

My breath caught and I had to force my lungs back into action. Violence begets violence; it always had. And violence against an innocent begets violence at a geometric rate. There was no use warning Gerrit to leave it alone, no use telling him revenge does no one any good, no use asking him to consider what a course of revenge would do to his career.

He knew all that. Knew it and didn't care.

I rose. "Take care of yourself, Gerrit."

But we both knew he wouldn't.

Chapter 12

"Conclusions?" Marina thumped her elbows on her kitchen table and put her chin in her hands. "I got mine. What are yours?"

Every name on my list was crossed off. Squinting, I studied my notes. "All of the guys I talked to were former teammates of Sam's. Todd played with him—"

Marina unstuck one hand from her chin and made rolling motions. "Conclusions, I beg you! Yon youths will waste of hunger ere they get fed if you go through every frigging minute of every conversation."

I drew breath to disagree, but looked at her wall clock—a recent present from her Devoted Husband, which had to be one of the most annoying clocks on the planet—and realized she was right. It was almost seven o'clock. If I didn't get the kids out of there soon I'd have to hear the noise Marina's DH had programmed: the sound of the kitchen smoke alarm going off. Seven times. One o'clock was the microwave beep. Two o'clock was the garage door going up, then down. Three was three rings of the telephone, etc., etc.

Marina loved the dreadful thing, and laughed until

she cried every time I headed for her microwave at one in the afternoon.

"All right, conclusions." I drummed my fingers on the table.

"Quit that." Marina slapped at my fingers. "And tell me what's bugging you."

I laid my hands flat. "Someone said . . ."

"Yeeessss?"

"That Sam used marijuana."

Marina's eyes bulged. "He what?! That's nuts. That's crazy. That's—" She stopped. "That was Denise, wasn't it? She tried the same thing on me last week."

"It's not true?"

"Puh-leeze. End of the summer Denise overheard Rachel talking to a friend about some baseball tournament. College alumni played a team of police officers, and I guess the grass wasn't cut right and a lot of guys were complaining."

I was trying out snippets of conversation. "Sam didn't like the cut of the grass." "The grass was bad; the police said it was a crime." Such a logical explanation, once you knew.

I relaxed, eked out a smile, and tossed my notepad on the table. "Conclusion number one."

Marina held up her index finger. "Ready and waiting."

"No one that Sam grew up with, played ball with, or who watched him grow up has the foggiest idea who might have killed him."

"I concur."

"Conclusion number two," I said, and Marina's middle finger went up next to finger number one. "In spite of Sam leading a charmed life, he was too nice to hate. His high school rivals were invited to his graduation party—and they all came. No one, but no one, hated him enough to kill him."

"Anything else?"

The harsh faces came back to me. "There's a lot of anger out there. Everyone from Flossie to Gerrit Kole is barely holding it in check. If the police find a what-do-they-call-them, a person of interest, I worry about his safety."

"You mean like this?" Marina held up an invisible noose, stuck her tongue out and made a choking noise. "Lynch mob," she croaked out.

"Put your tongue back in your mouth. You're creeping me out."

She made her eyes bulge.

"Stop that!"

Marina dropped the noose and reached across the table to pat my hands. "There, there. I'm sorry for scaring you. How about some milk and cookies to calm your tender nerves?"

I yanked my hands away. "It's not my fault my sisters made me watch horror movies when I was only six."

"Scarred you for life, poor thing." Marina's face was full of sympathy and understanding. "Older sisters are horrible creatures."

As she was one, she should know. "Yes, they are." I cast a glance up at the clock. Time to scamper. "Jenna!" I called. "Oliver! Time to pack up." I looked at Marina. "I take it your conclusions match mine?"

"Yup. Each and every one of the people I talked to assumes Sam was killed by a random stranger. All want a piece of said stranger before he gets put away." She smacked her fist into her palm. "For the health of our fair town, the killer needs to be found and put in jail. If not, the med center is going to be diagnosing a rash of ulcers induced by festering anger."

Fester. I shivered. What a nasty-sounding word.

"What's the matter?" Marina asked.

I wasn't about to admit that a word scared me. "Since

Sam wasn't killed by someone from his past, what's next? We still don't have a motive and we still don't have any suspects." We had nothing, and nowhere to go.

"What?" Marina sat up straight. "Do I detect a smidgen of doubt? An ounce of uncertainty? A dram of disbelief?"

I shook my head sideways. Yes, no, whatever.

"We know one thing." Marina raised one eyebrow. "We know this: 'Cowards die many times before their deaths; the valiant never taste of death but once.' "

A direct quote? *Julius Caesar*, if I remembered correctly. I gave my head a little shake. "Was that—"

"Of all the wonders that I yet have heard," she said, "it seems to me most strange that men should fear seeing that death, a necessary end, will come when it will come."

I looked at her curiously. "Aren't you scared of dying?"

"Everybody is. But like old Julius said, it is strange. We're all going to die; why are we so scared of it?"

"Easy." I stood, and as I called again for Jenna and Oliver, the memory of a line in an L. M. Montgomery book came to me. "Because it won't be what we're used to. It's the unknown, and there's not much scarier than that."

A loud beep went off above my head and Pavlov's reaction kicked into gear. Adrenaline coursed through me instantly. I jumped, sniffed the air for smoke, looked for smoke, looked for flames, noted the closest exits, gauged how long it would take to get the kids out—

The clock beeped again.

Seven o'clock.

Marina laughed. "You knew that was going to happen, and you were still scared."

Jenna, followed by Oliver, came into the room. Both were laden with backpacks that looked three sizes too heavy and both were wearing that "Feed me" look.

"Zip your coats," I said. "It's cold outside."

"Fraidy cat," Marina whispered.

"Better by far to face our fears and conquer them," I said, "than allow the worms of doubt to eat through our hearts."

"What's that from?" Marina asked, frowning. "It sure sounds like Shakespeare, but I don't remember seeing it in any of the quote books." Too late, she slapped her hand over her mouth.

I smiled. Smugly. I'd known all along that she hadn't been reading any of the plays. The odds of Marina reading *Richard II* from beginning to end were not nearly as good as the odds of me going to Jenna's next hockey game in a low-cut slinky gown and four-inch high heels.

"It's from 'Ode to Marina's Kitchen Clock,'" I said, "by Beth Kennedy." After I shooed the kids out the door I poked my head back into the kitchen. "Call me later, okay? I have an idea."

When I woke the next morning, Spot was nestled up against my feet in a warm, furry brown meat loaf shape. George was perched on the back of the nearby chair, one eye opening and closing every so often. I lay there, savoring the quiet calm, then sat up and started planning my day.

During a long conversation with Marina after the kids were in bed, I'd sat at the computer and made another list. Brainstorming 201, and the central idea was money. Not a very original idea for murder, but things became clichés because they happened so often.

Somewhere between writing my suggestion of "inheritance?" and Marina's of "hidden treasure?" something went *ping*.

"Oh," I said.

"What?" Marina demanded. "You had an idea. I can feel it from over here. You know who the killer is, don't you? I'm getting an image. Tomorrow you'll make a citizen's arrest and save Yvonne from Claudia Wolff and her thundering horde, convene a special meeting of the PTA and have her forcibly removed from the vice-presidency-ship, and when you're done with all that, find a job for Richard and help him mend relations with Jenna."

"Why is your fantasy world so much better than mine?"

"Because you have an unlimited capacity for guilt. Next question, please."

"Why do you have it in for Claudia?"

"A more pertinent question is why does she have it in for you? One more query. Then we must return to our labors."

"Is there really such a thing as a citizen's arrest?"

"Just make sure you catch him committing a felony."

I held the phone away from my head, stared at it, then put it back to my ear. "Do I want to know why you know that?"

She sighed dramatically. "Beth, you sooo do not watch enough television."

Whatever. "Have you picked up anything from your WisconSINs blog?"

"Nothing about Sam, but wait until I tell you about Viv Reilly. You remember we saw her with Dave Patterson? Well, he isn't the only one she's seeing. Would you believe—"

I sat back to listen. Marina's blog was important to her, and I knew if I dangled that shiny subject in front of her she'd veer away from my "oh" of surprise.

Marina was my best friend, my confidante, and the bosomest buddy of all time, but she didn't need to know everything.

"Where's Marina?" Debra O'Conner turned around in the booth and looked down the length of the restaurant. "It's not like her to be late."

I'd chosen the back booth of the Green Tractor to give us a modicum of privacy, but Debra wasn't with the program. She was waving and chatting with most of the patrons and all of the staff. I should have known better. As a vice president of Rynwood's biggest bank, Debra probably knew more people in town than anyone except my hairstylist.

This wasn't the quiet, heads-together lunch I'd tried to arrange without seeming to arrange it. Clearly, subtle subterfuge wasn't my strong suit.

Of course, lots of things weren't my strong suit. Baking with yeast, accounting practices that involved anything more than adding and subtracting, and the ability to touch my toes without bending my knees. Or calligraphy. I loved the curves and swirling arcs of inked letters, but every time I tried—

"Beth?" Debra had turned around. Her hair, once cut on monthly trips to Chicago, flowed carelessly to her shoulders. "Are you in there?"

Back in the dark ages, say about a year ago, I'd been overawed by Debra O'Conner. Bouncy blond hair straight out of a television commercial. Kind to animals and strangers. Picked up litter on the street. Rewarding and lucrative career, loving husband, well-behaved children, etc., etc. But a chance remark I'd made had set her on a different path.

The new path closely paralleled the old one: same career, same husband, same house and car, but the power suits and glossy hair were gone. She now dressed like an average middle-aged Midwesterner, had quit taking golf lessons, and publicly declared she didn't care if she ever tried zip-lining.

Happiness shone out of her skin, which was now absent of makeup. She said she owed her newfound contentment to me. The thought made me squirm a little, so I tried not to think about it.

"Is Marina coming?" Debra asked.

"Not today," I said.

"Oh?" Debra's eyebrows went up. "It's Tuesday, isn't it? Don't you have lunch with her today?"

How had I ended up such a creature of habit? Had it been motherhood, or being married to Richard? Or had the seeds of rutness abided in my psyche all my life and only recently come to full flower? I frowned, trying to remember. In high school I'd made lists of the clothes I wore, but that was to keep from wearing the same thing twice in a week. Rut-avoiding behavior, not rut-creating.

"Um, I didn't mean anything by that, Beth, okay?" Debra was biting her lower lip. "It's just you and Marina are such good friends that I don't want to horn in on anything. Some people can get possessive about their friends."

I made a very unladylike snorting noise. "Are we talking about the same Marina?"

"Maybe not." Debra put her index finger to her chin in a completely fake thoughtful pose. "The one I'm thinking about has red hair, a big laugh, big smile, and a big heart. Yours?"

Her kind words about Marina, a woman who at times could test the patience of a newly ordained minister, made me feel warm and fuzzy. But then I caught a glimpse of the coffee can Ruthie had placed by the cash register and remembered why we were there. Or at least why I was there; Debra didn't yet know I had an ulterior motive. "I did ask someone else to join us for lunch. That's okay, isn't it?"

"Sure." Debra put her purse on the wall side of the booth and started to slide over a little. "Any friend of yours is a friend of—"

"Beth!" a male voice called down the length of the restaurant. "Is that you way the heck back there? Ruthie, get me some provisions so I can make it without dying of hunger." His rich laughter boomed off the black-and-white-checked linoleum floor, off the ceiling, and off the mirror above the far wall.

I waved at him and Debra froze in midslide. "Is that—"

"Hey, sweetheart." Glenn Kettunen, husband to Christine, father of four, insurance agent for most of Rynwood, and owner of the baldest head in the county, slid in the seat across from me, almost squashing Debra against the wall.

"Hello, Glenn," she said.

This time I was the one who froze. It was the old Debra voice, the one that intimidated me to near speechlessness, the one that had toddlers do her bidding at a single command, the one that made cats stop shredding furniture.

"Ah, don't go all Debra on me." Glenn slung an arm around her shoulders. "Where's the Deb I know and love so much more?"

My wide-eyed gaze flicked from Glenn to Debra and back. What on earth had I done? This lunch, which had seemed like a brilliant idea last night, was suddenly in the running for Beth's Worst Idea Ever.

Debra tossed her head, flinging the ends of her hair into Glenn's eyes. "She disappeared the minute you told my husband that my life wasn't worth insuring since I stopped wearing Armani. 'Now that she wears plain old clothes,' you said, and I'm quoting here, 'there's no reason to make any big deal out of her.' "

Glenn chuckled, leaned over, and gave her a big smacking kiss on the cheek.

It was only then I noticed the grin lurking in the corner of Debra's mouth. She made a show of wiping her face. "Kissed by an insurance agent," she said. "Will I ever live this down?"

"Nope," Glenn said cheerfully. "Ah, Dorrie." He greeted our waitress and snapped his fingers. "Menu, young lady."

Dorrie, who'd stopped counting gray hairs years ago and had, instead, started making regular coloring appointments, gave Debra a glass of ice water, me a mug of hot water, and Glenn a mug of coffee. "You haven't used a menu in this place since 1991."

She pulled a tea bag from her apron pocket, put it next to my mug, gave us napkin-rolled silverware, then took out her order pad and started writing. "Rueben for you, soup of the day and house salad with Italian dressing for Debra, and a fish sandwich with coleslaw for Beth." She shoved the pad back in her pocket. "Twenty minutes."

"Twenty minutes?" Glenn asked.

"Mr. I've-Been-to-Cooking-School is being all persnickety about the fry batter." Dorrie rolled her eyes. "Like it's any different today than it's been any other day. Let me know if you need anything."

"When did Ian go to cooking school?" Debra asked. "I thought Ruthie hired him out of high school."

Glenn reached across her and picked five packets of sugar out of the wire rack against the wall. "The kid's been taking culinary classes." He leaned forward and dropped his voice to a nearly normal decibel level. "Says he wants to open his own restaurant someday."

Debra, wife, mother, and bank loan officer, looked thoughtful. "What kind, do you know?"

"One of those bistro-type places." Glenn unwrapped his silverware and stirred the sugar into his coffee. "Brick walls, uncomfortable chairs, a menu that changes every day, and a lot of talk about presentation."

"Could work."

Glenn took one sip of his coffee and grimaced. "In Rynwood?" He set down his mug and reached for three more sugar packets. "The kid would lose his shirt. Who's going to eat at a place like that? Auntie May?" He laughed, but Debra continued to wear the "I'm going to have to talk to Ian before he goes to another bank" look.

Before it wore off, I plunged in. "Speaking of money—"

"I hate it when people start conversations like that." Glenn waved his spoon around. "Second only to 'Promise you won't be mad.'"

"Or 'I forgot to tell you my parents are coming this weekend,'" Debra said.

The pair stared across the table at me and I felt my resolve slipping away. It had been a dumb idea, anyway. I didn't know how to investigate anything, I didn't know how to get people to talk, and I was a horrible liar. "It's about Jenna's hockey team," I said.

"Jenna plays soccer." Glenn made a head-butting motion. "Score!"

"And now she plays hockey," I said. "She was taking lessons all last summer and she's been playing with the Rynwood Raiders."

"Real hockey like on ice or field hockey like on grass?" he asked.

Debra gave him a look. "This is Wisconsin. What do you think?"

"Hey, I'm just an insurance agent. How am I supposed to keep up? Kids get older every year." He stabbed the table with every syllable. "Every year."

Debra shook her head. "What about Jenna's team?"

I dunked my tea bag. "I heard Sam Helmstetter was thinking about sponsoring. And now . . . well . . . I don't know what's going to happen." Which was true. What wasn't quite true was that I'd heard that Sam was thinking about a sponsorship. But since I'd said it, I'd now heard it, and I didn't have to think of it as a lie. Yes, it still was a lie, but rationalization and I could become close friends.

"Does her team need money?" Debra asked.

"Uniforms, pads, helmets." Glenn tapped the table with the end of his spoon at every item. "Skates, skate sharpening, tape, pucks, sticks. Ice time. Gas money. Food."

I could see dollar signs adding up in Debra's calculator of a brain. Once I'd watched her grab a lunch check, total it up, divide it up three ways, and add a twenty percent tip to each, all the while talking about a new muffin recipe she wanted to try. Later, Marina and I redid the math with a calculator. Debra had been right, down to the penny.

"Hockey isn't a sport for the poverty-stricken," Glenn said. "That's why I never played."

"You never played because you have the athletic ability of a soap dish," Debra said.

"I happen to know some very—"

"Who said Sam was thinking about sponsoring?" she asked.

My earlobes started to itch with heat. "Not sure."

"Hmm," she said. "Probably just a rumor."

Not a definitive statement, but it told me that Sam's company wasn't making the kind of money needed to fund a hockey team. And if they weren't making enough for that, they weren't making enough to make murder worthwhile. Sure, I knew in some places people were killed over a twenty-dollar bill, but not here in Rynwood. I hoped.

The chances that the Helmstetters carried their insurance locally were better than good. I looked at Glenn, who was reaching for another sugar packet. "Do you think it's worth asking Rachel?"

Clever Beth, to get Sam's banker and insurance agent at the same table at the same time. Guilt-ridden Beth, for asking them sly questions that would get me the answers I wanted without violating confidentiality issues.

Glenn tore off the top and slowly poured the sugar into the sticky mess that used to be coffee. "I wouldn't ask Rachel about donations for a few years. Say, twenty."

So, no nice big insurance policy. Nothing big enough to pay the mortgage, fund two college educations, and keep the kids in iPods. Poor Rachel.

I had one last straw to grasp. "How about Sam's partner? Do you think he would still be interested in sponsoring the team?"

Glenn shook his head. "I don't see how."

And no key person insurance. Not a huge surprise for a start-up company. Not a huge surprise for many small businesses, including mine.

The three of us stared at the table. What I saw in the scratched plastic laminate was a future for Rachel, Blake, and Mia that looked a lot like my nightmares. Cheap rooms above a downtown store. No store. No job. No health insurance. Nowhere to go. I'd end up sitting in front of the television all day, getting even fatter and ugglier and—

"I know what you're getting at," Glenn said.

"You do?"

"Sure. And I understand. Situations like these can be hard."

"Um . . . they sure are." Here I thought I'd been so clever, and Glenn had seen through me from the beginning. I glanced at Debra; she was nodding.

"In my experience," she said, "it's even harder for women."

Glenn laughed. "Hah. Some women find it easier than using speed dial to call Sabatini's for pizza."

"The exception that proves the rule." Debra tossed a sugar packet over to him.

On the outside, I kept a neutral expression on my face. On the inside, I was wondering what on God's green earth they were talking about.

Debra elbowed Glenn. "Look at the poor girl. She's afraid to ask, isn't she?"

"She's never done it," Glenn said. "Written all over her face."

"Beth." Debra put her elbows on the table and reached out for my hands. "Don't be scared. We're your friends."

"Um . . ."

"Cat must have snuck in when we weren't looking and stolen her tongue." Glenn looked under the table. "Here, kitty, kitty. Nope, cat's gone. We're going to have to talk for her."

Maybe they could do my talking the rest of the day. If I was asked a question, I'd step aside and let my newly appointed spokespersons take care of things. No saying anything stupid, no sounding like I didn't know what I was talking about. When Jenna and Oliver came into teenager-hood I wouldn't be able to say a single thing right; why not let Debra and Glenn say it for me?

It wasn't such a bad idea, really. The times I'd said the right thing at the right time were way outnumbered by the times I'd said the wrong thing, so why not—

"Hello?" Glenn snapped his fingers in front of my nose. "Did you hear me? I said I'd be glad to sponsor the Rynwood Raiders."

"You . . . would?"

"Sure. What's another ten bucks? Ow! Debra, quit kicking me."

The two started bickering about how much Glenn should donate. I sat back, trying to decide which reaction was on top. Dismay or amusement? Dismay, because I wasn't any closer to finding Sam's killer, or amusement, because I'd found a sponsor without trying.

Debra glared at Glenn. "If you don't give them enough money to buy new jerseys and keep their skates sharpened all season, I'll sic the chamber of commerce on you." She lifted her chin and reverted to the old Debra. "Do I know a potential donor for the summer fireworks? Why, yes, I do. Talk to Glenn Kettunen. He as good as told me he was willing to make a sizeable donation."

"Aw, Debra, you wouldn't."

"Want to try me?" With the eye that Glenn couldn't see, she winked at me.

Amusement. Definitely.

Which, as I listened to the two of them spar, slid back down to dismay. If Sam's death wasn't due to an old grudge and wasn't due to money, I was fresh out of ideas.

Chapter 13

The classroom echoed around the three of us. Erica looked at the wall clock, at the empty chairs, at Claudia's vacant spot, and at her watch. "It's seven o'clock," she said. "This special meeting of the Tarver Elementary PTA is now in session. Will the secretary call the roll?"

"Hale?" I asked.

"Here."

"Jarvis?"

Randy stirred. "Present and accounted for."

"Kennedy, here." I looked at the door, listened, waited, then said, "Wolff?"

"Mark her absent," Erica said. "If she's not—"

A door shut and footsteps hurried down the hall toward us. All three of us waited expectantly for Claudia to come through the door, tossing off excuses in place of apologies.

Summer Lang rushed through the doorway. "Sorry I'm late. Oh!" She stopped short at the sight of the mostly empty room. "Where is everybody? Isn't the dance committee supposed to give our report tonight?"

"Yes." Erica clipped the *s* on the end of the word

shorter than I would have thought possible for anyone except an auctioneer. "I hope you're prepared."

"Well, I guess so." She lifted the end of the sentence into a question. "I have the report. Is it okay if I just, you know, read it?"

Erica lifted an eyebrow. "Unless you were planning to sing it."

"To the tune of 'You Are My Sunshine,' then." Summer dropped her bag onto a chair, flung off her coat, and started singing.

This is my report
My only report.
It makes me happy
To have it done.
We made much money,
A lot of money.
Please don't make me do this again.

Erica burst into laughter. "Summer, you're a natural for the stage."

Summer blushed and sat in the second row. "Thanks. I tried, in high school." She put her hand on her stomach. "But my tummy felt funny for days before a performance. It was just too hard."

"I used to get that way before a court appearance," Erica said. "Beth, please finish the roll call."

The concept that Erica had ever been nervous—about anything—was going to take some getting used to. Could it be that she wasn't as strong and stable and self-assured as I'd always believed? And if so, did it make me happy to know she was an actual human, or did it frighten me? Because if iron-willed Erica had fears, what chance did I have of ever growing out of mine? "Wolff is marked as absent."

"Thank you," Erica said. "Did anyone hear from Claudia?" Randy, Summer, and I all shook our heads. "Summer, did anyone on the dance committee contact you?"

"Just Marina on Sunday to work on the report," she said. "Isn't she here?" Summer looked around the audience, as if expecting to find Marina under a child's desk. "Oh, she's probably in the gym with the kids, isn't she?"

"She's home with a bad cold," I said. A stuffed-up Marina had called me at work that afternoon, and I'd had to summon my emergency babysitter. And with the clock ticking at double pay for weeknight sitting, I hoped the meeting would be short.

"So where is everybody?" Summer asked.

"That's what I'd like to know." Erica looked like an attorney in the midst of an expensive courtroom battle. "Randy? Beth? Do you have any idea why all these chairs are empty?"

"Nope." Randy pulled a stick of gum out of his shirt pocket and unwrapped it. He shrugged.

A very unpleasant possibility crossed my mind, and its taste must have shown on my face.

"Beth?" Erica asked. "Do you know?"

I shook my head, and didn't say a word. Where were Debra and Glenn when I needed them?

"Why is she getting the good stuff?" Oliver pointed at Jenna's plate.

"Don't point," I said automatically. "What good stuff?" I was using tongs to put some egg noodles on Oliver's plate. Next to that was a piece of pot roast and next to that I'd put a tiny heap of peas. Oliver didn't like his food to touch, so I was concentrating on making sure the meat juices didn't leak over to the noodles.

"The clumpy ones." Oliver pointed, then jerked his finger away. "Those over there on the side of her plate. The ones all stuck together are the best. How come she gets them all?"

It was true. I had given the clumped noodles to Jenna. That I hadn't noticed any of the noodles were clumped, that I'd never known anyone wanted clumped noodles, and that I was slightly embarrassed that I'd cooked clumpy noodles wouldn't matter at all to my son.

"If there are clumpy noodles next time," I said, "I'll make sure you get them."

"I want them now." In the wink of an eye, Oliver's face, which had until now been sunny and cheerful, turned obstinate. He crossed his arms hard across his chest and slumped down in his chair.

Disciplining an eight-year-old was not in the evening's plans, but most of the things I'd done so far tonight weren't planned. Tonight's list didn't include cleaning up a Spot puddle or cleaning up after Oliver spilled red juice all over the kitchen counter, floor, and his formerly white shirt. I also hadn't planned to help Jenna with her English homework ("But, Mom, I don't know how to figure out what a theme is!"), and I hadn't planned on trying to repair the vase in the living room that had mysteriously broken.

"Oliver," I said patiently, "eat what's on your plate. There's nothing wrong with unclumped noodles."

"The clumped ones are the best."

"Why?" Jenna asked.

It was an excellent question. Jenna and I looked at the sole male in the room and waited for an answer.

"'Cause they're special." Oliver's chin slid forward. "There aren't hardly any of them."

There also weren't many peas on his plate, but that didn't seem to be an issue.

"Why does Jenna get all of them? I should get some."

"If you want them, take them." Jenna picked up the clump, and in front of my horrified eyes tossed them across the table to her brother, where they landed half on his plate, half off.

"Jenna!"

"He wanted the stupid clumped noodles; I gave them to him." She faced me with an overly innocent expression. "What's wrong with that?"

There were so many answers to her question that it took me a moment to come up with a first response. "You know perfectly well that we don't throw food at the table."

"No, I don't."

The innocent look was fixed in place. I closed my eyes and willed that time reverse itself. Not long, just enough for me to start dinner over again, to pay a little more attention to the noodle cooking and de-clump every noodle in the pot. Three times I wished it, the magic number for wishes. Unfortunately, when I opened my eyes, there were still noodles hanging off the edge of Oliver's plate.

"Jenna," I said quietly, "how many times have we talked about appropriate behavior at the table?"

"You've never said 'Don't throw food.' Ever." She smiled triumphantly.

Anger is always an ugly emotion, and when directed at a child it is monumentally so. I waited for the small wave to pass before speaking. "I thought you were smart enough, mature enough, and thoughtful enough that telling you something so obvious wouldn't be necessary."

"You've never told us," she said. "How can I be blamed for something I didn't know?"

"That's a good question," I said. "Why don't you go to your room and think about it? Make a list of five good reasons, and when you're done, bring me the list and we'll talk about them."

"But I haven't eaten hardly anything," Jenna said.

"Do I get to eat the clumpy ones?" Oliver asked.

The phone rang. If my luck was good it would be a telemarketer wanting to know if I had time to answer a twenty-minute phone survey. "Jenna, go to your room.

Your dinner will keep. Oliver, no one is eating those noodles."

As I picked up the phone, both kids were in full protest. "Hello, can you hold on a minute?" Without waiting for an answer, I put my hand over the receiver. "Oliver, be quiet and eat. Jenna, go to your room."

"But, Mom, I—"

"Mom, why can't—"

"Now!"

My shout surprised them to silence. They stared at each other and, after a short eternity, came to an unspoken agreement. Oliver picked up his fork and started eating. Jenna stomped out of the room and up the stairs. I listened to her thump down the hall and waited for her door to shut.

Bang!

The only noises in the room were the clock ticking away time and Oliver's overloud chewing.

I suddenly wanted three things very badly: a hot bath, a thick book, and a massage therapist to iron the kinks out of my neck after spending six hours in the tub reading. Instead, I took my hand off the phone. "Sorry about that."

"Difficulties with the children again?" my mother asked.

My hackles rose high. "What makes you say that?"

She laughed. "I'm your mother. The signs are all there. Covered phone, muffled shouts, slight delay before answering. Anything I can do to help?"

My hackles went halfway down. Maybe she wasn't judging me; maybe this time she wasn't going to remind me that the end of my marriage with Richard had been completely my fault.

"Thanks, Mom," I said, "but I have things under control."

She clucked. "It's too bad you don't have a man in the house any longer."

"We're in the middle of dinner," I said. "Can I call you back in half an hour?"

"You're eating rather late, aren't you? Such a late mealtime can't be good for the children."

I looked at the clock. Seven. Late, but not that late. "Mom, don't forget we're on central time here." The whole concept that I lived in a different time zone had never quite penetrated into my mother's consciousness.

"Ah, yes."

"When are you going to get here?" I asked. "Are you coming in on Tuesday or Wednesday?" How Thanksgiving had gotten so close so fast was a mystery, but there it was on the wall calendar: Thanksgiving Day.

I'd also written down names: Mom, Kathy, Darlene, Tim. I'd crossed off Kathy and Tim when they'd called to cancel, and the small square now looked like a half-done to-do list. So much for the nice big family Thanksgiving dinner at Beth's house.

"That's what I wanted to talk to you about," Mom said. "Thanksgiving."

"Don't worry. I'm still cooking the rutabaga."

"You are?"

"Well, sure. We always have rutabaga on the table at Thanksgiving. I don't want to be the first Emmerling to break with tradition." It'd probably bring me bad luck for thirteen years. "I'm making that pie you like with the pumpkin on the bottom and whipped filling on top. We're having green beans and squash, and mashed potatoes, and I want to try real cranberries this year."

The menu spilled out of me like water gushing from a broken pipe. Over the weekend I'd made my final final list and typed it into the computer. Set in stone. Almost. "And I was thinking of making that broccoli salad with bacon and raisins, but if you'd rather have a regular green salad, I can do that instead."

"Honey, there's something I have to tell you."

If I'd been standing, I would have sat down abruptly. Since I was already sitting, I sat up straight. No one had ever handed out good news by starting a conversation with "There's something I have to tell you." No, that was always the preface to bad news.

It was her health. She'd been diagnosed with terminal cancer and had only three months to live.

It was her house. There'd been a huge storm and a tree had crashed down on her house, making it uninhabitable, and, since she'd forgotten to renew her home insurance, irreparable without funding from her children.

It was her car. She'd crashed it against a telephone pole and the friendly police officers had taken her driver's license away from her. Without a car, she wouldn't be able to live in the house. She'd have to sell it and move to an assisted living facility unless one of us volunteered to take her in. My brother would assume one of his sisters would take care of things, and Kathy didn't have the room, so it was either me or Darlene, and I had the youngest grandchildren.

The first-floor study was the obvious place for Mom to stay. But where would I move its current contents? I was mentally rearranging furniture in my bedroom when Mom asked, "Beth? Did you hear me?"

"Um, sure. You said you had something to tell me."

"About Thanksgiving. I won't be able to make it down."

"You . . . won't?"

"No, I'm afraid not."

I swallowed. This was not personal. My family loved me. Kathy had a chance of a lifetime, that was all. And Tim's work schedule was out of his control. Nothing personal in any of that. "Are you okay?" I whispered.

Please let my mom be okay. Please don't let her be sick or hurt. Maybe we don't always get along, but I love her and would be lost without her guidance. I haven't told her about Richard's layoff. I haven't told her about Evan dancing with Jenna. Please let her be happy and healthy. Please . . .

"Certainly," she said. "Why? Do I sound sick?"

"No, but—"

"Honey, don't be such a worrywart." She laughed. "I'm sorry about Thanksgiving, but Gladys had a bad fall."

"Oh, no!" Gladys Pepper and my mom were next-door neighbors, best friends, and each other's security system. They had a complicated arrangement of lights on/lights off, curtains open/curtains closed that could mean anything from "I'm going to bed early so don't worry if all my lights are off" to "There's a serial killer in the house." Darlene lived barely twenty minutes away, but it was nice to know Mom and Gladys had each other. "Is she okay?"

"Yes, thank heavens, but she cracked some ribs and is bruised in all sorts of uncomfortable places. She'd been planning to fly to Texas to be with her son and his family for the holiday."

"She can't do that now," I said.

"No," Mom agreed. "And she doesn't have any family left in Michigan except for her sister in Pontiac, and her sister can't drive, so I said I'd make Thanksgiving for the two of us."

I swallowed. Mom was okay, inside and out. "You're a nice lady."

"Thank you, dear. And you're a nice daughter for not being upset about your dinner plans."

"Thanks, Mom." A warm feeling enveloped me. You never outgrow the glow that results from parental praise. Though what I was going to do with a twenty-pound turkey for five people, I didn't know.

"So, how are the children? I heard you scolding them. Was it Oliver? Jenna?" She clucked. "Don't tell me it was both."

The warm fuzziness evaporated immediately. Maybe it wouldn't be so bad to have only Darlene and her husband with us for Thanksgiving. At least Darlene wouldn't criticize my parenting skills, my divorce, my kitchen cleanliness, or my career choice.

I tried to listen to my mother suggest ways to improve my children, I really did, but most of me was stuck in worrywart mode. And, since there were a lot of things to worry about, I kept myself occupied all the way through my mother's lecture.

Being a worrywart had its bright side.

The front door of the store jingled open and Rachel Helmstetter came in. She thrust a flyer at me. "Here. What do you think?"

I took the bright white piece of paper, turned it around so I could read it without standing on my head, and started reading.

"Insurance might restore your financial losses, but who will restore your privacy? Once your customers have seen what you really look like, will they ever return? You can trust Rynwood Shredding to take care of your confidential documents with the utmost security. Call now to arrange for a free estimate. Annual, monthly, and on-demand contracts available."

Below the text was a large photo of a man sitting in the middle of a ransacked office. Drawers were pulled out, bookshelves toppled, chairs lying on their sides. The man sat behind a desk, and, above the waist at least, he was naked.

"So, what do you think?" Rachel asked.

"It's clever." I scanned it again and tapped the photo. "Memorable, too. You won't forget it easily."

She blew out a breath. "Really? That's great. You're the first person I've shown it to. But since you're the one who got me started, I figured it was only right."

Excellent. In addition to lighting the spark that changed Debra's life, I'd also managed to alter Rachel's. I made a mental note: Put duct tape over my mouth and let Glenn and Debra say everything that needed to be said.

I started to hand the flyer back, but Rachel waved her hands, making "stop" motions at me. "Keep it. If I'm really going to try and take Sam's place, I need to get used to handing out sales information."

Ever so slowly, the sun showed itself above the horizon and light dawned. "You're going to be partners with Brian Keller? How's he doing, anyway?"

"Okay." She moved her left arm and made a wincing face. "Anyway, we're going to try it for a few months. See how it goes. Brian's the operations guy. Sam . . ." She looked away, looked up at the ceiling, pulled in a gasping breath, and started over. "Sam was the sales guy. The idea guy. If I can do half of what Sam did, we might be able to make it work."

She was fiddling with her scarf, and the filter that usually kept my mouth from saying things my brain thought up suddenly stopped working. I blurted out a question I had no idea I'd ever had the courage to ask. "Rachel, how many scarves did Sam own?"

"Scarves?" She plucked at the orange one around her neck. "This was his Thanksgiving scarf. He had a gold one for Christmas, a red one for Valentine's Day, and a green one for St. Patrick's Day. And a black one for the winter solstice." She smoothed her husband's scarf. "He liked plaids for every day. Said they added spice to his weekdays."

That answered that question, but brought up another one. Why, with the plethora of Sam's scarves, hadn't I remembered that he regularly wore them? Chalk it up to yet more evidence that Beth Isn't Paying Enough Attention to Her Surroundings.

"Why do you want to know?" Rachel asked.

I shrugged. "Just wondered." True enough, but it was time for a diversion. "If you can come up with ideas like this"—I rustled her flyer—"you'll be just as good a marketer as Sam was. He never sent anything around downtown that I can think of." My brain suddenly kicked into high gear. "And I don't remember that he ever used his contacts to help him network."

Rachel frowned. "He was on Rotary and did the Toastmasters thing. He worked hard for the chamber of commerce, and you know he was active in the PTA."

"That's not what I mean." Judging from the hollow feeling of the store, we had a total of zero customers. Even so, I lowered my voice. "Sam was born and raised in Rynwood and figured he knew everybody without even trying. Which, for the most part, was true. But there are lots of new people in town."

"I suppose." Rachel sounded puzzled. "But the business was growing almost as fast as their business plan projected, so he didn't need to work super hard at marketing."

"That was Sam," I said. "You'll need a different approach."

"That's what this is all about." Rachel gestured at the flyer still clutched in my hand. "And I have some other ideas." Her voice drooped. "But I don't know if any of them will work."

"Half of all marketing dollars are wasted," I said. "It's just that no one knows which half."

Her smile came and went. "Maybe trying to run Sam's business is a bad idea. Maybe I should . . ." Her eyes took on that faraway look I'd seen so often on my mother's face after Dad died.

"Ask your friends to help," I suggested.

She shook her head. "They've already done too much. Cooked dinners, lunches, even breakfasts. Watched the kids. Watched me." This time her smile wasn't a smile at all.

"I can help," I said. "I'd like to."

"My freezer's packed full of casseroles already, but thanks."

I squinched my face. Casseroles weren't a food group I cared for. Whenever my mother had pulled the orange pot from the cupboard I knew I'd have to fill up on bread and butter. And I still didn't care for the color orange. "Not that kind of help." I rattled the flyer. "This kind of help."

Her mouth made a small round *o* of enlightenment. I smiled. Finally, I knew how to find Sam's killer.

And maybe, just maybe, find a little peace for Rachel, too.

Chapter 14

"What does Sabatini's Pizza have that's worth shredding?" Marina pulled a handful of her hair up to its full length, then let it drop. Since her thick, overly full locks didn't behave like normal hair, the hunk stuck in midair, making her look as if she'd just taken off a winter hat in dry air.

"Maybe he really is mobbed up," I said. "Maybe they're paying him to get rid of the evidence for a massive fraud perpetuated by . . ." I thought fast. ". . . by the costume industry. All these years we've thought of clowns as friendly creatures, but Sabatini's has been storing proof of a dastardly plot to take over the country."

Marina nodded. "I knew there was something off about clowns."

It was Friday night, the kids were with Richard, and Marina and I were seated at her kitchen table, scrutinizing Rynwood Shredding's client list. Rachel had hemmed and hawed when I'd first asked for a copy, but my argument that I could target downtown businesses better if I understood the client base convinced her. Which was good, because I didn't have a backup plan and would have had to keep repeating argument number one over and over until I wore her down.

"Mr. Sabatini goes on the list." Marina picked up her purple felt pen and wrote on a pink piece of paper.

Letting her write the names with the pen and paper of her choosing was the only way she'd agreed to tonight's list-making endeavors.

"I thought we were looking for a PTA connection, someone who knew about the meeting," I said. "Joe isn't married and he doesn't have any children."

"Not that we know about," Marina said darkly.

"If you're not going to be serious I'm going to take my lists and go home." And a dark, lonely house it would be with the kids at Richard's.

"Promise?" Marina clasped her hands together.

"Yes."

"Well, phooey." She sighed heavily, then brightened and scribbled on the pink paper.

I tried, unsuccessfully, to read her loopy handwriting upside down. "What's that?"

"Oh, just a name we should consider."

She was shooting for a casual, innocent tone. It didn't work. Marina was often casual, but she was rarely innocent. Matter of fact, the only time she'd been completely innocent was the Saturday night my house had been toilet-papered. Sunday morning I woke up to rain and soggy toilet paper over shrubbery, around porch columns, and even over the roof of the house.

I'd immediately called Marina, but she'd claimed zero knowledge. It took a few days of detective work to figure out that my house had been mistaken for the home of the high school starting quarterback.

"Let me see." I pulled the list around. "What? Marina Neff, you take Claudia's name off right now."

"Don't be such a spoilsport." Marina snatched back

the pen I'd taken from her. "It's my list and I can leave her on if I want to."

"Fine. I'll make my own."

"No, you won't. You said I could be list maker tonight." She wielded her purple pen like a tiny sword. "Back, back, back. Down, down, down."

"I thought this was a team effort."

"And I'm the captain."

"Okay, Captain Marina, sir, why would Claudia kill Sam?"

"That's easy," she said. "Because . . . well, because . . ." She perked up. "Because she was jealous of Sam's perfect life. Hers is so drab and unhappy in comparison that she couldn't take it any longer."

"And how about the police saying that the murder would have taken a man's strength?"

"Hmm." She pinched her nose as she considered the question. "Claudia and her sidekick Tina did it together. Each one held—"

"Tina went home that night right after the meeting."

Marina looked at me. "You are making that up."

"Nope. And I'm not going to say how I know, so don't bother asking." Marina heard the steel in my voice and didn't push. The only reason I knew anything about Tina was that she and the Helmstetters shared a backyard. The afternoon Rachel cried on my shoulder she'd sobbed that she knew something was wrong when she saw Tina letting the dog out and then Sam didn't come home. And didn't come home. And didn't come home.

"Oh, all right." Marina crossed off Claudia's name. "If she's off, who are we going to put on?"

I tapped the client list. "Remember these?"

She scrunched up her face. "Yah, but that looks like, you know, work. Say, what are you doing this weekend? Got a hot date with that pretty boy?"

I took the pages Rachel had printed out, kept half, and handed the other half to Marina. "We can work separately or we can work together. Which will it be?"

"Slave driver," she muttered.

Which might be true, but I knew that wasn't her real problem. She didn't want to look at these names—almost all of whom were people we knew—and try to link them to a murder. It was a silly game to play around with Claudia and Tina; it would be deeply ugly to seriously consider that someone we knew ended Sam's life.

"If we do not hang together," Marina said in dark tones, "we shall surely hang separately."

"That's Thomas Paine, not Shakespeare."

"Whatever."

"Ready?"

". . . I guess so."

We exchanged a long glance full of trepidation and fear.

Then we got to work.

"This I cannot believe." Paoze, arms crossed, stood at the store's front windows. His face was a complex mixture of disbelief, surprise, and anxiety. "It should not be."

"You're right." Lois laid a hand on his thin shoulder. "It shouldn't. I'm in complete agreement. Let's write a letter to the governor. Heck, we'll write letters to the entire state legislature and get them to sponsor a bill against this abomination. We'll start a grassroots movement, spur the entire populace into participating, and get immediate action. If we push hard enough we can get a law passed before Christmas."

Paoze didn't rise to her bait. "It should not be," he said stubbornly, still staring.

I laughed. "Oh, come on. You've seen snow before."

"Not so early." He was almost pouting. "Never November."

The three of us stood in a short row and watched the weather. Yesterday, the scene had been of storefronts, bare-branched trees, and a few evergreen shrubs. Today we couldn't read the sign on the shoe store across the street and the shrubs were swaddled in white. The few vehicles on the road were inching along cautiously, their drivers reacquainting themselves with winter driving skills.

"What you need is a car," Lois said.

Paoze used a bicycle to commute from Madison, five miles distant. Rain or shine, heat or cold, he was always on time, and was always dressed more professionally than ninety-nine percent of retail clerks in the country with his dark slacks and white shirts. The boy was a minor miracle.

He did need a car, but cars were expensive. The wages the bookstore could afford might stretch to paying for insurance, gas, and repairs, but a car payment? On top of tuition and fees and room and board? Wasn't going to happen. His parents couldn't afford to help him much, and the size of his student loans would be crippling when he graduated. Even worse, as an English major, his prospects of high wages were in the realm of zero.

"Mrs. Kennedy? You are okay?" Paoze asked.

I jerked out of my depressive reverie and realized that I must have sighed. "I'm fine." I looked out at the white swirling world. "But I have to go out in that and I didn't bring my boots."

Lois laughed. "Sucker. I tossed a pair in my trunk on Labor Day. Want to borrow them? All you have to do is go out to my car. It's in the parking lot way down by the grocery store."

"You are a cruel, cruel woman. To atone for your sins, I suggest you realphabetize the picture books." Picture books had been Marcia's favorite section, and her absence was showing. Task for tomorrow: Convince Yvonne that picture books were the love of her life.

By the time I zipped up my coat, pulled on my mittens, and tightened down my hood, Lois was deep into a conversation with Paoze concerning the pleasures of alphabetizing. I shook my head and left her to it. Paoze might or might not have read *The Adventures of Tom Sawyer*, but either way my guess was that he'd be sorting through picture books when I got back.

Outside, I gasped as the wind hit me full in the face. Paoze was right; this shouldn't be. I put my head down and struggled against the battering gusts. Step after step, snow and more snow insinuated itself between low-slung shoes and socks. I hated wet socks. Why had I believed the weather forecast enough to send the kids out in boots, but not enough to wear them myself?

I walked into the police station and stomped off the snow—twice with each foot, the classic northern tap dance—and asked for Gus.

"Do you have an appointment?" the officer asked. For once I did, and the young man ushered me down the short hall and into Gus's office. "Do you want me to shut the door, Chief?"

Gus looked at me. I nodded. Without another word, the young man withdrew and the door clicked shut. I pulled off my mittens, untied my hood, and unzipped my coat. "He's new, isn't he?" I asked, sitting in the vacant chair.

"Fresh out of the academy. My guess is two years, tops." The Rynwood Police Department had a tendency to rapid turnover. The city couldn't afford much of a wage, and after officers gained a year or two of experience, they were off for the bright lights of larger departments with more money, a wider variety of law enforcement opportunities, and room for advancement.

"Well," I said, opening my purse, "maybe he'll be the one who stays. Here." I handed Gus the pink piece of paper.

"What's this?" He held the paper at arm's length, squinted, then gave up and patted the piles of papers on his desk until he found his reading glasses. "Does this say Claudia Wolff?"

"Her name is crossed out," I said quickly. "Don't pay any attention to that. Marina was joking around."

Gus made a noncommittal grunt. "Marina. I should have known. Did she put you up to this?"

I assumed the question was rhetorical and didn't answer.

He read the rest of the names. "Wheeler's Autos. Stull Systems. Croftman Accounting. Bluegrass Construction." He let the paper fall to his desk and leaned back. "You said you had something important to tell me."

I inched forward. "That's right. Marina and I went through Sam's client list and those four names are ones who have strong PTA connections. We think—"

Gus put his hands behind his neck and leaned back. "That due to the timing of Sam's murder, the killer might have a connection to the PTA."

"Oh. Um . . ." Talk about taking the words out of my mouth. "That's right. The top salesperson at Wheeler's Autos is Janis Velona, and her youngest is still at Tarver. Eric Stull owns Stull Systems, and he has two daughters there." Rosie, Eric's wife, had hosted a PTA party or two, but I couldn't remember ever meeting Eric. "Andrew Bieber is—"

"The senior accountant at Croftman Accounting, with two boys and a girl at Tarver," Gus said. "And Floyd Hirsch, with three girls, is a crew leader at Bluegrass Construction."

My gaze slid away from Gus's kind one. Floyd's wife had been in the PTA for ages, but she'd gone back to college two years ago and I hadn't seen her since. "I didn't realize you knew all that."

"I'm the police chief," he said. "It's my job."

"Oh." It suddenly seemed very important to play with my snow-soggy mittens. "Um . . ."

"Leave the police work to the police, Beth." His words were kind, but firm. Kind of like a mom voice, only in this case Mom was a gray-haired male in a blue uniform who carried a gun. "The sheriff's department is doing all the right things. I appreciate what you're trying to do, but please don't. Besides the fact that you don't have any authority, you're not trained, you don't have any legal resources, and you don't have backup."

I hung my head. Evan had said much the same thing. He was right. They were both right. But how could I just leave this alone? How could I stand by and do nothing?

"Remember what happened last time." Gus sat forward, putting his elbows on the desk. "Oliver and Jenna were almost killed."

My mouth went weak at the memory. This time it was only the bookstore that was in danger; it was merely their financial future that was at stake. Maybe it would do them good to live on less; it would build character and make them stronger in the long run. "You're right," I whispered.

"That's my girl." Gus smiled and got up. "Now, you call Marina and tell her to take up macramé instead of investigating murders."

I stopped dead, my coat's zipper halfway through its metallic whoosh. "You can't be serious."

He laughed and opened his door. "I'd love to see her face if you did say that."

I flung my hood over my hair. "Pass. I'd like to live long enough to see my grandchildren."

Gus's full-throated laughter followed me down the hall, into the lobby, and out into the cold, where the snow was falling harder and the wind was whipping it around even faster.

"Goodness!" I said, but a chilling gust took the word away and carried it off, where, I did not know. Somewhere south, where it would whisper into the ear of some startled soul.

I amused myself with the thought as I walked back to the store, snow muffling all noise that the wind wasn't drowning out. Who would hear my startled syllables? A minister, maybe, who would search for a parishioner about to take the Lord's name in vain.

A car drove past, its engine noise nearly inaudible, its windows coated with white.

Or the person who heard my word might be a farmer out tending his cows. He'd jerk upright at the sound of a woman's voice, startling Bessy, which would cause her to kick out in alarm. Her hoof would catch the farmer on the seat of his pants and he'd be limping for a week thanks to a snowstorm in Wisconsin.

Head down, I started across the street.

Or it might be a woman in Georgia, walking down the street after completing an errand for her children's bookstore. She'd just picked up a box of doughnuts for her staff, when my word surprised her. She'd almost drop the box, but a handsome stranger would save it from plunging to the sidewalk. She'd invite him in, and a year from now

Something made me look up. Perhaps an angel tapped me on the shoulder. Perhaps it was pure chance. Whatever the reason, I did look up and saw a vehicle headed straight toward me.

For the merest fraction of a second, I couldn't—wouldn't—didn't—move.

He hadn't seen me yet, that's all. He was probably starting to swerve already, and if I moved I might move into his way and wouldn't that be a stupid way to die; Marina would never tire of teasing me about that one.

Then primal instincts shrieked at me: "Run! *Run!*"

Adrenaline activated my muscles and I was running. Or at least trying to run. The snow, wet and slippery, provided no traction and my street shoes couldn't find a grip. My feet wanted to move, but it was like one of those nightmares where you kept running and running and not going anywhere.

These shoes were going to kill me and it was going to be my own stupid fault.

Mad at myself, mad at the weather, mad at the world, I kicked off my shoes and ran stocking-footed through the snow, my toes gripping the thick white slop better than any boot would ever have done. Three lunging, running steps and I was up onto the curb. Two more and I was up and over the shrubbery. One more and I was safe against the wall of the antique mall.

Panting, I watched the back end of a white van fishtail down the street and out of sight.

Panting, I wondered what had just happened.

Panting, I tried not to think about what had almost happened.

Alan barreled out the door. "Beth? Are you okay? That guy headed straight for you!"

"Don't be silly." I tried to laugh, but it came out more like a cough. "He just couldn't see in the snow."

Alan shook his head vigorously. "I saw the whole thing. He was going slow, but when you started across the street, he speeded up. Gunned the engine, spun the tires, and aimed right at you."

"Don't be silly," I repeated, but even I could hear the doubt in my voice.

"You should go talk to Gus about it," Alan said.

"Mmm." He was right; I should. But what could Gus do? The license plate had been snow-covered. The van was white, and if any business name had been painted on the sides, it had been covered by sticky slush. If I went back to Gus now, all I'd get was another scolding.

No, thanks.

"The sooner the better," Alan said. "They say the first twenty-four hours are the most important for solving a crime."

But in this case it would be impossible to prove a crime had been committed. Even if we figured out who had been driving the white van, how could you disprove a statement of, "But, Officer, it was snowing so hard I couldn't see a thing. Sure, I gunned the engine a little. I was breaking through a snowdrift, that's all. I sure wasn't trying to hit anyone."

Alan looked at me, concern in his frown. "Do you want me to go with you? I was a witness."

Such a sweet man. "No, thank you," I said. "But I'll be sure to talk to Gus right away." Or Sunday at church. Whichever came first.

Chapter 15

"Who's that?" Yvonne asked.

"Who's what?" It was the next day, and I still hadn't told Gus about the Incident of the White Van. I hadn't told anyone, actually. Not even Marina. The more I thought about it the sillier it seemed. Alan was an excellent judge of antiques, but I wasn't so sure his eyes and ears, which were well past the enrollment age for AARP, were to be relied upon.

And why on earth would anyone want to run me over? The whole thing had obviously been an accident, and I wasn't about to make a fool of myself in front of Gus a second time.

"Outside," Yvonne said. "Right there in front of the store."

I looked through the window and saw a small circle of women huddled together. The huddling made sense, because while most of yesterday's snow had already melted, it was still cold and still windy. I started to turn away, but Yvonne's face stopped me. Her lips were tucked tight together and she was dusting the books in the front window display over and over and over again.

Hmm.

I moved closer to the window.

Oh, dear. This couldn't be good. There was no way this was good.

The red hat and black coat was Claudia, and the multicolored hat and pink coat was her sidekick Tina Heller. Either the other three women had bought new hats and coats or I didn't know them well enough for clothes recognition.

Tina turned her head away from the cluster and darted a look my way. The sheer venom in her glare was nearly tangible, fierce and ugly and raw.

I took an involuntary step backward. What had I ever done to deserve such a look? Okay, Tina wasn't my favorite person on the planet, but I couldn't recall doing any of the classic three things that would land me permanently on a woman's hit list: flirting with her husband, making fun of her new hairstyle, or telling her that she'd gained weight.

As Yvonne and I watched, another woman scurried down the sidewalk to join the others, her arms laden with an awkward arrangement of sticks and cardboard.

Lois, who could smell trouble even faster than she could come up with a story for Paoze, came up front. "What's going on?" She peered out the window. "Is that CeeCee Daniels? What's she got there? Wait a minute. Those are—"

"Signs," I said tonelessly. As my former friend CeeCee distributed the handmade signs around the group, I saw enough text to understand what was going on.

"They're picketing us?" Lois's voice rose almost to a shriek. "They can't do that! This is a public street. A public sidewalk! They can't do this, can they?" She turned to me, frowning, scared, angry. "Can they?"

Lois was looking at me, Yvonne was looking at me. I had a ferocious wish to be an employee again, and not the owner to whom the hard questions ultimately came.

I turned back to watch the goings-on. The snow piles tossed up by the city's plows were serving as a lumpy reminder of the coming winter, and into those snowbanks Claudia and her crew stuck handmade sign after handmade sign.

"Convicted Killer Inside."

"Make Rynwood Safe."

"Bookstore Harbors Convict."

"Can Your Children Be Safe There?"

Yvonne unpinned her name tag and held it out. "I'll leave by the back door," she said. "Then you can go out and tell them I'm gone. If you're lucky"—she gave a tiny smile—"they'll all come inside and start buying books."

I stared at her. "What?"

She shook the name tag and the loose point of the pin flapped around dangerously. "I'm quitting."

"No, you're not," Lois and I said.

Yvonne continued to hold out her tag and I continued to refuse to take it. "There's no quitting in bookstores," I said. Except for Marcia, but that hardly counted since I would have fired her anyway. "And no quitting right before the busiest season of the year."

"If this is the busy time," Yvonne said, looking around at the empty store, "I don't want to know what the slow season is like."

"This is an anomaly," I said firmly. "Claudia and her cohorts will get tired of standing out there in half an hour. They'll slink back to wherever they came from, and one by one they'll come back and shop. There isn't another children's bookstore this size within a forty-five-minute drive."

Yvonne's arm wavered, then dropped. "You think this will blow over?"

"Absolutely." Which was a complete lie, but if my earlobes were any guide, I was becoming accomplished at the task. "Put that tag back on. We'll have customers pouring in before we can get another round of tea brewed. Speaking of which, how about chamomile?"

As Yvonne headed to the teapot, Lois edged close. "Once Claudia gets a bee in her bonnet she might as well have it cast in stone."

"I know."

"So you don't really think they'll go away by lunchtime?"

We watched a man join the group. He carried a sign that read, "A Killer Is Roaming Free."

"No," I said. "I don't."

"What are you going to do?" Lois's voice was hushed.

"I'll think of something."

But what that something was, I had no idea.

"There's not much you can do," Evan said.

That was not what I wanted to hear. I gripped the phone receiver in my office tighter and hoped I'd heard wrong.

"If they're not physically blocking access to your store," he said, "for the most part they're within the law."

I latched on to the middle of his sentence. "For the most part? You mean there's a part where they might be breaking the law?" I envisioned a police van pulling up to the curb, officers tumbling out and handcuffing everyone.

He sighed a lawyerly sigh. "Constitutional law isn't my area of expertise, but I can tell you that fighting their right to free speech would be an expensive and costly proposition."

"I don't have that kind of money."

"And they could get support from many civil rights groups," Evan said. "I'm afraid yours is not the sympathetic side."

"But Yvonne didn't do anything." I was nearly shouting. "It isn't fair!"

The echo of my words thrummed in a hollow beat down through the memory of my childhood—through everyone's childhood. *It's not fair! It's not fair!* Which really meant, Make it fair, Mommy. Make it fair, Daddy. But even as we protested, even as children, deep down we knew the truth.

"Beth—"

"I know, I know. Don't expect life to be fair."

"You know that already. No, I was going to say that I could lend you money if you really want to fight this."

"You . . . would?"

"Of course." He sounded surprised. "What's important to you is important to me. I thought you knew that."

Tears stung my eyes. I'd known that he seemed to like spending time with me, that he enjoyed being with Jenna and Oliver, but that was all very different from writing a check. Especially a check the size that a project this size might require.

"Thanks," I said softly. "That means a lot to me."

"And you mean a lot to me."

I closed my eyes briefly, wanting to say the words back to him . . . but I couldn't. Or wouldn't. One of those.

"Why do you think I—" He stopped.

"Why what?"

". . . Nothing."

A couple of things went *click* in my head. Evan meeting with Debra. The money lavished anonymously on an elementary school dance. Money funneled through the bank. Evan stopping short of saying something. They all indicated one conclusion: Evan himself had paid for the dance decorations.

"Think about my offer," Evan said. "Okay? Just think about it."

And if he wanted to remain anonymous, I wasn't about to interfere. "I will. Thank you," I said. "Thank you very, very much."

My hand stayed on the phone after I disconnected. What a wonderful man. There were many reasons I was lucky to have Evan in my life, and putting a debt of money into the equation would complicate every single one of them. No, no matter how much money Evan had, borrowing money was out of the question. I'd just hope that Claudia and her followers wouldn't last long. Maybe this really would blow over.

"And maybe the Tarver Foundation will give the kids comic books for Christmas," I said. Then I put a solid smile on my face and went out to cheer up the troops.

The rest of the day went by with a constant ebbing and flowing of sign holders and a total of zero customers coming in the door. The second day was an exact replica of the first day, and by closing time I knew exactly what I had to do.

There was only one small detail to take care of.

Actually doing it.

Marina and I sat in my cramped office at the back of the store. "Here." Marina reached across my desk, four slips of paper in her hand. Thanks to a rash of colds and flu-like illnesses, all of Marina's daytime day-care charges were home in bed. And thanks to a Henry Vilas Zoo field trip, the schoolkids wouldn't arrive at her house until five o'clock. "Pick one," she said.

"You can't be serious."

"As a plate of corned beef. Pick one."

"Why is corned beef serious?"

"Have you ever taken a close look at the stuff? Please." She shook the papers and they fluttered in her self-created breeze. "If you don't pick one I'll do it for you."

"Fine." I plucked one at random.

"Don't tell, don't tell!"

Sometimes Marina acted about eight years old. "Wouldn't dream of it," I said.

She grinned. "I know. I'm acting like a ten-year-old."

"The thought never crossed my mind."

"Oh, sure. Now pick a second one and we'll work out a plan."

When we smoothed out the papers, Marina held Wheeler's Autos and Croftman Accounting. I had Stull Systems and Bluegrass Construction. Four PTA connections to Sam's shredding business, four companies to investigate.

"So what's the plan?" Marina looked around. "Where's your list? I know there's one here somewhere." She lifted the stacks of publishers' catalogs scattered all across my desk and looked underneath.

"No list."

Marina whacked her ears lightly with the palms of her hands. "Houston? Our communications are garbled. Can you repeat?"

Last night I'd lain awake with Spot snoring on my right side and George on my left, trying to fight off my fears, trying to think of a way to keep Yvonne from being convicted without benefit of trial, trying to figure out how to find a happy ending for everyone. All I'd gotten for my efforts were a lot of sleepless hours and pet hair all across the flannel comforter cover.

"There's no list," I said. "And cut the dramatics." She'd started the motion of clutching her hands to her chest in fake heart attack symptoms. "Without knowing more about these four, we can't make a plan." I put my fingers on my two pieces of paper and shuffled them back and forth. "My idea is this: We approach the companies as if we were prospective customers and—"

"And turn the conversation in the proper direction." Marina nodded. "Gotcha." She made faces at her picks. "Cars are easy, but how on earth am I going to come up with a reason to need an accountant?"

I smiled. "I'd planned to take that one and say the

store was thinking about switching accountants, but oh, no. You needed to make a game out of it. You were the one who said we had to draw papers. And we're not switching," I said as she started to take on a wheedling look. "Picks are picks."

She sighed. "I suppose you're right."

Being right should have made me feel good, or at least made me feel something, but I couldn't stop thinking about the protesters on the sidewalk, Yvonne's pinched look, and the cash register that hadn't rung in almost three days.

But all of that was eclipsed by the memory of the bleakness on Rachel's face.

"Hello?" I looked around the empty front office of Bluegrass Construction. Empty of people, anyway. There were rolls of blueprints, stacks of tile samples, piles of siding samples, even buckets of various-sized stones, but I didn't see a single human.

"Hello?" I called again. "Is anyone here?"

A sense of creepiness curled around my neck, and it occurred to me that it might have been wise to tell someone about the white van. It had been an accident, of course it had, but I could have told Marina.

Somewhere in the back a door slammed. A young woman walked into the office with long-legged strides. The scent of cigarette smoke clung to her clothes, and she was whistling as she unzipped her coat and tossed it over a chair.

"Oh, hi." She smiled. "Sorry. Have you been waiting long?"

"Not a bit." I smiled back, almost laughing at my silly self for getting all worked up over nothing. Mom had been right: My imagination was going to get me in trouble someday.

"Good." She held out her hand. "Gina. Office manager, head of sales, janitor, and lowest person on the totem pole."

I laughed. "At least you know where you stand."

"True enough." She sat down behind a desk covered with small squares of carpet. "What can I do for you?"

The half-truths I'd fabricated on the drive over started to slip away now that I was facing a real person. "Well," I said, "there's some work on my house I wouldn't mind having done." Which was true. I wouldn't mind hardwood floors on most of the main level. And I wouldn't mind a spa tub in the master bathroom. And I really wouldn't mind a sunroom like Erica's.

Gina was taking notes. "We do remodels all the time. Matter of fact, that's most of what we've been doing the last couple of years. What are you thinking? Kitchen? Bathroom?"

"Both would be wonderful," I said honestly, "but before I start anything, I need to get a rough idea of how much things cost." Also true.

"Sure. That makes sense," Gina said. "Costs are all over the map, though, depending."

"On what?"

I listened with half an ear as she talked about the variations in cabinet prices, windows, flooring, and fixtures.

When she paused to take a breath, I jumped in. "And what about labor costs? That can add a lot to the price, especially if the crew isn't experienced. How long have your guys been in the construction business?"

"Great question," Gina said approvingly. "Lots of people wouldn't think to ask that. Do you mean all the guys, or what?"

"Let's start with your foremen. The ones who run the crews."

"There's Bob Lowe. He's been with us for, oh, geez, forever. Ten years? And what's-his-name is new this year, but he worked as a finish carpenter for years and years."

"How about Floyd Hirsh?" a nonchalant Beth asked.

"Floyd's been here about three years. He started here just after I did."

I frowned. "And he heads up a crew?"

"Oh, he's been in the business a lot longer," she said easily. "Matter of fact, his dad ran a construction company, but retired a few years ago. Floyd came here because he didn't want the hassle of owning his own business."

"Makes sense to me," I muttered.

"Yeah?" Gina asked. "Do you know Floyd?"

"His daughters go to the same elementary school my children do."

"Oh, sure." Her gaze drifted down. "Then you probably knew Sam Helmstetter."

"Yes."

She sighed. "It's so horrible what happened to him. We didn't have much paperwork for him to shred, but I was told to give him whatever we could. 'Nice guys shouldn't always finish last,' the boss said, 'so let's help him out.' "

I was sure both of us were thinking the same thing, that this time a nice guy had indeed finished last. "That was generous," I said.

"Yeah, the boss is okay. He was upset about Sam's murder. Well, everyone was."

"Where I work it was all anyone talked about for a week."

"Same here," Gina said. "Bob said it must be some random thing because no one had any reason to kill Sam, but I don't know if that makes it better or worse. The boss figured it was some crazoid."

"What did Floyd say?"

"Oh, Floyd and his crew were at a site up in Sheboygan that week."

There was probably something appropriate for me to say, but nothing came out. "Um, I didn't know you worked that far away."

"Anywhere in the state," she said. "If you have funding, we'll travel." She rubbed her thumb against the tips of her fingers. "To get back to your renovation, how do you feel about granite countertops? They're kind of expensive, but they sure do look nice."

I tried to make appropriate noises while she talked on about my theoretical project, but all I could think was grateful thoughts that Floyd was in the clear.

As I was getting into the car, my cell phone rang. "It isn't Janis Velona," Marina said. "Turns out she was in the middle of selling a whole freaking fleet of cars to some company in Madison and was there half the night working."

I told her about Floyd. "Well, I didn't think he was right for it, anyway. Have you seen his stuff at the art shows? No one who takes pictures that pretty could kill anyone."

Before I could start arguing against her theory, she clicked off. Almost immediately, the phone rang again. Evan this time. I pulled Marina's list out of my purse and eyed it. "Hullo. What's up?"

"You have the kids this weekend, don't you?" he asked. "Do you have plans for Saturday night?"

The weekend was days away. How could I possibly know what was going on? "I'd have to check the calendar."

"I propose—"

Suddenly, I stopped breathing. Stopped thinking, stopped seeing, stopped everything.

"—that I take all four of us to dinner." He named a restaurant in Madison.

My breath started whooshing through my lungs again. "Jenna and Oliver have never been there." Mostly because eating there cost more than a weekend trip to Door County. "Are you sure? Oliver might be a little young for this."

"He'll be fine," Evan said. "He's a good kid. They're both good kids."

I knew that, but it was pure pleasure to hear other people say so. "Then it's a date." We set a time, chatted a little more, and when I hung up, I found a pen and drew a line through Wheeler's Autos.

Two down, two to go.

The front door of Stull Systems, Inc., stumped me. I stood in front of it, a damp cold breeze ruffling my hair, puzzling over how to get into the building. My knowledge of architecture was limited, but even I knew that the exterior doors of most commercial buildings opened outward. There should be hinges and a doorknob visible to the casual observer. Instead, what I saw was a mass of computer parts. Circuit boards and hard drives and fans and who knew what else covered every square inch of the door. There was nothing to indicate which way the door would swing, and no particular part shouted "Use me for opening!"

Whoever had designed the door had a warped and twisted sense of humor. On a nice summer day this might have been fun, but with a November wind breathing up my pant legs, I wasn't laughing.

I took a few steps backward. Doorknobs were all set on doors at roughly the same height, just a little higher than was comfortable for the average-sized woman, which made the most likely candidate for an opener to be . . . I put my gloved hand on a squarish chunk of circuitry, turned it, and was rewarded with a smooth click and a feeling of Open Sesame.

Inside, the lobby had hard surfaces that echoed each of my steps. Tile floor, hard drywall walls, and a ceiling of unrelenting white made the room feel cold and sterile. I checked the floor behind me to make sure I hadn't tracked in anything. Clean, which was good. Because I was already feeling guilty about the lie I'd prepared: Would Stull Systems consider creating special children's bookstore software? If so, how much might it cost? So much? Oh, dear. Thanks for your time, but I really can't afford that.

"Hi," said the young woman sitting behind the counter. "Can I help you? My name's Devon."

"Interesting door," I said.

"Mr. Stull says it's a test." Devon fiddled with one pen, had another pen tucked over one ear, and yet another pen shoved into her thick auburn curls. "Like, if you can get inside, then you're smart enough to use our software."

"I see."

"Not that it works." She smiled. "Just last week—" Her story was interrupted by the electronic ringing of a phone. "Stull Systems, this is Devon. How may I help you?" Listening, she put down the pen, picked up another, and made a note.

"I'm sorry, sir," she said, "but Mr. Stull is out of the office." She took his name and number and hung up. "Anyway, last week, this guy comes in and—" The phone rang again. "If that phone rings one more time this morning," she said, "I'm going to pull my hair out."

As she took another message, I wondered idly why she didn't send the caller to voice mail.

"Shoot." Devon had hung up and was frowning at a mark she'd made. "Wrong color."

"Color?" Then I noticed that her pens had inks of different colors. Red over her ear, black in her hand, and green in her hair.

"We have different colors for everything." She held up her hands and started ticking off on her fingers.

"There's six. Red, black, green, purple, brown, and orange. I have to write down everything in here." She thumped a thick three-ring binder.

"But you're a software company," I said. "Why aren't you using computers for all this?"

She rolled her eyes. "Tell me and we'll both know. I'm just a temp, and I'll be really glad when this assignment is over. They make me use a typewriter. And look at this." She waved a pink message pad.

"No voice mail?"

"They have it, but Mr. Stull says it can't be trusted. I have to write everything down, then make sure it's shredded later on."

The hairs on the insides of my ears sprang to attention. "You shred a lot of papers?"

"We used to, but now that—" The phone rang. "Excuse me again, okay?"

I looked around. A hallway behind her led to what I assumed were other offices. When she got off the phone, I gestured to the nether regions. "You seem awfully busy. Isn't anyone else here to help?"

"Don't I wish." She slumped a little. "Most of the programmers are at a conference. The vice president is home sick with the flu, and the only other person here is such a computer ge—" She stopped. "I mean, he's so into his work that he's not supposed to answer the phone."

I looked at her approvingly. Young, but tactful. If she knew anything about children's books, I'd have hired her myself. "Are you working a lot of hours with so many people gone?"

"Yeah. I'm supposed to be doing the books, too." She glanced at a teetering stack of papers. "My little sister, Tara? Her birthday is next week, and all I do is work. It's her sixteenth birthday and I wanted to help Mom make it really special."

"Tara?" I asked. "Tara Pettigrew?"

Devon cocked her head to the side. "Do you know her?"

I knew of her. She'd been the star forward on Jenna's hockey team when she was Jenna's age. Though she'd been gone from the team a few years, her legend lingered on. "My daughter is goalie for the Rynwood Raiders."

"Jenna Kennedy?" Devon's face brightened. "She's good."

I beamed. Clearly, Devon was an excellent judge of talent. "And she's only been playing hockey for a year."

"No kidding? That's great. If she keeps at it—" The phone rang again. "I should count all the calls," she said, looking at the phone with loathing, "and ask for a raise." Eyes crossed, she put the receiver to her ear. "Stull Systems."

This was obviously not a good time to talk. I waved and slipped out.

"It's him," Marina said. She plopped down in my office's company chair, squeezing her hips down between its narrow arms.

"Him who?"

"Andrew Bieber. The accountant. He's the one who killed Sam."

Her voice was full of excitement and certainty. The combination troubled me. "Why are you so sure?"

She leaned forward. "These." Her face went still and she stared at me with a concentration she didn't use on anything except rare sirloin steaks.

"Um . . ."

"Look again." She hopped the chair closer and stared at me a second time. "Don't you see?"

What I saw was her eyes starting to dry out from not blinking often enough.

"It's those serial killer eyes," she said impatiently, rubbing her eyelids. "That Andrew Bieber has them big-time."

"Serial killers have special eyes?"

"It's that intensity, that . . . that *look*. Charles Manson has them. Son of Sam has them. Jeffrey Dahmer had them."

I held up a hand to stop her horrible litany. The last thing I needed was more things to haunt my nights. "The way he looks isn't going to mean anything to the Dane County Sheriff's Department. We need evidence. We need proof."

"He has those eyes," Marina said stubbornly.

I flashed back on my morning visit to Stull Systems. Marina felt something was wrong with Andrew Bieber, and I felt a wrongness at Stull Systems. Though I wanted to poke holes all through the serial killer eyes theory, maybe her reaction was justified at a level too visceral to be quantified.

We had two down, and we still had two to go.

"There's something weird at Stull," I said.

"Stull Systems?" a quiet voice asked. "You mean Eric Stull?"

Chapter 16

Marina and I turned to look at Yvonne. She was holding a book in each hand and wearing an apologetic expression. "Sorry," she said. "I didn't mean to eavesdrop. I had a question about which of these would be better for a fourth-grade boy."

The books she held were *Indian in the Cupboard* by Lynne Reid Banks and *Snow Treasure* by Marie McSwigan. "Both are wonderful," I said, perking up at the thought of a real live customer. "Who's buying it for him?" A grandparent might be more inclined to buy *Snow Treasure* since it took place during World War II. A parent might lean more toward *Indian*, and since it was a trilogy, maybe the parent would buy all three and—

"No one," Yvonne said. "I'm just trying to learn our stock."

"Oh." I deflated down to normal size. "That's a great idea."

"Is Stull Systems in trouble?" Yvonne looked from me to Marina and back.

"No. Well, not that I know of."

She smiled at me, a slow quirk. "That didn't have the ring of sincerity."

If my cousin Bill were here, he'd confirm my conclusion: Yvonne had an excellent hooey detector. It was a term we'd come up with as children when one parent or another would claim that eating overcooked vegetables was good for us. "What a bunch of hooey," Bill said one Thanksgiving, and thus was born the hooey detector.

Thanksgiving. The thought was suddenly depressing. The overcrowded Emmerling Thanksgiving I'd been planning for so many weeks had diminished to a simple dinner for five. I wouldn't even have to get out the leaves for the table.

I pulled myself back to the present, where Marina was saying, "Beth? Insincere? What, pray tell, gave it away? The flag she was waving labeled 'I'm lying through my teeth'? Or was it the neon sign over her head flashing 'Liar' and a big red arrow pointing at her head?"

I considered the situation. Looked at Marina. Quirked my eyebrows and tilted my head to Yvonne. "Shall we add a third to the team?"

"Hmm." Marina focused her laserlike stare on the poor woman, who inched backward. Before she could escape, Marina gave a sharp nod. "Great minds think alike," she said, "and somehow so do ours. Young lady, come in and shut the door."

The door closed softly. Come to think of it, everything Yvonne did was quiet. She talked quietly, moved quietly, made only quiet noises. I wanted to ask if she'd always been like that, but was afraid I'd hear prison stories I didn't want to hear—chicken-livered Beth—so I'd never asked.

"What do you know about Stull Systems?" Marina demanded. "Stream of consciousness here. No thinking, just talking."

Yvonne stood there and didn't say a word.

"Come on, woman," Marina said. "You must know something!"

She shook her head. "Sorry. All I know is Eric Stull is president. The person I know there is Violet, the office manager."

"Not today," I said. "Devon Pettigrew is temping."

"She'll be there for a while," Yvonne said. "Violet's having a rough pregnancy."

"Waitaminnut." Marina shoved her cheeks together, mashing her face into an amorphous blob. "Is this Violet Demps you're talking about? She can't be having a baby—she's almost as old as I am."

Yvonne made a small shrug. "All I know is she's five months pregnant."

"How do you know all this?" Marina asked. "*I* didn't know it and Violet goes to my church."

"Well—" Yvonne stopped. "I can trust you, can't I? To keep quiet, I mean? Nothing bad," she said quickly. "It's just confidential."

"Cross my heart and hope to die." Marina drew her index finger across her chest.

I caught Yvonne's doubtful look. "She means it," I said. "She only pretends to be an overgrown thirteen-year-old. Inside she's a trustworthy adult."

"Okay." Her thin shoulders rose and fell. "Okay. Violet is my sponsor. She's a member of Innocent Behind Bars. Have you heard of them? They find people like me who were wrongfully imprisoned, do what they can to get us freed, then help us find our way back into a normal life."

"Sounds like a great group," I said.

"Oh, they are," Yvonne said, and there was more passion in her words than in anything I'd yet heard her say. "Without them I'd be—" She pulled back from herself. "Anyway, Violet helped bring me here and has been wonderful about getting me settled."

"So Violet," Marina said, "knows a lot about Stull Systems."

"She's run the office ever since they started up."

"Then we need to talk to her," I said decisively. "Marina, why don't you call and—"

Marina was shaking her head. "No can do. Remember how big my church is? I know people who know her, is all."

"She's not answering the phone these days anyway," Yvonne said. "Says talking on the phone makes her queasy."

"Oh." Marina looked pained. "One of *those* pregnancies."

"Poor woman." I wondered what our next step would be. If she saw two strange women standing on her front porch, she'd assume we were selling something and not come to the door.

"And she's not answering the door, either," Yvonne said. "Too many people with magazine subscriptions and whatnot, she says."

Marina and I looked at each other. There had to be a way; all we had to do was find it.

"I'll take you over," Yvonne said, "if you like."

"You will?" Marina clasped her hands. "Really, truly, totally, completely?"

Yvonne's shoulders hunched together a little, then relaxed. "Yes. I will."

I studied her. "Why are you doing this? Helping us, I mean."

"Why?" She got an owly look, round and deep and quiet. "Because I know you're trying to right a wrong. That means a lot to me." A flicker of a smile came and went. "But mostly because I owe everything to you two." She looked at her feet. "If you hadn't given me this job, if you hadn't been my friends, I'd still be sitting in that little house all by myself, trying to convince myself that everything will turn out right."

Marina's mouth twisted and I knew she was trying to

keep from crying. There were unshed tears in my own eyes, but they weren't from sentiment; they were out of anger for the sheer waste.

Thanks to the Emmerling ethics handed down from generation to generation, I couldn't stand waste. I used grocery bags multiple times and always made sure to eat leftovers. But the worst waste of all was of time. Yvonne, through no fault of her own, had been forced to throw away precious years. The idea that Claudia and her ilk wanted more of those years to be useless made me angrier than I'd been in a long time.

"Let's go." I stood abruptly.

"Right now?" Yvonne looked at the books still in her hands. "I'm scheduled to work until close."

"Lois can handle things." As if there were anything to handle.

"Hi, ho." Marina smiled, her frame of mind taking a hard turn. "It's the Three Musketeers. One for all and all for one!" Jumping to her feet, she stabbed an invisible foe with an imaginary sword. "Take that, yon knave!" With her foe vanquished, she leapt into a ghostly saddle, picked up her purse for reins, and off she went. "For Harry, England, and Saint George!"

Yvonne stared after her. "Is she always like this?"

"No. Sometimes she turns into Mae West."

"I hope she's not that loud around Violet," Yvonne said, pulling on her coat. "She's really not feeling very good."

"It'll be fine." At least I hoped so.

Violet's house was a lovely renovated bungalow. It was the kind of house that whispers, "Home." It summoned images of cozy fireplaces, window seats, and a kitchen where white cabinets climbed to the ceiling. I spun the brass tab of the old-fashioned doorbell and we listened to the quivering ring.

The three of us waited, and heard nothing.

"Let me do it," Marina said.

She elbowed around me and twisted the doorbell. Again we listened to a fading echo. I was just about to suggest going around to the back door, when Yvonne clutched at my sleeve. "What was that?"

"I didn't hear anything," Marina said.

"Beth, did you?" Yvonne's face was turned toward me, but her attention was focused inside the house. "It sounded like someone in pain."

I shook my head.

"Ooooo."

"There," Yvonne said. "You must have heard that."

But I already had my hand on the doorknob. "It's locked. Let's try the back."

The three of us clattered down the stairs, around the side of the house, and up the back steps. I pushed to the front of the pack and banged on the back door with the side of my fist. "Hello? Violet?"

As I called, I turned the oval doorknob. Unlocked. "Hello?" I pushed the door open and we hustled into the kitchen. Looking past the gray marble countertops and tall white cabinetry, I said, "I'll check upstairs. Marina, you look over there." I gestured to an open archway leading to dining and living rooms. "Yvonne, through there." I nodded at a smaller hallway.

We split like a river flowing around rocks. I clattered up the stairs and barged into a guest bedroom, study, and bathroom, searching quickly, looking carefully, wanting to hurry, wanting to be sure I didn't miss a woman who might be lying on a floor behind a desk, curled up in a small ball. Where was she, where was she . . . ?

"Down here!" Yvonne called.

I rushed down the stairs and followed Marina through the hallway and into a half bath. There, Yvonne was crouching on black and white hexagonal tiles, her arm around Violet's shoulders. Violet herself was kneeling on the floor, leaning over the porcelain toilet bowl and clutching the rim, heaving and gasping. She wore a loose T-shirt, loose sweatpants, and her hair was lank and stringy against her skull.

Marina and I exchanged a glance. I edged between the pedestal sink and the toilet and hunkered down. "Violet? Should I call 911?"

"No." She gulped down air. "My doctor said . . ." Her stomach spasmed, but whatever she'd eaten was long gone. She wiped her mouth with the back of her hand. "He said this would happen." She clutched her burgeoning midsection. "It'll pass . . . ooohh . . . in a minute. It always does."

Yvonne gave me a worried look. "Shouldn't we at least call her doctor?"

"No," Marina and I said.

"But she's sick!"

"Only in the morning," Marina said.

Yvonne frowned. "It's three thirty in the afternoon."

"Not if you're pregnant."

"If . . ." Yvonne looked at Violet with a dawning understanding in her eyes. "She has morning sickness."

"There's nothing morning . . . ahhh . . . about it." Violet closed her eyes. "Stupidest name ever."

"But we have to do something!"

Marina smiled. "We can tell childbirth stories."

"We will not," I said. "Yvonne, stay with Violet. Marina, come with me."

The two of us traipsed to the kitchen, where we opened drawers until we found some dishcloths. I ran cold water over two of them while Marina dug ice out of the freezer. "Quit with the childbirth stories," I scolded. "That's the last thing Violet wants to hear right now."

"Just passing on what was passed on to me," she said

airily. "I couldn't sleep for a week after my aunt Dorothy told me about—"

"Not listening." I twisted water out of the dishcloths and opened them flat on the counter. Marina laid down a wide row of ice cubes and I wrapped them up. Ice-wrapped cloths were Marina's best weapon for morning sickness recovery. If it didn't help, she always said, at least the cold would distract you.

We went back to the bathroom. Violet had slumped to a sitting position in the corner. I crouched beside her. "This is going to feel cold, okay?" I held the cloth against her forehead.

She groaned at the chill but didn't move away. The three of us waited, watching Violet's face. Her misery was etched into the grooves around her mouth and the set of her chin.

Please let this help, I thought. This poor woman needs some relief. Let the ice ease her misery. Let her lean on us. Let her accept our empathy. Let her baby be strong and healthy and happy.

"Oooo." Violet clutched the cloth with both hands, and my muscles tensed in readiness to move aside. I did not want to be between her and the toilet. "Oooo," she said again. "That feels good."

Marina and Yvonne and I smiled at each other. The newly formed Three Musketeers had saved the day. Hip, hip, hooray!

"Wow." Violet shifted the cloth around. "This feels incredibly good. I owe you guys. I'd offer you my first-born child, but I don't have one yet." She patted her belly and uncovered one eye. "Hey, Yvonne." The single eye darted at me, then Marina. "You go to my church. Marnie? No, Marina. That's it. Like with boats."

Her growing puzzlement was obvious. Why are these three women here? They may be saintlike in their ability to ease my pain, but why in the heck are they in my bathroom?

I gave her what I hoped was a reassuring smile. "My name is Beth Kennedy. I own the Children's Bookshelf."

"Oh. Sure. You hired Yvonne." She gave a very small nod. When in the throes of morning sickness, quick movements were not a good idea. "Nice to meet you."

A giggle tried to escape, but I caught it and sent it away. "I want to thank you," I said, "for helping Yvonne transition back into . . . into civilian life."

"You're welcome." She smiled faintly. "I've been involved with Innocent Behind Bars for years. It was wonderful to help someone personally."

"How wonderful?" I asked.

"Um . . ." She shifted the cloths. "Well, very, I guess. How do you mean?"

"What if Yvonne's job was in jeopardy? What if she wasn't sure she'd be able to make it in Rynwood? Able to make it anywhere?" I was laying it on a little thick, but sometimes exaggeration is the best way to get a point across. It was a technique I'd learned from my best friend.

Frowning, Violet looked from me to Yvonne to Marina and back around again. "What's wrong?"

"A very vocal group is boycotting the bookstore," I said. "Picketing. Their signs say the town won't be safe until Sam's killer is brought to justice. Worse, they imply that a killer works at the store. We haven't had a customer in days."

"Oh, no." Violet looked stricken. "It's been a week since I've left the house. I had no idea." She turned to look at Yvonne, wincing at the motion. "Is there anything I can do?"

"Help us put Sam Helmstetter's killer in jail," I said.

"Once he's put away, the boycott will disappear." The memories would linger, but I wasn't going to think about that.

"But I don't know anything about Sam's death." She was clearly bewildered.

I leaned closer and lowered my voice. "You might know more than you think. I spent some time at Stull Systems. The temp, Devon, was very helpful." I lifted my eyebrows. "It's interesting that none of the phone calls are logged into a computer. Did you work out that system, or did Eric Stull set it up that way?"

"Ooohh, nooo." Violet's face went a shade paler. I helped her up to a kneeling position. She grabbed the porcelain rim and hauled herself close. "I hate this I hate this I will never have another child why did I ever want a baby why"—she paused to take a heaving, gasping breath—"why does this happen why does anything happen? Ooooo . . ."

The three of us averted our eyes and tried not to hear the next event.

Wordlessly, Marina scooped the lukewarm dishcloths off the floor and rinsed them with cool water. I took them from her, went down on my knees next to Violet, and held them against her forehead. "What's going on at Stull?" I asked. "There's something wrong there, and I want to know what it is."

She shook her head, then went even paler. "I'm going to be sick again." She leaned over the toilet bowl and retched.

No morning sickness should be this bad. Holding her hair back, I looked up at my co-Musketeers, who were edging away. "I don't suppose either one of you knows the name of her doctor?" Marina and Yvonne shook their heads. "Go find it," I ordered. "Look for appointment cards. Kitchen calendar. The refrigerator. A desk. Look in her purse if you have to."

They shot out the door, leaving me to wipe Violet's forehead and murmur words of kind sympathy. "It'll be all right," I said. "We'll take care of you."

"No," she moaned. "It's a secret. Can't tell, promised I'd never tell. Ten years and I haven't told. It's Eric's secret, I can't tell, I can't—"

"Shhh," I whispered, stroking her hair. "I know you can't tell. A secret is a secret."

She moaned again. "So sorry. Sorry, sorry, sorry."

"I know." I put my arms around her quivering shoulders, and the two of us rocked back and forth. "I know you're sorry. It's okay."

"Got it!" Yvonne appeared in the doorway, waving a business card. "Marina's on the phone right now."

Ten minutes later we were buckling Violet into the backseat of Marina's van and I was calling Violet's husband, reassuring him that his wife was fine, telling him that he should meet us at the doctor's office. I clicked off my cell phone and clambered into the front passenger seat.

"You did it again," Marina said.

"Did what?"

But she only chuckled and drove us away.

Chapter 17

"Mom? Earth to Mom. Hello?"

It was bad enough when Jenna said that, but now Oliver was picking it up. I'd long ago decided that forbidding them from using the phrase wasn't a battle worth fighting, so I wrenched myself away from the theory that Violet became an Innocent Behind Bars volunteer to compensate for the secret she was keeping and smiled at my son. "Yes, dear?"

He looked at the waiter, who was poised, pen in hand. "He asked what you want."

"Twice," Jenna said.

I glanced at Evan, who was trying not to smile. "Sorry," I said to the waiter.

"No problem, ma'am. Would you like me to repeat tonight's specials?"

Evan chuckled and I repressed an urge to kick him under the table. The linen tablecloth would hide most of the movement, but Jenna's legs were getting long enough to be anywhere at any given moment, and I didn't want to hit the wrong person. "No, thank you," I told the waiter. "The trout will be fine. Rice instead of potato, please, and low-fat Italian dressing on the salad. Thank you."

I watched as Jenna ordered a steak, baked potato with sour cream, salad with ranch dressing, and nodded approvingly when she ended her order with a please and thank you. Oliver stumbled over the almandine part of his trout request, but sailed easily into a switch from potato to French fries and got a smile from the waiter when he requested "bluey cheese crumbles" on his salad. After Evan ordered his meal and we handed over the menus, the kids leaned toward me.

"Did I do it right?" Oliver whispered.

"You did fine."

"Maybe I shouldn't have asked for sour cream," Jenna said in a low voice. "I don't want to get fat."

Evan opened his mouth, but I jumped in first. "Honey, do you trust me?"

She gave me a look. "Most of the time."

"No, way down in your stomach"—I pointed at my own—"do you trust me? Do you believe that I want you to grow up strong and smart and fast? Do you believe that I'll do whatever I can to make sure you're the best goalie ever?"

"I guess so."

"Then believe me when I say you can have all the sour cream you want."

Her smile wiped all anxiety from her face. "Okay. Thanks, Mom."

I wanted to pull her close and give her a hard mothering hug, but the restaurant's ambiance didn't encourage such behavior. Instead I gave her a warm mom smile. "You're very welcome."

The waiter came by with crayons and heavy pieces of blank white paper for the kids. Jenna curled her lip briefly at such childish things, but when Oliver called for the blue crayon, she called for the red, and they were off.

"So I hear you took Violet Demps to the doctor the other day," Evan said.

"Um . . . that's right. We did." There were two reasons I hadn't told Evan about the incident. Number one, he'd have asked why I was there in the first place. Number two, he'd ask why I was there in the first place. "Beth," he'd say in that serious voice. "Remember what happened last time you got yourself involved in a murder investigation." I couldn't stand the serious voice; it reminded me of Richard.

"We?" Evan asked. "You and who else?" His mouth quirked up. "Let me guess. Marina."

"And Yvonne," I said.

He raised his eyebrows. "The woman from California? The one who—"

I cut in. "Yes. She knows Violet and . . . and wanted to introduce us to her." Not a complete lie, but I could feel my earlobes warming up. Maybe Evan wouldn't notice. But if the speculative look on his face was any indication, he already had and was in the process of formulating his next question.

"Hey, Beth."

I looked at the stranger standing next to the table, then something went *click*. "Hey, Pete."

Pete Peterson, almost unrecognizable in suit and tie, smiled at me and nodded at Evan. "Last time I saw you, you were in a tux."

I introduced the two men and started to ask Pete a vague social question about the weather, but Oliver started squabbling with Jenna over the crayons. "Let me have the brown."

"I'm using it."

"You are not!"

"I will in a second. Leave it alone."

Oliver's hand snaked out and I reached over to tap

his knuckles. "What did we talk about at home?" I asked quietly.

"No fighting in the restaurant," he said to the tablecloth.

"And are you?"

"All I want is—"

"Oliver," I said, "no fighting means no fighting. Okay?"

He nodded. I gave Jenna a stern warning look, and turned back to Pete. "Sorry. What are—" But I was talking to air. Pete was on the other side of the room, escorting a woman to a quiet table in a dark corner.

I watched him wave away the waiter and pull out a chair for his date. Though I couldn't see her face, she was slim and tanned. From here I couldn't tell if it was from a tanning booth or from an extended visit to sunny climates. Marina would be able to analyze such a thing at half a mile, but all I could tell was that I felt sickly white by comparison.

"How do you know him?" Evan was watching me watch Pete.

"What? Who?" A thought that was only half a thought flew away and was free, gone forever. "Pete? He runs Cleaner-Than-Pete's. I hired him last year."

"Before we met?" Evan smiled and reached for my hand.

As his warm skin touched mine, my cell phone started chirping. "Sorry." I reached for my purse. "Forgot. I'll turn it off." But I couldn't help looking at the display. I stood up. "Be right back. Kids, be good."

I hurried to the women's restroom and punched number 5 on my speed dial.

"Hey, sis," Darlene said. "Took you long enough."

"What's the matter?" She'd texted me with a call-soon-urgent message. "Are you all right? Is Mom okay?"

She laughed. "Why do you always assume the worst?"

"Because then I'll be prepared when it happens. What's so urgent that I had to leave my children alone with Evan in a restaurant with white tablecloths?"

Darlene whistled. "Is he going to propose?"

"Don't be silly."

"Don't be so sure. You're smart, funny, still relatively young, and almost pretty. I'm surprised he hasn't proposed already. Let's plan for a June wedding. I'll drive Mom down after Christmas and we can go to Chicago for your dress."

I raised my eyes heavenward. Sisters. "Darlene, I'm kind of busy. What do you want?"

She sighed. "I can't make it to Thanksgiving."

"You . . . what?" She couldn't have said what I thought she said. No way could every single member of my family have backed out on Thanksgiving dinner. It wasn't possible.

"Sorry, kiddo. I really am. But I just brought Roger home from the med center. He's got that horrible flu and they say it runs for at least a week. He's a mess." She paused. "Beth, are you there?"

I wanted to understand, and most of me did. But there was also a part of me that was hurt very badly. Words I wanted to say crowded into my mouth, and I put my hand over my lips to keep them inside, because saying them would burn wounds that might take years to heal.

How can you do this to me?

Why are you abandoning me?

Why is my happiness so easily traded away?

It was then that my half-formed thought circled around and came home to roost.

"No," I said slowly. "I'm not mad. Much."

She blew a big sigh into the phone. "Look, I want to be there, you know I do. And maybe we can get together for Christmas. I'll make a big batch of Grandma Emmerling's cookies; those were always your favorites." She talked on and on, but I wasn't listening.

Because I had an idea. And I was making a plan.

Monday morning I made up busywork tasks for Yvonne and Lois. Ten minutes later I was breezing through the intricate door of Stull Systems.

"Hi, Mrs. Kennedy!" Devon's smile was wide. "I hear your Jenna had an awesome game Saturday afternoon. Four to zero, that's so great."

"Shutout," I said proudly. "Her first ever." At dinner, Evan had proposed a toast to Jenna, and she'd blushed a brighter red than I'd thought possible. "The other day she asked if I thought she could get a college scholarship."

"Bet she could," Devon said.

"Really?"

"Sure. I've seen her in action. She's got natural instincts. Anticipates like crazy. She could go a long way."

Visions of Olympic medals danced in my head. "Are you sure?"

She grinned. "I'm assistant coach for the Madison Skippers. Believe me, I know Jenna's good."

I clutched the edge of the counter and fake gasped. "The enemy!"

Her laughter filled the lobby. "No, *you're* the enemy. Didn't you know?"

Her next question would be what could she do for me. Time to put the Plan into action. "When I stopped by the other day," I said, "I didn't tell you I own the Children's Bookshelf. I was wondering if Stull Systems would consider writing children's bookstore software. What we use is geared to full-range bookstores and we could use a new product."

Not a complete lie; we could use something different than the fifteen-year-old software running on rapidly aging computers. Of course, I didn't see how specialized software would help the store in any way, shape, or form, but it was a reason to talk to Devon.

"Oh, wow. I don't know." She opened a three-ring binder and started flipping pages. "This is the catalog. Everything Stull does is medical. Wait. Here's a . . . No, that's for veterinarians." She hummed as she turned pages. "No, nothing like that. Tell you what—"

The phone rang and she excused herself to answer. After she'd written a message, she put the slip atop a pile of similar slips, which was next to a towering pile of papers, which was next to another stack of papers. "There. Now, I was saying—" The phone rang again. She rolled her eyes, picked up the phone, and wrote down a message.

During my phone call with Darlene, the tiny lightbulb that occasionally blinked on in my brain had gone bright white. Devon had hockey knowledge that Jenna could use. Devon needed help with organization, help that I could provide, and in providing such, could gain knowledge that I could use.

Ostentatiously, I looked left and right, then leaned over the counter and beckoned her close. "Devon," I said softly. "How about a trade?"

Fifteen minutes later, I'd ensconced myself in Eric Stull's office with a foot-high pile of papers. When Devon had led me to a small conference room, I'd hesitated in the doorway. "I have an idea. What do you think about sorting these in Mr. Stull's office?"

She made a face. "I'm not supposed to touch anything in there."

"You wouldn't," I said soothingly. "And I won't. But that way I could see how he files things, and he made up the filing system, right?" Without waiting for an answer, I headed back down the hallway. "This is his office, isn't it?" I set the pile down carefully on the corner of Eric's empty desk and pulled up the guest chair. "All I'll do is peek into his files."

"Well, I suppose it might be okay."

"It'll be fine." I put on the special mom smile that was guaranteed to comfort and console. There's nothing less threatening than a mom in calming mode. The knowledge is one of our secret weapons. "What harm can I do?"

"That's true." Devon nodded. "Thanks a zillion for helping me out. I'll ask around for someone who'll give goalie lessons."

I smiled. The barter system was alive and well.

The phone rang. "Oh, rats," Devon said. "Got to go."

As soon as I saw the light on Eric's phone turn from blinking white to solid red, I jumped out of the chair and hurried around the large expanse of desktop. Eric's chair was tall-backed and leather and I felt like an imposter in it. Which I was, but I didn't like feeling that way.

I opened the large file drawer on the lower right side of the desk and rifled through its contents. Everything I could read had to do with clients or conferences or shareholders. Everything I couldn't read was in Spanish.

"Oh, dear." The only time I came close to using my three years of high school Spanish was at an ATM when I accidentally pressed the ESPAÑOL button instead of the ENGLISH one.

I opened the rest of the drawers and found office supplies, a pile of coins, and some empty candy wrappers. "Now what, smarty-pants?" I glanced at the phone. The light was still red, and there was another light winking away, so I ventured deeper into Eric territory.

The wall behind his desk was lined with bookshelves and cabinetry. The bookshelves were full of textbooks, software documentation, and three-ring binders filled with software coding. Behind the door of cabinet number one were stacks of paper much like the stack I'd put on his desk. Behind door number two was more paper, but also a framed photo of a man and two young girls.

I looked at the telephone—one red light, two white—and picked up the picture. It was taken on a lakeshore and all three were in swimsuits and life jackets. The man had his arms around the girls and they were all grinning hugely.

"So that's Eric Stull," I said quietly. It was the man at the dance who'd been in line in front of Jenna and me. The man who'd slapped down a hundred-dollar bill and then another fifty. His dark blond hair was cut short and his stomach was flatter than most men's his age. I studied the photo, trying to look into his head, read his thoughts, and analyze his personality, but all I saw was a father and his daughters after an afternoon of inner tubing.

As I put the photo back from whence it came, I realized there weren't any pictures of Rosie, his wife. Strange. Or not?

"What are you doing?" Devon stood in the doorway. "I thought you weren't going to touch anything." There was a note of censure in her voice.

I put on a reassuring smile and shut the cabinet door. "Just looking for some paper clips. It'll make sorting those papers easier if I have a way to keep similar topics together. Unless you want me to use a stapler."

"No staples. Mr. Stull says so. Paper clips are good, though. I'll be right back."

Mr. Stull had a lot of rules. I sat myself back in the guest chair. To meet my end of the bargain, I had to sort these papers into some semblance of order. I'd convinced Devon of my capabilities when I'd mentioned how much lists helped me organize my life.

"Mr. Stull loves lists," she'd said eagerly. "You must think like him. Let's give this a try."

Her confidence in me was heartening, and probably misplaced. But I couldn't tell her that, so I settled down and was busy sorting papers when she came back with a box of paper clips. She hovered, then went back out front when the phone rang.

Anything with a lot of numbers went into one pile. Anything in Spanish went into another. Phone notes here, mail there. Junk faxes I tossed into a recycling pile. No possible way could Mr. Stull want to know about a $99 cruise to the Bahamas. Order now for four days and three nights!

Half an hour later, I'd sorted through the main pile. I got up, stretched, and started in on the stack of numbers. I spread the sheets out across the large desk and tried to make sense of it all. Bills here, statements there. Undecipherable printouts from spreadsheets way over there.

I looked at it all from the point of view of a business owner and saw nothing out of the ordinary, other than some statements from banks with Spanish names. I tried to see it as a law enforcement officer—suspicious and looking for wrongdoing—and didn't see anything. But since I wasn't a member of the police force, maybe I wouldn't have known suspicious activity if it was in bright red letters.

Sighing, I paper-clipped the differentiated piles and stacked them to one side.

When the phone light was red, I got up and turned on Eric's computer. As I'd expected, it was password protected, and all the combinations I tried got me nowhere but nervous. What if he'd programmed the thing to take surreptitious pictures of someone trying to access his computer? I gave up and shut it down.

Next was the Spanish pile. Hadn't I seen . . . yes, there it was. A Spanish-English dictionary. Hooray for Beth's habit of examining all book titles in a room! With the dictionary and about two weeks of time, I'd be able to decipher every paper in the pile.

I scanned a few sentences of each sheet, then opened the dictionary and started searching for key words. I soon found out that Eric's dictionary didn't contain any of the words I wanted it to.

"Silly thing," I told it, and turned to the copyright page: 1989. Which could explain a lot if the words I was trying to translate were software-type words. I tried the same thing with other letters in the pile, and got as far as figuring out that somebody was trying to sell Eric a ranch in a remote location in an undisclosed country.

"Sure," I murmured. "I'll buy, too, if the price is right."

On to the phone messages. First I arranged them in chronological order, then I went through them slowly, looking for patterns, names, anything.

"Eva called." 10:15 a.m., Wednesday.

"Eva called." 11:05 a.m., Wednesday.

"Eva called." 11:25 a.m., Wednesday.

These I set aside. Some unfortunate soul must have been struggling with a tragic software problem. Poor woman.

I continued to sort. There were messages from computer dealers and messages from clients. There were lots of messages from salespeople, a couple of messages from Rosie, and a couple from the girls, Amelia and Chelsea, and a couple from someone named Chago.

I repressed an urge to toss all the slips into the air and run away before they landed.

"There has to be something here," I said.

Not true, of course. I just wanted there to be something. I needed something tangible, some slip of proof, some indication of . . . something.

Fatigue was creeping up my back. I stretched, gazing at the sorted piles of phone messages. There was a secret; Violet had said so. And I had it on good authority—

mine—that anything said in the midst of morning sickness was the absolute truth.

There was a secret here. All I had to do was find it.

"Right," I said. "Come out, come out, wherever you are."

"Are you okay?" Devon asked.

No, I wasn't. I was hungry, tired of looking at papers, scared for Yvonne, nervous for my finances, and terrified about the future in general. "Fine, thanks." I glanced at my watch. "If you wanted to run to get some lunch, I'll pay."

"Really?" Her eyes lit up. "Fast food or the Tractor?"

We settled on the Tractor. Soup and salad for me, burger and fries for her. I handed over a twenty-dollar bill. "Be right back," she said, and left me in Eric's office, where I'd be alone for a solid fifteen minutes.

I stood. If I was a secret, where would I hide? In a locked drawer, probably, but there weren't any here. Maybe it was a purloined secret, and all I had to do was open my eyes. I swept my gaze over walls, desk, and cabinetry. Nothing. The only thing on the walls were two framed Ansel Adams prints. In the name of being thorough, I looked at the backs of the prints. Nothing. The desk, when I'd arrived, had been empty of everything except a desk blotter–sized calendar.

Hmm.

I restacked the papers and exposed the month of November. The first and last weeks had red lines through them with the letters *SA* written at the left side. The rest of the weekdays were filled with cryptic notes. "NC mtg, 10." "Cnf cl, 2." "Stf mtg, 8."

Some of those I understood. Conference call. Staff meeting. But NC meeting could be a meeting in North Carolina, or it could be a new client meeting, or it could be a no charge meeting, or it could be a new code meeting for the company's programmers.

"Nothing, nothing, nothing," I muttered, restacking the papers. The breeze my frustration created sent a message twirling to the floor.

"Got it." Devon lunged and snatched it one-handed before it hit carpet. "Uh-oh. Purple. I'm supposed to shred all the purple ones." She set my lunch on the corner of the desk and laid the change on top of the white foam container.

A clue, Watson, a clue! "What's so special about the purples?"

She looked at the paper. "No idea. The whole color thing is goofy, if you ask me."

Yesterday she'd mentioned the color coding and I'd forgotten all about it. Bad Beth. "How do you know what color to use? Did Violet leave you directions?"

She shook her head. "Nothing on paper. Mr. Stull kept saying if I have to write things down, I wasn't right for the job. But, geez, how am I supposed to keep track of all this stuff?" She threw out her hands. "Red for billing. Black or blue for vendors. Green for . . . oh, shoot, what's green for? Oh, yeah. Clients. Purple is for people who don't leave a company name. Brown for nonpaying clients, and orange when anyone from the government calls."

"And what colors get shredded?"

"All of them," she said promptly. "Just at different times. Red at the end of the month. Green, when they're a week old. Purple, when they're older than one day. And I don't remember for brown and orange, I just don't." Her hair was coming down out of its braid. She shoved a strand back behind her ear, but it came right back out. "The last time I put a box out for Mr. Helmstetter, I'm sure some stuff went out that shouldn't have." She pushed at her hair. "I was so scared that something really important got shredded that I almost got sick. Mr. Stull seemed really mad until I said it was all stuff in Spanish."

My heart thumped hard against my rib cage. "Can you read Spanish?"

"Mr. Stull asked me that. I don't know any Spanish other than *uno*, *dos*, *tres*. I thought it might cost me the job, but he seemed okay with it."

Devon didn't read Spanish, but Sam did. Sam had often talked up the benefits of learning a second language. Sam's minor in college was Spanish. Sam had been featured in the newspaper annually for leading mission trips to Mexico. Everybody in town knew Sam could speak fluent Spanish.

And now Sam was dead.

"When is Mr. Stull expected back?" I asked. "According to his calendar he should be here today."

But Devon was shaking her head. "That's just the calendar he figures ahead with. Most of his appointments he doesn't even write down. Says they're safer in here." She tapped her temple with her index finger.

"Where is he?"

"At home. He said his wife was sick. And I think they're going away for Thanksgiving." She stood there, looking at the piles of papers. "Do you think he'll be mad at me? There's an awful lot I'm doing wrong."

Welcome to the club.

"You're doing your best," I said. "No one can fault you for trying your hardest."

"I am trying." She brightened a bit. "Really hard."

"Then you might as well stop worrying."

"Okay." She grinned. "Worrying doesn't do any good, anyway. I mean, if you can do something, go ahead and do it, right? If you can't do anything, what's the point of making yourself all nuts with worry?" She cocked her head. "Phone. Gotta go."

What was the point indeed? Devon was a lot smarter than I was.

I picked up the purple message she'd left behind. Red,

black, blue, green, purple, brown, orange. With a mind empty of ideas, I sorted the messages into piles of colored pens, then spread out the purple ones, one by one.

Why would purple messages want to be shredded after a day? I closed my eyes and thought of possibilities.

Because they weren't important.

Because they were top secret.

Because they were important and the calls would have been returned immediately.

Try as I might, I couldn't come up with any other reasons. I opened my eyes and looked at the purple names, none of which came with a last name or a company name. Rosie. Chago. Eva. Amelia. Chelsea. Rafael.

Rosie Stull, Eric's wife. No reason for her to leave a last name. Amelia and Chelsea, Eric's daughters. Same thing.

But who was Eva? And Chago and Rafael?

None of the slips from Rosie or the girls had a phone number, which made sense. Only one of Eva's slips had a number, and it had an extra set of digits at the front. An international call then, but since the only foreign country I'd ever set foot in was Canada, the number didn't mean anything to me.

Eva, Chago, and Rafael.

They could be South American clients. But if so, why wouldn't they leave a company name and a phone number?

Because they were really good clients and didn't feel the need?

I was never going to figure this out. Never.

"Eat," I told myself. "Food will help."

I slid the change Devon had returned into my purse and flipped up the white lid. A coin I hadn't noticed rolled off, onto the desk, and down onto the floor. The quarter rolled and rolled and rolled.

If it had been a penny, I wouldn't have moved. A

nickel probably wouldn't have inspired me to action, either, or even a dime. But a quarter? That was real money.

I went down on my hands and knees. Where had the little bugger gone? Ah. There. Waaaay over, directly under the middle of the desk. Naturally.

I turned to a sitting position, held the edge of the desk with one hand to keep my back off the floor, and stretched as far as my arm would stretch. "The things I'd do for a quarter." I stretched a little more.

My hand started to slip off the desk and I made a quick double grab. But instead of solidifying my grip, I latched on to Eric's calendar and pulled the whole thing onto the top of my head.

Papers that I'd just carefully organized came cascading down, and the two months left in the calendar fluttered like wings.

I sat there, papers surrounding me, and thought about joining the circus. Nothing bad ever happened in a circus. I could take tickets. The kids could learn acrobatics. A win-win situation for all.

"Are you okay?" Devon hurried in. "Oh, my goodness! What happened?"

"Um, I was reaching for . . ." The quarter, firmly caught between thumb and index finger mere seconds ago, was gone. "For something. And I fell." I gave her a sheepish smile. "Slid right off the edge of the chair. Silly, huh?"

Devon was already picking up the loose papers. "I did that once in the middle of biology class. Thought I was going to die of embarrassment."

"Everyone has . . ." Between the calendar's November and December pages, tucked in at the top, was a photo. I whisked it out of view. "Everyone has a moment like that in their life. With any luck you're already done."

"Hope so." Devon helped me to my feet. "Are you sure you're okay? You look a little red." She tapped her cheeks.

"Embarrassment will do that to you."

"Yeah. Give me a yell if you need anything." She ran off to answer the phone.

I slid the snapshot out from under the calendar and took a long, slow look at the people in the picture. Looked at the back. "Eva and the boys," someone had written. I laid the photo down next to Eric's calendar notes and studied them both. Same handwriting, no question.

Violet had said there was a secret here. I thought again about the purple message slips. Who wouldn't bother leaving a last name? A long-term client, a good friend, or a family member.

But clients were green.

I spread out the slips from Eva. She'd called every twenty minutes. What good friend would call that often? None. What family member would? Only a wife. A wife . . .

Eva and the boys.

"Oh . . ."

Things went *click* in my head.

Click.

Eric Stull ran an international software company.

Click.

The company was doing business in South America.

Click.

Eric had a second family there.

Click.

Sam was killed because he could have read about Eric's South American wife and children.

Click.

Eric's schedule said he was headed to South America next week.

And one last, solid *click.*

"He's never coming back," I said out loud.

Chapter 18

My fingers were fumbly with cold as I tried to speed-dial Marina's house. "C'mon, fingers, work." Though my car's heater was cranked to high, it was going to take a few minutes to combat the thirty-degree temperature. Finally, I pushed the right buttons. As soon as the line opened up I started talking as fast as I could.

"Marina, don't talk, just listen. Eric Stull killed Sam. Meet me—"

"You have reached the Neff household," Marina's DH droned. "Please leave a message and we'll—"

I clicked him off and pushed at the number for Marina's cell phone. Voice mail there, too.

I clutched my phone and yelled at it. "What good are you if I can't talk to anyone?" The phone made a satisfying *clunk* when I heaved it onto the passenger seat.

Now what?

I held my gloved hands in front of the lukewarm air pouring out of the vent and tried to think.

Where could Marina possibly be that she wasn't answering either of her phones? Fear twitched its hairy fingers and I shivered. What if Marina had gone outside for the mail and slipped on the ice? What if she was lying in the driveway, hidden from public view by the shrubbery? What if—

"You moron," I said out loud. It was a half day for Tarver. This morning at breakfast the kids had been all bouncy in anticipation of one of Mrs. Neff's surprise trips. These could range from stone-skipping contests to llama rides. Marina was undoubtedly at this very minute driving my children and the other day-care kids to an adventure they'd never forget. Marina, ultra-responsible while driving, would never answer her cell phone and might not check messages until all were home safe and sound.

So Marina was out. Should I talk to Gus? He'd take notes and promise to check things out, but would he take this seriously? Maybe, maybe not.

I could call Deputy Wheeler, but her response would be even more tepid than Gus's. If I'd cultivated a friendship with the deputy, things might have been different, but I couldn't get past the conviction that she thought I was a bubble-brained suburban mom who had nothing better to do than dream up wacko theories about my neighbors. No, Deputy Wheeler was way down on the list of people to call.

I put the car into Drive and headed to the Stulls' house. Maybe Rosie would be there. Maybe she'd have a rock-solid alibi for Eric and I could go on my merry way. Maybe talking to her—without giving away what I knew—would help me make sense of all this.

As I drove, snow started falling. First it came in flakes so scattered that you could pretend they didn't exist. Then the flakes came thicker and faster and wetter and I had to turn on the windshield wipers to see the road.

Swipe, swipe, swipe. At each swipe the windshield cleared, only to become completely obscured before the next time the wipers came around.

I flipped them to high and slowed way down. Safe

driving. "But I'm in a hurry!" I banged the steering wheel. "Why are you snowing? We never get two storms in November. We hardly ever get one!"

The snow paid no attention to me, so I slowed a little more and concentrated on my driving.

The few vehicles on the road in midafternoon on a suddenly snowy day were also driving slowly. At least most of them were. Every so often someone would pass, slopping windshields with slush and risking a multicar crash. I swerved to avoid an oncoming van. "Hope you have four-wheel drive," I scolded it. "And you better be wearing your seat belt."

Cars were rapidly pushing the snow into linear heaps that made driving difficult at best, dangerous at worst, and I was glad to turn onto the side road where the Stulls lived. If Rosie was home, I'd ask if she wanted to help with the mini-golf event. No? How about the senior story project? Easy enough to sidetrack into talk about her husband. Easy enough to ask some pointed questions.

I crept down the block, peering though the snow at all the large houses, which were all looking very similar under a layer of snow. I squinted at the house numbers. What was the Stulls' address? No idea. Their house was light gray, I remembered. Two stories, lots of dormer windows, a three-car garage. Which didn't exactly narrow it down in this neighborhood.

In one driveway a bundled-up figure was out snowblowing, flinging snow halfway across the yard in a long and chunky arc. If I couldn't find the Stulls' house, I could always stop and ask him.

But five drives farther down, someone was shoveling. Even in a thick coat, navy blue hat, and boots, he looked thin and frail. I took my foot off the accelerator and slowed. A nice quiet shoveler was much more approachable than a noisy snowblower.

As I was rolling to a stop, the person shoveling staggered, stood, staggered again, and fell to the ground.

I was out of the car in an instant, running up the driveway, trying to remember my long-ago lessons in CPR. Why, *why* hadn't I taken a refresher course? Every year people had heart attacks while shoveling snow. I just hoped that this little old man didn't die because of my lack of training.

I dropped to my knees in the snow. "Are you okay?" I touched his shoulder. "Do you need help?"

The navy blue hat turned to face me. "Beth?"

Not a little old man at all. I was such a moron. "Rosie, what's wrong?"

"Just a . . . little sick."

Her voice was weak. She started to push herself up and dropped back down. "Eric said I should . . . shovel before it . . . snowed too much. But I'm . . . so tired."

"Here, let me." I helped her sit up. "You okay like that? We have to get you up and inside. Ready?" With my inexpert assistance, she stood, wavered, gripped my hand, and finally stood almost steady.

"Um, is anyone else home?" I asked. If Eric Stull was home, letting his sick wife shovel, he was going to get an earful.

"No, Eric and—" She doubled over, groaning, clutching my hand as if it alone could save her.

"Let's get you lying down," I said. "I'll help you inside. Up the stairs, there you go. How about the couch in the living room? A few more steps and you'll be . . . there."

I pulled off her boots, slipped off her hat and coat, and laid her back against a pile of pillows. She clutched at a fuzzy blanket on the back of the couch and I spread it over her. The hand-to-forehead test showed she didn't have much of a fever, and she didn't seem to be in great distress.

"Have you been to the doctor?" I asked.

"No," she said in a faint voice. "It's just flu. Came on yesterday after supper."

I frowned. Flu meant fever. There were exceptions, but still. "Are you sure?"

She gave a small nod. "It's been going around."

"Aches and pains?"

"Dizzy a lot." She put her hands to her head, pushing her thick dark blond hair tight to her skull, then wiped at her eyes. "Even lying down . . ." Her voice trailed off. "Could you get me some water?" she whispered. "I'm really thirsty."

"Right away." I crossed the living room and formal dining room, and pushed the swinging door that led into the kitchen. Drinking glasses were in a glass-fronted cabinet next to the sink, and as I ran the water cold, I saw a laptop opened on a small desk next to the refrigerator.

Quickly, I typed Rosie's symptoms into a search engine and hit return. They were so generic I expected thousands of hits, and that's what I got.

I filled a glass with cold water and took it back to Rosie. "Is there anything else I can get you? Anything to eat?"

"No . . . not hungry."

"Let me get you some ice cubes for that water."

I hurried back to the laptop and added "loss of appetite" to Rosie's list of symptoms.

This time, there weren't nearly as many hits. And there was a common theme.

"Oh, no," I whispered. "He poisoned her."

I sat there, staring at the screen. Eric had poisoned Rosie. But how? With what?

Panic fluttered in my chest, but I ignored it. There was no time to be scared.

I ran the search engine a few more times, looking for

common household items that were poisonous. Prescription drugs, household cleaners, paint thinner, weed killer. The list was long, but I sensed the fastest way to help Rosie—and to show her what her husband had done—was to find some evidence.

"Beth?" Rosie called.

I ignored her and rushed down the hall to the master suite. The bathroom cabinet held only two prescriptions. One for birth control, and one for an antibiotic that had Amelia's name on it. Neither was likely to cause Rosie's symptoms.

I scrabbled through the bathroom garbage, looking for wrappers, receipts, anything, and found nothing but used facial tissues.

What next? I pressed my hands to the sides of my head. Where next?

Back to the kitchen. The last time I'd been here I'd tried hard not to envy Rosie her fancy kitchen with its six-burner cooktop and warming oven. Now, all trace of jealousy had been blasted away. Sticking with the garbage can theory, I looked under the sink. There was a garbage can, and it was empty.

Hmm.

"Beth?"

I ignored her for the second time and opened the garage door. A dark green garbage tote was in the corner next to the overhead door. I ran down the steps, across the concrete floor, and opened the lid.

Full to the brim.

Hardly thinking, I spun the tote around and tipped it over. Six garbage bags spilled across the floor. I swallowed my gag reflex, ripped open the plastic, and started pawing through the contents. Coffee grounds, egg shells, meat scraps, squash seeds. I pushed all of it to one side.

Nonrecyclable plastic, a ragged T-shirt, wadded-up paper towels. Nothing, nothing, nothing.

I was going through the last bag, the one that had been on the very bottom of the tote, and I was beginning to despair of finding any proof, when I found the very thing I needed.

"That's it." I picked up the small, but very empty, plastic bag and ran into the house.

Rosie pushed herself up on one elbow. "Fertilizer? But it's November. Why would Eric be using fertilizer now?"

I dragged a chair across the thick carpet and sat down in front of the couch. "Rosie, I have something to tell you. It'll be hard to hear, and it'll be scary, and I'm sorry, but you have to listen."

She dropped back down. "Later," she said, groaning. "Oh, I feel awful."

And she was going to feel a lot worse. "Where's Eric?"

"Airport."

"He's leaving for South America early?"

She shook her head slightly. "No, going to California. Thanksgiving. His parents."

"Without you?"

"I was supposed to, but . . ." She closed her eyes and took a few breaths. "But I got sick."

"Rosie, you're not sick," I said.

Her eyelids opened a fraction of an inch. "Thanks for . . . stopping, Beth. Let yourself out, okay?"

I took her hand between mine. She resisted, but didn't pull away. "You're not sick," I said quietly. "You've been poisoned."

"Don't . . . be silly."

"Common household fertilizer causes your symptoms exactly."

"How could I have eaten fertilizer?"

"Who made dinner last night?" I asked.

". . . Eric."

"How did it taste?"

"New recipe," she said slowly. "The girls had burgers, but Eric made pork for us. Heavy sauce. He wouldn't let me in the kitchen. It was . . . bitter. He said he might have added white pepper by mistake."

"And when did you start to feel sick?"

"Right after I finished the dishes." Her gaze of disbelief grew slightly less disbelieving. "Why would Eric poison me? If he didn't want me going with him and the girls, all he had to do was ask. I'd be fine with not visiting his parents."

On the drive over, a heart-stopping possibility had occurred to me, but I'd stuffed it down into the bottom of my brain. Now it came back and wouldn't go away. "Rosie, where are your daughters?"

"They're not sick. Just me."

I grabbed her shoulders and fairly shouted at her. "Where are the girls?"

"What's wrong with you?" She jerked away. "They're with Eric. They're on their way to California."

I stared at her, aghast. "Right now?"

"They left not long before you got here."

A white van had sped past me half a mile from the Stulls' house. A white van had tried to run me over. I'd forgotten all about the white van parked near the school the night Sam was killed. It could have been a white van that hit Brian Keller. Maybe Eric was afraid Sam had shared his secret with Brian.

"Does . . ." My voice croaked and I started again. "Does Eric drive a white van?"

She nodded. "Why?"

And a white van was taking two young girls away from their mother. "Rosie, he's kidnapping Amelia and Chelsea."

She smiled faintly. "He's their father. Why would he need to kidnap them?"

"He's taking them to South America. He has a second

family there and he killed Sam Helmstetter to cover up a mistake and now he's . . ."

But Rosie was shaking her head. "Where are you getting that? A second family? That's . . . silly. Eric and I have been having problems, sure, but what couple doesn't?" She spoke in complete sentences. Either the poison was working itself through her system or her increasingly emotional state was burning it out fast.

"Do you have passports for the girls?" I asked. "Where are they?"

"Passports?" Rosie tried to get up. "Kitchen desk. But . . ." She put her hand to her forehead and fell back. "So dizzy . . ."

"Where are they?" I stood.

"Right side," she said, panting. "Second drawer."

I ran to the kitchen and yanked open the drawer. Papers of all sorts, but no little blue passport books. I rifled through the drawer's entire contents. No passports. I opened the rest of the drawers, pulled cookbooks off shelves, flipped through telephone books. No passports. "They're not here," I called.

"No," Rosie said. "They wouldn't be. We carry them when we go across state lines."

Frustration clawed at me. She had to believe me. What could I do to convince her? I paced the floor, balling my hands into fists until my knuckles ached. Think, Beth. Think! We didn't have time for me to trot out all the evidence I'd gathered. What would convince her? Who would convince her?

Bingo.

I grabbed the cordless phone off the wall, ran it into the living room, and thrust it into her face. "He has his cell phone, doesn't he? Call him. Call Eric. Ask him about Eva. And Chago and Rafael. Ask him about the purple ink. Ask him about the picture in his desk blotter. Go ahead, ask him."

Rosie's hand lifted, hesitated, then took the phone from me. As she punched in the numbers, we stared at each other wordlessly. She didn't want any of this to be true. She wanted everything to be the way it was yesterday, and she wanted me to be stark, raving mad.

"Eric?" she asked. "Are the girls with you?"

I leaned close enough to hear his reply.

"Right here," he said. "Did you want to say good-bye?"

She smiled at me. "That's right. Put Amelia on, will you?" She gave a few mom endearments and kissing noises to her daughters.

"Ask him about Eva," I whispered.

"Have a good time with the palm trees, honey," she said. "Now let me talk to your dad again."

"Rosie," Eric said, "we're getting ready to go through security. I have to hang up."

Ask him! I mouthed, making hurry-up motions with my hands.

"Rosie?" Eric asked. "Did you hear me? I have to—"

All in a rush, in a tumble of words and feelings and doubt and fear, Rosie asked a single question. "Eric, who's Eva?"

There was a short silence. So very short, but long enough to tell long tales of lies and betrayal and untold amounts of heartbreak. Then there was a click and the line went dead.

I took the phone from her. "Let me call the poison control center," I said. "First thing is to make sure the poison won't—"

Tossing off the blanket, she grabbed the phone out of my hand and flung it out of reach. "First thing—the *only* thing—is getting my daughters back."

She ran for the door, and I was right behind her.

Chapter 19

"Can't you go any faster?" Rosie begged.

Since I was already driving faster than any rational human being should drive in three inches of wet, sloppy snow, I didn't answer. For years I'd driven like . . . well, like a mother carrying precious cargo. I hadn't pushed the edge of my driving capabilities in over a decade. Lucky for Rosie, I'd learned to drive in an area of Michigan that got a hundred and fifty inches of snow a year. Some things you never forget.

At least I hoped so.

We were headed west on Highway 30, chunking over the rows of slush kicked up by passing cars and large blocks of snow dropping off fenders.

Stay on target. Stay on target. . . .

The car began sliding right, starting to turn, starting to spin out of control, and Rosie's hands shot out and latched on to the dashboard. "Beth! Watch out! Beth! *Beth!*"

"Got it," I said calmly. Or as calmly as I could. My right foot had come off the accelerator when the car started slipping. I desperately wanted to whip the wheel left, but knew I couldn't. "Turn into the direction of the skid," my father's voice said. "Don't fight thc slide—work with it."

The car slowed, I turned slightly right, hoped my seat belt was on tight, prayed that the air bags wouldn't injure us too much, wondered if I'd paid the car insurance bill, and, above all, wished I was home in bed.

We slid for a year and a day, through a white blurry world, through a soundless universe, and just before the car went into the ditch, I felt control come back to my hands. I eased the wheel left and there we were, driving along in the right lane as if nothing had happened.

"Just like riding a bike." I swallowed down the bitter taste of fear.

"What's that?" Rosie asked. "This is taking too long." She pounded the dash. "Can you go any faster?"

I risked a glance at my passenger. Nothing but large eyes, white showing all around. "Why don't you call 911?" I asked. "Maybe we can get some police help."

"Right." She rustled around in the purse she'd grabbed as we'd run out her front door.

She was still explaining the situation to the dispatcher when we drove into the Dane County Regional Airport. "We're at the airport right now," she said. "He said they were going to Denver first. What airline? Um . . ." She pressed the tips of her fingers into her forehead. "Um . . . United? Pretty sure it's United. Departure time?" She gave me a wild look. "I don't remember. I don't remember!"

Panic was starting to grab hold of her, which would do none of us any good. I risked taking a hand off the wheel and gave her arm a gentle, reassuring squeeze.

"Okay," she was saying. "I'm taking a deep breath. Okay. Yeah, I'm okay. Eric left late because I was sick"—her eyes narrowed to the thinnest of slits—"and in this snow it might have taken twice as long to get here, so they could be flying out any minute. How long before someone can get here?" She paused, listening, and any semblance of calm vanished. "You want me to *what*?" She thumbed off the phone and threw it into her purse.

"Um . . ." Hanging up on a 911 call couldn't be a good idea.

"I know," Rosie said, "I shouldn't have done that. But she was telling me to stay outside. To wait for the police to arrive!"

Either the dispatcher didn't have children or she was just doing what her job told her to do. No mother worth the name would willingly stand idle while her children were in danger. It was a physical impossibility and cruel to even ask.

Just shy of the second entrance to the terminal, the closest entrance to the United ticketing desk, I started braking into a sloppy stop. Even before the car stopped moving forward, Rosie and I had opened our doors and were out in the cold, running as fast as we could.

"Ma'am, I'm sorry," a skycap said, "but you can't leave your vehicle there. Ma'am? Ma'am!"

Rosie and I rushed into the building, brushing the edges of our shoulders on the too-slow automatic doors. Inside, we came to an instant stop. All was bedlam. Children screeching, adults scolding, teenagers sulking, airport personnel looking harried and worn. It was Thanksgiving week, and the mass movement of Americans had begun.

Rosie ran forward, stopped, took two fast paces, and stopped again. "We're never going to find them," she said, looking left and right and up the escalator. "It's too late. They're gone. I'll never get them back."

Her words, full of despair and hopelessness, spurred me to action. I stepped in front of her and grabbed her shoulders. Looking straight into her eyes, I said, "You're their mother. They need you. They will always need you. Are you going to give up this easily?"

She shook herself out of my grip. "Of course I'm not," she snapped. "Come on." Elbowing aside young and old alike, she bullied to the front of the line, ignoring all shouts and protests, and slapped her driver's license on the counter. "I'm Rosie Stull. Are my daughters on one of your planes?"

"Ma'am?" The well-groomed woman smiled blandly.

Rosie leaned forward and spoke in a low voice. "My soon-to-be-ex-husband has my daughters and I want them back. Amelia and Chelsea Stull." She stabbed her license with her forefinger. "S-t-u-l-l. They're traveling with a piece of pond scum named Eric who won't be my husband much longer. He no longer has my permission to have the girls unattended. I want them back."

"Oh, dear." The woman's fingers flew across her keyboard. "Oh, dear," she said, frowning. "Mrs. Stull, I'd really like to help you, but there isn't anyone named Stull flying with us today."

"But there has to be!"

I tugged at Rosie's elbow. "Did you ever see the tickets? Eric might not have been telling the truth about the airline." Or the departure time or the destination, but I didn't say any of that.

"The rat fink," she said through gritted teeth, and allowed me to pull her away from the counter. "He kept the tickets in his briefcase. I never thought to look. Why didn't I? Why?"

But there'd been no reason for her to, and now wasn't the time for her to waste time beating herself with the imaginary hammer so many women carry around. "Time to split up," I said. "You check with the other airlines, and I'll go—"

"No," she interrupted. "It'll take too long." And before I could argue with her, she was off. Weaving in and out of the mass of people snaking in lines through the light-filled space, she trotted back and forth, calling the names of her daughters. "Amelia? Chelsea? Amelia? Chelsea!"

As plans went, it was better than many. I rushed to catch up to her, and trailed in her wake, looking for tall men with dark blond hair. Which, unfortunately for us in an area settled by Germans, was two out of three men. And half of those were holding at least one child by the hand.

"Chelsea? Amelia!"

Heads turned, but none turned with the alacrity of a child hearing her mother's voice. There was no answering call, and there was no retreat by a father figure.

"Amelia?"

Pieces of me were starting to break into tiny shards of sorrow. Maybe they were already gone. Maybe Eric was already in the air with the girls, winging southward, never to come home, never to see their mother, never to—

I shook my head. No. That wouldn't happen. It. Would. Not.

"Chelsea?" Rosie's voice was starting to go hoarse. "Amelia?"

There had to be a better way. There just had to be.

Suddenly I saw what it was. I grabbed Rosie's sleeve and pushed through the crowd to an information counter. "Excuse me," I said to a blue-jacketed woman. "My daughters have wandered off. Can you please make an announcement for Amelia and Chelsea to meet their mother at the baggage claim?"

Rosie clutched the edge of the counter. "Amelia and Chelsea Stull," she said.

The woman looked at me and I nodded. She picked up a telephone receiver upside down and held the mouthpiece to her lips. "Would Amelia and Chelsea Stull please meet their mother at the baggage claim? Amelia and Chelsea Stull, meet your mother at the baggage claim."

Rosie and I half ran, half trotted to a vantage point halfway between the conveyor belts and the escalator, heads turning, eyes searching, our senses at full alert, our hopes and fears wrapped up into this one instant.

Were they here? Were they gone? They must be here.

But what if they were gone?

For the briefest of seconds I imagined a day in which I'd be torn forever from Jenna and Oliver. It was the worst second of my life.

"Amelia?" Rosie called. "Chelsea?"

No replies. No answers. No daughters, no reunion. No joy.

Nothing but the black void of an empty life.

Nothing but nothing forever and ever and ever.

"Amelia?" Rosie's voice was raspy and dry. She turned in a circle, looking, searching, crying. "Chelsea?"

I swallowed. Maybe security would let us through upstairs. But so much time had passed already. By the time we'd talked our way through the guards, the girls would be long, long gone.

"Amelia!" Rosie's neck cords stood out. *"Chelsea!"* She called again and again and again until her voice could no longer be heard.

People walked past, their glances sliding toward us and away. What's wrong with that poor woman? Someone should call security.

Tears stung my eyes. What do you do after you've already done everything you can do? "Rosie . . ." I put out a hand, but she pulled away before I touched her.

"Amelia! Chelsea!" Her voice was only a croak, but she kept calling their names, would keep on calling until the stars fell from the sky. "Amelia," she whispered, finally allowing me to put an arm around her. "Chelsea . . ."

I hugged her hard, and was ready to speak painful platitudes when the miracle occurred.

"But you're wrong, Daddy," Chelsea called in a clear, young voice. "It *is* Mommy." The girl ran down the escalator, coming down from the second-floor secure area, the escalator's big moving steps making her short gait awkward and adorable.

"Mom!" Amelia was right behind Chelsea. "Are you coming with us?"

The two poured down the stairs in a rush of blond hair and happiness. Rosie knelt, gathering the girls to her in a large hug, but her gaze was trained on me, and there were question marks in her eyes. For we'd both seen Eric on the escalator behind the girls, and he was already walking rapidly to the exit.

I paused just long enough to say, "Don't let them watch," and started after him.

He looked over his shoulder, saw me leave Rosie's side, noted my determined stance, and broke into a run.

One step, two, and then I was in top gear, chasing down the man who'd killed Sam, the man who'd caused Yvonne undeserved anguish, the man who'd caused all this pain. Run? Oh, yes, I'd run. I'd burn my lungs to fire, I'd run until I couldn't run any longer, I'd run until the world ended to catch this man and put him where he belonged.

He dodged people carrying garment bags and carry-ons and wheeled suitcases, and I was right behind him. He hurdled a baggage cart awkwardly, and I gained a yard with my clean jump.

The automatic door slid open just ahead of him and we both went through it at a dead run.

He was bigger and stronger and my one small advantage was footwear. The slick bottoms of his dress oxfords couldn't compete against the safe tread of my sensible shoes. Which wasn't much of an advantage, but I'd make it work. I had to.

With a bare look at traffic, he started across the street.

If he made it to the parking garage, he could use any of a hundred ways to escape. Run across the open fields and make his way into the city. Commandeer a car and drive away. Hide under vehicles or behind posts until the search ended, then slip away in the dark and—

No. That would not happen.

It. Would. Not.

My fierceness added a spurt of speed to my panting run. I was close, so close, I could almost touch him.

No! He's starting to pull away, he's going to get away, I'm not going to—

And then he slipped. His right shoe lost its purchase in the lumpy slush and he lost his balance. Just for one step, but one step was all I needed.

I pushed off with all my might into a flying horizontal leap. Arms outstretched, head down, I hurtled my body forward and tackled Eric Stull, grabbing him about the waist and bringing him to the wet sloppy ground.

Behind us, police car sirens wailed to a stop. Doors opened and officers piled out with a speed that was a great comfort at this moment in my life.

"Hello, Mrs. Kennedy." Deputy Wheeler helped me to my feet. "Nice tackle. To be honest, I didn't know you had it in you."

I watched as two of her fellow officers handcuffed a struggling Eric. "That's what I used to think," I said.

She looked at me curiously, but I just smiled.

And, after a moment, she smiled back.

Epilogue

"Mom?" A red-faced Jenna looked up from the pot of potatoes over which she was toiling. "Are these mashed enough?"

"Let me see." I gave the gravy one more stir and turned the heat to low. A strand of hair had escaped my ponytail and I pushed it back behind my ear as I crossed the kitchen for inspection duties. Inside the pot the potatoes were a lumpy mess. "Perfect," I said, and gave her a floury hug. "Best mashed potatoes ever."

"Are you sure?" Jenna looked dubious. "They're a little chunky."

"Shows they're not out of a box," I said. "Three more mashes and you're done."

"Mom?" Oliver looked up from the plate of raw vegetables he was assembling at the kitchen table. "Does this look okay?"

I trotted back to the gravy, stirred it, and went to my son. The carrots were arrayed in a half circle, celery in a jumble at the opposite side of the plate, a few pieces of broccoli in the center, and two radishes on either side of the broccoli.

"It's a face," Oliver said. "See?" He held up two radishes. "These are the eyes, the carrots are the mouth. Like this." He grinned horribly, lips drawn wide and high.

"Very nice. Jenna, let's get those potatoes in something nicer." I handed her a china bowl and, after giving the gravy one last stir, poured it into the stainless steel gravy boat.

"Okeydoke, kids. I think we're about ready. Jenna, you have the potatoes. Oliver, you have the vegetables, and I have the gravy. Is there anything we're forgetting?" I put on a haunted look. "It seems as if there is, but I can't remember."

Oliver bounced in his chair. "The turkey, Mom. The turkey!"

"And the stuffing." Jenna pointed at the oven, where I'd put the carved-up turkey and stuffing to keep warm.

I smiled at my children. "Silly old me. What would I do without the two of you?"

Oliver slid off the chair and came to my side. "You'd be bored."

"Yeah," Jenna said, drawing near. "And who would wake you up on Saturday mornings?"

I laughed and pulled them into a tight hug. "That settles that. I guess it's a good thing I have you." For without them, I wouldn't be whole. I wouldn't be Mom, I'd just be Beth, and that wasn't a reality worthy of contemplation.

"Okay," I said, giving them a last squeaking squeeze. "Let's get this food on the table."

The three of us made a small parade as we trekked out of the kitchen, Oliver in front, Jenna next, and me last, each of us carrying food-laden plates. When we reached the dining room, loud applause broke out.

"It looks wonderful!" Yvonne exclaimed.

"Beth, this is great." Rachel Helmstetter's smile was the first real one I'd seen on her in weeks.

"Mrs. Kennedy?" Blake asked. "Who gets the wishbone in your house?"

In a droning tone, Jenna and Oliver simultaneously said, "Whoever washes the most dishes."

"And there are a lot of them," Lois said, spreading her hands. "Just look at all this food!"

Last week she'd repeated her annual complaint that her very extended family Thanksgiving dinner, held in a rented hall, just wasn't what Thanksgiving should be. She'd accepted my invitation gladly and asked if she could bring a guest. Now, she looked across the table to him. "I'm told we can't get up from the table until it's gone."

Paoze's eyes went wide. "We are going to be here all night!"

"No way," Jenna said. "I like turkey. Lots and lots."

"You can have my turkey if you want," Zach said. "My favorite is the stuffing."

"Forsooth, verily," Marina said, winking at me. "This is a feast for the eyes as well as the mouth. You did good, Beth. The DH will be seriously bummed that he was too sick to come over."

Rachel leaned to one side and her daughter whispered in her ear. "I'm not sure," Rachel said. "How about if I ask?" She looked at me. "Mia and I are interested in your centerpiece. Is it a tradition in your family?"

"You could say that." Smiling smugly, I admired my own handiwork. Last night I'd cooked the Emmerling rutabaga casserole. This morning I'd spooned it all into a clear glass bowl, alternating a layer of rutabaga with a layer of colored sand from one of the kids' long-ago art projects. Rutabaga, orange sand. Rutabaga, brown sand. Rutabaga, maroon sand. I'd topped the whole thing with a few dried hydrangea heads I'd clipped from the front yard, and bingo bango bongo, I had a Thanksgiving centerpiece. If any of my missing family members quizzed me on my menu, I'd be able to honestly say that, yes, rutabagas had been on the table.

"Shall we pray?" I asked. Everyone bowed their heads, and I took the hands of Jenna and Oliver, seated at my right and left.

"Dear Father," I said. "Thank You for this special day, a day to remember Your goodness. We thank You for the pleasure of coming together for this meal and we thank You for all the gifts of love we've had. We pray that You'll help us to carry on and live as You would have us. This we ask in Your name. Amen."

Rachel wiped away a tear. "Amen."

"Amen," breathed Yvonne.

"Amen," said Lois quietly.

Marina thumped her fist on the table. "So be it, let's eat!"

Trust my best friend to lighten a mood. "Turkey, anyone?" I started the platter on its way. "There's more of everything, so feel free to load up."

Around went Oliver's vegetables and Jenna's potatoes and the gravy and the cranberries and the green bean casserole and the Jell-O salad and the onion wraps and the stuffing and sweet potato casserole and the dinner rolls and the fruit salad.

Around went my life and love to these friends old and new, all of us wounded by recent events, all of us putting things back together again, all of us moving ahead, onward and upward.

"Aren't we doing the Thanksgiving thanks?" Blake asked his mother.

"Oh, honey . . ." Rachel looked flustered.

"What's that?" Jenna asked.

"At our house," Blake said, "each of us gives thanks for something before we eat."

"That's a nice idea." I smiled at him, at Rachel, at everyone in the room, at the whole world. My heart was full and happy and I had so much to be thankful for. Amelia and Chelsea were safe and sound, Yvonne's reputation was restored, business was coming back to the bookstore, Richard had called and said he had two job interviews next week, Jenna and Oliver were healthy and happy, and Evan was taking me to a Minnesota Wild hockey game next weekend. "I'm thankful for such wonderful children."

"Oh, Mom," Jenna said, rolling her eyes. "I'm thankful for Mr. Kettunen's insurance company. My hockey team gets new jerseys next week."

"I'm thankful for Spot," Oliver said. "He sleeps with me now and he's really warm."

"For my new kitten." Mia's smile was a mile wide. "She purrs!"

"For piano lessons," Blake said. "It's fun playing with my mom."

"For kind people," Paoze said.

"For a loving family that's on the other side of town." Lois grinned.

"For good friends," Rachel said.

"For new friends," Yvonne said, her eyes shining.

"A toast!" Marina cried, and rose to her feet. "To the woman who gathered us here for this most special of meals, the woman to whom we all owe so much, the woman we all want to be when we grow up. To Beth Kennedy!"

"Don't be silly," I murmured, but everyone stood and clinked glasses while I sat in hot embarrassment at the head of the table.

"To Beth!"

"To Mom!"

"To Mrs. Kennedy!"

They sat, laughing and talking as they rattled their silverware free of napkins. Marina caught my eye. "What?" I asked.

"You're not mad, are you?" she whispered.

"About the toast? No. Mortified, but not mad."

"A little mortification is good for the soul." She gave a wise nod.

"One of these days I'm going to mortify you and we'll see how you like it."

Her eyes sparkled. "Me, mortified? What fun!"

I shuddered to think of the events that would require Marina mortification. "Thanks, but I think I've had enough excitement in the last year to last a lifetime."

She quirked an eyebrow. "Really?"

I looked out across my Thanksgiving table. Friends, food, and family. What more could I want? "No more excitement," I said firmly.

Well, at least for a little while.